辦公室英語會話必勝課

職場溝通即戰力

EVERYDAY OFFICE ENGLISH

作者 Michelle Witte　譯者 謝雅婷／劉嘉珮／黃詩韻　審訂 Helen Yeh

Contents

Part 1 認識工作 Learning About Your Job

Part 2 公司內部溝通 Communication in the Office

Part 3 使用硬體設備 Using Office Appliances

Part 4 工作事務 Discussions, Meetings, and Proposals

Part 5 對外的聯絡 Outside Correspondences and Contacts

Part 6 人事相關事宜 Personnel Matters

Part 7 社交與旅遊 Socializing and Travel

Part

1 認識工作 Learning About Your Job

UNIT 01 新人報到 Arriving at a New Job

(1) R Receptionist K Katharine A Ann

1 Katharine arrives at her new office and introduces herself to her colleagues. 凱薩琳到達新公司並向同事自我介紹。

R Hi there, may I help you?

K Yes, hi. I'm Katharine Sylvester, the new **research assistant**[1]. I was told to ask for Jacob Smith when I **got in**[2].

R Ah, of course. I'm Barbara. It's nice to meet you. Jacob's not available just yet, but he asked me to hand you over to Ann while you wait for him. She's in the **conference room**[3] around the corner.

K OK, thank you.

R 您好，我能為您效勞嗎？

K 您好，我是新來的**研究助理**凱薩琳·西爾維斯特。有人告訴我**到了**以後找雅各·史密斯。

R 當然。很高興見到妳，我是芭芭拉。雅各目前走不開，但他有吩咐，在等他時把妳交給安。她人就在轉角的**會議室**。

K 好的，謝謝。

2 She walks to the conference room. 她走向會議室。

K Hi, I'm Katharine. Are you Ann?

A Yes, nice to meet you.

K Pleasure to meet you.

A Did you **have** any **trouble**[4] getting here?

K Oh, no. Actually, it's a very easy **commute**[5].

K 您好，我是凱薩琳。您是安嗎？

A 我是，很高興見到妳。

K 很榮幸見到您。

A 妳到這裡會**很麻煩**嗎？

K 噢，不會。其實**通勤**滿方便的。

Useful Expressions

A Self-introduction 自我介紹 2

1	James Brady, nice to meet you.	我是詹姆士·布雷迪，很高興見到你。
2	I'm Sara Cooper. It's a pleasure to meet you.	我是莎拉·庫珀，很榮幸見到你。
3	I'm your newest **analyst**[6], Brian Sandhurst.	我是新來的**分析師**布萊恩·桑赫斯特。
4	My name's Leslie Cooper. I believe I'm supposed to be meeting with Aaron Cantor to get started.	我叫萊斯莉·庫珀。我想我應該要找亞倫·康圖爾報到。

B Making small talk 閒聊

5	Welcome to the office! We're glad to have you **onboard**[7].	歡迎來到公司！我們很高興有你的**加入**。
6	Don't worry, the first day is always a little **nerve-wracking**[8].	別擔心，第一天總是有點**緊張**。
7	The weather looked beautiful on my way in. Is it still nice out?	在我進來的時候天氣似乎很好，現在還是嗎？
8	Is this your first time in our office?	這是你第一次到我們公司嗎？

1 **research assistant** 研究助理
2 **get in** 到達
3 **conference room** 會議室
4 **have trouble doing sth.** 做某事有所困難
5 **commute** [kə`mjut] (n.) 通勤
6 **analyst** [`ænl̩ɪst] (n.) 分析師
7 **onboard** [`ɑn,bord] (adj.) 加入的
8 **nerve-wracking** [`nɝv,rækɪŋ] (adj.) 令人不安的

Ways to Commute 通勤方式

by MRT 搭捷運

by bicycle 騎腳踏車

by driving a car 自行開車

on foot 步行

by bus 搭公車

by taxi 搭計程車

by train 搭火車

C Talking about yourself 談及自身 (3)

9	I'm from Seoul originally, but I've been living in the US for the last four years.	我是首爾人，但在過去四年來一直住在美國。
10	I just graduated from business school, and I'm really excited to be able to **put my skills to work**[1].	我剛從商學院畢業，期待**將所學運用於實務工作**上。
11	I've been working in sales for a number of years.	我當業務已有幾年的時間了。

D Introducing someone to his or her work 介紹工作內容

12	We're hoping you can **hit the ground running**[2], as we've got a lot to do here.	由於這裡事情很多，我們期望你能**立即上軌道**。
13	Your **supervisor**[3] will **brief**[4] you on our current status.	你的**主管**會向你**簡短說明**我們的現況。
14	For now, we would like you to focus on learning our **customer service**[5] policies.	目前我們希望你將重點放在**顧客服務**的規章上。

Review Questions

Listen to the conversations and answer the questions below.

4 **1. Why does the man come to the office?**

- Ⓐ He has a job interview there.
- Ⓑ He has a meeting with the boss there.
- Ⓒ He is working there.
- Ⓓ He has a friend there.

2. Who does the man speak to most likely?

- Ⓐ The vice president.
- Ⓑ The receptionist.
- Ⓒ The accountant.
- Ⓓ The cleaner.

5 **3. What are the man and the woman talking about?**

- Ⓐ They are discussing politics.
- Ⓑ He is asking her questions.
- Ⓒ They are making small talk.
- Ⓓ They are talking about transportation.

6 **4.** **A** Hi there, I'm Gerald Butler. I was told to come to this conference room for a ________________ on the current project.

B Hi, Gerald, we've been expecting you. I'm Jane Wu and this is Brian Kane. I'm ________________ this project and Brian is assisting me with it. We're hoping you can hit the ground running and get ________________ into some of the work we need to get done.

A Pleased to meet you both. I'm here to work!

Ans C, B, C, briefing, managing, straight

1 **put sb's skills to work** 學以致用
2 **hit the ground running** 立即展開行動
3 **supervisor** [ˋsupɚ͵vaɪzɚ] (n.) 主管
4 **brief** [brif] (v.) 簡略說明
5 **customer service** 客戶服務

UNIT 02 歡迎與介紹新人
Welcoming and Introducing the Newcomer

7 J Jacob B Babara K Katharine J Jason S Samantha

1 Katharine is being introduced to her coworkers[1] by her supervisor[2], Jacob Smith, on her first day of work.
上班第一天，凱薩琳的主管雅各·史密斯將她介紹給同事們認識。

J You might have met Barbara Polley on your way in. She's our **receptionist**[3] and she'll tell you who's in, who's out, where to find us . . . she pretty much **runs the place**[4].

B Hi, Katharine.

K Nice to meet you, Barbara.

J And this is Jason Smollet, another research assistant here. You'll probably **end up**[5] working together a lot of the time. He's a good person to go to with questions or problems, before you ask someone else.

J Welcome to ABC Tech, Katharine.

K Thank you, it's a pleasure to meet you. Maybe I can **set up**[6] a time to **pick your brain**[7]?

J Any time. I know it can be confusing around here at first!

J And that's Samantha Barnet, our **Human Resources**[8] Manager, just walking in. She'll probably be coming around to help you set up your **paperwork**[9], right, Samantha?

J 妳進公司時，可能就已經見過芭芭拉·波利了。她是公司的**接待員**，告訴妳誰進誰出、哪裡找得到我們……她幾乎**一手包辦大小事**。

B 妳好，凱薩琳。

K 很高興見到妳，芭芭拉。

J 這是另一位研究助理傑森·斯墨列特，你們以後或許會長時間共事。有任何疑難雜症需要詢問別人前，問他就對了。

J 歡迎加入 ABC 科技公司，凱薩琳。

K 謝謝，很榮幸見到你。或許我可以**安排**個時間**向你請教請教**？

J 沒問題。我知道在這裡剛開始可能會有點混亂！

J 現在走進來的是我們的**人資部**經理薩曼莎·巴內特。她可能會來幫妳建立妳的人事**資料**，對吧，薩曼莎？

2 Samantha walks over. 薩曼莎走了過來。

S Good morning, everybody. Welcome, Katharine. Yes, I'll come by later today to make sure we've **dotted the i's and crossed the t's**[10].

J Thanks, folks. Now, Katharine, let's go to your **cubicle**[11].

K OK—nice to have met all of you!

J And here is where you'll be working. Barbara will show you how to **set up**[6] the telephones, and she'll **give you the rundown on**[12] the computer, passwords, and anything else you'll need to know to get going. I think I'll call her now so you can get started. Is that alright? Do you have any questions?

K No, not **at the moment**[13], thanks. I'm happy to get started.

S 早安，各位。凱薩琳，歡迎。沒錯，我晚點會來**確認一切無誤**。

J 謝啦，各位。凱薩琳，我們去妳的**位子**吧。

K 好，很高興認識大家！

J 這是妳工作的地方。芭芭拉會過來教妳如何**設定**電話，**大概說明**電腦、密碼，還有其他妳工作需要了解的東西。我想我現在就打電話叫她，這樣妳才能開始工作，好嗎？有其他問題嗎？

K **目前**沒有。謝啦，很高興能開始工作了。

1 **coworker (= co-worker)** [ˋkowɝkɚ] (n.) 同事
2 **supervisor** [ˋsupɚvaɪzɚ] (n.) 主管
3 **receptionist** [rɪˋsɛpʃənɪst] (n.) 接待員
4 **run the place** 安排一切大小事物
5 **end up** 最終成為
6 **set up** 安排；設定
7 **pick sb's brain** 向某人請教
8 **human resources** 人力資源
9 **paperwork** [ˋpepɚˏwɝk] (n.) （特定事務所需的）所有文件資料
10 **dot the i's and cross the t's** 仔細檢查
11 **cubicle** [ˋkjubɪkl] (n.) 隔間
12 **give sb. the rundown on sth.** 向某人概述某事
13 **at the moment** 目前

Useful Expressions

A Introductions 介紹 (8)

1 Let's **get acquainted with**[1] the rest of the team.
我們來**認識**團隊裡的其他人吧。

2 Katharine, meet Barbara, our receptionist.
凱薩琳，來見過我們的接待員芭芭拉。

3 Katharine, Barbara. Barbara, Katharine. Katharine is our new research assistant.
凱薩琳，這是芭芭拉。芭芭拉，這是凱薩琳。凱薩琳是我們新進的研究助理。

4 I don't believe you've met Lance yet. Lance is an analyst.
我想你還沒見過蘭斯吧。蘭斯是一位分析師。

5 I'd like you to meet Jason, a senior analyst. Jason is **a wealth of information**[2] on finance. You and he should set up a time to meet. He will be a big help in getting you **oriented**[3] here.
我要你來見過資深分析師傑森。傑森可是位財經**達人**。你與他應該約個時間碰面，他會對你**適應**這裡的環境助益良多。

常見職稱

- Chairman 總裁
- President 董事長
- General Manager 總經理
- Director 處長
- Special Assistant 特別助理
- Factory Chief 廠長
- Assistant Manager 副理
- Junior Manager 襄理
- Chief Engineer 首席工程師
- Advisory Engineer 顧問工程師
- Section Manager 課長
- Principle Engineer 策畫工程師
- System Engineer 系統工程師
- Specialist 專員
- Administrator 行政人員
- Supervisor 主任；組長
- Representative 代表
- Operator 作業員；技工
- Team Leader 領班

B Describing your position 敘述職位

6	Ⓐ So you're the new girl? Ⓑ Yes, I'm just **getting my feet wet**[4].	Ⓐ 所以妳就是那個新來的女生囉？ Ⓑ 是，我還是**生手**。
7	I just started this week.	我這禮拜才開始上班。
8	I just started working as a project manager.	我剛擔任專案經理一職。
9	I work in the sales department as a customer service **technician**[5].	我在業務部擔任客服**技師**一職。
10	I'm in **real estate**[6].	我從事**不動產業**。

1 **get acquainted** [əˋkwentɪd] **with** 認識／結識某人
2 **a wealth of information on sth.** 通曉某事
3 **orient** [ˋorɪɛnt] (v.) 使適應；使熟悉情況
4 **get sb's feet wet** 初嘗某事
5 **technician** [tɛkˋnɪʃən] (n.) 技師；技術人員
6 **real estate** 不動產

C Offering assistance 提供協助 9

11	Please come to me if you have any questions.	有任何疑問請儘管向我詢問。
12	If there's anything I can do to help, just let me know.	有任何需要我幫忙的地方，儘管跟我說。
13	George is always willing to give a helping hand.	喬治總是樂意幫忙。
14	Barbara will help you **get settled**[1] in here.	芭芭拉會幫你把這裡**安頓好**。
15	Barbara will **bring you up to speed**[2].	芭芭拉會**協助你進入狀況**。

D Politely declining[3] the offer of more assistance 婉拒更多協助

16	Thanks, but I think I'm all set **for now**[4].	謝了，不過**目前**一切都可以了。
17	Thank you. I think that's all I need for now.	感謝你，我想目前我只需要這些了。
18	I feel pretty comfortable with everything now.	目前我覺得都很好。
19	I'm ready to get to work.	我準備好要一展身手了。

1 **get settled** 安頓妥當
2 **bring sb. up to speed** 使某人跟上進度／了解最新狀況
3 **decline** [dɪˋklaɪn] (v.) 婉拒
4 **for now** 目前；暫時

Review Questions

Listen to the conversations and answer the questions below.

10 **1. Who is farther away, Robert or John?**

Ⓐ Robert. Ⓑ John.

2. Who is a research assistant?

Ⓐ Robert. Ⓑ John. Ⓒ The speaker.

11 **3. Who is not an accounts administrator?**

Ⓐ Leslie. Ⓑ Bill. Ⓒ June.

4. Where are the sales offices?

Ⓐ On two floors. Ⓑ On the 4th floor.
Ⓒ On the 3rd floor. Ⓓ Next to the accounts office.

5. What did Leslie mean when she said "You'd never know it from Bill, though" ?

Ⓐ Bill isn't often in the sales offices.
Ⓑ Bill is often in the sales offices.
Ⓒ Bill is often on the floor.
Ⓓ Bill is often out of town.

12 **6. What is the situation?**

Ⓐ An university orientation.
Ⓑ A lunch meeting.
Ⓒ An interview.
Ⓓ A new employee training session.

7. Who will run the training session?

Ⓐ Christine. Ⓑ George. Ⓒ Gloria. Ⓓ John.

Ans B, B, B, C, A, D, C

UNIT 03 會見老闆或上司 Meeting Your New Boss or Supervisor

(13) J Jacob K Katharine

Katharine goes to her new supervisor's office to introduce herself.
凱薩琳到新主管的辦公室自我介紹。

J Come in, welcome.

K It's very nice to see you.

J And you. How are you settling in so far? Has Barbara got you all set up?

K Oh yes, she's been really helpful. Everyone has. I'm working on **learning the ropes**[1] now and getting as involved as I can.

J That's what we need from you, so that sounds great. Have you got any questions for me right now?

K No, I don't think so. I'm sure I will have some as soon as I continue working, though. If I have questions about the **database**[2], I should go to Ann, right?

J Yes, Ann's the lead on that project. And **my door is** always **open**[3]—though I do **have a lot on my plate**[4] at the moment, so I may not always be in my office!

K Thank you!

J 請進，歡迎妳。

K 非常高興見到你。

J 我也是。目前適應得如何？芭芭拉都幫妳處理好了嗎？

K 是的，她幫了很大的忙。大家都是。我目前正努力**學習基本功**，盡量讓自己幫得上忙。

J 很好，這正是我們需要的。現在妳有任何問題要問我的嗎？

K 我想沒有。不過我確定繼續工作以後就會有問題要問了。如果我對**資料庫**有疑問，要去問安，對嗎？

J 對，安是專案的負責人。**有問題儘管問我**，但**我目前很忙**，所以可能會常常不在辦公室。

K 謝謝你！

Useful Expressions

A Asking how someone is settling in at work 詢問上班情況 (14)

1	How is everything going so far?	目前都還好嗎?
2	Are you **getting a handle on things**[5] yet?	一切**掌握**得還順利嗎?
3	Are you **getting the hang of**[6] the database?	你**掌握**到資料庫使用的**訣竅**嗎?
4	Is everything starting to make sense?	一切都懂了嗎?
5	Are you getting used to things yet?	你開始習慣了嗎?

B Describing being new to a position 表示新到職

6	I'm a **rookie**[7] who doesn't know anything yet.	我是**新人**,什麼都不懂。
7	I'm learning all the time.	我一直在學習。
8	I'm doing my best to **absorb**[8] all the new information.	我盡我所能**學習**所有新資訊。
9	I think I'm **getting into the swing of things**[9].	我覺得自己越來越**進入狀況**了。
10	I'm just going to **wing it**[10] until the new training program starts next week.	下星期的訓練課程開始之前,我都要**臨場應變**。

1 **learn the ropes** 學習做法;掌握竅門
2 **database** [ˋdetəˏbes] (n.) 資料庫
3 **sb's door is open** 某人隨時歡迎
4 **have a lot on sb's plate** 某人很忙碌
5 **get a handle on sth.** 掌控
6 **get the hang of sth.** 抓到訣竅
7 **rookie** [ˋrukɪ] (n.) 新手
8 **absorb** [əbˋsɔrb] (v.) 學習;理解
9 **get into the swing of things** 進入狀況;投入
10 **wing it** 臨場反應

Office 辦公室

reception 接待處

corridor 走廊

elevator 電梯

stairway 樓梯間

hallway 門廳

escalator 手扶梯

restroom 廁所

C Asking questions about new duties 新工作相關問題

11	Who should I talk to about the telephone system?	我要找誰詢問電話系統的問題？
12	If I have a question about the data, should I speak to George?	若我對資料有疑問，是要問喬治嗎？
13	Who is the **go-to person**[1] on the project?	這個案子的**負責人**是誰？

1 **go-to person/guy** 負責人

Review Questions

Listen to the conversations and answer the questions below.

15 1. **Who is the woman?**

(A) The man's colleague.
(B) A new employee.
(C) A client.
(D) The man's friend.

2. **Why does the man like to talk to new employees?**

(A) Because he likes to take care of others.
(B) Because he likes to hear new opinions.
(C) Because he is often out of the office.
(D) Because he is often too busy to talk later on.

3. **How does the man treat new employees?**

(A) He tries to be available to new employees.
(B) He is not available to new employees.
(C) He cannot help new employees.
(D) He is indifferent to new employees.

16 4. (A) Jeff, why don't you tell me a little bit about yourself?

(B) Gladly. Well, I'm a bit of ________________. I have two dogs at home and I ________________ at the animal ________________ on the weekends.

Ans B, D, A, dog nut, volunteer, shelter

UNIT 04 認識辦公室環境 Learning About Your Office

(17) B Babara K Katharine

Barbara is explaining the office layout[1] to Katharine.
芭芭拉正在向凱薩琳說明辦公室格局。

B It can be easy to **get turned around**[2] here, so let me show you around. The office is set up in two long **corridors**[3] that begin at reception. The managers' offices are on the right; everything else is on the left.

K I see.

B Here's the kitchen, just **down the hall**[4] from your **cubicle**[5]. Across from the kitchen is the mail room. That's where the fax and scanners are. If you need to send a letter, post it and put it into one of these **cubby holes**[6] in the middle of the room. There are separate places for local, domestic, and international mail.

K Got it.

B The bathrooms are at the very end of this corridor. The door after the bathroom is the emergency exit, which goes to a stairway. Be careful, because that door locks automatically. If you get locked out, you have to walk down to the first floor and take the elevator back up.

K Good to know!

B The fifth floor of this building is ours, too; that's where the **executives**[7] are. We share this floor with a consulting firm. The second and third floors are a small publishing company, and the first floor is all building maintenance. And, back to your cubicle. Your computer **is hooked up to**[8] a printer that is just around that corner. Have you seen it?

K Yes, I'm pretty comfortable with this area by now. Thanks for the tour.

B 這裡很容易**迷路**，所以我先帶妳到處逛逛。從接待處這裡開始，辦公室在兩條**長廊**上。經理辦公室在右邊，其他人的辦公室在左邊。

K 知道了。

B 從妳的**座位沿著走廊**走就是茶水間。茶水間對面是收發室，放置傳真機和掃描機的地方。要寄信的話，把信放到房內其中之一的**信箱**中，本地、國內其他地區與國際信件分別放不同的地方。

K 了解。

B 洗手間在這條走廊的盡頭，洗手間後方的門是通往樓梯的緊急逃生口。這扇門會自動鎖上，如果妳被鎖在門外，要走到一樓再搭電梯回來，這點要注意。

K 多虧妳告訴我！

B 此棟大樓的五樓也是我們的，是**主管們**辦公的地方。我們和一家顧問公司共用此層。二、三樓是一家小型出版社，一樓則是建築維護管理處。然後回到妳的座位，妳的電腦**連接**到轉角的印表機，有看到嗎？

K 有的，我現在對環境很了解了。謝謝妳的導覽。

1 **layout** [ˋleˏaʊt] (n.) 格局；布置
2 **get turned around** 迷路
3 **corridor** [ˋkɔrɪdɚ] (n.) 走廊
4 **down the hall** 沿著走廊
5 **cubicle** [ˋkjubɪkl̩] (n.) 隔間
6 **cubby hole / pigeonhole / mailbox** 信箱
7 **executive** [ɪgˋzɛkjʊtɪv] (n.) 行政主管
8 **be hooked up to** 連接

emergency exit 緊急出口

cubicle 工作隔間

executive's office 主管辦公室

mail room 收發室

Useful Expressions

A Describing the location of things inside a building (18) 描述建築內的物品位置

1	His office is the first door on the left.	他的辦公室位於左邊第一間。
2	The conference room is down the hall on the right, across from the vending machine.	會議室在走廊盡頭右側，販賣機的對面。
3	The elevators are on the other side of the **courtyard**[1].	電梯在**庭院**的另一邊。
4	Please wait in the waiting room, which is through the door next to this reception counter.	請在等候室等待，從這個接待櫃檯旁邊的門進去。
5	The executive offices are directly above us, on the third floor.	**主管**辦公室就在我們樓上三樓。
6	The cafeteria is two floors down.	自助餐廳在往下兩層樓。

B Asking where things are 詢問位置

7	Can you tell me where the staff **lounge**[2] is?	可以告訴我員工**休息室**在哪裡嗎？
8	Is there a bathroom on this floor?	這層樓有洗手間嗎？
9	Are the elevators before or after the **stairwell**[3]?	電梯在**樓梯間**的前面還後面？
10	Excuse me, is this the way to Conference Room 2?	不好意思，請問這是往二號會議室的路嗎？
11	Where can I find a water fountain?	哪裡有飲水機？

1 **courtyard** [ˋkortjɑrd] (n.) 庭院
2 **lounge** [laʊndʒ] (n.) 休息室
3 **stairwell** [ˋstɛrwɛl] (n.) 樓梯間

Office 辦公室

water dispenser/cooler 飲水機

drinking/water fountain 飲水機

vending machine 自動販賣機

courtyard 庭院；天井

waiting room 等候室

staff lounge 員工休息室

Review Questions

Listen to the conversations and answer the questions below.

(19) 1. **Where are the bathrooms?**

Ⓐ They are on the left. Ⓑ They are on the second floor.

Ⓒ They are to the left of the stairway. Ⓓ They are on this floor.

(20) 2. **What happened to the man?**

Ⓐ He is on the wrong floor. Ⓑ He is in the wrong building.

Ⓒ He is in the wrong suite. Ⓓ He is taking the elevator.

(21) 3. **What probably happened to the woman?**

Ⓐ She is lost. Ⓑ She is hungry or thirsty.

Ⓒ She is busy. Ⓓ She is bored.

(22) 4. Ⓐ Sorry, I've forgotten where the ______________ is. Could you point the way for me?

Ⓑ Sure. Go to the end of this ______________ and turn right. The mail room is ______________ the emergency exit at the end of the hall.

Ans B, A, B, mail room, corridor, opposite

UNIT 05 認識公司週遭環境
Learning About Locations Near Your Office

23 Ⓚ Katharine Ⓑ Barbara

Katharine wants to go out for lunch. She asks Barbara about restaurants nearby. 凱薩琳要外出吃午餐，她向芭芭拉詢問這附近的餐廳。

Ⓚ I was wondering if there are any places to eat within **walking distance**[1]?

Ⓑ Well, across the street from the building is a shopping center. There's a Mexican restaurant there, and a sandwich shop, and there's a supermarket that has a pretty good salad bar.

Ⓚ That sounds good.

Ⓑ Then if you go out and turn right and head down to Apple Ridge Road—it's the first light—**catty-corner**[2] from you is a bakery that has good croissants and coffee. There are a bunch of restaurants along Apple Ridge Road, but you couldn't walk to them.

Ⓚ What kind of restaurants?

Ⓑ Oh, about a mile down there's a sushi place. Further along, near the **highway exit**[3], is a good Chinese **takeout**[4] and a Peruvian place.

Ⓚ Great, thanks. Can I ask you one more thing? Is there a dry cleaner nearby?

Ⓑ Yes. From here, you go out and turn left; then keep on this road for three blocks. You **go through**[5] one set of traffic lights. At the second set of lights—it's a big **intersection**[6]—you turn right. That's Plum Tree Road. Go down Plum Tree Road for another few blocks and it's on the left.

Ⓚ Thank you!

Ⓚ 我在想，這附近有**走路就能到**的用餐地點嗎？

Ⓑ 這個嘛……公司對街有一間購物中心，裡面有墨西哥餐廳、三明治店，還有間超市，它的沙拉吧很不賴的。

Ⓚ 聽起來還不錯。

Ⓑ 如果妳出去右轉，走到蘋果脊路，到第一個紅綠燈時，妳的斜對面有一間麵包店，他們的牛角麵包跟咖啡滿好的。蘋果脊路上有好幾間餐廳，不過步行沒辦法到達。

Ⓚ 什麼樣的餐廳？

Ⓑ 大約一哩路外，有一家壽司店。再過去，接近**高速公路出口**處有間中式**外賣餐館**和祕魯餐廳。

Ⓚ 太棒了，謝謝。可以再問一個問題嗎？這附近有乾洗店嗎？

Ⓑ 有。妳從這裡出去左轉，沿著此路過三條街，妳會經過一個紅綠燈，到第二個紅綠燈會有個大十字路口，向右轉就是李樹路了。沿著李樹路走過幾條街後，就在左邊。

Ⓚ 謝謝妳！

1 **walking distance** 步行距離
2 **catty-corner/catercorner** 斜對面
3 **highway exit** 公路出口
4 **takeout** [ˋtekaʊt] (n.) 外賣餐館
5 **go through** 穿越
6 **intersection** [͵ɪntɚˋsɛkʃən] (n.) 十字路口

Types of Restaurant 餐廳種類

ethnic restaurant 異國風味餐廳

fast food restaurant 速食餐廳

food stall 食物攤販

bistro 餐酒館

buffet (restaurant) 自助式吃到飽餐廳

diner 餐館

cafeteria （公司或學校附設的）自助餐廳

café 咖啡店

pub 酒吧

food court 美食街

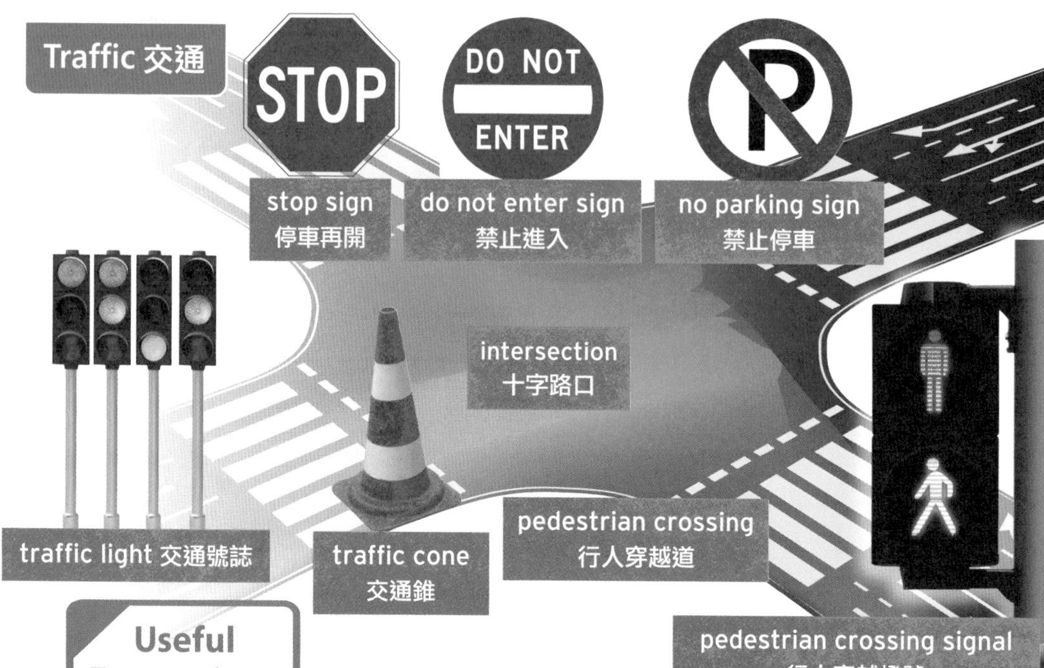

Useful Expressions

A Describing locations outside the office 敘述辦公室外的地點 (24)

1	The parking garage is under the building.	停車庫在大樓地下。
2	The gas station is on the next block, past the **four-way stop**[1].	加油站在下一條街，**四方停車指示**路口再過去。
3	The restaurant is three blocks down Charles Street.	沿著查爾斯街過三個街區就到餐廳了。
4	The florist is across the street.	花店就在對街。
5	The hotel is about a mile north of here.	旅館大概在北邊一哩遠處。

B Giving directions 指路

6 To get to the restaurant, go straight out from the parking garage. Turn right at the first **stop sign**[2] and it's on your left.

要前往餐廳的話，出停車庫後直行，看到第一個**停止標誌**右轉後，就會看到餐廳在左邊。

7 To get to the highway, turn left out of the building. Follow Main Street for three or four blocks, then turn right onto Elm Street. The exit is another kilometer or so down Elm Street.

要到公路的話，出大樓後向左轉，沿著緬因街經過三或四個街區，再右轉榆樹街，沿著榆樹街再開車約一公里左右就到出口了。

8 Take the highway exit toward **Route**[3] 13, going north. You'll be on that road for about five minutes. Make a left on Maple Street. Go through three sets of **stoplights**[4]. We're the first building on the right after the third stoplight.

在往 13 號**公路**的出口下交流道，朝北前進。大概開了 5 分鐘左右，在楓樹街左轉。過三個**紅綠燈**後，我們就在過第三個紅綠燈的右邊第一棟。

1 **four-way stop** 四方停車指示牌
2 **stop sign** 「停車再開」標誌
3 **route** [rut] (n.)（美國的）公路
4 **stoplight / traffic light** 紅綠燈

Review Questions

Listen to the conversations and answer the questions below.

25 **1. How far away is the Turner Building?**

- Ⓐ Around the corner.
- Ⓑ A few blocks.
- Ⓒ At the next traffic light.
- Ⓓ It is on the next blocks.

26 **2. Where is the post office?**

- Ⓐ It is on the same street as the building.
- Ⓑ It is on Rosebud Street.
- Ⓒ It is at the traffic light.
- Ⓓ It is on the woman's right.

3. Which directions should the woman go?

- Ⓐ The woman should turn right out of the building.
- Ⓑ The woman should turn left out of the building.
- Ⓒ The woman should walk straight out of the building.
- Ⓓ The woman should walk south out of the building.

27 **4.** Ⓐ Could you please tell me how to get to the ________________?

Ⓑ Sure. Come out of the ________________ and turn right. Go straight through the first light and you'll see a sign for ________________ 12. Take Highway 12 north. The hotel is just off of Exit 9. You can see it from the road.

Ans B, B, B, hotel, parking lot, Highway

UNIT 06 認識公司組織
Learning About Your Company's Organization

Randal is talking to his supervisor, Lawrence, about the company's organization. 藍道正與主管羅倫斯討論公司的組織。

L Here's our **organizational chart**[1], Randal. As you can see, in the end we **are** all **accountable to**[2] the Board of Directors. Glenn Wilson deals with them most of the time, and Penelope Granger handles more of the operations side of things.

R OK.

L Anne Handley manages our group. I meet with her every week and with Joyce Sterne a little less often. Anne, Joyce and I meet with Yu-Fong on an **as-needed basis**[3] to **give her a heads-up**[4] on what's happening in our departments. She's got the final say on what happens in our department.

R Does she ever meet with the rest of the staff?

L Yes, occasionally she will come to one of our program **wrap-up**[5] or **kick-off**[6] meetings. You'll meet her before too long.

R Oh, good.

L Here is the **HR**[7] set up. You'll have met our HR contact, Sarah. Her boss is Barry, but you'll probably never need to meet with him. Sarah does a good job of taking care of us. And I think that's that. Do you have any questions about our setup here?

R No, I don't think so. Thanks for showing me this.

Ⓛ 藍道,這是我們的**組織圖**。如你所見,最後大家都要**對**董事會**負責**。大多時候都由葛倫·威爾森負責董事會相關事務,潘妮洛普·格蘭潔則處理營運方面事務。

Ⓡ 知道了。

Ⓛ 安·韓德里管理我們的團隊,我每週都和她開會,和喬伊絲·史登就沒那麼頻繁。安、喬伊斯與我**在需要時**也會和玉鳳開會,**告知**她部門目前的狀況。而她擁有我們部門的最終決定權。

Ⓡ 她曾經與其他員工開會嗎?

Ⓛ 她偶爾會在與**總檢討**會議與**誓師**大會上出席,你不久後就會見到她。

Ⓡ 太好了。

Ⓛ 這是**人資部門**,你以後會見到我們的人資部聯絡人莎拉。她的上司是貝瑞,不過你應該不會見到他,莎拉把我們照顧得很好。我想大概就這樣了,對我們組織還有什麼疑問嗎?

Ⓡ 我想沒有,謝謝你告訴我這些。

1 **organizational chart** 組織圖
2 **be accountable to** 對……負責
3 **as-needed basis** 有需要時
4 **give sb. a heads-up** 提醒或警告某人
5 **warm-up** [ˋræp͵ʌp] (adj.) 總結的
6 **kick-off** [ˋkɪk͵ɔf] (adj.) 開始的
7 **HR (= human resource)** 人力資源

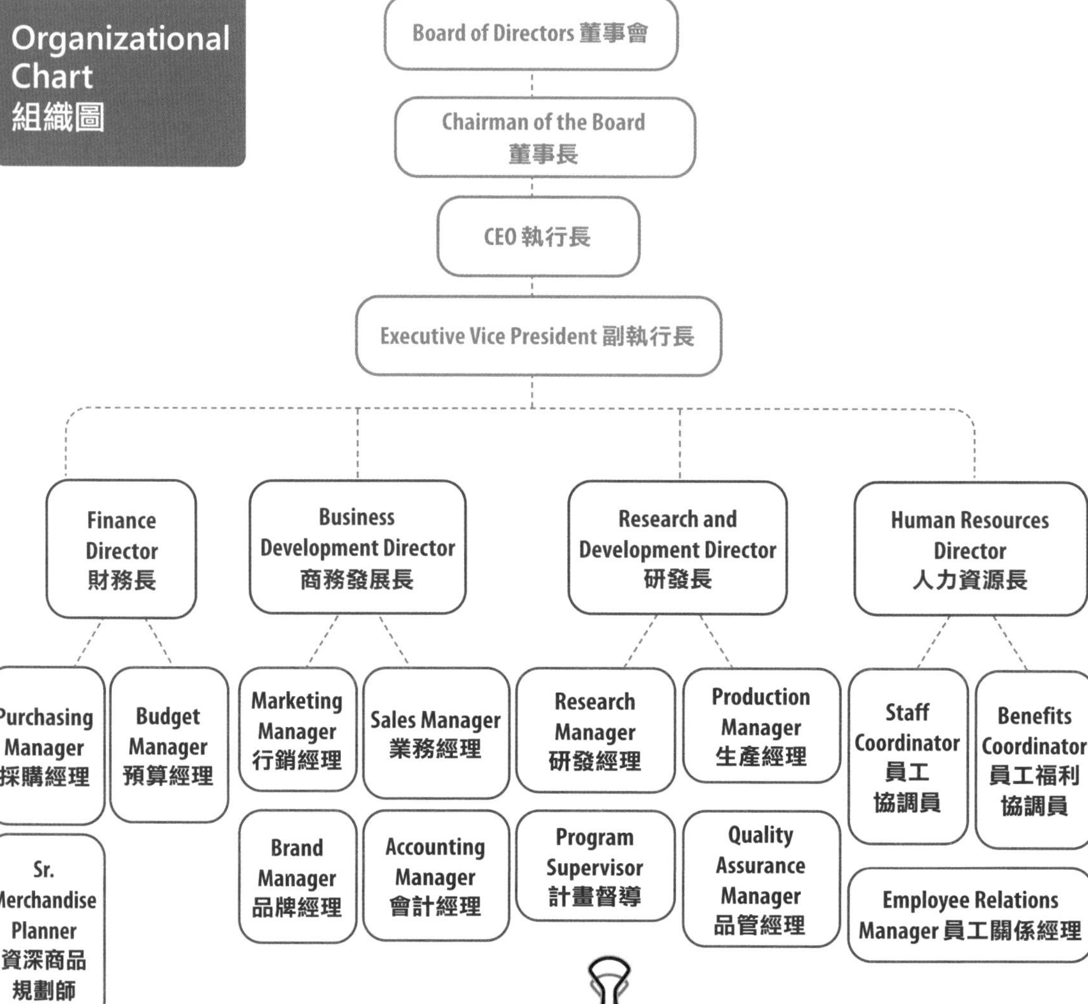

職稱字首大寫的注意事項

❶ 大多的職稱手冊上指出，職稱的字首**不一定需要使用大寫**。

❷ 當**職稱**跟著**人名**一同出現，字首才需要**大寫**，且職稱通常在**人名前**，例如：

- Africa **Regional Manager** Andrea Sterne
  非洲區經理安德雅・史登
- **Professor** Marshall
  馬歇爾教授
- **Finance Director** Michael O'Dell
  財務主管麥可・歐戴爾

❸ 若職稱置於姓名後則無須大寫，例如：

- Sanaz Kumar, **human resources director**
  沙納茲・庫馬，人事部主管

Useful Expressions

A Describing positions 說明職位 29

1 The budget manager **oversees**[1] and approves budgets for company projects.

預算經理負責**監督**與批准公司專案的經費。

2 Human resources handles hiring and firing employees and **administrating**[2] benefits.

人力資源部負責聘用和解僱員工，以及**管理**員工的福利。

3 The regional managers are responsible for all of the company's projects in their region.

地區經理要為他們區內所有的案子負責。

4 Program analysts work on individual projects with research assistants.

電腦程式分析師與研究助理一起合作處理個別的案子。

5 Marketing Manager Yu-Tian Han establishes marketing **strategies**[3] and oversees all staff and activities in the marketing department.

行銷經理韓羽恬負責規劃行銷**策略**，與監督行銷部門的員工與活動。

1 **oversee** [ˌovɚˋsi] (v.) 監督
2 **administrate** [ədˋmɪnəˌstret] (v.) 管理
3 **strategy** [ˋstrætədʒi] (n.) 策略

B Describing relationships 說明關係

6 **CEO**[1] Glenn Wilson **is accountable to**[2] the Board of Directors.
執行長葛倫·威爾森要向董事會負責。

7 The finance director, business development director, international relations director, and human resources director all report to the CEO.
財務主管、業務發展主管、國際關係主管，與人資主管都要向執行長報告。

8 The international relations director has the **last word**[3] on all health projects in every region.
國際關係主管對各區域的健保計畫有決定權。

9 How many staff work under the budget manager?
預算經理的下屬有多少人？

10 Where do accounts managers fall in the **hierarchy**[4]?
會計經理是屬於哪一階層的？

Review Questions

Listen to the conversations and answer the questions below.

30 1. **Who in the conversation has the highest rank?**

Ⓐ Anne. Ⓑ Joseph. Ⓒ Bob. Ⓓ Aaron.

2. **Who answers to Aaron?**

Ⓐ Anne. Ⓑ Bob. Ⓒ Joseph. Ⓓ The speakers.

31 3. **What does the man want to do?**

Ⓐ He wants to speak to Gloria.
Ⓑ He wants to speak to Ron.
Ⓒ He wants to get his project approved.
Ⓓ He wants to figure out who's in charge.

4. **Who must approve the project before it can begin?**

Ⓐ Ron. Ⓑ Gloria Shue.
Ⓒ The woman speaking. Ⓓ The man speaking.

32 5. **A** Who should I talk to about a problem with my ____________?
B That would be HR's ____________.
A Can I speak to anyone in the department?
B Well, I'd talk to Sally, the ____________ for our group. Or you could go over her head and talk to the HR manager.

Ans D, C, C, B, insurance, responsibility, administrator

1 **CEO (Chief Executive Officer)** 執行長
2 **be accountable to** 對⋯⋯負責
3 **last word** 決定權
4 **hierarchy** [ˋhaɪərɑrkɪ] (n.) 階層

UNIT 07 詢問與說明職務 Asking/Answering Questions About Your Duties at Work

(33) K Katharine J Jacob

Katharine is asking Jacob about her responsibilities.
凱薩琳詢問雅各自己的職務。

K Jacob, can you tell me what I should do to finish this data entry project? I know that my main duties will be **centered around**[1] analyzing the data, but should I start in on that right away? Should I write up a report on what I've done first?

J Oh, it's not necessary to write a report on that. But before you start the analysis, I want you to read some of our previous reports, to get a sense of what we look for and how our analysis is organized, because you're going to be responsible for setting up the database that organizes our results. Because this is your first time, please show me the database before you start the analysis. I might want to make some changes.

K OK. And will I be working on writing for this project?

J I want you to stay focused on the data for now, so no, not this time. You'll get a chance to write soon, but in this position you are mainly going to be doing **data-crunching**[2].

K 雅各，你可以告訴我要做什麼好完成資料輸入嗎？我知道我主要的工作是資料分析，但是要立刻開始嗎？我需要寫工作紀錄嗎？

J 噢，不用寫那個。不過由於妳將要負責建立結果整理的資料庫，所以要開始分析前，我想要妳先讀過以前的報告，好對我們需要什麼、如何組織報告有個頭緒。因為這是妳第一次做，請先讓我看過資料庫之後，妳再開始分析，我或許會想做些修正。

K 好。那我要替這個專案寫報告嗎？

J 這一次不用，我要妳目前專心於數據就好。妳很快就有機會寫了，不過妳這個職位主要是要做**資料運算**。

1 **center around** 以……為中心
2 **data-crunching / number crunching** 資料運算

Useful Expressions

A Describing responsibilities 說明職務 (34)

1	Our division works on building **brand identity**[3], **market shares**[4], and **brand-marketing strategies**[5].	我們的部門負責建立**品牌識別**、**市佔率**與**品牌的行銷策略**。
2	I was hoping you could take care of the meeting set-up so I can work on my presentation.	我希望你能負責安排會議，如此一來我才能準備我的簡報。
3	Julie's going to **handle**[6] the layout, so you don't need to worry about that.	茱莉會**負責**安排，你就不用擔心了。
4	All our research budgets fall **under the authority of**[7] the finance department.	我們所有的研究經費都**由**財務部**掌控**。

B Asking about responsibilities 詢問職務

5	Who is **in charge of**[8] marketing?	誰**負責**行銷？
6	Who is responsible for making travel arrangements?	誰負責安排旅遊？
7	What should I be focusing on now?	我目前應該以什麼為重？
8	What should my priorities be in this position?	此職位的優先工作為何？

3 **brand identity** 品牌識別
4 **market share** 市佔率
5 **brand-marketing strategy** 品牌行銷策略
6 **handle** [ˋhændl̩] (v.) 處理
7 **under the authority of** 由……支配
8 **in charge of** 主掌；負責

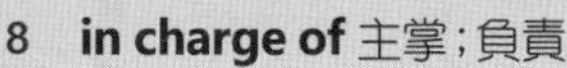

Conference Equipment 會議使用的設備

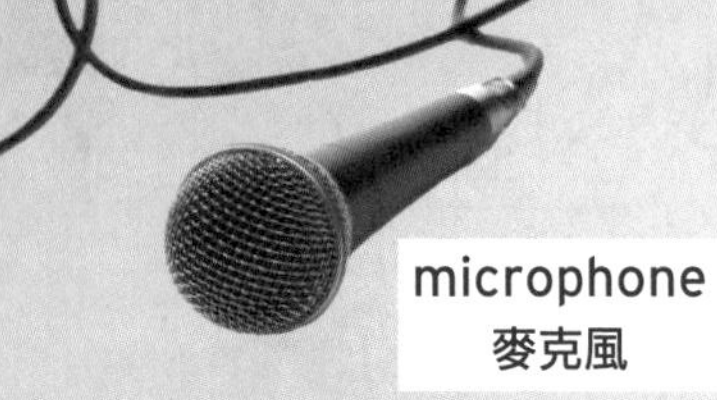

microphone
麥克風

computer cable 電腦傳輸線

tablet 平板電腦

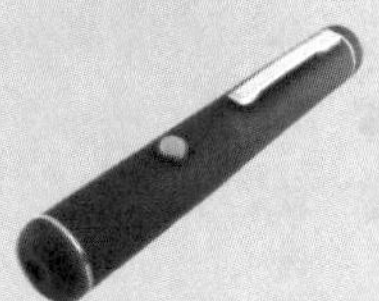

laser pointer 雷射筆

loudspeaker 喇叭

laptop 筆記型電腦

remote clicker
簡報筆

webcam
網路攝影機

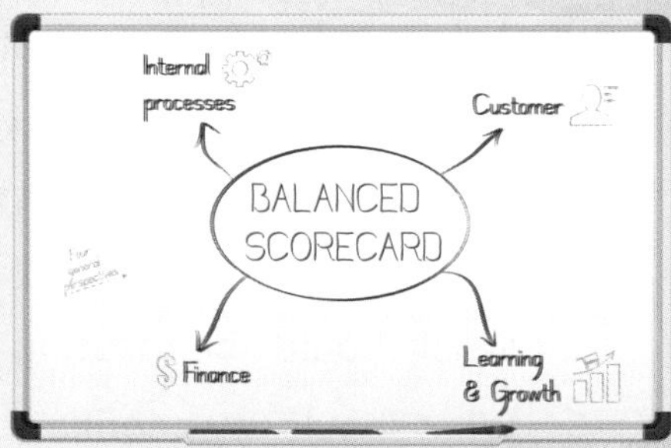

interactive whiteboard 互動式電子白板

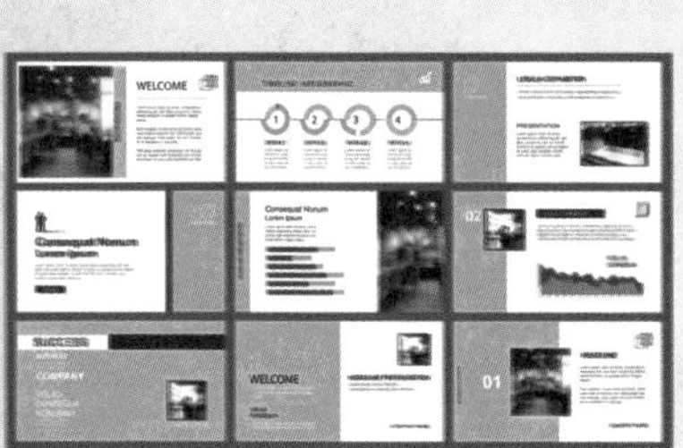

presentation slide 簡報投影片

projector 投影機

projection screen
投影屏幕

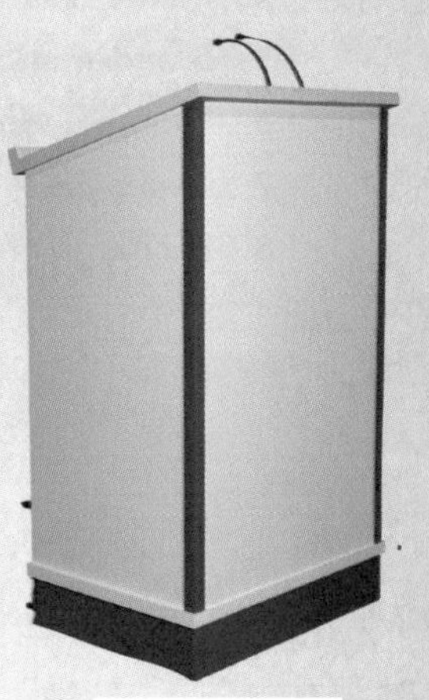

lectern 講台

videoconferencing software
視訊會議軟體

Skype

Zoom

Google Meet

Review Questions

Listen to the conversations and answer the questions below.

(35) 1. **What didn't the woman do?**

Ⓐ The woman didn't complete her work.
Ⓑ The woman didn't understand what she was supposed to do.
Ⓒ The woman didn't direct the report to the right person.
Ⓓ The woman didn't wait to find out what to do.

2. **Who is in charge of reviewing reports?**

Ⓐ The man. Ⓑ The woman.
Ⓒ The manager. Ⓓ The marketing team.

(36) 3. **What is most likely Chloe's job?**

Ⓐ A receptionist. Ⓑ A CEO.
Ⓒ An accountant. Ⓓ A budget director.

4. **What do they need a temp to do?**

Ⓐ Call the agency. Ⓑ Be responsible for the office.
Ⓒ Call to Chloe. Ⓓ Handle the phones.

(37) 5. **A** Hey, I need some help—we're in the middle of a meeting here and the ____________ with our presentation on it just crashed. Can you help me get it to work again?

B Gosh, I usually only ____________ routine maintenance. Let me call Leah, who's ____________________ emergency repairs.

A Alright. Just ask her to come quickly.

Ans B, C, A, D, laptop, deal with, in charge of

UNIT 08 辦公室的基本問候語 Greetings and Small Talk in the Office

 B Barbara K Katharine A April C Carl

Colleagues are talking about their weekends on a Monday morning. 星期一早上，同事們互相討論著上週末的活動。

B	Good morning, Katharine. How was your weekend? I saw your pictures on Facebook; it seems like you had a good time!
K	Oh, it was pretty nice. I went outside and enjoyed the sunshine a lot. How about you?
B	I enjoyed the sun, too. I mostly worked in my garden over the weekend. I'm not much of a partyer.
A	Good morning, ladies.
K B	Hi, April.
A	Hi. Mondays, ugh. I need some more coffee.
K	**Late night**[1]?
A	It was a busy weekend. Fun, but busy. I had some friends visiting from out of town, and I **went** totally **overboard**[2] showing them a good time. I think I need about ten more hours of sleep before I'll be any use to anyone.
C	Hi, you all.
B	Hi, Carl. How are you doing? You **don't look so hot**[3].
C	I'm beat. I was sick all weekend and I still haven't managed to **shake it**[4].
K	Oh dear! I think I have some vitamin C, if you want some.
C	I think I'm OK for now. I'm going to go hide in my **cube**[5].
K	Feel better! OK, **back to the grind**[6], I guess.

B 凱薩琳早安。週末過得如何?我在臉書上面看到妳的照片,看起來妳玩得很愉快!

K 噢,還不錯,我出門曬了很多太陽。妳呢?

B 我也享受了陽光,幾乎整個週末都在院子裡東弄西弄。我實在不是派對咖。

A 早安啊,小姐們。

K B 早,艾波。

A 又到星期一啊。我需要多點咖啡提神。

K 妳**玩到很晚**?

A 週末真是忙翻了,又忙又好玩。我和幾位外地來的朋友簡直是**玩瘋了**,我看我要再睡上十小時才有辦法幫你們任何人的忙。

C 大家早。

B 早啊,卡爾。你**看起來很疲累**,怎麼啦?

C 我累斃了。整個週末都在生病,到現在都還沒**痊癒**。

K 噢我的天啊!你需要的話,我這裡有些維他命 C。

C 我現在還好,我要去窩在我的**座位**上了。

K 早日康復!好吧,我想該**回去繼續工作**了。

1 **late night** 熬夜
2 **go overboard** 玩瘋了
3 **not look so hot** 看起來很疲倦
4 **shake sth.** 擺脫某事
5 **cube** [kjub] (n.) 辦公室座位小隔間
6 **back to the grind = back to work** 繼續工作

Common Social Networking Sites 常見社群網站

Useful Expressions

A Asking about the past weekend 詢問上個週末 39

1	How was your weekend?	週末過得好嗎？
2	What did you do this weekend?	你這週末做了什麼？
3	Did you have a good weekend?	週末玩得開心嗎？

B Asking about plans 詢問計畫

4	What are you up to this weekend?	你週末打算要幹嘛？
5	What are you going to do over the vacation?	你放假要做什麼？
6	Do you have plans for the holiday?	你放假有何計畫？

C Asking about someone's health 詢問某人健康狀態

7	How are you feeling today?	你今天還好嗎？
8	Are you OK? You look tired / **worn out**[1] / **under the weather**[2].	你**滿臉倦容**，還好吧？＊
9	Are you feeling any better?	你好點了嗎？

＊ 有些人會忌諱被他人說滿臉倦容或臉色不佳，因此評論同事的外表時，要格外注意。

D Commenting on someone's appearances 評論他人外表 (40)

10	You look like you're **on the mend**[3].	你似乎**正在好轉中**。＊
11	Anne looks very well-rested today.	看起來安今天好好休息過了。
12	John looks like he's been **run ragged**[4].	約翰看起來**很累**的樣子。
13	That's a beautiful dress you have on.	你身上穿的洋裝好漂亮。
14	I love your new shoes! Where did you get them?	我愛死你的新鞋了！哪裡買的？

＊ 頌讚同事外表時也必須注意。雖然批評他人的外表很不禮貌，但刻意恭維可能顯得虛情假意，或有拍馬屁之嫌。

1 **worn out** 筋疲力盡的；極累的
2 **under the weather** 身體不適
3 **on the mend** 在好轉中
4 **run ragged** 使筋疲力竭

E Talking about holidays, weekends, and events
談論假期、週末和活動

15	I had a really relaxing holiday.	我有個超悠閒的假日。
16	My weekend was **jam-packed**[1].	我的週末事情排得**滿滿的**。
17	We had an incredible vacation.	我們有個超棒的假期。
18	We've got **big plans**[2] for next month's trip.	有關下個月的旅行，我們已經擬了**重大的計畫**。

1 **jam-packed** [ˋdʒæmˋpækt] (adj.) 塞滿的
2 **big plan** 重要計畫

Review Questions

Listen to the conversations and answer the questions below.

41 **1. Why did the woman stay in bed all weekend?**

- (A) She was tired.
- (B) She was sick.
- (C) She was working.
- (D) She wanted to waste her time.

2. Why did the woman say her weekend was wasted?

- (A) Because she was too sick to enjoy it.
- (B) Because she had to work during the weekend.
- (C) Because she didn't go to any events.
- (D) Because she slept too much.

42 **3. What are the women talking about?**

- (A) They are talking about shoes.
- (B) They are talking about work.
- (C) They are talking about shopping.
- (D) They are talking about time.

4. What is the condition of the shoes?

- (A) They are new.
- (B) They are old.
- (C) They are borrowed.
- (D) They are broken.

43 5. **A** Hey, Claire! I saw your pictures on Instagram last night! It seems you had a really cool party. Did you ________________ anything yesterday?

B Oh, yes. It was my boyfriend's birthday, so we ________________ a room at a KTV for it.

A Wow, I bet you had a great time!

B Indeed. Everything was great, except my ________________ is killing me now. I definitely need more coffee!

Ans B, A, A, B, celebrate, reserved, hangover

UNIT 09 電話禮儀 Telephone Etiquette[1]

(44) B Barbara S Shannon C Caller

1 Shannon, the new temp[2], is taking on Barbara's telephone duties.
新來的約聘員工雪儂代理芭芭拉的職務。

B OK, Shannon, I'm on my way out. **Are** you **up to**[3] dealing with the phones?

S **No sweat**[4].

B 雪儂，我要出去一趟，妳**可以**幫忙接電話嗎？

S **小事一樁**。

2 Shannon answers the phone. 雪儂接聽電話。

S Good morning, ABC Industries. This is Shannon speaking; how may I help you?

C Hello. I'm trying to reach Amazonia Textiles.

S I believe you've dialed the wrong number—this is ABC Industries.

C **My mistake**[5]. So sorry.

S That's alright. **Wrong numbers**[6] happen! *(Shannon hangs up.)*

S 這裡是 ABC 企業。您好，我是雪儂，請問有什麼可以為您服務的嗎？

C 您好，我要找亞馬遜尼亞紡織。

S 這裡是 ABC 企業，您可能打錯電話囉。

C **我的錯**，不好意思。

S 沒關係，誰都會**打錯電話**。*(雪儂掛上電話。)*

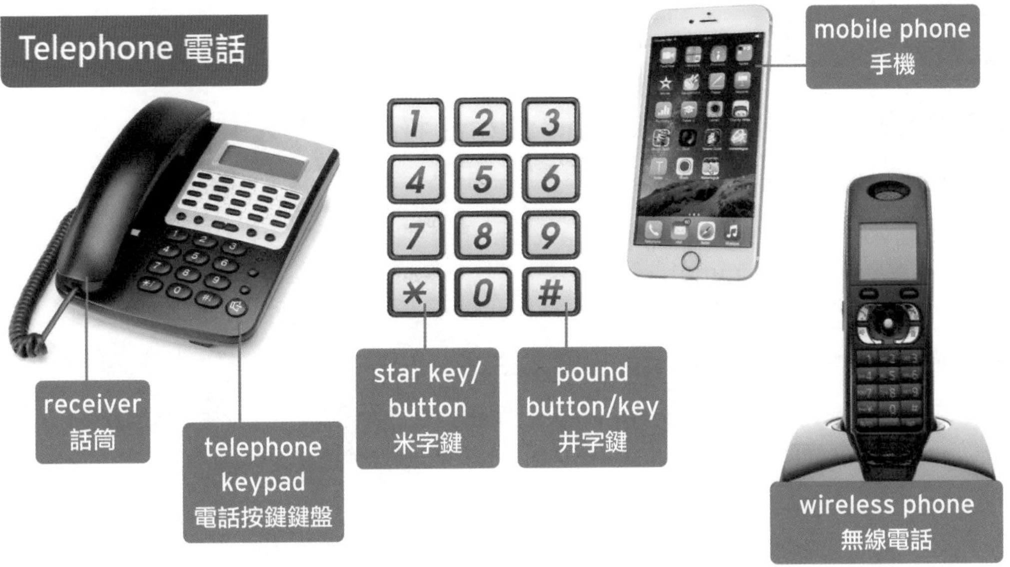

3 Shannon answers the phone again. 雪儂又接了一次電話。

Ⓢ Good morning, ABC Industries. This is Shannon speaking; how may I help you?

Ⓒ Jacob Smith's office, please.

Ⓢ May I tell Mr. Smith who's calling?

Ⓒ Yes, this is Jordan Jeon of Top Design.

Ⓢ Please wait one moment and I'll **transfer**[7] you.

Ⓢ ABC 企業，您好。我是雪儂，有什麼能為您服務的嗎？

Ⓒ 麻煩請找雅各．史密斯的辦公室。

Ⓢ 請問是哪裡找史密斯先生？

Ⓒ 我是頂尖設計公司的喬登．田。

Ⓢ 請稍等，我將為您**轉接**。

1 **etiquette** [ˋɛtɪkɛt] (n.) 禮節；禮儀
2 **temp** [ˋtɛmp] (n.) 短期約聘人員
3 **be up to (sth.)** 能夠（做某事）
4 **no sweat** 小事一樁
5 **my mistake** 我的錯
6 **wrong number** 打錯電話
7 **transfer** [trænsˋfɝ] (v.) 轉接（電話）

Useful Expressions

A Reaching someone on the phone 打電話給某人 (45)

1	I'll **buzz**[1] Joe this afternoon.	我今天下午會**打給**喬。
2	Can you **ring**[2] Isabelle for me and tell her I'll be over in a few minutes?	你可以幫我**打給**伊莎貝爾，告訴她我等一下會過來嗎？

B Answering the phone 接聽電話

3	Good morning/afternoon/evening, ABC Industries. (This is) Sean speaking.	早安／午安／晚安，這裡是 ABC 企業。我是尚恩。
4	Helix Industries, may I help you?	這裡是黑力克斯公司，可以為您效勞嗎？
5	Good afternoon, Jean Otas' office, Knot speaking.	午安，這裡是吉恩·歐塔斯的辦公室，我是諾特。
6	Sean speaking. How can/could/may I help you?	我是尚恩。有什麼能為您服務的嗎？
7	You've **got/dialed the wrong number**. = You **have the wrong number**[3].	您**打錯電話**了。

C Making a phone call 撥打電話

8	May I speak to Jean Otas, please?	我可以請吉恩·歐塔斯先生聽電話嗎？
9	This is James Warbler of Helix Technologies calling for Jean Otas.	我是黑力克斯科技公司的詹姆斯·沃布勒爾，想要找吉恩·歐塔斯先生。
10	Hi, I'm trying to reach Jean Otas.	嗨，我想找吉恩·歐塔斯先生。
11	I'd like to speak to someone in your human resources department, please.	我想請貴公司人力資源部門的人聽電話，麻煩您。

D Asking for the caller's name/information 詢問來電者姓名／資訊 (46)

12	Who's calling, please?	請問您是哪位？
13	Could/May I take/have your name, please?	請問大名？／ 請問怎麼稱呼您？

14	May I tell her who's calling?	我可以告訴她是哪位打來的嗎？
15	May I ask who you are calling, please?	請問您要找誰？
16	Who shall I say is calling?	請問是哪位？等會兒我好回話。
17	May I ask what this is regarding?	請問有什麼事嗎？

E Asking the caller to wait 請來電者稍等

18	Could you hold on a moment/minute, please?	請稍等一下。
19	Just a moment/minute, please.	請稍待片刻。
20	Please hold on.	請稍待一下。
21	I'm not sure if he's in yet. Hold on and I'll check for you.	我不確定他回來了沒。請稍等，我為您確認一下。
22	Sorry. I've got another call coming in. Can I call you later?	不好意思，有另外一個電話插播，我等一下再回電給你，可以嗎？

F Saying someone is busy or out 告知某人沒空或不在 (47)

23	Carl isn't in (the office) at the moment.	卡爾目前不在（辦公室）。
24	Andy is away **on business**[4] until Wednesday.	安迪**出差**到週三。
25	John **is out of the office**[5] today.	約翰今天**不在辦公室**。
26	Mr. Laurie **is away from his desk**[6] at the moment.	勞里先生目前**不在座位上**。
27	John has just stepped out for a moment.	約翰才剛出去一會兒。
28	John is not expected back until early next week.	約翰預計要到下星期初才會回來。
29	I'm sorry, he's in a meeting now.	抱歉，他現在正在開會。
30	I'm sorry, Carl is not available now. Would you like his voice mail?	很抱歉，卡爾目前沒空。您要不要留言在他的語音信箱？

1 **buzz** [bʌz] (v.) 打電話給……
2 **ring** [rɪŋ] (v.) 打電話給……
3 **get/dial the wrong number** = **have the wrong number** 打錯電話
4 **on business** 出差
5 **be out of the office** 外出；不在公司
6 **be away from sb's desk** = **be not at sb's desk** 不在座位上

31	Carl is not able to take your call right now; may I take a message?	卡爾目前無法接電話，要幫您留言嗎？
32	Carl is away from his desk at the moment. Is there someone else who can help you?	卡爾目前不在座位上，還有別人可以幫您嗎？
33	She is on the phone / on another line / on another call right now. Please call back later.	她現在在電話中，請稍後再來電。
34	He is on his lunch break.	他在午休。
35	He has left for the day.	他已經下班了。
36	He is not at this company anymore.	他不在這間公司了。
37	She is off / on leave / not on duty today. I'm her **substitute**[1]/**deputy**[2].	她今天休假，我是她的職務代理人。
38	He is on annual leave. I'm his substitute/ deputy today. How can I help you?	他休年假，我是他的職務代理人。有什麼可以幫忙的嗎？

G Transferring a call 轉接電話 (49)

39	**Hold on**[3] one moment while I **put you through**[4] to Anne Handley.	**請稍等**，我將幫您**轉接**給安·韓德里。
40	Please hold and I'll transfer you to Mr. Jacob's office.	請稍候，我會馬上把您的電話轉接到雅各先生的辦公室。
41	I'll connect you to Jacob Smith now.	我現在就幫你把電話轉給雅各·史密斯。
42	Mr. Smith? I've just got a Mr. Jordan Jeon on the line for you from Top Design. Will you take the call?	史密斯先生嗎？我剛接到一位來自頂尖設計公司的喬登·田先生來電，你要接嗎？
43	I'm getting a **busy signal**[5] at Mr. Jacob's office. Can I transfer you to someone else?	雅各的辦公室正忙線中，我可以把你的電話轉給其他人嗎？

H Finishing a conversation 結束通話

44	Thank you for calling, Mr. Black. Goodbye.	謝謝您來電，布萊克先生。再見。
45	Thank you for calling ABC Industries. Have a nice day!	感謝您致電 ABC 企業。祝您有個美好的一天！
46	Let's keep in touch. Goodbye.	讓我們保持聯絡。再見。

Review Questions

Listen to the conversations and answer the questions below.

50 **1. Who is the caller?**

Ⓐ Leah Hammer. Ⓑ Jonathan Busey. Ⓒ Phoenix Pharmaceuticals.

2. Who does the caller want to speak to?

Ⓐ Leah Hammer. Ⓑ Jonathan Busey. Ⓒ Phoenix Pharmaceuticals.

51 **3. What will the caller do?**

Ⓐ He will leave a message. Ⓑ He will call again later.
Ⓒ He will send an email. Ⓓ He will leave a voice message.

4. Where is Mr. Dover?

Ⓐ He is at a meeting. Ⓑ He is at lunch.
Ⓒ He is out of the office. Ⓓ It is not known.

52 **5. What will the receptionist do?**

Ⓐ The receptionist will take a message.
Ⓑ The receptionist will leave a message.
Ⓒ The receptionist will leave a voice mail.
Ⓓ The receptionist will transfer the call to Rachel Ravin.

6. What is Ms. Raven doing now?

Ⓐ She is in a meeting. Ⓑ She is out to lunch.
Ⓒ She is going to pick up the call. Ⓓ She is very busy.

Ans A, B, B, D, A, D

1 **substitute** [ˋsʌbstəˏtjut] (n.) 代理人
2 **deputy** [ˋdɛpjətɪ] (n.) 代理人
3 **hold on** 稍等
4 **put sb. through** 幫某人轉接（電話）
5 **busy signal** 忙線中的信號

Part 2 公司內部溝通 Communication in the Office

UNIT 10 記錄留言 Taking Messages

Shannon is handling the telephones at ABC Industries.
雪儂正接聽 ABC 企業的一通來電。

S Good morning, ABC Industries. This is Shannon speaking; how may I help you?

C Hello, I'd like to speak to Bob Carmody, please.

S I'm sorry, Mr. Carmody isn't **available**[1] at the moment. Would you like his voice mail?

C Actually, could I leave a message with you? I don't think Bob checks his voice mail that often.

S Of course. Who's calling, please?

C This is George Simian from Utmost Contractors.

S Would you spell your last name for me?

C Sure, that's S-I-M, M as in man, I-A-N, N as in Nancy.

S Thank you. What is the message you'd like to leave?

C Please let Bob know that the shipping times have been **pushed back**[2], and the materials for the Houston project won't arrive until Tuesday afternoon, not Monday. Everything should still arrive in plenty of time for the **kick-off**[3] meeting.

S OK, let me read that back to you: the materials for the Houston project will arrive on Tuesday afternoon, not Monday, but everything should still arrive in time for the kick-off.

C That's it. Thank you. Oh, and have him call me when he gets a chance.

S **Will do.**[4] Thank you.

S ABC 企業。您好，我是雪儂，請問有什麼能為您效勞的？

C 您好，請找鮑伯．卡莫迪。

S 很抱歉，卡莫迪先生目前無法接聽電話。您要不要在他的語音信箱留言？

C 您可以替我留言給他嗎？事實上，我認為鮑伯不太會去查看自己的語音信箱。

S 當然沒問題。請問是哪位找他？

C 我是「極致承包商」的喬治．斯緬。

S 可以麻煩拼出您的姓氏嗎？

C 沒問題，是 S-I-M，man 的字首 m；I-A-N，Nancy 的字首 n。

S 謝謝。請問您的留言是？

C 請告訴鮑伯，休士頓一案的出貨時間**延後**了，材料要到星期二下午才會抵達，而不是星期一。不過在專案**啟動**會議前，貨物還是有充足時間可以抵達。

S 好的，我唸一次給您聽：休士頓案子的材料要到星期二下午才會抵達，而不是星期一。不過在專案啟動會議前，貨物還是能即時送達。

C 沒錯，謝謝。對了，請他有空撥個電話給我。

S **沒問題**。謝謝。

1 **available** [ə`veləbl] (adj.) 有空的
2 **push back** 延遲
3 **kick-off** [`kɪk͵ɔf] (adj.) （活動）開始的
4 **Will do.** 沒問題。

Useful Expressions

A Asking to leave a message 請求留言 (54)

1	Could you **pass on**[1] a message for me?	可以麻煩您替我**傳**個話嗎？
2	Can I give you a message for her?	能請您替我留言給她嗎？
3	Could I leave a message, please?	請問是否可以留言呢？
4	Could you tell her that her friend Kyle called?	可以請您告知她，她的朋友凱爾打給她嗎？
5	Could you ask her to call me when she is available? My number is 2233-0756.	可以請您告訴她有空時回電給我嗎？我的電話號碼是2233-0756。

B Offering to take a message 幫忙留言

6	Can I take a message?	要留言嗎？
7	Would you like to leave a message?	您要留言嗎？
8	Can I give Mr. Jones a message from you?	要幫您留言給瓊斯先生嗎？
9	If you'd like to give me your number, I'll ask him to call you back.	如果您願意留下您的電話號碼，我會請他回電給您。

C Asking for information 詢問資訊

10	Could you tell me what this is regarding?	能請您告訴我這與什麼有關嗎？
11	May I have your name, please?	請問您貴姓大名？
12	Who shall I say is calling?	請問哪裡找？
13	What message would you like me to give him?	請問您要我傳什麼話給他？
14	Please tell me your phone number. Is it a direct line, or do you have an **extension**[2]?	請問您的電話是多少？直撥即可，還是有**分機**號碼？

1 **pass on** 傳遞　　2 **extension** [ɪkˋstɛʃən] (n.) 分機

D Clarifying information 說明資訊 (55)

15	Would you please spell that for me?	可以請您拼給我聽嗎?
16	**Come again?**[3] Could you repeat that for me?	**您說什麼?**可以再說一次給我聽嗎?
17	Please let me read this back to you.	我覆述一次給您聽。
18	Before you go, let me **double check**[4] this information.	您掛電話前,我**再確認一次**資訊。
19	Excuse me, is this a **solicitation**[5]? We don't accept solicitations over the phone.	請問,這是**推銷**嗎?我們不接受電話推銷。

E Telephone problems 電話問題

20	The line is very bad . . . could you speak up, please?	線路不太穩……可以請您大聲一點嗎?
21	I think I lost you. Are you still there?	我想電話斷線了,您還在嗎?
22	I'm afraid I can't hear you.	恐怕我聽不到您的聲音。
23	Sorry. I didn't catch that. Could you say it again, please?	對不起,我沒有聽到,可以請再說一次嗎?

3 **Come again?** 你說什麼?
4 **double check** 再次確認
5 **solicitation** [sə͵lɪsɪˋteʃən] (n.) 推銷;拉客

Review Questions

Listen to the conversations and answer the questions below. 

1. Important Notice

For	
Date	Time ________ a.m. / p.m.
M*	
Of*	
Phone	

Follow-up action:

- ☐ Please call
- ☐ Wants to meet
- ☐ Will call again
- ☐ Needs attention

Message

Signed

*M in this case stands for Mr., Mrs., or Ms.; the title of the person who has called.
*Of indicates the company the caller works for.

Ans Important Notice

For	Office manager (name)
Date	Time ______ a.m. / p.m.
M*	(Ms.) Gloria
Of*	Strong Telecom
Phone	(07) 285-3394, extension 19

Follow up action:

☑ Please call ☐ Will call again
☐ Wants to meet ☐ Needs attention

Message

Please call back to discuss VOIP (Voice Over Internet Protocol) service that can save half on monthly phone bills and most of long distance bills.

Signed *(Shannon's initials)*

57

2. Important Notice

For	
Date	Time ________ a.m. / p.m.
M*	
Of*	
Phone	

Follow-up action:

☐ Please call
☐ Wants to meet
☐ Will call again
☐ Needs attention

Message

Signed

Ans **Important Notice**

For	Barbzara
Date	Time ______ a.m. / p.m.
M*	(Ms.) Sue Granger
Of*	Your Way Caterers
Phone	

Follow up action:

☐ Please call ☐ Will call again
☐ Wants to meet ☑ Needs attention

Message

Confirmed that she will be here next Thursday to set up at 10:45 a.m., as agreed. Please call with any changes.

Signed *(Shannon's initials)*

UNIT 11 請假 Taking a Day Off

1 Katharine wants to take a day off to visit with her parents.

凱薩琳想休一天假去見父母。

MESSAGES

From:	Katharine Sylvester (sylversterk@abcindustries.com)
To:	Jacob Smith (smithj@abcindustries.com)
Subject:	Requesting leave next Friday, February 19

Dear Jacob,

As I might have mentioned, my family will be coming for a visit next weekend. They are flying in from Montana and will be arriving at the airport late Friday morning. I would really appreciate it if I could take a **personal day**[1] on Friday to pick them up at the airport and get them settled in at my apartment. This will be their first visit to Virginia and our first visit in a year, so I want to spend as much time with them as possible.

Of course, I don't want to **disrupt**[2] our work or the progress of any projects. Please let me know if there is anything you would like me to finish before Friday, or if there is anything I can do to make sure things go smoothly without me.

Thank you,
Katharine

寄件人：Katharine Sylvester (sylversterk@abcindustries.com)
收件人：Jacob Smith (smithj@abcindustries.com)
主旨：2 月 19 日下星期五請假

親愛的雅各：

我或許之前有提過，下週末我的家人要來看我。他們從蒙大拿搭飛機過來，會在下星期五早上抵達。如果星期五能請**事假**去機場接他們回我家，我會很感謝您的。這將是他們第一次來維吉尼亞州，也是我們今年首度見面，所以希望能儘量與他們多相處些時間。

當然我也不希望**影響**到工作或案子的進度，所以，若您有任何事務需在星期五前完成的，請一定要跟我說；或請告訴我為確保我不在的時候一切順利，是否有任何事是我能先做的。

謝謝您。

凱薩琳

Leave 請假

- personal leave 事假
- sick leave 病假
- official leave 公假
- annual leave 年假／特休
- marriage leave 婚假
- funeral leave 喪假
- injury leave 傷假
- maternity leave 產假
- paternity leave 陪產假
- menstrual leave 生理假
- paid leave 有薪假
- unpaid leave 無薪假
- take (a/an) . . . leave 請……假
- ask . . . for leave 向……請假
- take + 天數／星期 + off 請幾天／星期幾的假
- grant leave 准假
- on leave 告假中
- leave request form 假單
- come in late 遲到
- leave early 早退

2 Jacob stops to speak with Katharine about her request.

雅各停下手邊工作，與凱薩琳討論她的申請。

J Hi, Katharine. I got your email and I think taking Friday off will be fine. You aren't getting close to any project **deadlines**[3] right now, are you?

K No, nothing is due for the next few weeks. We seem to **be on track**[4].

J Yes, you seem to **be** really **on top of things**[5]. All I need for you to do before you go is write up a **quick note**[6] about where you are on your tasks and where any important files are, so people can find them while you're gone. You can give the note to Barbara on Thursday. I hope you have a good time with your family!

K Great. Thanks very much!

J 凱薩琳，我收到妳的信了，休星期五我想是沒問題的。妳最近沒有在趕任何案子的**截止日**吧，有嗎？

K 沒有，接下來的幾個禮拜都沒有要趕截止日。我們一切都**很順利**。

J 很好，看起來妳的進度很不錯。我只要妳在離開前把妳的工作進度和重要文件的擺放位置寫在一張**小紙條**上，這樣妳不在時同事才找得到。妳星期四再把便條交給芭芭拉吧。希望妳和家人玩得開心！

K 太好了，謝謝！

1 **personal day = personal leave** 事假
2 **disrupt** [dɪsˋrʌpt] (v.) 使中斷
3 **deadline** [ˋdɛdlaɪn] (n.) 截止日
4 **be on track** 平順；進行順利
5 **be on top of things** 跟上進度
6 **quick note** 內容簡短的便條

Useful Expressions

A Asking for time off 請求休假 (60)

1 I would like to take a personal day on March 3.
3 月 3 日我想請一天事假。

2 I've got a dentist **appointment**[1] on April 15. Would it be alright if I took the morning off?
我 4 月 15 日有**預約**看牙醫，可以請上午的假嗎？

3 I'm planning a trip to the beach and I'd like to use five of my vacation days.
我正在籌劃去海邊旅行，想請五天的年假。

4 I'd like to use my ten vacation days in August, but I can be **flexible**[2] on the exact dates.
我在 8 月想要請十天的年假，但確切的日期還不確定。

5 My sister is getting married on November 1. I'd like to take the day as a **paid holiday**[3].
我姊 11 月 1 日要結婚，當天我想要請一天**年假**。

B Calling in sick 請病假

6 I'm sorry, I feel awful. I think I'm going to have to take a **sick day**[4].
很抱歉，我身體不適，要請一天**病假**。

7 I just don't feel well enough to come in. I'd like to take the day off, but I'**m** so **backed up**[5]. I think I'll just work from home.
我覺得不舒服要請一天假，不過待辦事項嚴重**落後**，我想還是在家中做好了。

8 I have to stay in bed for the next three days. I guess I'll have to use all of my **sick leave**[6].
接下來三天我都會臥病在床，我想我應該要請完全部的**病假**了。

9 I've already used my all my sick leave, but I can't come in with a broken ankle. I hope that I can take some **unpaid leave**[7].
我的腳踝受傷還無法上班，但已把所有病假用完了，希望能放幾天**無薪假**。

10 Bob's not here; he **called in sick**[8].
鮑伯沒來，他**打電話請了病假**。

Review Questions

Listen to the conversations and answer the questions below.

61 **1. What does John want the woman to do?**

Ⓐ John wants the woman to take her day off after Tuesday.
Ⓑ John wants the woman to take a day off this week.
Ⓒ John wants the woman to take a day off whenever she wants.
Ⓓ John wants the woman to take a day off immediately.

2. What is the problem that their office is facing?

Ⓐ Their office is very slow right now.
Ⓑ Their office is very busy right now.
Ⓒ Their office is approaching a deadline.
Ⓓ Their office is expanding operations.

62 **3. Who is sick?**

Ⓐ Joe. Ⓑ Sara.
Ⓒ Alex. Ⓓ Gilbert.

4. Who is Alex most likely to be?

Ⓐ Joe's friend. Ⓑ Joe's supervisor.
Ⓒ Sara's employee. Ⓓ Sara's assistant.

63 **5.** Ⓐ Hey, Jim, I just wanted to remind you that I've got a dentist ____________ next week, so I won't be in on Tuesday. Is there anything you need me to do before we finish the report?

Ⓑ Oh, thanks for ____________ me. Yes, on Monday would you ____________ the drafts one last time?

Ⓐ Sure.

Ans A, B, A, B, appointment, reminding, proofread

1 **appointment** [əˋpɔɪntmənt] (n.) 預約
2 **flexible** [ˋflɛksəbl] (adj.) 有彈性的
3 **paid holiday = paid vacation = paid leave** 給薪假；年假；特休
4 **sick day** 病假
5 **be backed up** 落後
6 **sick leave** 病假
7 **unpaid leave** 無薪假
8 **call in sick** 打電話請病假

UNIT 12 說明遲到原因
Explaining Reasons for Being Late

Katharine is late for work. 凱薩琳上班遲到了。

K Hi, Jacob. I'm so sorry I'm late—there was terrible traffic. There had been an accident and they **shut down**[1] both lanes of Route six for an hour. Traffic was **backed up**[2] for miles!

J Oh wow. That must have been annoying. I'm glad you're here—we were just worried about you. Next time, please call if you're going to be late. We don't mind—everybody **oversleeps**[3] sometimes. Just let us know.

K Yes, I'm sorry about that. I wanted to call, but I forgot to charge my phone last night and it **died**[4].

J Never mind. Thanks for stopping by. Have a good day.

K You too. Sorry again.

J Oh, and why don't you **pop by**[5] Ann's desk and let her know you're in? I know she'll have some tasks for you later today.

K 早，雅各。很抱歉我來晚了，交通狀況很糟。路上發生車禍，6 號公路雙線道路都因此**關閉**了一小時，交通一團糟，**塞車**塞到好幾哩外！

J 哇塞，這樣一定很煩。很開心妳還是到達了，大伙們都在擔心妳呢。下次如果妳發現妳會遲到，請記得要打電話。我們不會介意的——誰沒**睡過頭**過呢？只要知會一聲就好。

K 我知道了，真是不好意思。本來要打電話的，但昨晚忘記充電，手機**沒電**了。

J 沒關係。謝謝妳還來跟我說，希望妳有個愉快的一天。

K 你也是，真的是很抱歉。

J 對了，妳何不**去找**安，讓她知道妳進公司了？我知道她今天有工作要交付給妳。

Useful Expressions

A Explaining being late through your own fault (65)
說明因自身問題而遲到的理由

1 I'm so sorry I'm late! I **slept** straight **through**[6] my alarm.
對不起我遲到了！我**完全沒聽到鬧鐘響**。

2 I really apologize for just getting here! I lost my keys and had to **turn the house upside down**[7] to find them.
剛剛才來，真的很對不起！我弄丟鑰匙，**找遍整間房子**才找到它們。

3 I couldn't get out the door this morning—I've become so **scatterbrained**[8]. I had to run back for my keys, then my laptop, and then my lunch!
我今早一直出不了門，**丟三落四的**。回去拿了鑰匙、筆電，還有我的午餐！

4 I just couldn't **get going**[9] this morning.
今早我就是不想**出門**。*

* 對上司而言，這種理由表示員工的工作態度消極，因此只適合用於同事間的閒談。

1 **shut down** 關閉
2 **back up** 堵（車）
3 **oversleep** [͵ovɚˋslip] (v.) 睡過頭
4 **die** [daɪ] (v.) 沒電；因沒電而停止運轉或報廢
5 **pop by** 短暫拜訪
6 **sleep through** 無視……繼續睡
7 **turn sth. upside down** 將……弄得天翻地覆
8 **scatterbrained** [ˋskætɚbrend] (adj.) 丟三落四的
9 **get going** 出發；開始

這些遲到的理由較為合情合理，且無法避免。

B Explaining being late through someone else's fault
説明因他人問題而遲到的理由

5 You would not believe the traffic today! It took me more than an hour to get here.

你不會相信今天的交通有多可怕！我多花了一小時才到公司。

6 When I went to start my car this morning, it wouldn't work. I had to call a friend to come **give me a jump**[1].

今天早上我發動車子時，車子完全沒反應。我只好打電話請朋友來**幫我替車子充電**。

C Explaining being late through someone else's fault on the phone
在電話上說明因他人問題而遲到的理由

7 I woke up this morning and discovered that my basement had flooded in the night. I've got to wait for the **plumber**[2] to show up, but I'll be in as soon as I can.

早上起床發現地下室在晚上時淹水了，我需要等**水管工人**過來，但我會儘快趕到公司。

8 I'm sorry, but my daughter is really sick this morning and I'm going to have to take her to the doctor. I'll call you when I know what is happening and I'll get in as soon as I can.

很抱歉，但今早我女兒病得很嚴重，我要帶她去看醫生。等我確認情況後我會再打給你，並儘快到公司。

9 Hi, there. I'm on my way in, but I just **got into**[3] a **fender-bender**[4]. I'm fine, but we have to wait for the police and call the **insurance**[5] companies. I'll be there as soon as we finish.

嘿，我已經在路上了，但剛剛**發生了小擦撞**。我沒事，不過要等警察來並通知**保險**公司，結束後我會儘快到公司。

1 **give sb. a jump** 幫某人的車子充電
2 **plumber** [ˋplʌmɚ] (n.) 水管工
3 **get into** 涉入（事件或情況）
4 **fender-bender** [ˋfɛndɚˋbɛndɚ] (n.) 車子的小擦撞
5 **insurance** [ɪnˋʃurəns] (n.) 保險

Review Questions

Listen to the conversations and answer the questions below.

66 1. **Why did Leslie call?**

Ⓐ Because Carla is late.
Ⓑ Because she is still at home.
Ⓒ Because she got into an accident.
Ⓓ Because she will be late.

2. **When will Leslie get to the office?**

Ⓐ She doesn't know.
Ⓑ At 10:30.
Ⓒ Before the meeting.
Ⓓ At noon.

67 3. **Why will Margaret be late coming back from lunch?**

Ⓐ Because of the traffic congestion.
Ⓑ Because the restaurant's service is slow.
Ⓒ Because her car got towed.
Ⓓ Because she forgot that she still has to work.

4. **When will Margaret get back to the office?**

Ⓐ At 1:15.
Ⓑ Before her next client comes in.
Ⓒ Right away.
Ⓓ It will be uncertain.

5. **What does Margaret want Gail to do?**

Ⓐ Call the towing company.
Ⓑ Call her client to change the meeting location.
Ⓒ Call her client to postpone their appointment.
Ⓓ Meet the client for her.

Ans D, A, C, D, C

UNIT 13 公司內部的電子郵件
Email Correspondence Within the Company

68

MESSAGES

From:	Jacob Smith (smithj@abcindustries.com)
To:	Joyce Stern (sternj@abcindustries.com)
Subject:	Tentative work plan for the Myers report
Attachment:	Myers report work plan.doc

Dear Joyce,

Attached is the **tentative**[1] **work plan**[2] for the Myers report, as promised. After I receive your comments, I'll **distribute**[3] it to the staff and get their **two cents**[4].

Thanks,

Jacob

Jacob Smith
ABC Industries, Inc.
smithj@abcindustries.com
(303) 885-6600, ext. 558

寄件人：	Jacob Smith (smithj@abcindustries.com)
收件人：	Joyce Stern (sternj@abcindustries.com)
主旨：	麥爾斯報告的暫定工作計畫
附加檔案：	Myers report work plan.doc

親愛的喬伊絲：

附件是我之前允諾關於麥爾斯報告的**暫定工作計畫**。收到妳的評論後，我會**發給**員工們並詢問他們的**意見**。

謝謝妳。

雅各

雅各・史密斯
ABC 工業公司
smithj@abcindustries.com
(303) 885-6600, 分機 558

MESSAGES

From:	Joyce Stern (sternj@abcindustries.com)
To:	Jacob Smith (smithj@abcindustries.com)
Subject:	Re: Tentative work plan for the Myers report

Dear Jacob,

The work plan looks good. I didn't have any changes to make, so feel free to get **input**[5] from the staff and then **implement**[6] it. As long as you don't make major schedule changes, I won't need to review it again; just please send me the final plan for my files.

Thanks,
Joyce

Joyce Stern, Research Manager
ABC Industries
sternj@abcindustries.com
(303) 885-6600, ext. 446

寄件人：	Joyce Stern (sternj@abcindustries.com)
收件人：	Jacob Smith (smithj@abcindustries.com)
主旨：	Re: 麥爾斯報告的暫時工作計畫

親愛的雅各：

工作計畫沒問題，我沒有什麼要修改的。你就詢問員工**意見**，放手**實行**吧。只要時間表不要有太大的變動，我就不需要再看了。只要最後寄份最終計畫給我備檔即可。

謝謝你。

喬伊絲

研究經理　喬伊絲・史登
ABC 工業公司
sternj@abcindustries.com
(303) 885-6600, 分機 446

1 **tentative** [ˋtɛntətɪv] (adj.) 暫定的
2 **work plan** 工作計畫
3 **distribute** [dɪˋstrɪbjut] (v.) 分發
4 **two cents** 想法；意見
5 **input** [ˋɪnpʊt] (n.) 意見
6 **implement** [ˋɪmpləmənt] (v.) 實行

MESSAGES

From:	Jacob Smith (smithj@abcindustries.com)
To:	Katharine Sylvester (sylversterk@abcindustries.com), George Carlton (carltong@abcindustries.com), Anne Salisbury (salisburya@abcindustries.com)
Subject:	Myers report work plan
Attachment:	Myers report work plan.doc

Dear team,

As you know, the deadline for the Myers report is next month. Attached is a work plan that I've drawn up, which **divvies up**[1] responsibilities among the four of us. Because I'll be away for the next two weeks, it's very important for us to be **on the same page**[2] in terms of duties and time lines.

Please review the duties I've **allotted**[3] to each of us and think carefully about how you can achieve each in the time given. I welcome your **feedback**[4] on the plan, and I will be happy to make any necessary changes. If you want to change the schedule or ask me about your part of the work, please get in touch with me before the end of the day tomorrow. I will **incorporate**[5] all your **suggestions**[6] as best as I can. Then we can **touch base**[7] on the final plan on Thursday morning. I've booked the **conference**[8] room for 10 a.m.

Thank you all,
Jacob

Jacob Smith
ABC Industries, Inc.
smithj@abcindustries.com
(303) 885-6600, ext. 558

MESSAGES

寄件人：	Jacob Smith (smithj@abcindustries.com)
收件人：	Katharine Sylvester (sylversterk@abcindustries.com), George Carlton (carltong@abcindustries.com), Ann Salisbury (salisburya@abcindustries.com)
主旨：	麥爾斯報名工作計畫
附加檔案：	Myers report work plan.doc

親愛的夥伴們：

如各位所知，麥爾斯報告的截止日在下個月。附件是我擬好的工作計畫，上面**分配**好我們四人的工作。又由於我下兩個禮拜不在公司，所以我們在職務與計畫上能**達到共識**是非常重要的。

麻煩看完我**分配**給各位的工作，並仔細思考如何才能於指定時間內完成每個任務。我樂意接受各位對於計畫的**意見**，必要時也可做調整。若你想調整時間表或向我詢問你的工作職責，請在明天下班前和我聯絡。我會盡我所能將各位的**建議納入**其中，這樣一來便能在星期四早上**詳談**最後的定案。我已預約早上十點的**會議**室。

感謝各位。

雅各

雅各．史密斯
ABC 工業公司
smithj@abcindustries.com
(303) 885-6600, 分機 558

1 **divvy up** 分攤；均分
2 **on the same page** 達成共識
3 **allot** [əˋlɑt] (v.) 分配
4 **feedback** [ˋfid͵bæk] (n.) 反饋
5 **incorporate** [ɪnˋkɔrpə͵ret] (v.) 包含；將……納入
6 **suggestion** [səˋdʒɛstʃən] (n.) 建議
7 **touch base** 聯繫（某人）；（與某人）見面交談
8 **conference** [ˋkɑnfərəns] (n.) 會議

Useful Expressions

A Talking about email messages 談論電子郵件 (71)

1	Did you get the email I sent this morning?	你有收到我今早寄給你的電子郵件嗎?
2	The message I sent **bounced back**[1]. I must not have the right address.	我寄出的信**被退回來了**,一定是郵件地址錯了。
3	Can you call Nancy and tell her the materials are on their way—and then send an email to confirm, so she has it in writing?	你可以打給南西,跟她說貨物已在運送途中了,然後寄封信去確認,讓她有書面紀錄嗎?
4	As soon as I have a chance to go over the **agenda**[2], I'll email you my comments.	等我一看到**議程表**,我就會將我的意見寄給你。
5	Include Jason on the update email. He'll want to know what's going on.	將傑森加入更新的電郵名單中,他會想知道事情的最新發展。

B Talking about attachments 談論附加檔案

6	Please find the scans for the book design attached.	附檔為書籍設計的掃描檔案。
7	Attached are the drafts you requested.	附件為您要求的草稿。
8	I've attached the first five account summaries here.	我已將前五則的帳目摘要夾帶在檔案中。

C Talking about responding to email 談論電子郵件回覆

9	Please confirm your receipt of this message.	請確認您有收到此信。
10	Please respond as soon as possible.	請儘快回覆。
11	Please respond by email or by phone.	請以電郵或電話回覆。
12	Please do not hit "**reply all**[3]" when you respond, unless you have a comment for the entire list.	除非您想回覆給所有人,否則回信時請勿按「**全部回覆**」。

13 I will be out of the office from October 2-4. I will check my email when I return on October 5. For urgent questions, please contact Sonia Hendrickson at sonia.h@designplus.com.

我從 10 月 2 號到 4 號不在公司,一直到 10 月 5 號回到公司才會開信箱。如有緊急問題,請聯絡索妮雅·韓德克里森,郵件地址為:sonia.h@designplus.com。

Review Questions

Listen to the conversations and answer the questions below.

72 1. **What is strange according to the man?**

Ⓐ That the man has been at his computer all day.
Ⓑ That the man wanted to make design changes.
Ⓒ That the man hadn't gotten the woman's email.
Ⓓ That the man didn't send the design changes.

2. **Did the woman respond to the man's email?**

Ⓐ No.　Ⓑ Yes.

73 3. **Who will the email be addressed to?**

Ⓐ The whole office.　Ⓑ The woman.
Ⓒ The man.　Ⓓ The cleaners.

4. **What else does the woman want the man to do?**

Ⓐ Reply to her.　Ⓑ Forward the email to the cleaner.
Ⓒ Delete her from the message.　Ⓓ Cc her on the message.

74 5. **What is the man going to do?**

Ⓐ Forward the email to the woman.
Ⓑ Forward the email to Frida.
Ⓒ Respond to the woman's email.
Ⓓ Respond Frida's email.

Ans C, B, A, D, A

1 **bounce back** 退回
2 **agenda** [ə`dʒɛndə] (n.) 議程表
3 **reply all** 全部回覆

Part 2 公司內部溝通 Communication in the Office

UNIT 14 會議準備事項 Setting up a Meeting

75  

J Jacob　　K Katharine

Jacob is talking with Katherine about setting up a meeting.
雅各正與凱薩琳討論會議準備一事。

J I've been looking at the **progress reports**[1] on the project. Rather than give you feedback individually, I think we should meet as a team.

K Alright. When were you thinking of meeting?

J Well, I'm not sure of everyone's **schedules**[2], but I'd like to do it soon. Tomorrow afternoon, if possible, or Wednesday morning. Do you think you could speak to everyone and set an exact time?

K Certainly. You want to meet with the whole team, right? Do you want to include Barbara?

J I don't think we need Barbara for this one. We can **fill her in**[3] afterward.

K OK. I'll **touch base with**[4] everyone now and see if we can do two or three o'clock tomorrow. I have another meeting at four, so I can't do anything later than that. If not, I'll try to arrange something for Wednesday. Is any time before eleven alright?

J Yes. Thanks, Katharine.

J 一直以來我都有在看專案的**進度報告**，與其分別回饋意見給大家，我想我們應該開個團體會議。

K 好的，你想哪時候開會？

J 這個嘛，我不確定大家的**時間表**，但還是儘快舉辦吧。可以的話就明天下午或星期三早上。妳可以先跟大家說並訂個確切的時間出來嗎？

K 當然沒問題。你是要跟全體人員開會對吧？芭芭拉也要嗎？

J 這一次不用。之後再**告訴她**。

K 好，我會**聯絡**大家，看明天下午兩點或三點行不行。我四點有其他會議要開，所以之後的時間不行。不行的話，我再安排星期三的時間，11 點前可以嗎？

J 可以。謝啦，凱薩琳。

Meeting Seating Format 會議室的座位安排形式

theater-style 劇院型

classroom-style 教室型

hallow square-style 中空型

U-shape style U 字型

boardroom-style 董事會型

Useful Expressions

A Arranging a meeting 安排會議 (76)

1	I'd like to schedule a meeting with the design team.	我想找時間和設計團隊開會。
2	I need to meet with the **accountants**[5] before I leave.	在我離開前要先與**會計師**們開個會。
3	I want to do our project updates **face-to-face**[6].	我想**面對面**了解專案的最新消息。
4	Let's meet for a project update before the holiday.	我們在放假前先來開個專案最新進度的會議吧。

1 **progress report** 進度報告
2 **schedule** [ˋskɛdʒul] (n.) 時間表
3 **fill sb. in** 告知某人
4 **touch base with** 與……聯繫
5 **accountant** [əˋkaʊntənt] (n.) 會計師
6 **face-to-face** [ˋfestəˋfes] (adv.) 面對面地

B Discussing dates and times 討論日期與時間

5	Will you **be available**[1] next Friday?	下星期五你**有空**嗎？
6	**Are** you **free**[2] Thursday afternoon?	星期四下午你**有空**嗎？
7	How does Monday morning sound? Say, 9 a.m.?	星期一早上九點如何？
8	Can you do Monday at ten?	星期一早上十點可以嗎？
9	Tuesday morning is better for me.	星期二早上我比較有空。
10	I'm afraid Monday **is out**[3]—I'll be at the dentist.	星期一恐怕**不行**，我會去看牙醫。
11	Four o'clock isn't great for me.	四點我不行。
12	The afternoon is no good, but I'm free in the morning.	下午不行，不過早上我可以。
13	No one can make it this week. We're all **overwhelmed**[4]. We'll have to try for next week.	這禮拜沒有人可以，大伙都**忙翻**了。下星期才有辦法。

1, 2 **be available = be free** 有空的

3 **be out** 不可能

4 **overwhelmed** [ˏovɚˋhwɛlmd] (adj.) 難以承受的；窮於應付的

Review Questions

Listen to the conversations and answer the questions below.

77 **1. When did the people originally want to meet?**

Ⓐ Friday morning. Ⓑ Friday afternoon.
Ⓒ Thursday morning. Ⓓ Thursday afternoon.

2. When is the meeting set for?

Ⓐ Friday morning. Ⓑ Friday afternoon.
Ⓒ Thursday morning. Ⓓ Thursday afternoon.

78 **3. Who will the man contact?**

Ⓐ The contractors only. Ⓑ The project managers only.
Ⓒ Both of them. Ⓓ Neither of them.

4. When will the meeting be set?

Ⓐ This Tuesday. Ⓑ This Thursday.
Ⓒ Next Tuesday. Ⓓ Next Thursday.

79 **5. Why does the man want to meet the team?**

Ⓐ Because of the project reports.
Ⓑ Because of the project cost.
Ⓒ Because of the team members.
Ⓓ Because of the project schedule.

Ans B, C, B, C, D

UNIT 15 申請文具 Applying for Stationery

80 K Katharine B Barbara

Katharine needs stationery, and she's asking Barbara for help.
凱薩琳需要文具，她正向芭芭拉請求協助。

K Hi, Barbara. I'm sending out business letters and I'm going to need **letterhead**[1] and envelopes, but I can't find any in the copy room. Do I have to apply for **stationery**[2]?

B Oh, yes. There should be some forms you can use to apply in one of your desk drawers, but I've got some right here. Just check the boxes for the type of paper and the amount you need.

K Wow, I've never seen these terms before. What's a "**quire**[3]"?

B Oh, they're just terms for measuring amounts of paper. Since you'll probably be sending lots of business letters, why don't you just get a **ream**[4]? Then you can keep it at your desk and not bother with applying over and over again.

K That sounds good. Oh, and I need a box of pens, too. And probably a **stapler**[5]. Somehow I don't have any of that stuff!

B You can order all of that. And while we're at it, let's order you some business cards!

K 芭芭拉，我在寄商業信函，要用到**有信頭的信紙**跟信封。影印室裡都沒有了，我需要申請**文具**嗎？

B 噢，要，妳抽屜裡應該有用來申請的表單。不過我這裡就有幾張，只要在紙類與需要數量的小方框打勾就行了。

K 哇，沒看過這些用語耶。什麼是「**一刀**」？

B 那是計算紙張數量的用語。既然妳會寄很多商業信件，何不申請**一令**擺在桌上呢？這樣就不用一而再、再而三的申請了。

K 聽起來不錯。我還需要一盒筆，大概也需要一台**釘書機**，不知怎的，我完全沒有那些東西！

B 妳就全部申請吧，等我們要申請時再替妳申請一些名片！

1 **letterhead** [ˋlɛtɚˋhɛd] (n.) 印有信頭的信紙
2 **stationery** [ˋsteʃən͵ɛrɪ] (n.) 文具
3 **quire** [kwaɪr] (n.) 一刀（24 或 25 張紙）
4 **ream** [rim] (n.) 一令（25 刀或 480／500 張紙）
5 **stapler** [ˋstepl̩ɚ] (n.) 釘書機

Office Supplies 辦公用品

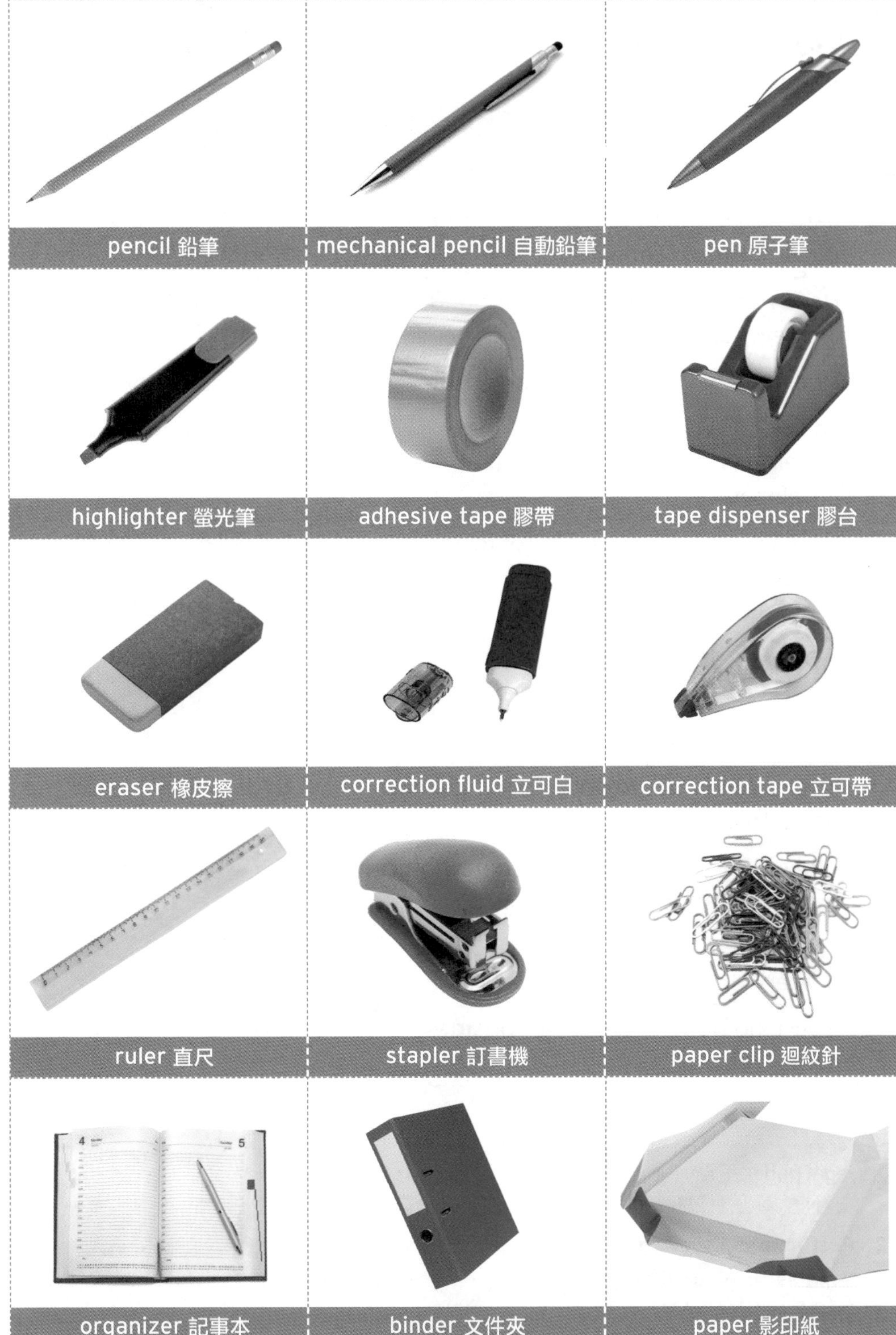

Useful Expressions

Post-It note 便利貼

legal pad 拍紙簿

A Talking about stationery 談論文具 (81)

1	Barbara, I'm going to need a few **legal pads**[1] for the meeting.	芭芭拉，我需要**拍紙簿**，會議上會用到。
2	Have you got a red pen lying around? There are never any of those when you need them!	你手邊有紅筆嗎？需要用的東西總是找不到！
3	Does anyone have extra **Post-It notes**[2]?	有人有多的**便利貼**嗎？
4	I'd like to get two boxes of **window envelopes**[3] and a box of standard envelopes.	我要兩盒**橫式開窗信封**跟一盒標準信封。
5	Have you got a few **sheets**[4] of **letter paper**[5]?	你有幾**張 letter 尺寸的紙**嗎？

B Applying for materials 申請用具

6	I need a new **mouse pad**[6]. Do we have those in the supply room?	我需要新的**滑鼠墊**，用品室裡有嗎？
7	Who should I talk to about getting a new office chair?	我要向誰申請新的辦公椅？
8	What is the process for getting new office supplies? I'**m out of**[7] everything!	申請辦公用品的流程是什麼啊？我東西全**用光**了！
9	What do I have to do to get a working printer?	申請能用的印表機需要什麼手續？
10	How long does it take to get **business cards**[8] printed?	印製**名片**要花多久時間？

1 **legal pad** 拍紙簿（一種上面印有橫線的可撕式黃色便條紙）
2 **Post-It note = sticky note** 便利貼
3 **window envelope** 橫式開窗信封
4 **sheet** [ʃit] (n.) 紙張
5 **letter paper** 尺寸 21.6 * 27.9 公分的紙
6 **mouse pad** 滑鼠墊
7 **be out of sth.** 用完某物
8 **business card** 名片

envelope 信封

window envelope 橫式開窗信封

Review Questions

Listen to the conversations and answer the questions below.

82 **1. What is the man probably going to do?**

Ⓐ Print a letter. Ⓑ Mail a letter.

Ⓒ Receive a letter. Ⓓ Copy a letter.

83 **2. What does the man want to do?**

Ⓐ He wants to print letters. Ⓑ He wants to print envelopes.

Ⓒ He wants to print a poster. Ⓓ He wants to apply for stationery.

3. What did the woman give the man?

Ⓐ A ream of paper. Ⓑ A quire of paper.

Ⓒ A sheet of paper. Ⓓ A few sheets of letterhead.

84 **4. What does the woman want to do?**

Ⓐ She wants to write on paper. Ⓑ She wants to fasten paper together.

Ⓒ She wants to erase marks. Ⓓ She wants to cut something off.

5. Where are the office supplies usually kept?

Ⓐ Sally usually keeps them. Ⓑ They usually are under the copier.

Ⓒ They usually are in the cabinet. Ⓓ They usually are in the hallway.

Ans B, A, D, B, C

UNIT 16 提出公務申請並請求批准
Making Requests Related to Your Work and Asking for Permission

 Ⓚ Katharine  Ⓙ Jacob

Katharine is asking Jacob for permission to make changes to her supplies and work routine. 凱薩琳問雅各她是否能替換用品與改變工作例行事務。

Ⓚ I think that in the future, when I start to travel more, it will be much easier to work from a laptop than to **transfer**[1] all my files—so **would it be possible**[2] for me to switch from my current desktop to a laptop?

Ⓙ I don't see why not. Barbara has computer **assignment**[3] paperwork; ask her for it and I'll sign it and we can get you switched.

Ⓚ Thanks, that's great. And another thing: I don't know what the office policy on working from home is. On days when the weather is bad, like it has been this week, or if I don't want to infect other people in the office when I'm sick, could I ever **work from home**[4]?

Ⓙ I don't know about that. So far, I've found that it's hard to manage people working from home, and it's so difficult for them to stay **on top of changes**[5] in the office that it's a struggle to get anything done. I think if you're sick enough to stay home, just take a day off. Maybe we'll **revisit**[6] the idea of working from home later, but for now it's not really an **option**[7].

Ⓚ OK, just checking. And one last question—the **glare**[8] through my window really **bugs**[9] me in the mornings. Can I move my desk to face a different direction?

Ⓙ You can move your desk to face anywhere you want!

1 **transfer** [træns`fɝ] (v.) 轉移
2 **would it be possible** 能否
3 **assignment** [ə`saɪnmənt] (n.) 分配
4 **work from home** = **telecommute** 在家工作
5 **on top of sth.** 掌控
6 **revisit (an idea, concept, etc.)** 重新考慮
7 **option** [`ɑpʃən] (n.) 選擇
8 **glare** [glɛr] (n.) 刺眼的強光
9 **bug sb.** 使困擾

K 我想，等以後需要在外奔波時可能用筆記型電腦比較方便，就不用把檔案**傳**來傳去，所以**可以**把我目前的桌上型電腦換成筆電嗎？

J 可以啊，芭芭拉負責電腦的事務，妳去跟她說，我會簽核。我們就可以幫妳換了。

K 太好了，謝啦。還有一件事，我想請問公司對於在家工作的政策為何？像是這禮拜以來天候不佳，或是我生病時不想傳染給其他同事，可以**在家工作**嗎？

J 這我不清楚。目前我認為管理在家工作的人很困難，他們也很難**掌控**公司內的任何變動，要做好事有點難。我認為，若妳不舒服到要在家中休息，就請假吧。或許之後我們會**再考慮**在家工作的想法，但目前不考慮。

K 好，只是問問看而已。最後一個問題——早上從我窗戶照進來的**陽光**讓我很**困擾**，我可以把桌子轉到別的方向嗎？

J 妳想面向哪都不是問題！

Office Supplies 辦公用品

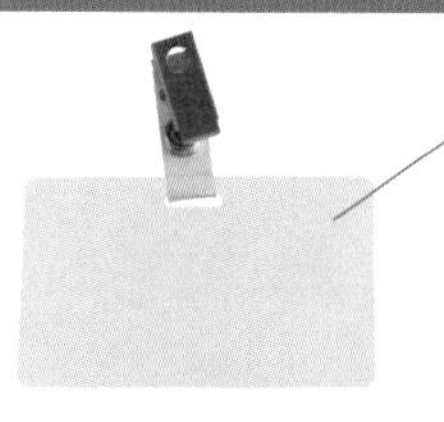

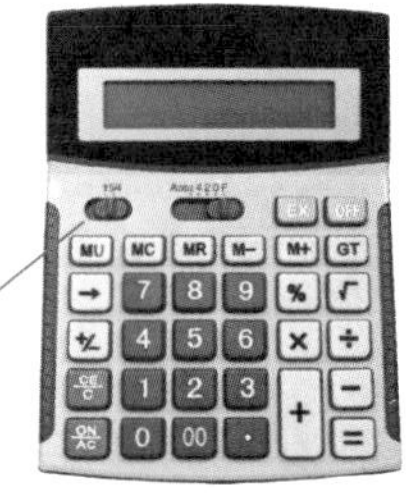

ID badge 識別證

staple remover 拔針器

stamp 橡皮章

calculator 計算機

corkboard / bulletin board 軟木告示板

box cutter 美工刀

L folders L 夾

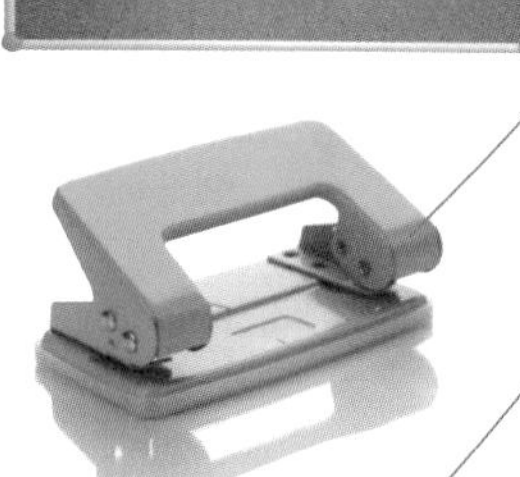

hole puncher 打孔器

scissors 剪刀

folders 資料夾

pencil cup 筆筒

trash bin 垃圾桶

binder clip 長尾夾

clipboard 板夾，帶夾寫字板

filing case 文件盒

bookend 書檔

business card 名片

Useful Expressions

A Making requests with "can" 用 can 提出要求

1	Jordan, can I speak with you before **close of business**[1]?	**下班**前能跟你談談嗎，喬登？
2	**Can I ask you to**[2] move that table a little to the left?	**可以請您**將桌子稍往左移嗎？
3	Can we change the meeting time to three o'clock?	我們可以將會議時間改到三點嗎？

B Making polite requests with "could" and "would" 用 could 與 would 禮貌地提出要求

4	George, could you print out the meeting **agenda**[3], please?	喬治，可以麻煩你印出會議的**議程表**嗎？
5	Anna, would you handle **distributing**[4] the **workshop**[5] materials?	安娜，麻煩妳將**研討會**的資料**發下去**。
6	John and Sara, I'd like it if you two could **coordinate**[6] travel for the team.	約翰和莎拉，我要麻煩你們**合作**為小組安排行程。

1 **close of business** 辦公時間結束
2 **Can I ask you to . . . ?** 能請您……？
3 **agenda** [əˋdʒɛndə] (n.) 議程表
4 **distribute** [dɪˋstrɪbjut] (v.) 分發
5 **workshop** [ˋwɝkʃɑp] (n.) 工作坊；專題討論會
6 **coordinate** [koˋɔrdn̩et] (v.) 協調；合作

ink pad 印泥

staple 釘書針

C Asking for permission 請求批准

7	I was hoping that I could speak to you after the meeting.	我希望會後能與您談談。
8	I was wondering if I could be **reimbursed**[1] for my commuting expenses.	不知道我的通勤費用是否能**報帳**？
9	I'd appreciate it if I could bring my laptop home over the weekend.	如果週末可以將筆電帶回家，我會很感激。
10	Is there any way I could change the dates of my vacation?	有任何辦法能改變我休假的日期嗎？
11	I'd really like to attend the meeting, if I may.	要是可以，我真的很想出席會議。
12	Is it OK if I skip this meeting to work on the **budget report**[2]?	我可以不去開會，繼續做**預算報告**嗎？

1 **reimburse** [͵riɪm`bɝs] (v.) 報銷；核銷
2 **budget report** 預算報告

laptop 筆記型電腦

desktop 桌上型電腦

Review Questions

Listen to the conversations and answer the questions below.

87 **1. What is the man working on?**

(A) A report. (B) A letter.
(C) An email. (D) A business.

2. When will the man submit the report?

(A) The next day. (B) Later in the day.
(C) By 2:30. (D) Immediately.

88 **3. What does the man want?**

(A) A new desk. (B) A new computer.
(C) A new chair. (D) A new mouse.

4. Whom does the woman tell him to check with?

(A) The boss. (B) Sam. (C) Reception. (D) Herself.

5. The man can buy his own chair and be repaid.

(A) True. (B) False.

Ans A, B, C, B, B

UNIT 17 使用傳真機 Using a Fax Machine

89 B Barbara J John

Barbara is explaining fax procedures to a new employee.
芭芭拉正向一名新進員工解釋傳真的步驟。

B As you can see, we've just received our new fax machine, and it works a little differently than the old one. The dialing **procedures**[1] will be the same, though.

J So we still dial nine to get an outside line?

B Right. This is where you **feed**[2] the documents you want to fax, and on this machine you have to put them **face down**[3]. Then everything is like any other fax machine—hit start, and send the papers through. The **paper tray**[4] is under here.

J If there's a problem, will the machine **redial**[5] automatically?

B Yes, I think . . . the **manual**[6] says it will redial five times. There's also a **speed dial**[7] on this machine, so I'm going to print a list of the most commonly used fax numbers, set them on the speed dial, and post the list above the machine. We're also going to connect this machine to the network, so you should be able to fax from your computers now. I'll come around and help you get hooked up to the machine if there are any problems.

B 如你所見，我們剛收到新買的傳真機，這台和舊的操作有些不同，但撥號**步驟**是一樣的。

J 所以打外線一樣是撥 9 囉？

B 對。這裡是你**放置**要傳真文件的地方，在這台機器文件那**面要朝下**，其他就跟別的傳真機沒兩樣了——按下開始鍵，傳送文件。**紙匣**在下面這裡。

J 如果傳送有問題，機器會自動**重撥**嗎？

B 我想是會的，**說明書**上說它會重撥五次。傳真機上還有速撥功能，我會把最常用的傳真號碼設成**速撥鍵**，印一張清單貼在傳真機上。我們還會將它連上網路，這樣你應該就能從電腦上直接傳真。要是有問題，我會過來幫你連線。

1 **procedure** [prəˋsidʒɚ] (n.) 步驟
2 **feed** [fid] (v.) 放入
3 **face down** 面朝下
4 **paper tray** 紙匣
5 **redial** [riˋdaɪəl] (v.) 重撥
6 **manual** [ˋmænjʊəl] (n.) 手冊
7 **speed dial** 快速撥號鍵

Useful Expressions

A Asking questions related to the fax machine (90) 詢問傳真機相關問題

1	Do I need to load the paper **face up**[8] or face down?	我需要把紙**面朝上**還是朝下放?
2	Is there an easy way to send a **double-sided**[9] fax?	有可以傳**雙面**傳真的簡單辦法嗎?
3	Why do I keep getting this **transmission**[10] error message? I know I have the right number!	為什麼會一直收到**傳送**錯誤的訊息呢?我的號碼明明是對的!
4	Do I need to dial nine before entering the fax number?	撥傳真號碼前我需要先按 9 嗎?
5	Where are the ink **cartridges**[11] for the new machine?	新傳真機的**墨水匣**在哪裡?

B Explaining the fax machine 說明傳真機

6	We aren't getting any faxes because the machine is out of paper!	我們收不到傳真是因為機器沒紙了!
7	I think the problem is that the paper is **jammed**[12].	我認為問題是**卡紙**了。
8	I think we need to change the **toner**[13] on the fax.	我想我們該換傳真機的**碳粉**了。
9	You've loaded the paper backward.	你把紙放反了。
10	This fax is really blurry—I think I need to change the **resolution**[14] on the machine.	這張傳真真的很模糊,我想是需要重設**解析度**了。
11	You can use **scrap paper**[15] for writing faxes.	你可以使用**廢紙**寫傳真。

8 **face up** 面朝上
9 **double-sided** [ˋdʌblˋsaɪdɪd] (adj.) 雙面的
10 **transmission** [trænsˋmɪʃən] (n.) 傳送
11 **cartridge** [ˋkɑrtrɪdʒ] (n.) 墨水匣
12 **jam** [dʒæm] (v.) 卡紙
13 **toner** [ˋtonɚ] (n.) 碳粉
14 **resolution** [ˏrɛzəˋluʃən] (n.) 解析度
15 **scrap/waste/used paper** 廢紙

Office Appliances 辦公設備

time clock/recorder 打卡鐘

fax machine 傳真機

punch/clock in 打卡上班
punch/clock out 打卡下班

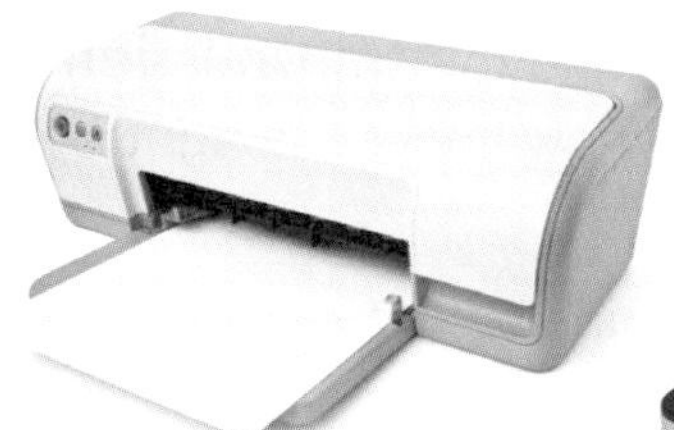

inkjet printer 噴墨印表機

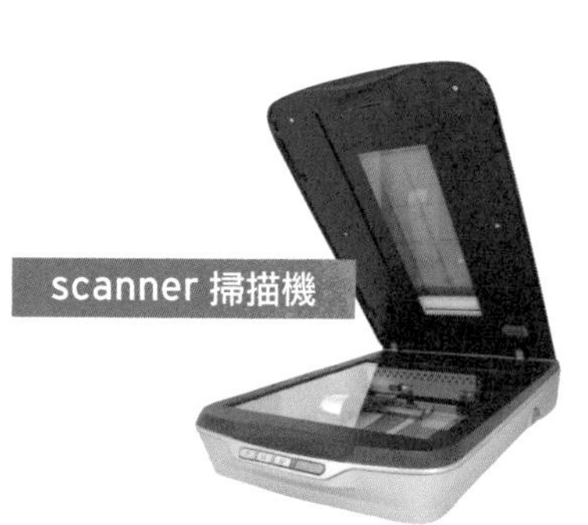

scanner 掃描機

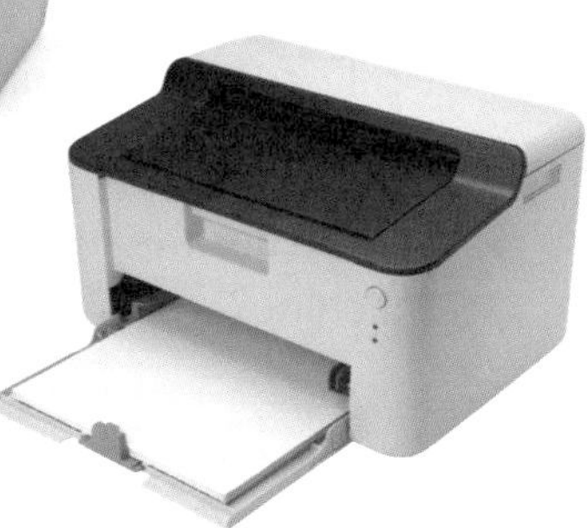

laser printer 雷射印表機

laminating machine 護貝機

shredder 碎紙機

copy machine / copier 影印機

Review Questions

Listen to the conversations and answer the questions below.

91 **1. Why cannot the man send the fax?**

- Ⓐ Because there is a fax receiving.
- Ⓑ Because there is a fax sending.
- Ⓒ Because the man didn't follow the instruction.
- Ⓓ Because the fax machine is broken.

92 **2. What will the man do next?**

- Ⓐ He will send a fax.
- Ⓑ He will read the fax.
- Ⓒ He will receive a fax.
- Ⓓ He will write a fax.

3. What was the woman doing?

- Ⓐ She was sending a fax.
- Ⓑ She was waiting for a fax.
- Ⓒ She was using speed dial.
- Ⓓ She was answering the man's question.

93 **4. What does the woman want to do?**

- Ⓐ She wants to send a fax.
- Ⓑ She wants to receive a fax.
- Ⓒ She wants to fix the fax machine.
- Ⓓ She wants to add paper to the fax machine.

5. What is the right way to load the paper according to the man?

- Ⓐ The paper should be loaded face down.
- Ⓑ The paper should be loaded face up.
- Ⓒ The paper should be loaded from the top loader.
- Ⓓ He doesn't know at all.

Ans B, A, A, D, A

UNIT 18 使用影印機 Using a Copy Machine

 B Barbara J John

Barbara is showing John the copy machine.
芭芭拉正在教約翰如何使用影印機。

B To start with, you should load any recycled paper in **tray**[1] two, and load it face down.

J Got it.

B If you're copying a long document, instead of copying page by page on the glass, you can use the **top-loader**[2]. There's an option here to **collate**[3] the documents or sort them by page.

J Great. Can it staple, too? I've seen copiers that staple.

B Yes, it can! Moving on . . . do you know how to **shrink**[4] and **enlarge**[5] documents? Those functions are here—the machine will **prompt**[6] you to change the paper size and tray if you need to. We usually keep A3 or B3 paper in the bottom tray, but you can load it anywhere. Letterhead should go in the side loader, so we don't waste it.

J OK, thanks. I think I'm pretty familiar with what else the machine can do. I have one question, though—can anyone use the copier, or is there an **access code**[7] I have to put in?

B Oh, there aren't any codes. Anybody in the office can use it.

B 首先，將回收紙放在二號**紙匣**，要印的那一面朝下放。

J 知道了。

B 要是你要影印的文件頁數很多，不用一頁一頁放，可以用**頂端送紙匣**。這裡有可以**整理**文件順序或分頁的選項。

J 太好了。這也可以裝訂嗎？我看過有裝訂功能的影印機。

B 這個可以！然後……你知道如何**縮放**文件嗎？那些功能都在這——有需要的話，影印機會**提醒**你更換紙的尺寸與紙匣。我們通常把 A3 或 B3 大小的紙放在底部紙匣，不過你要放哪都可以。有信頭的信紙要放在手送紙匣，才不會浪費。

J 謝啦，我想我大概知道其他的功能了。但我還有一個問題，所有人都能使用影印機嗎？還是說我要輸入**密碼**才能使用？

B 不用，不需要任何密碼，辦公室的人都能使用。

Useful Expressions

A Asking questions related to the copy machine (95)
詢問有關影印機的問題

1	Do you need collated stacks, or **stacks**[8] of each page?	你是要每份分成**一疊**，還是將相同頁數分成一疊？
2	Does anyone know how to deal with a **paper jam**[9]?	有人知道**卡紙**要怎麼辦嗎？
3	How can I get the machine to make double-sided copies?	我要怎麼影印成雙面文件？
4	Does this machine make color copies?	這台影印機有彩色影印功能嗎？
5	Can I load recycled paper into the main tray?	我可以把回收紙放到主紙匣嗎？

1 **tray** [tre] (n.) 紙匣
2 **top-loader** [ˋtɑpˋlodɚ] (n.) 頂端送紙匣
3 **collate** [kəˋlet] (v.) 整理（紙張）
4 **shrink** [ʃrɪŋk] (v.) 縮小
5 **enlarge** [ɪnˋlɑrdʒ] (v.) 放大
6 **prompt** [prɑmpt] (v.) 提示；提醒
7 **access code** 認證碼
8 **stack** [stæk] (n.)（疊放整齊的）一堆／疊
9 **paper jam** 卡紙

Copy Machine 影印機

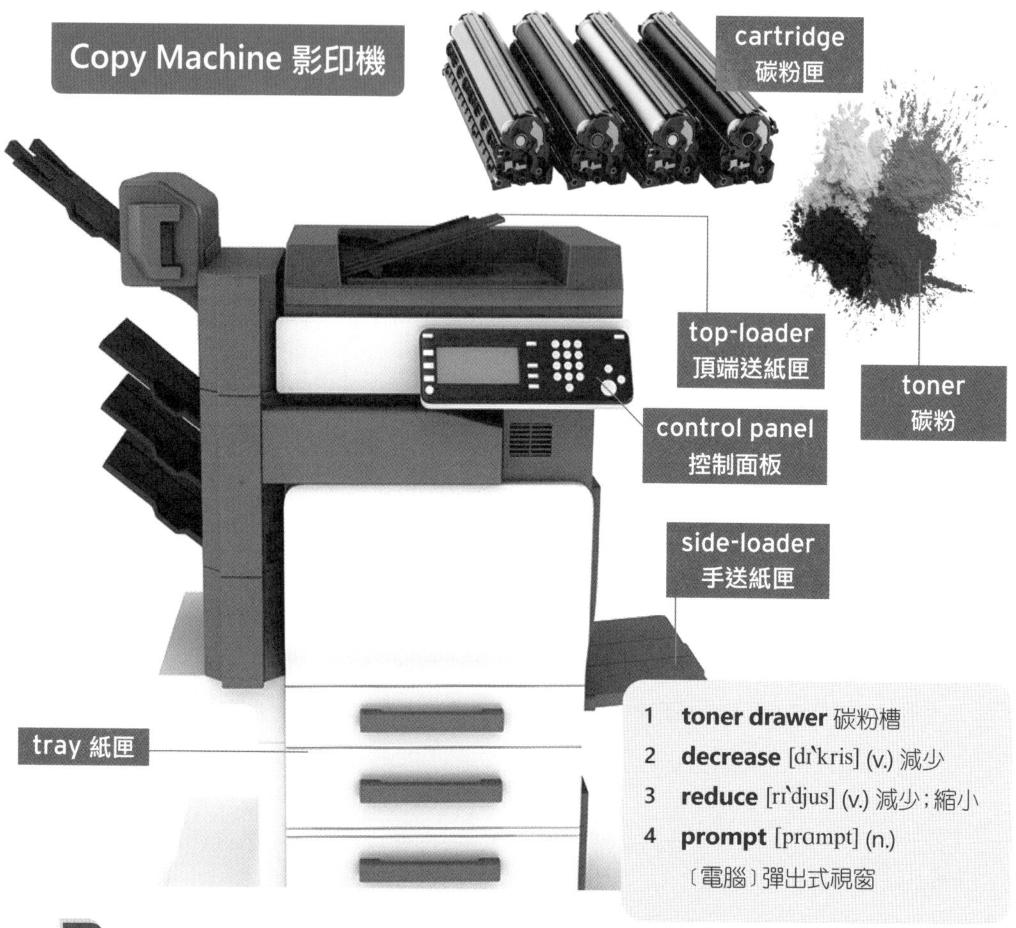

1 **toner drawer** 碳粉槽
2 **decrease** [dɪˋkris] (v.) 減少
3 **reduce** [rɪˋdjus] (v.) 減少；縮小
4 **prompt** [prɑmpt] (n.)
〔電腦〕彈出式視窗

B Explaining the copy machine 說明影印機

6 The copy machine is getting low on toner. To change it, open the **toner drawer**[1] and follow the instructions inside.

影印機的碳粉快沒了。要更換碳粉匣，打開**碳粉槽**，按照裡面的說明更換。

7 Your job printed on letterhead because someone left a stack of it in the paper tray!

有人把一疊有信頭的紙留在紙匣，所以你的影印文件都印到信頭紙上了！

8 To **decrease**[2] the size of the image you want to copy, select "**reduce**[3]" on the menu and follow the **prompts**[4].

要**縮小**欲影印的影像，選擇選單上的「**縮小**」，再依照**彈出視窗**指示進行。

9 I would use tray one. For some reason, printing from tray two tends to make the machine jam.

我會用一號紙匣，不知道為什麼，用二號紙匣影印很容易卡紙。

Review Questions

Listen to the conversations and answer the questions below.

96 1. **How will the woman print the meeting agenda probably?**

(A) She will print the meeting agenda single-sided.
(B) She will print the meeting agenda double-sided.
(C) She will print the meeting agenda colored.
(D) She will print the meeting agenda black and white.

2. **How many copies does the man need?**

(A) Five. (B) Ten. (C) Fifteen. (D) Twenty.

97 3. **What happened to the woman?**

(A) She doesn't know how to use the fax machine.
(B) She doesn't know the access code of the copy machine.
(C) She doesn't know where to put the toner.
(D) She doesn't know how to print the right way.

4. **What is the man's suggestion?**

(A) The woman should use A4 paper.
(B) The woman should use the top-loader.
(C) The woman should use tray two.
(D) The woman should load the letterhead face up.

98 5. A What's the ________________ size of paper this machine can hold?

B B3, I think.

A Thanks. I need to make this picture bigger to use it on a ________________.

B I see, then don't forget to change the ________________; otherwise the picture may be too blurry.

A Will do.

Ans A, B, D, C, biggest, poster, resolution

UNIT 19 電腦的基本功能 Basic Computer Functions

99 B Barbara J John

Barbara is showing John some computer functions.
芭芭拉正在教約翰一些電腦的基本功能。

B You're going to be doing a lot of editing of long documents. I assume you can **cut**[1], copy, and **paste**[2] text easily?

J Yes, of course. I'm used to **inserting**[3] pictures in documents, creating tables, all of that.

B Great. And have you ever used **styles**[4]? Styles let you apply the same formatting—like fonts, numbering, and other things—to different areas of your document, so the document is **consistent**[5].

J No, I haven't.

B They're pretty simple. The styles menu allows you to choose styles and apply them to text. You can change styles with the "**modify**[6] styles" option. It's pretty easy to figure out.

J OK.

B We also often use the "track changes" function when we edit documents. Go to the "Tools" menu and choose "track changes." Now choose "record changes." Now, if I cut something or type something new or make any other changes in this document, it's recorded so you can see it.

J I see! But how do I get the changes to stay?

B You go back to "track changes" and select "accept or reject." Then you can go through the whole document and incorporate the changes or not.

J That seems very easy.

B Oh, it is. You'll find it really **handy**[7]. Then, with the changed document, use the "save as" function and save it under the name "document **version**[8] A," rather than using the "save" function to save over your original.

J And then you can keep track of the different versions of the document, right?

or New Document
dit View Insent Format Tools Help
Open Sans 14 B I U A x x

3 2 1 1 2 3 4 5 6 7 8 9 10 11 12 13

B 你將要編輯許多長篇幅的文件，我想「**剪下**」、「複製」跟「**貼上**」對你來說應該不難吧？

J 當然不難。我很習慣在文件中**插入**圖片，做表格之類的。

B 太棒了，那你用過「**樣式**」嗎？「樣式」可以讓你在文件不同的部分使用同種格式——像是字型、編號與其他東西等等，可以保持文件**一致**。

J 我沒用過耶。

B 這還滿簡單的。你可以從樣式選單選擇，並套用到文字中。利用「**修改**樣式」的選項來更改樣式，這不難理解。

J 好。

B 我們編輯文件時也常會用到「追蹤修訂」的功能。到「工具」選單中選擇「追蹤修訂」，再選「記錄修訂」。要是我剪下、打上新文字或者做修改，都會記錄在文件中，你就能看到了。

J 我懂了！那要如何保留變更呢？

B 回到「追蹤修訂」，選擇「接受變更」或「拒絕變更」，便能選擇套用或拒絕整份文件的修改了。

J 好像很簡單。

B 是很簡單。你會發現這很**方便的**。再來用「另存新檔」功能將修改過的文件另存，檔名存成「文件版本 A」，而不是用「儲存檔案」的功能存下原檔。

J 這樣一來就能追蹤所有不同版本的文件了，對吧？

1

1 **cut** [kʌt] (v.) 剪下
2 **paste** [pest] (v.) 貼上
3 **insert** [ɪnˋsɝt] (v.) 插入
4 **style** [staɪl] (n.) 樣式
5 **consistent** [kənˋsɪstənt] (adj.) 一致的
6 **modify** [ˋmɑdə͵faɪ] (v.) 修改
7 **handy** [ˋhændɪ] (adj.) 隨手可得的；方便的
8 **version** [ˋvɝʒən] (n.) 版本

Useful Expressions

A Asking questions about editing functions 詢問編輯功能相關問題

100

1 Can you help me **export**[1] this document?
你可以幫忙我**匯出**這份文件嗎?

2 Do you know how to use styles?
你知道要怎麼使用樣式嗎?

3 Can you please help me with this **spreadsheet**[2]? I want to **format**[3] the numbers as dates, but I can't find that option.
你可以幫我看看這**試算表**嗎?我想將數字格式**設**為日期,卻找不到這個選項。

4 Can you help me turn off this automatic **spell-checker**[4]?
你可以幫我把自動**拼字檢查**的功能關掉嗎?

B Asking about other computer functions 詢問其他電腦功能

5 Do you know how to change the **desktop**[5] background?
你知道要怎麼更換桌布嗎?

6 Can you help me change my menus from lists to **icons**[6]?
能替我將選單的列表改成**圖示**嗎?

7 Oh no! My computer just **crashed**[7]! Do you think I can **recover**[8] the file I was working on?
不!我的電腦**當機**了!有辦法把我剛剛在做的檔案**回復**嗎?

C Describing computer functions 描述電腦功能

8 To **adjust**[9] the **margins**[10], find out where you can make modifications to a whole page. It's usually under the "page **layout**[11]" option.
要**調整頁面邊界**的話,需要找出能修改整頁的地方,通常就在「**版面配置**」的選項中。

9 Thank goodness for cut and paste; otherwise, we'd have to type everything **by hand**[12]!
多虧有了「剪下」跟「貼上」的功能,不然我們全部文字都要**用手**打了!

10 That program should **install**[13] on its own once the installation **wizard**[14] comes up.
安裝精靈一旦出現後,該程式便會自動**安裝**。

11 Use **bold**[15] text to make your **headers**[16] stand out more. It's in the formatting menu.
使用樣式選單上的**粗體字型**來更凸顯你的**頁首**,它在「格式編排」的選單裡。

Review Questions

Listen to the conversations and answer the questions below.

101

1. **What is the man probably doing?**
   - (A) Copying a letter.
   - (B) Editing a document.
   - (C) Cutting paper.
   - (D) Playing video games.

2. **What is the man probably using?**
   - (A) A word processing program.
   - (B) A printer.
   - (C) A copy machine.
   - (D) A scanner.

3. **What has the woman probably made?**
   - (A) A new word processing document.
   - (B) A new song.
   - (C) A new image file.
   - (D) A new spreadsheet.

4. **What will the woman probably sent the new expense report sheet as?**
   - (A) A fax.
   - (B) An email message.
   - (C) An email attachment.
   - (D) An SMS.

5. **A** I need to ________________ this new program, but I can't get the installation wizard working.

   B Do you know the reason?

   A No, I don't, and I don't have time to figure it out. Can you just help me do it ________________?

   B Sure. It might take a ________________.

   A That's fine. Thank you very much.

Ans B, A, D, C, install, by hand, minute

1 **export** [ɛks`port] (v.) 匯出
2 **spreadsheet** [`sprɛd͵ʃit] (n.) 試算表
3 **format** [`fɔrmæt] (v.) 編排
4 **spell-checker** [`spɛl͵tʃɛkɚ] (n.) 拼字檢查
5 **desktop** [`dɛsktɑp] (n.) 電腦的桌面
6 **icon** [`aɪkɑn] (n.) 圖示
7 **crash** [kræʃ] (v.) 當機
8 **recover** [rɪ`kʌvɚ] (v.) 回復
9 **adjust** [ə`dʒʌst] (v.) 調整
10 **margin** [`mɑrdʒɪn] (n.) 頁邊空白；邊界
11 **layout** [`le͵aʊt] (n.) 版面編排
12 **by hand** 以手工的方式
13 **install** [ɪn`stɔl] (v.) 安裝
14 **wizard** [`wɪzɚd] (n.) 小幫手；安裝精靈
15 **bold** [bold] (adj.) 粗體的
16 **header** [`hɛdɚ] (n.) （位於文件或書籍每頁頂端的）頁首

UNIT 20 內部網路與資源共享 FTP and Networks Inside the Company

Katharine needs to access[1] some programs and files.
凱薩琳需要使用一些程式與檔案。

K Can you help me with something? You asked me to save this file to the server, but I'm not exactly sure how to do it.

J Sure. It's really simple. All our computers **are hooked up to**[2] a **network**[3] that connects this whole office. All of us can access files on the server. Saving a file to the server is easy. Open the folder that says "Shared Files;" you'll see folders named for all our current projects and an **archive**[4] for the old ones. Then you should be able to see where I would want you to save the file.

K Great, thanks!

J You'll also need to learn to use **FTP**[5]. We use this to share files from our website, or to share large files that would take a long time to pass around. I'll show you how to set up your account, and then you'll be able to access and upload from it.

K OK.

J You will need to know how to use **cloud storage**[6] as well. The cloud storage is really convenient, providing us with immediate access to upload or download files. We use both Dropbox and Google Drive, later I will let you know how to **register**[7] and use them.

database 數據庫

K 你可以幫我一下嗎？你要我把這個檔案存到伺服器上，不過我不確定要怎麼做。

J 當然沒問題，這很簡單。我們所有的電腦都有**連上**全公司的**網路**，所有人都可在伺服器上存取檔案。要把檔案存到伺服器上很簡單，找到「共用檔案夾」，打開後妳會看到以目前各個專案命名的資料夾與舊專案的**檔案庫**。應該就會看到我要妳存檔的地方。

K 太好了，謝啦。

J 妳還要學習如何使用 FTP。我們用此來共享我們網站上的檔案，或是共用需費時傳送的大檔案。我會教妳如何設立帳戶，這樣一來，就可以在上面存取和上傳檔案了。

K 好的。

J 妳也需要學會用**雲端硬碟**，雲端硬碟真的很方便，讓我們可以即時上傳與下載檔案，Dropbox 和 Google Drive 我們都有使用，待會我會教妳怎麼**註冊**和使用它們。

1 **access** [ˋæksɛs] (v.) 〔電腦〕讀取；使用
2 **be hooked up to** 連接
3 **network** [ˋnɛtˏwɝk] (n.) 電腦網路
4 **archive** [ˋɑrkaɪv] (n.) 資料庫
5 **FTP (File Transfer Protocol)** 檔案傳輸協定
6 **cloud storage** 雲端硬碟
7 **register** [ˋrɛdʒɪstɚ] (v.) 註冊

Useful Expressions

A Talking about computer networks and FTP 談論電腦網絡與 FTP

105

1	Who is on this network?	有誰在網上?
2	Because our office is small, we can use a **peer-to-peer network**[1].	由於我們的辦公室很小,便可使用**點對點網路**。
3	Tomorrow we'll create a network account for you.	明天我們會幫你建立一個新的網路帳號。
4	I can't access the network. I think there might be something wrong with one of my cables.	我連不上網絡,可能是有條線路出問題了。
5	This wireless network is so much easier than fussing around with cables used to be.	跟以前亂糟糟的有線網路相比,無線網路來得方便多了。
6	We don't have an FTP program yet, but we can get one from **freeware**[2] or **shareware**[3].	我們還沒有 FTP 的程式,但可從**免費**或是**共享軟體**中取得。
7	You'd better start your upload soon or your session is going to **time out**[4]!	你最好趕快上傳,不然連線就要**逾時**了!
8	Who is our FTP **host**[5]?	我們 FTP 的**主機**為何?

B Talking about cloud storage 談論雲端硬碟

9 How much **capacity**[6] do we have in our cloud storage?
我們的雲端硬碟有多少**容量**?

10 Could you share the link to your cloud drive with me so I can view the file?
你可以分享雲端硬碟的連結給我,讓我看檔案嗎?

11 I have changed your **status**[7] on the drive—now you can edit the document as well.
我修改了你在雲端硬碟裡的**權限**——現在你也可以編輯文件了。

12 There is a new plan of Dropbox that you can have unlimited storage for just $60 per year! And You can start your 3-month **free-trial**[8] right now!
Dropbox 有個新方案,每年只要 60 美金,就可以享有無限的容量!而且你現在就可以**免費試用**三個月!

1 **peer-to-peer network (P2P)** 點對點網路　　2 **freeware** [ˋfriwɛr] (n.) 免費軟體

Review Questions

Listen to the conversations and answer the questions below.

(106) 1. **What did the man need to do?**

Ⓐ He needed to write an email.
Ⓑ He needed to access a document.
Ⓒ He needed to distribute a large document.
Ⓓ He needed to create a network account.

2. **What kind of assistance will the woman offer to the man?**

Ⓐ She will help him upload a file.
Ⓑ She will help him to download a file.
Ⓒ She will help him to copy a file.
Ⓓ She will help him to delete a file.

3. **Why couldn't the man use the FTP by himself?**

Ⓐ Because he didn't copy the right files.
Ⓑ Because he didn't use the network.
Ⓒ Because he didn't send an email.
Ⓓ Because he didn't know if he has a username or password.

(107) 4. **Which device did the woman want to use?**

Ⓐ The database. Ⓑ The server.
Ⓒ The project. Ⓓ The folder.

5. **Why did the woman tell the man "not to use the his own folder"?**

Ⓐ Because he didn't know how to do it.
Ⓑ Because the files are organized.
Ⓒ Because he didn't have the access to do it.
Ⓓ Because he didn't set up an account yet.

Ans C, A, D, A, B

3 **shareware** [ˋʃɛrwɛr] (n.) 共享軟體
4 **time out** 逾時
5 **host** [host] (n.) 主機
6 **capacity** [kəˋpæsətɪ] (n.) 容量
7 **status** [ˋstetəs] (n.) 能使用某物的身分；權限
8 **free-trial** [ˋfri͵traɪəl] (n.) 免費試用期

UNIT 21 使用網路 Using the Internet

  Jacob  Katharine

Jacob needs Katharine to perform an Internet search for him.
雅各要凱薩琳替他搜尋網路。

J Clients have been telling me that our company is hard to find, like it doesn't come up in Internet searches. I want to find out why. Could you do a search with some **keywords**[1] that people might use when they're looking for a company like ours and see what comes up?

K Sure. I wonder why our site doesn't come up.

J I don't know. I think there may be a way to buy keywords on **search engines**[2] to help move our company to the top of the list.

K I see. Do you want me to look into that, too?

J Yes, why don't you? And take a look at the websites that come up when you search for ours. If they're our competitors, we should see what they're doing.

K Will do.

J And make sure you check a few different search engines!

J 一直有客戶告訴我，網路上很難搜尋到我們公司。我想找出原因，可以請妳用一些搜尋我們這類公司可能會用到的**關鍵字**找找看，看看會出現什麼嗎？

K 當然沒問題，我也想知道為什麼我們的網站沒有被搜尋到。

J 我不知道。我想或許可以購買**搜尋引擎**的關鍵字，讓公司出現在搜尋結果的最上面。

K 知道了。你要我也去了解一下這個嗎？

J 好啊，有何不可？順便看看搜尋我們公司時，也會出現的網站。如果出來的是我們的競爭對手，看看他們在做什麼。

K 好的。

J 記得要多用幾個不同的搜尋引擎！

1 **keyword** [ˋki͵wɝd] (n.) 關鍵字
2 **search engine** 搜尋引擎
3 **google** [ˋgugl̩] (v.) 以 Google 搜尋引擎搜尋
4 **image search** 圖片搜尋

More Terms About the Internet 網路相關用語

- **URL** 網址
- **HTML** 超文件標示語言
- **hyperlink** 超連結
- **Web 2.0**
- **paywall** 付費牆
  （對線上內容付費閱讀的模式）
- **server** 伺服器
- **host (hosting)** 網頁寄存服務
- **cookie** 小型文字檔案
- **search engine optimization (SEO)**
  搜尋引擎最佳化
- **crowdsourcing** 群眾外包

Useful Expressions

A Talking about search engines 談論搜尋引擎 (109)

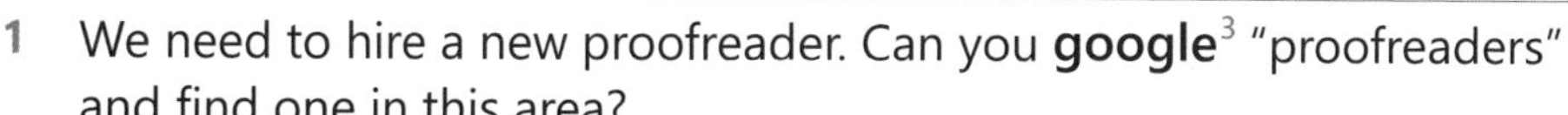

1 We need to hire a new proofreader. Can you **google**[3] "proofreaders" and find one in this area?

我們要新聘一位校對人員，你可以上網**用 Google 搜尋**關鍵字「校對人員」來找一位這個領域的人嗎？

2 I have no idea what magnolia flowers look like. Do you think we can do an **image search**[4] and find out?

我完全不知道木蘭花長什麼樣子，你覺得可以用**圖片搜尋**來找嗎？

B Talking about websites 談論網站

3 There are so many **pop-ups**[1] on the local paper's website. I can't even read it anymore.

當地報紙的網站有一堆**彈跳式視窗**，多到根本沒辦法看。

4 That website was so helpful—please **bookmark**[2] it so we can find it again!

那個網站很實用，請**加入書籤**，方便之後再尋找！

5 Would you send me the **link**[3] to that cheap airlines website?

能請你將該廉價航空公司的**網站連結**寄給我嗎？

6 This month our website registered 1,000 more **hits**[4] than last month!

本月我們的網站比上個月多了 1,000 位**訪客**。

C Talking about Internet browser 討論網路瀏覽器

7 You should try the free **browser**[5] I just downloaded. It's much faster than the one we're using now.

你應該用用看我剛下載的免費**瀏覽器**，速度比我們目前所使用的快多了。

8 If I want to look at two websites at once, should I open a new window or a new **tab**[6]?

若要同時觀看兩個網站，是要開啟新視窗還是新**分頁**？

9 Wait, I want to see that page again. Hit "**back**[7]."

等等，我要再看一次該網頁。按「**回上一頁**」。

10 Would you **refresh**[8] the page, please? I think it's been updated.

可以請你**重新整理**嗎？這網頁應該已經更新了。

11 If you **right-click**[9] the link, you can open it in a new tab.

若你對這個網址**按右鍵**便可以在新分頁開啟該連結。

12 That's a useful image. Would you **save it as**[10] a file?

這是個很常用到的圖片，可以請你**另存新檔**嗎？

13 Should I use the **cached**[11] option or click on the website?

我應該要選**頁庫存檔**選項還是直接點選網址？

14 You can open an **incognito window**[12], so what you browsed won't be in history.

你可以使用**無痕視窗**，這樣你瀏覽過的內容就不會出現在歷史紀錄裡。

Review Questions

Listen to the conversations and answer the questions below.

110 1. **What is the man looking for?**

(A) An email address. (B) A web page.

(C) A browser. (D) A click.

2. **Why might the man have a problem?**

(A) Because he might not remember the keyword.

(B) Because he might not remember the name of the browser.

(C) Because he might not remember the name of the search engine.

(D) Because he might not remember the name of the website.

111 3. **What did the woman want to know?**

(A) Internet searching. (B) Service booking.

(C) Hook repairing. (D) Book repairing.

4. **What did the man suggest to the woman?**

(A) To search online by keys. (B) To search online by alphabets.

(C) To search online by browser. (D) To search online by keywords.

112 5. **A** Why can't I get to my personal email ________________?

B I think the company ________________ all social websites.

A Wow! So I can't even check personal email on my ________________?

B I guess not.

Ans B, D, D, account, blocked, lunch break

1 **pop-up** [ˋpɑp,ʌp] (n.) 彈出式視窗
2 **bookmark** [ˋbʊkmɑrk] (v.) 加入書籤
3 **link** [lɪŋk] (n.) 連結
4 **hit** [hɪt] (n.) 訪客數；點擊數
5 **browser** [ˋbraʊzɚ] (n.) 瀏覽器
6 **tab** [tæb] (n.) 分頁
7 **back** [bæk] (n.) 回上一頁
8 **refresh** [rɪˋfrɛʃ] (v.) 重新整理
9 **right-click** [ˋraɪt,klɪk] (v.) 按右鍵
10 **save sth. as** 另存新檔
11 **cached (as in data)** 頁庫存檔
12 **incognito window** 無痕視窗

Part 3 使用硬體設備 Using Office Appliances

UNIT 22 使用通訊軟體 Using Instant Messengers for Correspondence

113 J Jacob K Katharine

Jacob is discussing the company IM program and policy with Katharine. 雅各正在和凱薩琳討論公司對即時通訊軟體的處理方式。

J Katharine, are you using the office **IM**[1] program?

K No, I haven't been. Actually, I thought that most offices **frowned on**[2] using IM.

J Oh, no, we find it really useful, especially for people who are working from home or working in our other offices. It's much faster than email.

K I'll get on it, then. I have a few IM **handles**[3]; I'll see if the office is using one of the programs I'm already registered with or if I have to sign up to it.

J Good. When you do, please send an email around letting us know your username so we can all add you.

K I will.

J 凱薩琳，妳有在使用辦公室的**即時通**軟體嗎？

K 我從來沒用過耶。其實我以為公司大多都**不贊成**使用即時通訊軟體。

J 噢，不會。我們公司覺得相當方便，尤其是對在家工作，或是在其他辦公室工作的同事來說，比電子郵件快多了。

K 這樣的話我就登入了。我有幾個即時通的**帳戶**，我看看公司用的是否是我已經註冊過的，還是我要重新註冊。

J 太好了。等妳弄好了，麻煩寄信告訴大家妳的用戶名，我們才可以加妳。

K 好的。

1 **IM (instant messaging)** 即時通訊
2 **frown on** 不贊成
3 **handle** [ˋhændḷ] (n.) （在社群媒體網站或論壇上的）使用者名稱
4 **distract** [dɪˋstrækt] (v.) 使分心
5 **invisible** [ɪnˋvɪzəbḷ] (adj.) 顯示離線的
6 **status** [ˋstetəs] (n.) 狀態
7 **profile** [ˋprofaɪl] (n.) （社交網站等的）個人資料
8 **invite** [ɪnˋvaɪt] (v.) 邀請
9 **chat** [tʃæt] (v.) 線上聊天
10 **on the record** 保存通訊紀錄
11 **off the record** 私下的

Useful Expressions

A Talking about instant messenger service options 談論即時通的服務選擇

1 All the messages from friends are starting to **distract**[4] me. I'm going to have to go **invisible**[5].

朋友們傳的訊息已經開始讓我**分心**了，我要改**顯示成離線**。

2 I usually find when I set my **status**[6] to busy, people leave me alone.

我發現若我的**狀態**設為忙碌的話，大家就不會來吵我。

3 You should add a picture to your messenger **profile**[7]!

你應該在你即時通的**個人資料**中加張照片。

4 I need to remove some people from my contact list.

我要從我的連絡人名單中移除幾個人。

5 I'm going to **invite**[8] you to **chat**[9], so add me when you see the message.

我要**邀請**你**聊天**，所以看到這則訊息時請加我。

6 Keep this session **on the record**[10], so we can refer to it later if we need to.

把這段聊天**紀錄留下來**，若以後需要才能參考。

7 Let's chat **off the record**[11].

我們來**私下**聊天吧。

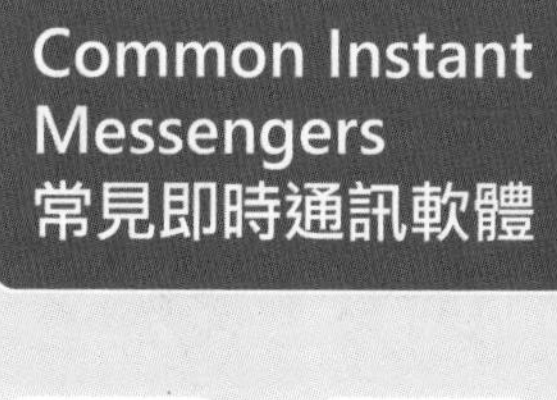

LINE Telegram WhatsApp

Snapchat

Skype

Messenger

Facetime

WeChat

Slack

B Talking about sending instant messages 談論發出即時通訊息

8 How much time do you spend IMing each day?

你一天花多少時間使用通訊軟體？

9 We're only allowed to use IM to communicate with colleagues.

我們被規定通訊軟體只能用來與同事聯絡。

10 I'm going to be working from home for the next two days, but I'll be in touch over IM.

我在接下來兩天會在家工作，不過我會在線上。

11 Can I send a picture through the office instant messenger?

我能用辦公室的通訊軟體傳照片嗎？

C Talking about group IM functions 談論即時通的群組功能

12 Do you know how to set up group chat?

你知道如何建立群組聊天嗎？

13 We're going to do a **group chat**[1] today, instead of an in-office meeting.

我們今天不舉行公司內部會議，要改以**群組聊天**方式進行。

14 You'll be able to get into the group chat as soon as I invite you.

等我邀請你，你就能加入群組聊天了。

15 To invite someone, click on "options" and then "group chat." You'll be prompted to invite whoever you want.

要邀請他人的話，點選「選項」，再點「群組聊天」，就能看到詢問你要邀請誰的選項了。

1 **group chat** 群組聊天

Top 10 Popular Emojis

face with tears of joy

red heart

rolling on the floor laughing

thumbs up

loudly crying face

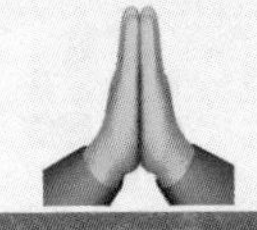

folded hands

face blowing a kiss

smiling face with hearts

smiling face with heart-eyes

smiling face with smiling eyes

Review Questions

Listen to the conversations and answer the questions below.

115 **1. What does the man want the woman to do?**

(A) He wants her to use her email more often.
(B) He wants her to become available over IM.
(C) He wants her to use her computer like everyone else.
(D) He wants her to block her IM.

2. Why is the woman surprised?

(A) Because she thought the program would be blocked.
(B) Because she thought her colleague was rude to ask her to use IM.
(C) Because she thought she was already using IM.
(D) Because she thought everyone has already used IM.

116 **3. What might be the reason why Sylvia won't see the IM?**

(A) Because she must be out of the office.
(B) Because she seems to be out to lunch.
(C) Because she will not come back.
(D) Because she appears to be away from her computer.

4. What indicates that Sylvia is away?

(A) Her message.
(B) Her email.
(C) Her status.
(D) What the man just said.

117 5. **A** I just ________ my computer ________. Can you see if John is ________ on messenger?

B Sure. Yep, he's there.

A Great. Can you just tell him that I can meet at nine tomorrow? I'll see him in his office.

B ________.

Ans B, A, D, C, shut, down, available, Sure thing

Part 3 使用硬體設備 Using Office Appliances

UNIT 23 使用印表機 Using a Printer

  Katharine B Barbara

Katharine is going to print some documents. 凱薩琳正準備要列印一些文件。

K Hi, Barbara. A quick question: I'm about to print a really long document. Should I just use the **default**[1] printer, or is there another machine I should use for long stuff?

B How long is it?

K 65 pages.

B Yes, maybe you should print to the copier in the mail room. It should be an option in your printer menu, just not your default printer. I think the name is HQ330 or something.

K Alright, I'll check for that one.

B And make sure no one's left letterhead in it before you send the **job**[2]!

K 嘿，芭芭拉。問妳一個小問題：我要印一份頁數很多的文件，是要用**預設的**印表機，還是有多頁數文件專用的印表機？

B 有幾頁？

K 65 頁。

B 那也許妳要用收發室中的印表機來印。那台機器不是預設印表機，但應該會在妳的印表機選單中，名稱好像是 HQ330 還是什麼的。

K 好，那我來看看。

B **列印**前，要記得確認沒人把有信頭的列印紙放在印表機中。

1 **default** [dɪˋfɔlt] (adj.) 系統預設的
2 **(print) job** 列印工作

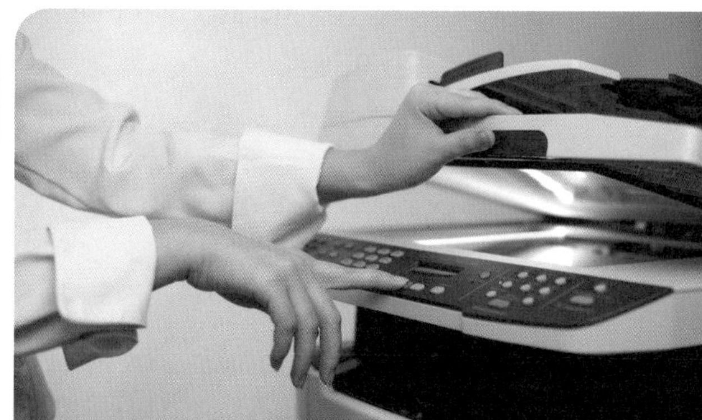

Useful Expressions

A Connecting printers and computers 119
連接印表機與電腦

1	I need to **install**[3] the new printer before I can use it.	我要先**安裝**好新的印表機才能使用它。
2	My laptop still won't recognize the new printer.	我的筆記型電腦還是無法辨識新的印表機。
3	I think I'm going to change my default printer.	我想我要更改預設的印表機。
4	Does only one printer serve our whole network?	我們整個網路只共用一台印表機嗎？

B Printing documents 列印文件

5	Print me ten copies of page one, please.	第一頁要印十張，麻煩您。
6	The first few pages are fine, but four to nine need to be reprinted.	前幾頁可以，但從第 4 頁到第 9 頁要重印。
7	You should make sure you change the **orientation**[4] of the paper before you print that.	列印前你應先確認有調整紙張的**方向**。
8	I always **preview**[5] my documents before I send them to the printer.	在列印前，我通常會先**預覽**文件。

3 **install** [ɪnˋstɔl] (v.) 安裝
4 **orientation** [ˏorɪɛnˋteʃən] (n.) 列印方向
5 **preview** [ˋprivju] (v.) 預先瀏覽

Printer Types and Supplies 印表機的種類和零件

inkjet cartridge 墨水匣

laser toner 碳粉匣

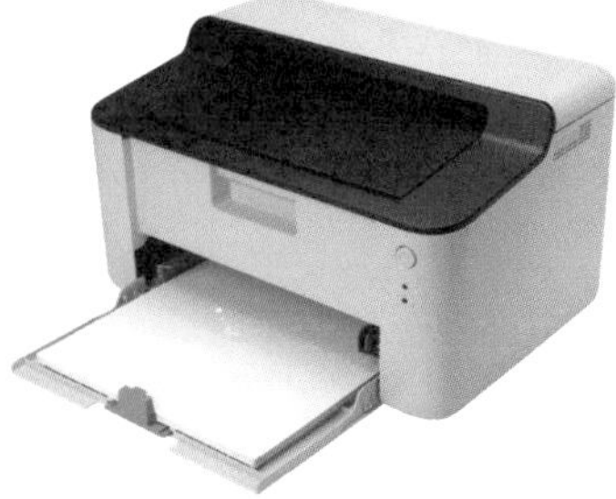

laser printer 雷射印表機

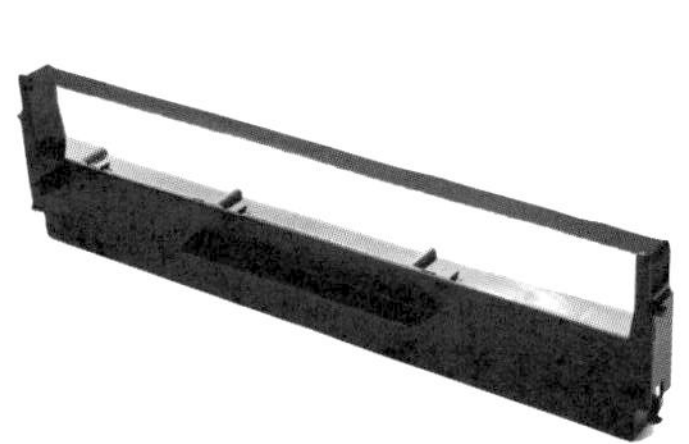

fabric ribbon 色帶

inkjet printer 噴墨印表機

paper 列印紙

C Printing problems 列印問題

9 The printer ran out of toner in the middle of my report.

我的報告印到一半，印表機的碳粉就用完了。

10 Do you know how to add colored ink to the printer?

你知道要如何更換印表機的彩色墨水匣嗎？

11 I feel like my documents look **slanted**[1]. Maybe there's a problem with the **paper feed**[2].

我的文件好像**歪歪的，送紙器**可能有問題。

12 I think there's a **scrap**[3] of paper stuck in the printer. I've pulled out as much paper as I could see, but it still says there's a jam.

我猜想可能有**紙片**卡在印表機裡。我已盡可能拉出看得到的紙了，卻仍然顯示卡紙。

1 **slanted** [ˋslæntɪd] (adj.) 傾斜的；歪斜的
2 **paper feed** 送紙器
3 **scrap** [skræp] (n.) 碎片；小塊

Review Questions

Listen to the conversations and answer the questions below.

120 **1. What does the man ask the woman?**

(A) Whether she has messages to send.
(B) Whether she is going to print anything.
(C) Whether she is connected to the printer.
(D) Whether she wants to wait for him.

121 **2. What will the woman have to do?**

(A) Print her document again.
(B) Connect to the printer again.
(C) Recycle her printer.
(D) Preview her document.

3. Why does the woman asks if the man needs recycled paper?

(A) Because she bought some recently.
(B) Because she will recycle his paper.
(C) Because she can't use the document she just printed.
(D) Because she is an environmentalist.

122 **4.** A: Do you want me to make copies of the ________________, Jim?

B: Thanks, but I'm actually not finished with it yet. I'm just running spell check now, but then I've got to ________________ it and make sure nothing's gone wrong with the formatting. I wouldn't want to make you wait around.

A: Oh, alright then. I guess I'll just see you at the ________________ then. Let me know if you need any other help.

Ans B, A, C, agenda, preview, meeting

UNIT 24 使用電子郵件 Using Email

  Jacob  Katharine

Jacob wants Katharine to help him send some materials to other people in the company. 雅各要凱薩琳替他寄資料給公司的其他人。

J Katharine, I need to send the proposed book design to headquarters. Can you make ten color copies of the front and back cover designs and **overnight**[1] them to Stan at headquarters?

K Sure. I assume it's urgent?

J Yes, the designer fell behind and just gave it to me today. Now, if I want the thing to be approved, I need to get it to **HQ**[2] so they can review it and send it back to me with enough time to have it printed before the due date.

K I'll be happy to overnight the copies, but why don't I also scan it and email them the scans?

J Why didn't I think of that? Great idea. I'll send you all the email addresses you'll need. Thanks a lot.

J 凱薩琳，我要把書籍設計的提案寄到總公司。可不可以請妳把封面與封底各影印十份，再**寄隔日件**給總公司的斯坦？

K 好，我想這很緊急吧？

J 對。設計師進度落後了，到今天才給我設計。如果提案要通過，就要先寄到**總公司**讓他們看過再寄回給我，才有時間在截止日前送印。

K 我很樂意隔日寄送提案，但我們何不也掃描提案，直接寄掃描檔給他們就好？

J 好點子，我怎麼沒想到？我會把所有需要的郵件地址寄給妳，多謝妳啦。

1 **overnight** [ˋovənaɪt] (v.) 隔夜送達
2 **HQ (= headquarters** [ˋhɛdkwɔrtəz]**)** (n.) 總部；總公司

Useful Expressions

3 **fire off** 急速寄出(言辭激憤的郵件)
4 **shoot** [ʃut] (v.) 寄
5 **forward** [ˋfɔrwəd] (v.) 轉寄
6 **in the loop** 在決策圈內

A Talking about sending email messages 談論寄送電子郵件

1	I've got to **fire off**[3] an email to the new insurance representative.	我要**快速寄**一封電子郵件給新來的保險專員。
2	**Shoot**[4] me a message as soon as you read my comments, will you?	看過我的評論後，請立即**寄**訊息給我好嗎？
3	Would you **forward**[5] that email to Stan, please? He'll want to be kept **in the loop**[6].	可以麻煩你將信**轉寄**給斯坦嗎？他會想知道情況的。
4	I'll **bcc**[7] you on the incident report I am sending to Human Resources.	我會將我寄給人資部的事件報告**用密件副本寄**給你。
5	Please **cc**[8] Sylvia when you send the new schedule around.	發新的進度表時，也請**寄副本**給席薇亞。

B Talking about attachments 談論附加檔案

6 Can you send that as an email and attachment, not a fax?
你可以在電子郵件夾帶附件給我，而不要用傳真嗎？

7 For some reason, I can't get this document to attach to the email I've written. Would you look at it for me?
不知道為什麼，我無法將此文件夾帶到我寫的郵件中，能請你替我看看嗎？

8 Claire sent the schedule as an attachment, but it's a type of file my machine doesn't recognize and I can't download it.
克萊兒以附件寄出時間表，但我的電腦無法讀取這種檔案類型，也無法下載。

9 The attachment he sent was too big—my whole computer **froze**[9] when I tried to open it.
他寄的附件檔案太大了，當我要打開檔案時，整台電腦就**當機**了。

10 Don't send the description as an attachment, please; just paste it into the body of your message.
請勿將說明文字以附件寄送，貼到信件內文中即可。

7 **bcc (blind carbon copy)** 寄密件副本(收件者 [to] 看不到此項內的收件人及其電子信箱)
8 **cc (carbon copy)** 寄副本
9 **freeze** [friz] (v.) 當機

General Internet Abbreviations 一般網路縮寫

- **AFK (away from keyboard)** 暫時離開電腦
- **AKA (also known as)** 也被稱為；又名
- **ASAP (as soon as possible)** 盡快
- **BTW (by the way)** 順帶一提
- **CU (See you.)** 再見
- **F2F (face to face)** 面對面
- **FWD/FW (forward)** 轉寄
- **FYI ([just] for your information)** 供你參考的資訊
- **GR8 (great)** 很好
- **IDK (I don't know.)** 我不知道。
- **IMO (in my opinion)** 在我看來
- **L8R (later)** 晚點
- **N/A (not available/applicable)** （用於填寫表格）不適用
- **NAZ (name, address, ZIP)** 姓名、地址和郵遞區號
- **OIC (Oh, I see.)** 噢，我懂了。
- **Pls (please)** 請
- **POV (point of view)** 觀點
- **Q&A (question and answer)** 問與答
- **RSVP**（來自法文 **répondez s'il vous plaît**，英文為 **request for responses**）請回覆
- **TBA (to be announced)** 待公布
- **TBC (to be continued/confirmed)** 待續／待確認
- **TBD (to be determined)** 待決定
- **thx (thanks)** 謝謝
- **TTYL (talk to you later)** 待會再聊
- **SIM (Subject is message.)** 主旨即訊息內容
- **SRY (sorry)** 抱歉

C Other email issues 其他電子郵件問題

11 I've been getting so much **spam**[1] lately. Someone must have **gotten hold of**[2] my address.

最近我常收到**垃圾信件**，一定是有人**拿到**了我的郵件地址。

12 The **temp**[3] we let go last month has been sending me strange emails every day. I'm going to **block**[4] her address and report her to Human Resources.

我們上個月解聘的**約聘員工**每天寄給我奇怪的信件，我要**封鎖**她的郵件地址，並回報給人資部。

13 For some reason, email from our overseas office often ends up in my junk mail folder. I'm going to have to add their address to my **safe list**[5].

海外辦公室所寄的電子郵件不知為何總會分到我的垃圾郵件匣中，我要把他們的郵件地址加到**安全清單**中。

14 For some reason, my emails to Jane keep **bouncing back**[6]. I wonder if her inbox is full.

我寄給珍的電子郵件總是不知怎麼**被退回**，不知道是不是她的收件匣滿了。

Review Questions

Listen to the conversations and answer the questions below.

125 **1. What problem is the man having?**

(A) He can't open an attachment.
(B) He can't start his computer.
(C) He can't access his email.
(D) He can't change his password.

2. Why does the woman suggest the man call tech support?

(A) Because tech support is trained to handle computer problems.
(B) Because tech support should be informed of computer problems.
(C) Because tech support is visiting the building.
(D) Because tech support cooperates with their department.

126 **3. What does the woman want?**

(A) An address.
(B) An email address.
(C) A name.
(D) A phone number.

4. What is probably the name of Glenda Harris's company?

(A) It is impossible to know.
(B) Harris Shipping.
(C) Global Shipping.
(D) Glenda Harris.

5. Which symbol is in Glenda Harris's email address?

(A) A hashtag.
(B) A hyphen.
(C) A question mark.
(D) An underscore.

Ans C, A, B, C, D

1 **spam** [spæm] (n.) 垃圾信件
2 **get hold of** 得到
3 **temp** [tɛmp] (n.) 短期約聘人員
4 **block** [blɑk] (v.) 封鎖
5 **safe list** 安全清單
6 **bounce back (as an email)** (電子郵件)被退回

UNIT 25 電腦中毒與疑難排解 Viruses and Troubleshooting

127 K Katharine B Babara

Katharine's new computer is running slowly. 凱薩琳的新電腦速度很慢。

K Barbara, my computer is really slow to start up. There must be something I can do to get it cleaned up.

B I bet there are a lot of unnecessary programs on that computer. You could uninstall some of them. Use the add/remove programs option.

K Yes, I'll take a look at that. But there are a lot of programs I don't really need that open when I start up.

B I can take a look at your **startup settings**[1] later, if you want.

K That would be terrific. No rush.

B OK, I'll come by later. **In the meantime**[2], run a **virus scan**[3], make sure you aren't running more than one messenger service at once, and start a **disk defrag**[4].

K 芭芭拉，我的電腦開機很慢，一定有辦法能清理吧。

B 我猜是電腦裡有很多用不到的程式。妳可以用「新增／移除」的選項來解除安裝。

K 好，我會看看。不過我開機時，很多用不到的程式都會跟著打開。

B 妳要的話，晚一點我可以幫妳看看妳的**開機設定**。

K 太好了，不急喔。

B 好，我晚點再過來。**同時**也**掃描**一下**病毒**，確認沒有一次開一個以上的通訊軟體，再做**磁碟重組**。

1 **startup settings / startup options** 開機設定／開機選項
2 **in the meantime** 與此同時
3 **virus scan** 病毒掃瞄
4 **disk defragmentation (defrag)** 磁碟重組

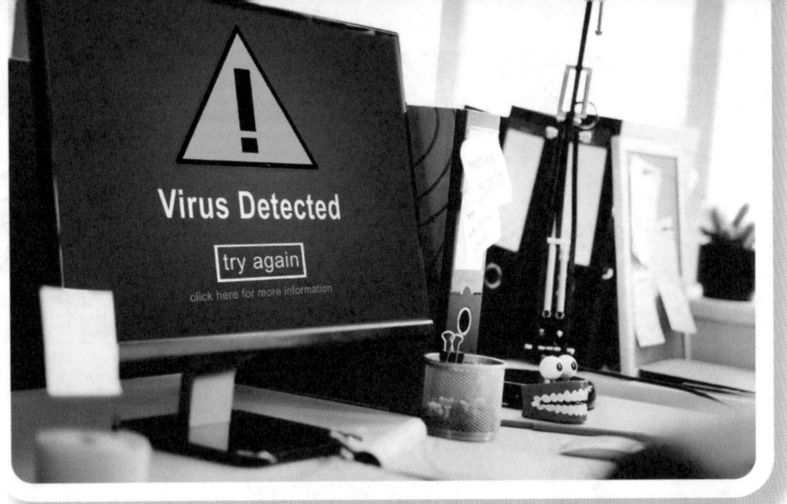

Useful Expressions

A Talking about troubleshooting[5] options 

談論疑難排解的選擇

1 Start your computer in **safe mode**[6] so we can see what the problem is.
在**安全模式**下開啟電腦，我們才能知道問題出在哪裡。

2 **Reboot**[7] your computer and see if it'll work after that.
將電腦**重新開機**，看開機後是否能正常運作。

3 You probably need to do a **system restore**[8].
你可能要將**系統還原**。

4 Maybe you should see if too many programs are taking up your memory.
你可能要看看是不是有太多程式佔掉你的記憶體。

B Talking about computer problems 談論電腦問題

5 I'm getting an error message that says **illegal operation**[9].
我收到一則錯誤訊息，上面寫著**操作不當**。

6 I keep getting this **runtime error**[10].
我一直收到**執行發生錯誤**的訊息。

5 **troubleshooting** [ˋtrʌbl̩ˌʃutɪŋ] (n.) 疑難排解
6 **safe mode** 安全模式
7 **reboot** [riˋbut] (v.) 重新開機
8 **system restore** 系統還原
9 **illegal operation** 不當操作
10 **runtime error** 執行時發生錯誤

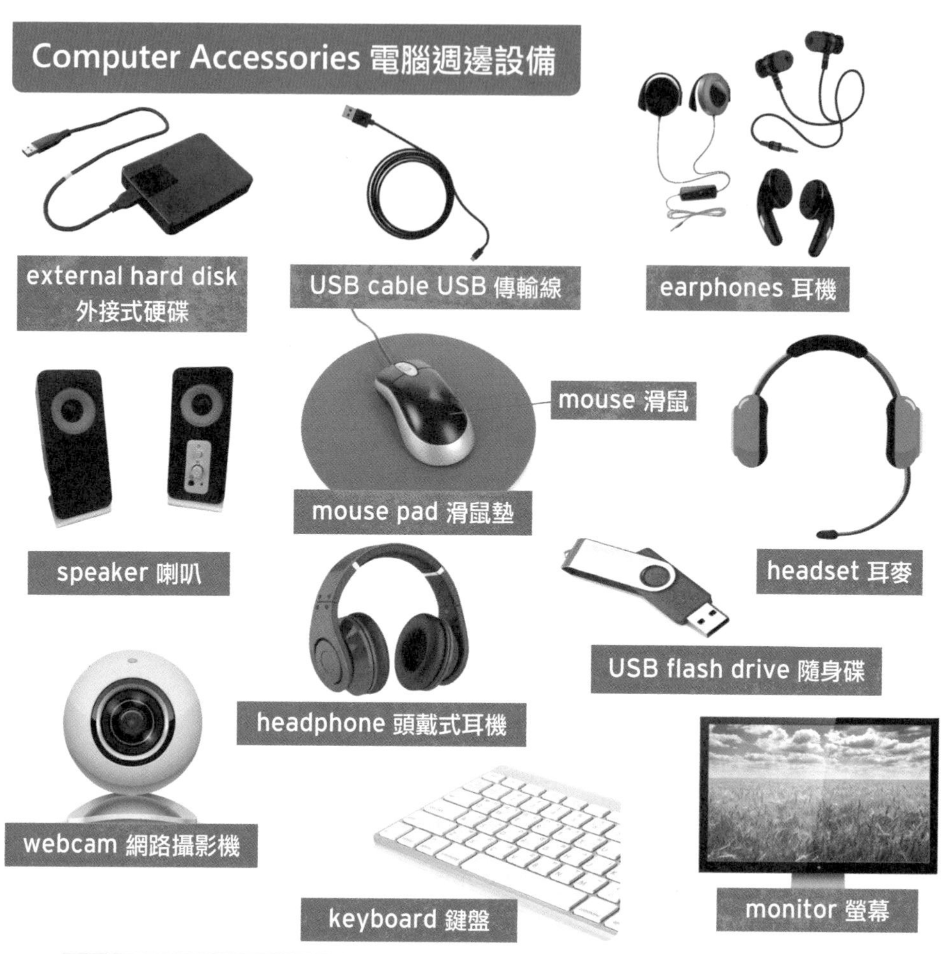

7 I'm getting a low disk space message. I guess I need to close some programs.
我不斷收到磁碟空間不足的訊息，我想可能要關掉一些程式。

8 My computer says "bad command or file name." What should I do?
我的電腦顯示「指令錯誤」，我要怎麼辦？

9 What is a "**syntax error**[1]"? 什麼是「**語法錯誤**」？

10 I think my computer is overheating, but I don't know what to do about it.
我覺得我的電腦過熱，卻不知道該怎麼辦。

C Talking about viruses and anti-virus software
談論病毒與防毒軟體

11 I think you ought to get a better **anti-virus program**[2].
我認為你應該去買個更好的**防毒軟體**。

12 My computer is running really slowly. I think I need to run a virus scan.
我電腦跑得超慢，應該要來掃毒了。

13 Oh no! I think I just opened an email with a **worm**[3] in it.
噢不！我想我剛剛開了一封夾帶有**蠕蟲病毒**的郵件。

14 You've really got to be careful opening email with **attachments**[4] these days.
最近你開啟信件時要多加注意夾帶**附件**的電子郵件。

1 **syntax error** 程式語法錯誤
2 **anti-virus program** 防毒軟體
3 **worm** [wɝm] (n.) 蠕蟲病毒
4 **attachment** [əˋtætʃmənt] (n.) 附件

Review Questions

Listen to the conversations and answer the questions below.

129 1. **What happened to the man's computer?**
Ⓐ It is probably started. Ⓑ It is probably burned.
Ⓒ It is probably crashed. Ⓓ It is probably rebooting.

2. **What kind of assistance will the woman offer to the man?**
Ⓐ Troubleshooting. Ⓑ Checking for viruses.
Ⓒ Startup setting. Ⓓ Cleaning up the computer.

130 3. **What is the woman worried about?**
Ⓐ Hits. Ⓑ Syntax errors.
Ⓒ Networks. Ⓓ Virus.

4. **What is the man's suggestion?**
Ⓐ He tells her to speak to management.
Ⓑ He tells her to reboot the computer.
Ⓒ He tells her to find better software.
Ⓓ He tells her to trust the current software.

131 5. Ⓐ Have you ever seen this? It says "______________ 451."
Ⓑ No, sorry. I don't know what that means.
Ⓐ I get so ______________ with computer problems. Do you think I need to call tech support?
Ⓑ I'd try ______________ your computer first. Maybe it's nothing.

Ans C, A, D, C, error code, frustrated, restarting

UNIT 26 提議 Making Proposals

J Jacob　K Katharine　A Ann　G George

Katharine and the team are meeting to discuss the project's progress. 凱薩琳與團隊正在開會討論案子的進度。

J Let's talk about how we're going to approach this testing cycle. We've been overnighting the results back to this office for **analysis**[1]. Is this the way we want to continue?

K Why don't we do the analysis **on-site**[2]?

J How do you mean?

K Well, the testers have a certain understanding of the raw results we're getting, right? More than someone back here who hasn't seen the subjects, anyway. Why don't we do the **initial**[3] analysis on-site?

A We'd have to test fewer subjects in one day, to give the **analysts**[4] time to do the extra work . . . but I don't think that would be a problem. We could add one day to each trip, but do more work before we get back.

G So the schedule wouldn't be affected.

J Well, what do you all think? It sounds like a good option to me.

J 我們來討論要如何處理這次的測試週期。我們已將結果連夜送回公司做**分析**，這是我們想要繼續進行的方式嗎？

K 我們何不**現場**分析呢？

J 妳的意思是？

K 這個嘛……測試員對於我們拿到的原始結果比那些沒見過實驗品的人來得有概念，那何不先現場做**初步的**分析呢？

A 我們一天會測試較少的實驗品，好讓**分析師**有時間去完成外加的工作……但我不認為這會是問題。我們送一趟可以多給一天的時間，但在東西送回來前多做一些事。

G 這樣一來就不會影響到進度了。

J 那麼，大家覺得如何？我覺得是個不錯的方案。

1 **analysis** [ə`næləsɪs] (n.) 分析
2 **on-site** [`ɑn`saɪt] (adv.) 在現場地
3 **initial** [ɪ`nɪʃəl] (adj.) 最初的
4 **analyst** [`ænl̩ɪst] (n.) 分析師

Useful Expressions

A Making proposals[5] 提議 

1	I have an idea I wanted to **throw out**[6] there.	我有個點子要說。
2	I've been thinking about making some changes to the design and I wanted to **run them by all of you**[7].	我一直想對該設計做些修改，而我想**聽大家的意見**。
3	I think we should **outsource**[8] all of the design.	我認為我們應該**外發**所有的設計。
4	Can I propose that we **shelve**[9] this for now and discuss it further when we have more information?	我可以提議目前先**暫緩**此事，等有進一步消息再討論嗎？
5	I suggest we change all the dates.	我建議更改所有日期。
6	What about using a different **contractor**[10]?	換一位不同的**承包商**如何？

5 **proposal** [prəˋpozḷ] (n.) 提議
6 **throw out** 提出
7 **run sth. by sb.** 向某人徵求對某事的看法
8 **outsource** [ˋaʊtˌsors] (v.) 外包；委外
9 **shelve** [ʃɛlv] (v.) 擱置；暫緩
10 **contractor** [ˋkɑntræktɚ] (n.) 承包商

Diagram Types 圖表種類

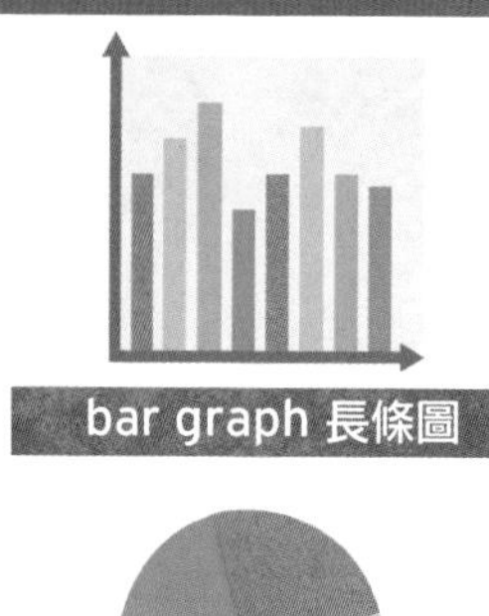

bar graph 長條圖

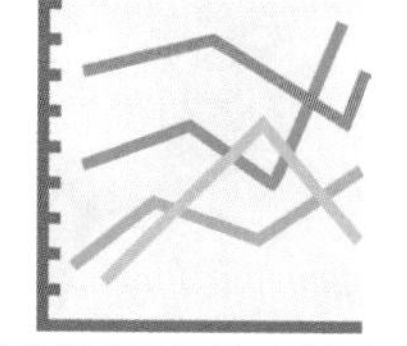

line graph 折線圖

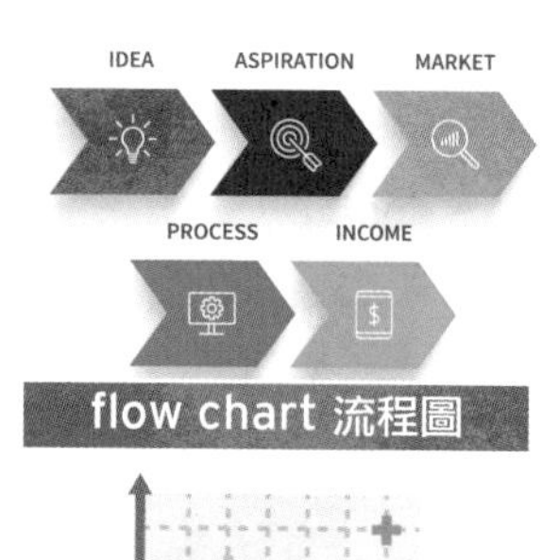

flow chart 流程圖

pie chart 圓餅圖

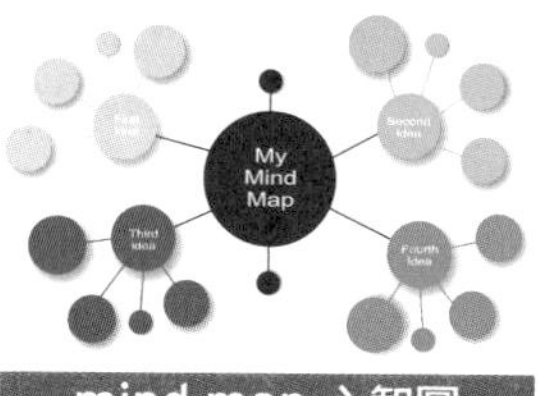

mind map 心智圖

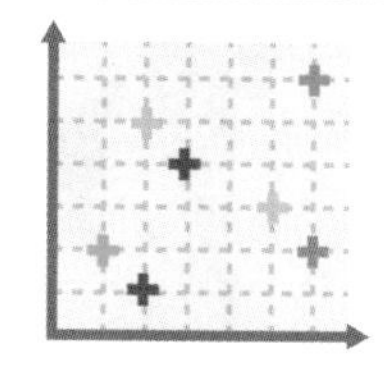

scatter diagram 散布圖

B Talking about proposals 談論提議

7	What do you think about Carol's suggestion?	你覺得卡蘿的提議如何？
8	Let's think about Tom's proposal.	我們來想想湯姆的提案。
9	The idea of changing the format is interesting.	這個更改格式的點子很有趣。
10	I'm not sure this proposal will work, but let's consider it.	我不確定這提議行不行得通，不過我們還是可以考慮。

C Accepting proposals 接受提議 

11	An **open house**[1] is a great idea.	**開放參觀**真是個好點子。
12	I think that sounds **promising**[2]. Let's talk about it some more.	我認為這聽起來**大有可為**，我們再進一步談談吧。
13	This sounds like something that could work. It could really **generate**[3] great **word of mouth**[4].	這聽起來行得通，可能會**產生**極佳的**口碑**。

D Rejecting proposals 拒絕提議

14	Jennifer's idea is good, but we've tried it before and it hasn't worked out.	珍妮佛的想法很好，但我們之前嘗試過卻沒有成功。
15	I think it would be too hard to **implement**[5] that suggestion.	我認為此建議太難**實行**。
16	I'm afraid we don't have the budget for that.	我們恐怕沒有預算做這個。
17	We should try that in another project, but not this one.	我們可以將此用在別的案子上，但不是這一個。

Review Questions

Listen to the conversations and answer the questions below.

135 1. **What does the man suggest?**
- (A) Changing the way they make travel arrangements.
- (B) Letting him make travel arrangements.
- (C) Changing their travel plans.
- (D) Canceling the travel plans.

2. **Why is the woman surprised?**
- (A) Because the man was rude.
- (B) Because she thought the man was joking.
- (C) Because she thought they were going to be traveling.
- (D) Because she thought the issue had already been settled.

3. **Why does the man think his suggestion is good?**
- (A) Because it will give work to others.
- (B) Because it will get him overtime.
- (C) Because it will save them time.
- (D) Because it will save them money.

136 4. **What did Bob do just before this conversation occurred?**
- (A) He made an agenda.
- (B) He made a suggestion.
- (C) He made a comparison.
- (D) He made a deal.

5. **What does the woman want to know?**
- (A) What the idea would cost.
- (B) Who the man would invite.
- (C) What the others' thoughts are.
- (D) More detailed about what they do.

Ans A, D, C, B, C

1 **open house** 開放參觀
2 **promising** [ˋprɑmɪsɪŋ] (adj.) 有希望的；有前途的
3 **generate** [ˋdʒɛnə͵ret] (v.) 產生
4 **word of mouth** 口碑行銷；口耳相傳
5 **implement** [ˋɪmpləmənt] (v.) 執行

UNIT 27 進行會議 Conducting a Meeting

137 J Jacob K Katharine A Ann G George

1 **Katharine and the team are meeting to discuss the project's progress.** 凱薩琳與團隊正在討論案子的進度。

J Good morning, everyone! I'm glad to have this chance to sit down with all of you. I think we're all pretty well aware of the project's progress so far, but it's always **valuable**[1] to update each other face-to-face. My aim today is to get an informal status report from each of you, to hear about any problems you are facing or **anticipating**[2], and to talk about any lessons you've learned so far that may help the rest of us. Before we begin, do any of you have any other specific topics you'd like to add to our **agenda**[3]?

K None here.

A G Nope.

J Fine. Now, Ann, you're first on the agenda. Can you give us a brief overview of where you are in your work right now?

J 早安，各位！很高興有機會和大家一同坐在這裡。我想大家對案子目前的進度都相當清楚，但面對面互相說明最新狀況總是很**重要的**。我今天打算要聽你們每個人報告狀況、知道你們面臨或**預期**的問題、談談你們目前學到且對我們可能有所助益的經驗。在開始之前，有沒有人對特定主題有興趣，要加到**議程表**中的？

K 沒有。

A G 沒有。

J 那好。現在，安妳是議程表上的第一位，可以請妳簡短報告妳目前的進度嗎？

1 **valuable** [ˋvæljuəbl] (adj.) 重要的；有價值的
2 **anticipate** [ænˋtɪsə͵pet] (v.) 預期
3 **agenda** [əˋdʒɛndə] (n.) 議程表
4 **concrete** [ˋkɑnkrit] (adj.) 具體的
5 **convene** [kənˋvin] (v.) 集會；聚集
6 **wrap up** 〔非正式〕結束某事

2 Later in the meeting. 會議稍晚時。

G If there's nothing to add on this topic, I think we can move on.

J Great. Now, let's discuss the last item on the agenda: "New Project." It looks like we may be getting a new contract very soon. We'll have to start thinking about how we can manage our current workload while taking on new work. Unfortunately, we haven't got anything **concrete**[4] to go on now; I just wanted to make you all aware of the fact that this new work may be coming. As soon as I've got any more information, we'll **convene**[5] again.

For now, though, looks like we've covered our main topics. If there aren't any questions or issues I've forgotten about, I think we can **wrap up**[6].

G 若對此主題沒什麼要補充的話，那我們可以繼續到下一個主題了。

J 太好了，現在來討論議程最後一個事項——「新案子」。我們似乎很快又要有新合約了，要思考如何同時接新案子和處理目前的工作量。不過我們目前尚未有**實際的**想法，我只是要讓各位事先知道接下來可能會有新工作。一旦有更多消息，我們要再次**開會**討論。

那現在主要的議題我們似乎都討論到了，如果沒有我沒提到的問題或議題，我想我們可以**結束**會議了。

Useful Expressions

A Welcoming and introducing attendants 
歡迎與介紹與會者

1	Welcome, everyone, and thank you for coming.	歡迎各位，感謝大家的蒞臨。
2	Good afternoon! I'm glad you could all **make it**[1] today.	午安！很高興你們今天都**能準時出席**。
3	I'd like to introduce Gloria, our new account manager.	我要介紹新來的客戶經理葛洛莉亞。
4	I want to welcome Jonathan Hamm, who has traveled from Idaho to be here today.	我要歡迎今天從愛達荷州過來的強納生·漢。

B Opening a meeting and stating objectives
開始會議與說明主旨

5 I think we're all here, so let's get started.

我想全員到齊，可以開始了。

6 We have a lot to cover today, so let's **commence**[2].

我們今天要討論許多議題，就**開始**吧。

7 Let's **get down to business**[3].

我們開始**進入正題**吧。

8 Our goal today is to determine how to handle this **dispute**[4] between the office manager and the building administrator.

我們今天的目標，是要決定如何處理公司經理與大樓管理員的**糾紛**。

9 Our main aim today should be to come up with ideas for the board meeting agenda.

我們今天的主要目標，是想出董事會會議議程的點子。

1 **make it** 做或完成某事
2 **commence** [kəˋmɛns] (v.) 開始
3 **get down to business** 進入主題；討論正題
4 **dispute** [dɪˋspjut] (n.) 爭執；糾紛

10 As you can see from the agenda, the focus of this meeting will be **lessons learned**[5].

如各位在議程表上看到的，此次會議將著重於**學到的經驗**。

C Suggesting procedures or ground rules[6] 
建議流程或規則

11 I'd like to keep to the order on the agenda today.

今天我想按照議程順序走。

12 If you all agree, I think we should discuss the new business before we get to the project updates.

若各位同意，在報告專案的最新狀況前，我想我們應先討論新的業務。

13 Because we have so much to get through, I hope each report can be kept to 10 minutes.

由於我們有太多事要討論了，我希望每個報告能控制在十分鐘。

14 We're very tight on time today, so I need to stress that you bring any outside problems to my attention later and today **adhere to**[7] only what will affect all of us.

由於我們今天的時間緊湊，所以我要強調，今天只談會影響到全體的事項，其他問題晚點再說。

5 **lessons learned** 學到的經驗或教訓
6 **ground rules** 基本規則
7 **adhere to** 遵守；堅持

D Keeping a meeting moving 繼續會議

15 If that's what we've decided to do, let's make sure it's added to the **minutes**[1] and then move on to the next topic.

若我們決議如此，確認有寫進**會議紀錄**中並接著討論下一個主題。

16 Has everyone had a chance to **contribute**[2]? Yes? OK, then let's continue.

大家都發表過意見了嗎？有嗎？好，我們繼續吧。

17 I suggest we close this topic until we've all had time to consider it, and move on to other items.

我建議先停止討論此議題，等到大家都有時間考慮再討論，現在先討論其他事項吧。

E Closing a meeting 結束會議

18 I think we've addressed everything on the agenda now.

我想我們已討論過議程上的所有事項了。

19 Unless anyone has anything to add, I suggest we stop things here.

除非有人還有事要補充，不然今天就到此為止。

20 I know we could spend a lot longer talking about this, but we've run out of time.

我知道我們能再多花些時間討論此事，不過時間已經不夠了。

21 I know you're all busy and we've come to the end of our time. Why don't I set up a time, as soon as possible, to continue working through the unresolved items?

我知道各位很忙，會議也快要進入尾聲了。我們要不要儘快定個時間繼續，討論未決事項？

1 **minutes** [ˋmɪnɪts] (npl.) 會議紀錄或摘要
2 **contribute** [kənˋtrɪbjut] (v.) 貢獻

Review Questions

Listen to the conversations and answer the questions below.

140 **1. What is the man doing?**

Ⓐ He is opening a meeting.
Ⓑ He is closing a meeting.
Ⓒ He is setting up a meeting.
Ⓓ He is rejecting a proposal.

2. What does the man want to go over?

Ⓐ The meeting rules.
Ⓑ The items on the agenda.
Ⓒ The schedule.
Ⓓ The minutes.

141 **3. What does the speaker want to do?**

Ⓐ She wants to change the order of some agenda items.
Ⓑ She wants to change the time of the meeting.
Ⓒ She wants to ask Jason to leave early.
Ⓓ She wants to ask Jason to miss the discussion.

142 **4.** Ⓐ I wish we could spend more time on this point, but we've got a lot to get to today. I'd like to suggest that we ________________ this discussion in order to get into it in more detail later.

Ⓑ Can I ________________ that we make this the focus of our next meeting?

Ⓐ Great idea. Karl, make sure the minutes ________________ this, please. Now, our next topic is publications . . .

Ans A, B, A, shelve, propose, reflect

UNIT 28 討論行銷策略
Discussing Marketing Strategies

The members of a small company are going to meet to discuss their marketing plan. 一間小公司的成員要開會討論他們的行銷計畫。

143

MESSAGES

From: Suleiman Khalil (skhalil@exectraining.com)
To: Bob Newcastle (rnewcastle@exectraining.com), Jenny Sun (jsun@exectraining.com), Bess Reinhardt (breinhardt@exectraining.com), Albert Blithe (ablithe@exectraining.com)
Subject: Agenda for Marketing Meeting, April 28th, 9:30 a.m.
Attachment: Detailed Agenda 4-28.doc

Dear colleagues,

Attached please find a detailed agenda for our marketing meeting next Tuesday, April 28. I have included all of the hot topics we **identified**[1] from our **preliminary**[2] **brainstorm**[3] of April 20. Please let me know if you have any questions or any topics to add before the meeting.

Thank you,
Suleiman

Suleiman Khalil
Junior Analyst
Executive Training Inc.
www.exectraining.com
skhalil@exectraining.com

MESSAGES

寄件人： Suleiman Khalil (skhalil@exectraining.com)
收件人： Bob Newcastle (rnewcastle@exectraining.com), Jenny Sun (jsun@exectraining.com), Bess Reinhardt (breinhardt@exectraining.com), Albert Blithe (ablithe@exectraining.com)
主旨： 4 月 28 日早上 9:30 的行銷會議議程
附加檔案： Detailed Agenda 4-28.doc

親愛的同事們：

附件為下星期二，也就是 4 月 28 日要召開的行銷會議詳細的議程表。我已將我們在 4 月 20 日的初步腦力激盪中所想到的點子都囊括進去了。若各位有任何疑問或是有想補充的主題，請於開會前告知我。

謝謝。

蘇萊曼

蘇萊曼・哈林
初級分析師
決策訓練公司
www.exectraining.com
skhalil@exectraining.com

1 **identify** [aɪˋdɛntəˏfaɪ] (v.) 確認；發現
2 **preliminary** [prɪˋlɪməˏnɛrɪ] (adj.) 初步的
3 **brainstorm** [ˋbrenˏstɔrm] (n.) 腦力激盪

Meeting Agenda: Updating the Marketing Plan

Date and location: April 28, 2023, 9:30-11:00 a.m., Executive Training Offices
Attendees: Bob Newcastle, Bess Reinhardt, Suleiman Khalil, Jenny Sun, Albert Blithe

1. **Call to order: Bob Newcastle**
2. **Correspondence[1]**
3. **Minutes from last meeting: Suleiman Khalil**
4. **Topics**

(A) Defining our objective: Company growth? Increased profits per project? New clients? Bigger projects? What is our USP[2] ?

(B) What is our market: public sector[3], private sector, or both?
- Attracting private sector clients
- **Diversifies[4]** our business
- Possibly more **lucrative[5]**
- No real market share now
- Penetrating deeper into public sector / Federal government
- Build on positive word of mouth
- More long-term, **high-profile[6]** projects

(C) How should we communicate with potential[7] clients?
- Update website.
- Attend government small business panels? Who? When?
- Host a training open house? Phone calls?

(D) Should we set aside[8] a marketing budget?
What expenses should we expect? Who will manage the budget?

(E) What is our pricing strategy?
Skim pricing[9] ? Penetration pricing[10] ?

議程表：行銷計畫最新消息

日期與地點：　2023 年 4 月 28 日，早上 9:30 到 11:00，主管訓練辦公室

與會者：　Bob Newcastle, Bess Reinhardt, Suleiman Khalil, Jenny Sun, Albert Blithe

1. **宣布開會：**Bob Newcastle
2. **聯絡人**
3. **前次會議紀錄：**Suleiman Kahlil
4. **主題**

(A) 界定我們的目標：公司的成長？各個案子所增加的收益？新客戶？更大的專案？我們獨特賣點為何？

(B) 我們的市場為何：公部門、私部門，還是兩者皆是？

- 吸引民營企業的客戶
- **多角化**經營
- 更多**有利可圖的**賺錢方式
- 現在沒有真正的市佔率
- 深入瞭解公營事業／聯邦政府
- 建立正面的口碑行銷
- 建立長期、**備受矚目的**計畫

(C) 如何與潛在客戶聯絡上？

- 更新網站
- 參加政府的小型商業小組？誰參加？參加時間？
- 舉辦免費訓練會？電訪？

(D) 應該撥出行銷預算嗎？

我們的預定費用？誰負責預算？

(E) 訂價策略為何？

吸脂訂價策略？ 滲透訂價策略？

1 **correspondence** [͵kɔrəˋspɑndəns] (n.) 聯絡人

2 **USP (= unique selling proposition)** 獨特賣點

3 **sector** [ˋsɛktɚ] (n.) 部門

4 **diversify** [daɪˋvɝsə͵faɪ] (v.) 使多樣化；從事多角化經營

5 **lucrative** [ˋlukrətɪv] (adj.) 賺錢的；有利可圖的

6 **high-profile** [͵haɪˋprofaɪl] (adj.) 備受矚目的（**low-profile** 低調的；低姿態的）

7 **potential** [pəˋtɛnʃəl] (adj.) 潛在的

8 **set aside** 撥出（金錢）

9 **skim pricing** 吸脂訂價策略（將產品的價格定得較高，儘可能在產品壽命初期或在競爭者研製出相似的產品以前，儘快收回投資，並且取得相當的利潤。）

10 **penetration pricing** 滲透訂價策略（以低於生產成本加平均利潤的價格訂價，能夠迅速擴大市場占有率，讓同行感到利潤率不高，不積極仿製，使產品保持競爭優勢。）

Meeting agenda: Updating the Marketing Plan, April 28, 2023 (continued)

Topics

(F) What are our targets? What are our ratios[1]?

- Setting targets—Quarterly[2]? Yearly? What makes sense for us?
- Defining ratios—What percent of inquiries[3] become prospects[4]? What percent of prospects become clients?

1. Tracking inquiries and prospects—create a log[5]? Review entries at weekly meeting? Follow up[6] more thoroughly?
2. Create a spreadsheet[7] with marketing outlays[8] and returns[9]?
3. New staff—hire new administrative staff to handle this aspect[10] of marketing? How much expertise is needed?

(G) How will we measure results?

New clients, profit from projects, new private sector expansion, business growth?

Situation Analysis 狀況分析 指管理人員用來分析組織內部和外部環境，以了解組織能力、客戶和業務環境的方法。

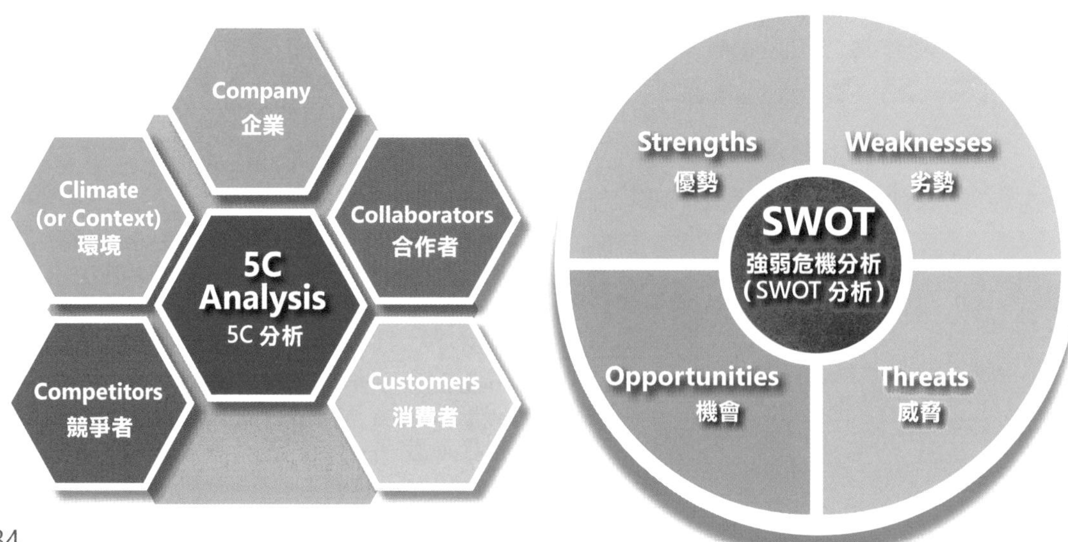

議程表：行銷計畫最新消息
2023 年 4 月 28 日（接續）

主題

(F) 我們的目標為何？比例為何？

- 設定目標——每季？每年？什麼對我們而言是重要的？
- 界定比例——有多少比例的受訪者成為潛在客戶？又有多少潛在客戶成為真正的客戶？

1. 追蹤受訪者與潛在客戶——建立工作日誌？在每週例會上檢閱紀錄？持續追蹤後續發展？
2. 製作行銷費用與收益的試算表？
3. 新員工——聘請新行政人員來處理此方面的行銷？人員的專業程度要到哪？

(G) 如何評估結果？

新客戶、案子的收益、新民間企業的擴展、業績的成長？

Useful Expressions

A Discussing market strategies 討論行銷策略

1 This conference will be a great **networking**[11] opportunity.
此會議將是個很棒的**交流**機會。

2 We need to be very careful about how we **position**[12] ourselves.
我們要非常謹慎的**定位**我們的產品。

3 Should we consider providing a **guarantee**[13] for all our services?
我們應該要考慮對所有服務提供**保證**嗎？

1 **ratio** [ˋreʃɪo] (n.) 比例
2 **quarterly** [ˋkwɔrtəlɪ] (adv.) 每季度地
3 **inquiry** [ɪnˋkwaɪrɪ] (n.) 調查；詢問
4 **prospect** [ˋprɑspɛkt] (n.) 潛在客戶
5 **log** [lɔg] (n.) 工作日誌
6 **follow up** 進度控制；後續追蹤
7 **spreadsheet** [ˋsprɛd͵ʃit] (n.)〔電腦〕試算表
8 **outlay** [ˋaʊt͵le] (n.) 費用；支出
9 **return** [rɪˋtɝn] (n.) 收益；利潤
10 **aspect** [ˋæspɛkt] (n.) 方面
11 **networking** [ˋnɛt͵wɝkɪŋ] (n.) 交流
12 **position** [pəˋzɪʃən] (v.) 定位
13 **guarantee** [͵gærənˋti] (n.) 保證

4 I don't think that **cold calling**[1] will win us any new customers.
我不認為**電話行銷**會替我們帶來任何新客戶。

5 We should send out a **press release**[2] about our latest award.
我們應發布有關最近得獎消息的**新聞稿**。

6 We need to start a **viral marketing**[3] **campaign**[4].
我們應該開始**病毒式行銷的宣傳活動**了。

7 We really need to **motivate**[5] our **sales force**[6].
我們真該**激勵**我們的**業務人員**。

B Discussing marketing processes 討論行銷過程

8 It's time for a detailed **situation analysis**[7].
該是時候做詳細的**狀況分析**了。

9 Our most important objective is to increase quarterly sales by 15%.
我們最重要的目標為增加 15% 的季營收。

10 We plan to review our **pricing strategy**[8] in the new year.
我們打算在新的一年重新檢視我們的**訂價策略**。

11 Do you have the data from the **SWOT**[9] report? 你有 **SWOT** 分析報告的資料嗎?

C Discussing market shares 討論市佔率

12 We need to **reposition**[10] the product in our **target market**[11].
我們應**重新定位**我們**目標市場**的產品。

13 There isn't another company to challenge our **market share**[12].
沒有其他公司能挑戰我們的**市佔率**。

14 We are doing very well with government contracts, but we don't have any private sector **penetration**[13] to speak of.
我們與政府合作得非常順利,在民營企業的**佔有**率卻是零。

1 **cold calling** 電話行銷;促銷電話
2 **press release** 新聞稿
3 **viral marketing** 病毒式行銷策略,即將一些廣告直接從一個用戶傳播到另外一個用戶,普遍運用於現在的網路行銷。最常見的是透過網路社群和各種媒體,早期用在電子郵件行銷(email marketing)。
4 **campaign** [kæm`pen] (n.) 宣傳活動
5 **motivate** [`motə͵vet] (v.) 激勵
6 **sales force** 業務人員
7 **situation analysis** 狀況分析
8 **pricing strategy** 訂價策略

Review Questions

Listen to the conversations and answer the questions below.

145 1. **Why is the woman cold calling?**

Ⓐ Because it is the season for calling.
Ⓑ Because she has finished her other work.
Ⓒ Because she is a new hire.
Ⓓ Because it is in her schedule.

2. **Why doesn't the woman like cold calling?**

Ⓐ Because she doesn't think it's effective.
Ⓑ Because she thinks it's boring.
Ⓒ Because she has to wait on the line.
Ⓓ Because she has to come up with some marketing ideas while doing this.

146 3. **What are they trying to sell?**

Ⓐ A new technology. Ⓑ A new plan. Ⓒ A new game. Ⓓ A target.

4. **What does "grown men who understand gaming" mean to the woman and the man?**

Ⓐ Their marketing plan. Ⓑ Their target market
Ⓒ Their commercials. Ⓓ Their hard market.

5. **Why does the man suggest rethinking their marketing plan?**

Ⓐ To attract more men. Ⓑ To attract more commercials.
Ⓒ To attract more children. Ⓓ To attract more women.

Ans B, A, C, B, D

9 **SWOT (strengths, weakness, opportunities and threats) SWOT** 分析法，為用於分析企業的優點、缺點、處於競爭環境中的機會和威脅，進而能夠提前規劃未來發展和決策的一種方法。
10 **reposition** [rɪpə`zɪʃən] (v.) 重新定位
11 **target market** 目標市場
12 **market share** 市佔率
13 **penetration** [͵pɛnə`treʃən] (n.) 佔有；滲透

Part

4 工作事務 Discussions, Meetings, and Proposals

UNIT 29 提出新企畫 Proposing a New Project

 J Joyce J Jacob A Andrew S Sara

Jacob is meeting with Joyce and the other managers to discuss new business. 雅各正與喬伊絲和其他經理們討論新的業務。

J And that's the rundown on our current projects. Now for the new ideas.

J I've got a proposal to make **regarding**[1] our department's website. **For all intents and purposes**[2], we don't have a website, do we? Our page on the company's main site is hard to find and doesn't contain much information. I think we are losing business because our prospects **tune out**[3] and go elsewhere before they can learn about us.

A You think we need our own website?

J Yes! We need a site in our name, explaining our work. I propose that we spend some time **summarizing**[4] what we can do for clients, and put that information, with our **mission statement**[5], into a website that will attract new business.

S I don't know. I'm not **convinced**[6] that websites actually bring in that much business.

J I think if you look at some of our competitors' sites, you'll change your mind.

J I think this is a great idea, Jacob. We're out of time now, but why don't you put this idea together in more detail this week? Give us some idea of the **scope**[7] of the website project, the cost, and some of the ways you can see it adding to business. Does that work for the rest of you? To **reconvene**[8] next week?

1 **regarding** [rɪˋgɑrdɪŋ] (prep.) 關於
2 **for all intents and purpose** 實際上
3 **tune out** 不理睬
4 **summarize** [ˋsʌməˏraɪz] (v.) 概述
5 **mission statement** 企業理念聲明

J 這就是我們目前案子的概要。現在，輪到大家說說新想法了。

J 我對我們部門的網站有個提議，**實際上**我們部門沒有網站，對吧？我們在公司主要網站上的網頁難以搜尋，資訊也很少。我認為這樣會使潛在客戶在還沒來得及了解我們之前，就**失去興趣**到別家公司去了，造成生意損失。

A 你是說我們部門要有自己的網站？

J 沒錯！我們需要有自己部門名稱的網站，說明我們的業務。我建議我們花點時間**概述**對客戶的服務項目，連同**企業理念**一起放上網站，來招攬新業務。

S 我不知道。我不認為網站能對我們的業績有多大的幫助。

J 我想，若你看到對手們的網站，你就會改變想法了。

J 雅各，我覺得這是個好主意。現在沒時間了，但你這禮拜何不把此想法的細節整理好？向我們大略說明網站一案的**範圍**、花費，還有一些你認為對業務有幫助的方式。下禮拜**再開一次會**，其他人都可以嗎？

Useful Expressions

A Proposing a project 提議一項企畫

1 I propose a survey project to reevaluate our current customer base.
我提議計畫一項調查，用來再評估我們目前的消費族群。

2 My proposal outlines a way to cut the budget without losing necessary functions.
我的提案扼要介紹了一種方法，既能刪減預算，卻又不失應有功能。

3 This project will help us **get back in the game**[9].
這項計畫能幫我們**東山再起**。

4 I've **worked up**[10] a proposal that addresses our **infrastructure**[11] needs.
我**擬定**了一項提案，能解決我們**基礎建設**的需求。

6 **convinced** [kənˋvɪnst] (adj.) 確信的
7 **scope** [skop] (n.) 範圍
8 **reconvene** [rɪkənˋvin] (v.) 再次集合（開會）
9 **get back in the game** 東山再起
10 **work up** 擬定；制定
11 **infrastructure** [ˋɪnfrəˏstrʌktʃɚ] (n.) 基礎建設

B Asking questions about a new project 詢問與新企畫有關的問題

5	Who are the **stakeholders**[1] for this project?	誰是此專案的**利害關係人**？
6	What exactly is the scope of the new IT project?	新資訊科技企畫案的範圍到底是什麼？
7	What's the project budget?	專案的預算是多少？
8	I think the concept **is right on**[2], but I'm not sure I understand how you're going to implement it.	我想你的概念**完全正確**，但我不確定是否了解你實行的方式。
9	Can you give us some more details about how your proposal will work?	你可以對你的提案如何運作再詳加說明嗎？
10	How does this proposal fit in with our **vision statement**[3]?	此提案要如何與我們的**願景聲明**一致？

C Planning for a new project 策畫新企畫

149

11	We need a strong mission statement.	我們需要一個強烈的企業理念聲明。
12	We're going to have to think carefully about the **questionnaire**[4] in order to keep it within the scope of the project.	我們要審慎地製作**問卷**，讓它不致偏離專案主題。
13	Determining the right audience is going to be the most difficult part.	決定準確的顧客群將會是最困難的部分。
14	Let's talk about a time line for the PR project.	我們來討論公關專案的時間規劃。
15	We're going to need a lot of **buy-in**[5] from the top to make this successful.	我們將需要高層的大力支持才能使其成功。

D Agreeing or disagreeing with project ideas 贊成／不贊成企畫的想法

16	I think you've hit on something really important.	我想你點出了非常重要的地方。
17	If we get the right buy-in, this could really **take off**[6].	若我們獲得恰當的支持，這可能真的會**成功**。
18	I'm afraid I can't quite **get onboard**[7] yet.	我恐怕是不怎麼**贊成**。
19	I don't think this is the right direction for us right now.	我認為現在對我們來說，這似乎不是對的方向。

Review Questions

Listen to the conversations and answer the questions below.

150 1. **What do all the participants have a copy of?**
   (A) The main points. (B) The proposal.
   (C) The market. (D) The main burden.

2. **Who would do the printing and layout?**
   (A) The team of five. (B) The outsource.
   (C) A contractor. (D) The man.

3. **What is the time frame for the project?**
   (A) Three months. (B) Three weeks.
   (C) One month. (D) It is not mentioned.

151 4. **What is the project's scope?**
   (A) International. (B) Regional.
   (C) City-wide. (D) Only in this building.

5. **What does the man want to hear more about?**
   (A) Potential audiences. (B) Potential fundraisers.
   (C) Potential branches. (D) Potential advertisers.

6. **What will be moved under this proposal?**
   (A) Advertisers. (B) Branches.
   (C) Warehouses. (D) This region.

Ans B, C, A, B, D, C

1. **stakeholder** [ˋstekˏholdɚ] (n.) 利害關係人，指參與專案者，以及會被專案影響或對專案有興趣者
2. **be right on** 完全正確
3. **vision statement** 願景聲明
4. **questionnaire** [ˏkwɛstʃəˋnɛr] (n.) 問卷
5. **buy-in** [ˋbaɪˏɪn] (n.)（對意見）同意，接受
6. **take off** 成功
7. **onboard / get onboard** 贊成

UNIT 30 介紹新產品 Presenting a New Product

Jared, in the product development department, presents a new product to shareholders[1] with a slide show. 在產品開發部門的傑瑞德，正用簡報向股東們介紹新產品。

J As you all know, our Ethersole athletic shoe has been a huge hit. We believe our new children's line, with its first design, the Etherkid, will help us **capitalize on**[2] that success. As you can see from this slide, the Etherkid is based on the Ethersole design, but it comes in a wider color range and with **iron-on initials**[3]. We think kids are going to **go nuts for**[4] these initials.

This slide explains the **profit margins**[5] we **predict**[6] for the Etherkid, which we plan to **roll out**[7] in Fall 2022. Having the existing infrastructure means our production costs for this product will be much lower, giving us a higher profit margin. We think the Etherkid is going to be a **gold mine**[8].

S Who's your target here?

J Well, we don't want to stray too far from the Ethersole brand, which was marketed toward serious runners. Therefore, we're aiming the Etherkid at children who are interested in athletics and style—and parents who want their kids to have the best equipment.

S And does the research show that the market will support another product like this?

J Oh, absolutely. Our market research found that there is a huge, **unmet**[9] demand for a shoe like this.

1 **shareholder** [ˋʃɛr,holdɚ] (n.) 股東
2 **capitalize on sth.** 從……中獲益
3 **iron-on initials** 用熨燙法燙上去的首字母
4 **go nuts for** 為……瘋狂
5 **profit margin** 淨利率；毛利率
6 **predict** [prɪˋdɪkt] (v.) 預期
7 **roll out** 推出

J 如各位所知，我們 Ethersole 運動鞋向來非常暢銷。我們深信首次設計新的兒童產品線 Etherkid，會讓我們享受到豐碩成果。你能從這頁簡報中看到，Etherkid 是以 Ethersole 的設計為基礎，但有更多顏色可供選擇，還有**燙印首字母**。我們認為小孩們一定會**為**這些燙印首字母**瘋狂**。

這頁簡報則說明了我們對在 2022 年秋季**推出**的 Etherkid 所**預估**的**淨利率**。既然設備都是現有的，就表示我們生產的成本會低得多，帶給我們更高的淨利率。我們認為 Etherkid 將會是個**金雞母**。

S 你的目標客戶是誰？

J 這個嘛，我們不想與主打認真跑步的 Ethersole 品牌區隔過大，所以我們將 Etherkid 定位在喜愛運動、跟隨流行的孩子，和希望小孩能使用最好用品的父母。

S 那研究有顯示市場會接受這樣的商品嗎？

J 當然有。市場調查顯示正急需這種鞋子。

8 **gold mine** [ˋgold͵maɪn] (n.) 財源	9 **unmet** [ʌnˋmɛt] (adj.) 未滿足的

remote clicker 簡報筆

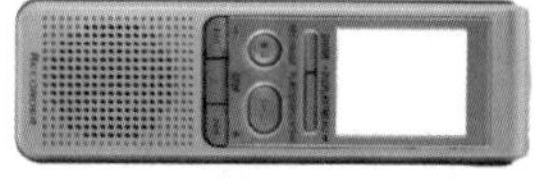
voice recorder 錄音筆

projector 投影機

laser pointer
雷射筆

projection screen
投影屏幕

digital camera
數位攝影機

presentation slide 簡報投影片

laptop 筆記型電腦

Useful Expressions

A Talking about a new product's potential 談論新產品的潛力

153

1	I don't really see a lot of sales potential here.	我不覺得這裡有何銷售潛力。
2	This product is going to open up a whole new market for us.	此產品將為我們打開一個全新市場。
3	This is going to **extend our brand**[1].	這將會**推廣我們的品牌**。
4	We're offering a product no one else is selling.	我們將要推出一個現在沒有人在銷售的商品。
5	We believe this product will appeal to an **untapped market**[2].	我們相信，此商品將會吸引**未開發市場**的注意。
6	This is going to appeal to a **niche market**[3].	這將會吸引到**利基市場**的注意。

B Asking questions about a new product 詢問新產品相關問題

7	What would the profit margin be for this line?	此系列商品的**淨利率**會有多少？
8	What's going to make this product **stand out**[4]?	此產品的傲人之處在哪裡？
9	How is this going to affect our **bottom line**[5]?	這將會如何影響我們的**損益**？
10	Isn't the market **saturated**[6] with these products?	這些產品市場是否**飽和**了呢？
11	Does this product fit our image?	這產品符合我們的形象嗎？
12	Can you sell it to **impulse buyers**[7]?	你能將這賣給**衝動型的消費者**嗎？
13	Are you going to go for penetration pricing?	你要選擇滲透訂價策略嗎？

1 **extend brand** 推廣品牌
2 **untapped market** 未開發市場
3 **niche market** 利基市場
4 **stand out** 突出；出眾
5 **bottom line** 盈虧
6 **saturate** [ˋsætʃə,ret] (v.) 使飽和
7 **impulse buyer** 衝動買家

Review Questions

Listen to the conversations and answer the questions below.

154 **1. How was the previous model compared to the Skinny Phone?**

Ⓐ It is smaller.
Ⓑ It is longer.
Ⓒ It is bigger.
Ⓓ It is shorter.

2. What does the man want to know?

Ⓐ The difference between the phone and the previous model.
Ⓑ The similarity of the phone to the one before.
Ⓒ The color of the phone.
Ⓓ The capability of the phone.

155 **3. How is the new model?**

Ⓐ It is more expensive than the original.
Ⓑ It is more complex than the original.
Ⓒ It is less expensive than the original.
Ⓓ It is less complex than the original.

4. Why is the man unsure?

Ⓐ Because he is not convinced that there is a market for the product.
Ⓑ Because he is not convinced there is a new product.
Ⓒ Because he is not convinced that there is competition.
Ⓓ Because he is not convinced that there is a saturated market.

5. Why does the woman think the product will sell?

Ⓐ Because it is faster.
Ⓑ Because it is cheaper.
Ⓒ Because it is brand new.
Ⓓ Because people like the brand.

Ans C, A, C, A, D

UNIT 31 討論問題的解決方案 Discussing Solutions to a Problem

  Ⓚ Katharine Ⓖ George

Ann, George, and Katharine are discussing problems they are having with the new project leader, Caroline.
安、喬治與凱薩琳正在討論他們和新的專案負責人卡洛琳之間的問題。

Ⓐ I think we need to talk to Caroline about our problems with her before we go to Jacob.

Ⓚ Agreed. We shouldn't **ambush**[1] her. I think Caroline can do a good job—she's just trying to change things too much. We need to **come to grips with**[2] this issue or she's going to **run** this project **off the rails**[3].

Ⓖ Exactly. Yesterday she was talking about a whole new system of organizing our data. She hadn't **thought it out**[4]; it was just an idea, but I had to listen to her talk about it when I really needed to be finishing my analysis. Now I'm afraid she's going to tell me I have to use her new system!

Ⓐ We have our own ways of doing things here.

Ⓚ And I'm willing to listen to new ways to do things, but not in the middle of a project that we're behind on already!

Ⓖ Right. But somehow, when I try to explain this to her, she doesn't get it.

Ⓐ We have to request a meeting with her and Jacob. We can't go on avoiding the problem. I think we should tell them both that we have concerns about the project's management and we want to address them before they become more serious.

1 **ambush** [ˋæmbuʃ] (v.) 暗中陷害
2 **come to grip with** 設法解決;認真對待
3 **run sth. off the rails** 搞砸;走樣
4 **think sth. out** 仔細考慮
5 **hurdle** [ˋhɝdl̩] (n.) 障礙;困難
6 **can of worms** 燙手山芋;難題
7 **pressing** [ˋprɛsɪŋ] (adj.) 急迫的
8 **hardware** [ˋhɑrd͵wɛr] (n.)〔電腦〕硬體
9 **blow sth./sb. off** 對……置之不理
10 **micromanage** [ˋmaɪkrə͵mænɪdʒ] (v.) 大小事都要管

Ⓐ 去向雅各報告之前，我認為我們應先向卡洛琳說明我們的問題。

Ⓚ 我贊成，我們不應該暗算她。我認為卡洛琳能勝任這件事，但她太想要改變了。我們要**想辦法解決**這個問題，要不然她一定會**搞砸**這件案子。

Ⓖ 沒錯。昨天她還在談論一個全新的資料整理系統。那只是個想法而已，她根本還沒**想清楚**。當我忙著要完成分析時，卻要聽她滔滔不絕說著想法。我現在很擔心她會要我使用她的新系統！

Ⓐ 大家都有自己做事的方法。

Ⓚ 我是很願意聽取做事的新方法，不過不是在專案進行到一半、我們進度落後的時候！

Ⓖ 對。不過不管我怎麼跟她說明，她就是不懂。

Ⓐ 我們得跟雅各還有她開個會，我們不能一直逃避這個問題。我認為要告知他們兩位我們對專案管理的擔憂，在問題變得更加嚴重前先通知他們。

Useful Expressions

A Identifying problems 發現問題 (157)

1	One problem is that new staff don't understand our procedures well enough.	有一個問題就是新員工對我們的流程不夠了解。
2	The biggest **hurdle**[5], I think, is Sara's lack of experience.	我想最大的**問題**，在於莎拉經驗不足。
3	The budget is the real **can of worms**[6] here.	預算才是最**棘手的問題**。
4	The most **pressing**[7] issue seems to be the outdated **hardware**[8].	最**急迫的**問題似乎是**硬體設備**老舊。
5	I disagree; I think the underlying trouble is actually poor training.	我不贊同；我認為潛在的問題其實是出於訓練不佳。
6	I've been trying to get management's attention and they're **blowing me off**[9].	我一直想引起管理高層的注意，但他們都**置之不理**。
7	She's slowing everyone down by **micromanaging**[10] us.	她對我們**管東管西**，造成大家進度落後。

open a can of worms 製造不必要的麻煩（惹來一身腥）

open a can of worms 意思是「打開一罐（can）的蟲子（worms）」。釣客常用蟲子做為釣餌，如果把裝滿蟲子的罐子打開，蟲子就會四處亂爬、製造髒亂，很難再一條條抓回罐子。因此這個俚語就引申為「招惹麻煩」、「沒事找事」，造成問題更加棘手。a can of worms 如單獨使用則指「複雜難解的問題」。

B Asking for solutions 詢問解決方案

8 What should we do about the **mess**[1] in **accounting**[2]?

我們要怎麼處理**會計**的**問題**?

9 Does anyone have a suggestion for the **predicament**[3] we're in at Site Three?

有人對我們在「三號地點」遇到的**問題**有建議嗎?

10 We need to brainstorm ways to **put out the fire**[4] at HQ before we do anything else.

在做出任何事之前,我們要先腦力激盪,想出**解決**總公司**問題**的辦法。

11 Let's talk about solutions for our staffing problems.

我們來討論人員配置問題的解決辦法。

12 Has anyone figured out how to fix the formatting problems on the report?

有誰想出怎麼處理報告中的格式問題?

C Suggesting solutions 建議解決方案 158

13 I think it's time we **reevaluated**[5] our training procedures.

我想是時候**重新評估**我們的訓練流程了。

14 We need to set up a meeting between accounting and management right away. They need to resolve their problems.

我們要立即召開會計部與管理部門的會議。他們必須要解決他們之間的問題。

15 The only way to move forward, in my opinion, is to accept that this project will be over-budget and go from there.

我個人認為,要繼續下去的唯一辦法就是接受此專案會超出預算的事實,然後再進一步討論。

16 If we can get the staff to agree to a week of overtime, we'll **be in good shape**[6].

若我們能讓員工同意加班一星期,我們就**不會有問題**。

17 To settle this, the first thing we need to do is change designers.

要解決這件事,首先要做的就是換掉設計師們。

18 We can't clear this mess up without involving the executives.

我們無法不藉助主管的力量來解決這問題。

Review Questions

Listen to the conversations and answer the questions below.

159 **1. What problem is the woman having with her computer?**

Ⓐ It's slow and it crashes.
Ⓑ It's slow and it has viruses.
Ⓒ It's hot and it's old.
Ⓓ It's old and it has viruses.

2. Who is Thomas, probably?

Ⓐ Their colleague.
Ⓑ Their friend.
Ⓒ Their supervisor.
Ⓓ Their contractor.

3. What does the woman want?

Ⓐ A meeting with Thomas.
Ⓑ A new computer.
Ⓒ A visit from a computer expert.
Ⓓ An anti-virus program.

160 **4. Who made the mistake?**

Ⓐ The man.
Ⓑ The woman.
Ⓒ Sophia.
Ⓓ It is not mentioned.

5. What is the solution to the problem?

Ⓐ To resend the same invitation.
Ⓑ To change the date.
Ⓒ To make Sophia apologize.
Ⓓ To send another letter.

Ans A, C, B, C, D

1 **mess** [mɛs] (n.) 問題
2 **accounting** [əˋkaʊntɪŋ] (n.) 會計
3 **predicament** [ˌprɪˋdɪkəmənt] (n.) 困境
4 **put out a fire** 解決問題
5 **reevaluate** [rɪɪˋvæljʊˌet] (v.) 重新評估
6 **be in good shape** 情況良好

UNIT 32 討論工作疏失 Discussing a Mistake

 Joyce 

Joyce discovers that Katharine has made a mistake in her research.
喬伊絲發現凱薩琳的調查中有個錯誤。

Joyce: Hi, Jacob. I've been going over some of Katharine's research for the website proposal, and I need to talk to you about something.

Jacob: What is it?

Joyce: It looks like most of the website designers she's listed are out of our price range. I think she must have misread some of the budget numbers.

Jacob: Uh oh. That's going to **set us back**[1] a bit.

Joyce: Only as long as it'll take her to redo the research. Otherwise, everything looks great.

Jacob: Well, that's good. OK, I'll make her aware of the error and have her start over on that part of the research. I hope the results are as promising when she uses the correct numbers!

Joyce: 雅各，我看了一下凱薩琳針對網頁提案所做的調查，我需要與你談談。

Jacob: 什麼事？

Joyce: 她列出的網頁設計師大多都超出我們的價格範圍。我猜她可能看錯預算數目了。

Jacob: 糟糕，這會造成我們**進度延後**。

Joyce: 除了要她重做調查，不然其他都沒有問題。

Jacob: 那就好。我會告訴她錯誤的地方，讓她重做該部分的調查。希望她修正數字後，出來的結果是樂觀的。

1 **set sb./sth. back** 使……受到延誤／阻礙

Useful Expressions

A Identifying a mistake 發現錯誤 

1	The mistake on the **brochure**[2] was a major **setback**[3].	**手冊**上的錯誤是個重大問題。
2	I just noticed that there's a **typo**[4] in the letter we sent to Doctor Yurick's clinic.	我注意到在要寄給尤里克醫師診所的信上有**字打錯**了。
3	It looks like Adam forgot to reserve our rooms.	亞當好像忘了訂我們的房間了。
4	I can't believe I did all that work and forgot to send the file.	我真不敢相信我完成全部的工作，卻忘了寄出檔案。
5	Esther never sent the final **drafts**[5] to headquarters to review and they're furious.	埃絲特不曾把最終**草稿**寄給總公司審查，他們對此勃然大怒。
6	Helen really **botched**[6] that report, in my opinion.	我認為海倫真的把報告給**搞砸**了。

2 **brochure** [broˋʃur] (n.) 小冊子
3 **setback** [ˋsɛt͵bæk] (n.) 失敗；挫折
4 **typo** [ˋtaɪpo] (n.) 打字錯誤
5 **draft** [dræft] (n.) 草稿
6 **botch** [bɑtʃ] (v.) 搞砸

Emotions About Mistakes 面對犯錯的情緒反應

guilty 自責的

anxious 焦慮的

sad 難過的

astonished 震驚的

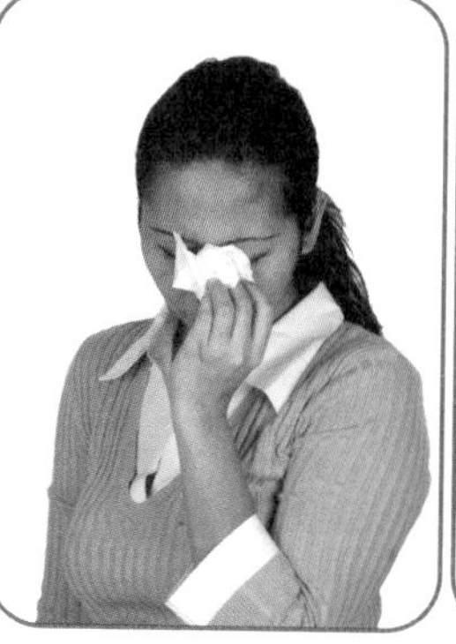

B Discussing the cause of a mistake 討論錯誤的原因

7 Tracy must have **misunderstood**[1] what we wanted.
崔西一定**誤解**了我們想要的。

8 The team didn't take into account what would happen at high temperatures.
這個團隊沒有把高溫下會發生的情況給考慮進去。

9 Somehow, confirming with the board must have **fallen through the cracks**[2].
不知何故，和董事會確認一事肯定是**被忽略**了。

10 With all the excitement about the new product, quality control just **fell by the wayside**[3].
因對新產品的興奮之情，而**疏忽**掉品管。

11 Beth and Jeanette were just too inexperienced to **pull** that presentation **off**[4].
貝絲與珍奈特因經驗不足而無法**成功完成**簡報。

12 Confirming with the caterer just **slipped my mind**[5].
我**忘了**要跟外燴業者確認。

1 **misunderstand** [ˌmɪsʌndɚˋstænd] (v.) 誤解

2 **fall through the cracks** 忽略

3 **fall by the wayside** 遭到忽視；遭受失敗

4 **pull sth. off** 達成；成功完成

5 **slip sb's mind** 被（某人）忘記

barrassed 窘迫的

doubtful 懷疑的

furious 憤怒的

depressed 沮喪的

Review Questions

Listen to the conversations and answer the questions below.

163 1. **When was the last month the numbers were correct?**

Ⓐ March. Ⓑ April. Ⓒ May. Ⓓ June.

2. **What was wrong with the budget?**

Ⓐ It ended up being too much. Ⓑ It ended up being too little.
Ⓒ It was in a quarter. Ⓓ It was perfect.

164 3. **How many things have gone wrong so far?**

Ⓐ One. Ⓑ Two. Ⓒ Three. Ⓓ Four.

4. **What is the man trying to organize?**

Ⓐ A conference. Ⓑ A meeting.
Ⓒ A convention center. Ⓓ A product presentation.

5. **Who is going to cancel?**

Ⓐ Joan.
Ⓑ Keith.
Ⓒ The keynote speaker.
Ⓓ The man.

Ans A, B, C, A, C

UNIT 33 接受批評與承擔責任 Accepting Criticism and Taking Responsibility

165 J Jacob K Katharine

Jacob talks to Katharine about her mistake. 雅各與凱薩琳談論她的錯誤。

J Hi, Katharine. I wanted to talk to you about this research for the website. You did a great job getting a lot of information, and I appreciate the accessible format you put it into. There's one problem, though. I think somewhere you must have misread the amount we'd budgeted for designers.

K Oh dear, really?

J Yes, so it looks like almost all the designers you turned up are going to be out of our range.

K I can't believe I did that! I'm so sorry.

J It's OK, just please be careful in the future. This research will be relatively easy to redo, but on other projects it might not be.

K I understand. It won't happen again.

J I'm sure it won't. Don't worry about it too much; we all make mistakes. Just remember, always check dates, amounts, and numbers first. They're the most important things to get right!

K I'll remember. Now, I guess I should get back to work on this research.

J That's right—**get back on the horse**[1]!

J 凱薩琳，我要跟妳談談有關這網站的調查。蒐集資訊方面妳做得很好，我很欣賞妳使用便於理解的格式。不過有個問題，那就是妳弄錯我們請設計師的預算。

K 哎呀，真的嗎？

J 是的。所以妳找的設計師幾乎都超過我們的預算。

K 真不敢相信我弄錯了！真的很抱歉。

J 沒關係，以後注意點就好了。這次調查要重做相對來說比較容易，但其他專案就不見得了。

K 我明白，以後不會再發生了。

J 我知道不會。我們都會出錯，別太放在心上。只要記住要先檢查日期、數量跟數目，那是最重要的部分，一定要正確才行！

K 我會記住的。我想我現在應該回去繼續完成調查了。

J 沒錯，**從頭開始**吧！

Useful Expressions

A Apologizing 致歉 

1 I'm sorry I made you wait for so long.
很抱歉讓您等這麼久。

2 We sincerely apologize for the **inconvenience**[2] this has caused you.
此事造成您的**不便**，我們深表歉意。

3 Please accept my **apologies**[3] for the delay in your order.
延誤您所訂購的商品，請接受我的**道歉**。

4 Please forgive me for leaving your name off the guest list.
請原諒我在客人名單中遺漏掉您的姓名。

5 I wish I could take back the **ignorant**[4] comments I made.
我真希望能收回曾經說過的**無知**話語。

1 **get back on the horse** 振作起來；重新出發
2 **inconvenience** [ˌɪnkən`vinɪəns] (n.) 不便
3 **apology** [ə`pɑlədʒɪ] (n.) 道歉
4 **ignorant** [`ɪgnərənt] (adj.) 無知的

B Taking responsibility 承擔責任

6 The formatting problems were my fault. I didn't double check the layout.
格式有問題是我的錯，我沒有再檢查一遍版面。

7 The **miscalculation**[1] was my mistake. **Mea culpa**[2].
算錯是我的不好。**是我的錯**。

8 I **take** full **responsibility for**[3] the shipping problems.
我對運送問題**負起**全**責**。

9 I **take the blame for**[4] the oversight.
我**對**這個疏忽**負責**。

10 I'll **take the heat**[5] for this one—after all, I was the last one to see the missing file.
畢竟我是最後看到遺失文件的人，我會**承擔**此次的**責任**。

11 We deeply regret the inconvenience we have caused.
對於我們所造成的不便，我們深感到抱歉。

C Acknowledging criticism 接受批評 

12 You're absolutely right about the problems with the letter.
關於這封信件的問題，你百分之百是對的。

13 I understand why you're so upset. Please tell me what I can do to try and fix things.
我能理解你如此生氣的原因，請告訴我要如何補救。

14 Obviously, I didn't perform up to your standards. Please help me understand what I can do to improve.
顯然我的表現未能達到您的標準。請教我要如何改善。

15 Next time, I will follow your advice. 下次我會遵從你的意見。

D Offering restitution[6] 提供彌補

16 How can I make it up to you? 我要怎麼補償你？

17 I will **rectify**[7] it as soon as possible. 我會儘快**改過來**。

18 He really wants to **make amends**[8]. He's going to work overtime until he can fix it.
他真的很想**補償**，他要加班到處理好為止。

19 What can we do to **redress**[9] this issue?
要怎麼做才能**改正**這個問題呢？

Review Questions

Listen to the conversations and answer the questions below.

168 **1. What are they talking about?**

Ⓐ A report. Ⓑ A letter.
Ⓒ A deadline. Ⓓ A responsibility.

2. What does the man take responsibility for?

Ⓐ The projects. Ⓑ Other projects.
Ⓒ The state. Ⓓ The schedule problems.

3. Has the man had other problems with deadlines?

Ⓐ Yes. Ⓑ No. Ⓒ We don't know.

4. What was wrong with the quotation?

Ⓐ It was too high. Ⓑ It was too low.
Ⓒ It was serious. Ⓓ It was miscalculated.

5. Why does the woman want to look at her files?

Ⓐ To find her mistake. Ⓑ To find Mr. Ryan.
Ⓒ To avoid blame. Ⓓ To complain about the situation.

Ans A, D, B, B, A

1 **miscalculation** [mɪsˌkælkjəˋleʃən] (n.) 計算錯誤；失算
2 **mea culpa** 〔拉丁文〕是我的錯
3 **take responsibility for** 負責……
4 **take the blame for** 承擔……責任
5 **take the heat** 承擔責任
6 **restitution** [ˌrɛstɪˋtuʃən] (n.) 補償
7 **rectify** [ˋrɛktəˌfaɪ] (v.) 改正
8 **make amends** 補償
9 **redress** [rɪˋdrɛs] (v.) 補救；改正

UNIT 34 責任歸屬與工作分配 Distribution of Work and Responsibilities

Ann, Katharine, George, Jacob, and Caroline are discussing the distribution of work for the project. 安、凱薩琳、喬治、雅各還有卡洛琳正在討論案子的工作分配。

C Alright, let's look at the new work plan for the project. Ann and George, you'll be doing the data collection at the first site. You'll also both be doing the analysis. When you get back to the office, though, George, you will write up the report while Ann, you help Katharine and myself get ready for our trip to the second site. Then, when we return, the two of us will do the analysis, but Katharine will take on the writing while I'll help prepare for the third site.

J And while you are gone, I'll be responsible for writing up the **methodology**[1], updating the clients, and finding a printer.

K What happens after the third site is done?

C George and Ann will move on to other projects, when their work on this one is done. It will **fall on**[2] you and me to put the pieces of the report together.

Ⓒ 那我們現在來看看專案的新工作計畫。安跟喬治，你們倆負責在第一地點蒐集資料與做分析。等你們回到公司，喬治會負責寫報告，安則是幫忙我跟凱薩琳安排前往第二地點的行程。等我們回來時，我們之中有兩個人會一起做分析，凱薩琳負責寫報告的同時，我則是為第三地點做準備。

Ⓙ 妳不在時，我會負責寫**方法**說明、更新客戶資料，還有尋找印刷廠商。

Ⓚ 第三地點結束後要做什麼？

Ⓒ 喬治跟安等此案的工作結束後會接著處理其他專案。這個案子剩下的就會**由我跟妳**合力**完成**。

1 **methodology** [ˌmɛθəˋdɑlədʒɪ] (n.) 方法
2 **fall on sb.** 落到某人頭上；由某人負責

Useful Expressions

A Describing work distribution 說明工作分配 (171)

1 I feel like I'm doing more than my **fair share**[1]. 我覺得我好像做超出分量的事。

2 I'll handle the cold calling if you'll draft the sales literature.
如果你要寫銷售資料，那我就負責電話訪問。

3 Jane's going to be **hard-pressed**[2] to get to anything but meetings this week. Can you **pick up** some of **the slack**[3]?
珍本週的**工作繁重**，除了會議外一律無法參加。你能幫忙**接手**一些工作嗎？

4 Lauren will **tend to**[4] the new clients while you concentrate on the new logo.
羅倫將**負責**新客戶，你則專心做新的商標。

5 Because Julia is going to **be** so **wrapped up with**[5] the sales report, I'm **delegating**[6] some of her work to Thomas.
由於茱莉亞將要**忙**銷售報告，我便將她的一些工作**分派**給湯瑪斯。

6 This is a complex project, so we need to be thorough when we **set dependencies**[7]. 這是個複雜的案子，所以我們要仔細**分派工作**。

7 Karen's really got a lot **on her shoulders**[8]. 凱倫的**手頭上**有許多工作要做。

8 As the **low man on the totem pole**[9], you get the most boring work.
身處**基層**的你，得到的是最枯燥的工作。

B Talking about responsibility 說明職責

9 Who's going to **spearhead**[10] the radio campaign? 誰要**帶領**廣播宣傳活動？

10 If the new tool is a bust, it'll **be Arthur's head**[11]. 若是新工具失敗了，亞瑟就要**頭疼**了。

11 George is the **head honcho**[12] at TechPlus. 喬治是 TechPlus 的**老闆**。

1 **fair share** 公平的分量
2 **hard-pressed** [ˋhardˋprɛst] (adj.) 工作繁重的
3 **pick up the slack** 接手
4 **tend to** 照料
5 **be wrapped up with** 忙於……
6 **delegate** [ˋdɛləget] (v.) 指派
7 **set dependencies** 分配負責工作
8 **on sb's shoulders** 工作落在某人肩上
9 **low man on the totem pole** 最低階的人（美國原住民會將人臉刻在圖騰柱上，許多人誤解越下面的圖騰代表地位越低，但其實並無地位高低之分。）
10 **spearhead** [ˋspɪrhɛd] (v.) 領導
11 **be sb's head** 面臨麻煩事
12 **head honcho** 老闆

C Disputing[13] responsibilities 否認**職責**

12	I really don't think that emptying the trash is in my job description.	我不記得我的職務說明內有倒垃圾這項。
13	Both departments are claiming that the problem is out of their **jurisdictions**[14].	兩個部門皆聲稱此問題不在他們的**管轄範圍**內。
14	I really think that questions about the manufacturing of our product line are beyond my **purview**[15] as a customer service representative.	我真的認為，有關商品線生產的問題，身為客服專員的我並沒有管理的**權限**。
15	We don't think it is fair to expect us to take on the duties of a whole separate department.	我們認為，期望我們去分擔整個獨立部門的工作是不合理的。

13 **dispute** [dɪˋspjut] (v.) 不贊同
14 **jurisdiction** [ˏdʒurɪsˋdɪkʃən] (n.) 管轄範圍
15 **purview** [ˋpɝvju] (n.) 權限

Review Questions

Listen to the conversations and answer the questions below.

172 1. **Who does the woman want to speak to?**
Ⓐ A salesman. Ⓑ A supervisor. Ⓒ A client. Ⓓ A receptionist.

2. **Why can't the man help her?**
Ⓐ Because he is new. Ⓑ Because he is angry.
Ⓒ Because he is impatient. Ⓓ Because he is a temp.

173 3. **What is Joel responsible for?**
Ⓐ The research. Ⓑ The program.
Ⓒ Answering to Tim. Ⓓ Communication with the client.

4. **Why did the man choose Linda to be the onsite representative?**
Ⓐ Because she likes to do research. Ⓑ Because she likes to travel.
Ⓒ Because she likes to correspond. Ⓓ Because she likes to report.

5. **Who will the male speaker be working with?**
Ⓐ Joel. Ⓑ Linda. Ⓒ Jade. Ⓓ Tim.

Ans B, A, D, B, C

UNIT 35 工作過量與抱怨 Feeling Overworked and Making Complaints

174 G George A Ann

Ann is overwhelmed and talking to her colleague about her problems.
安覺得壓力過大，正在向同事談論她的難處。

G How are you doing, Ann?

A Honestly, I'm **at the end of my rope**[1].

G Is the project getting to you?

A Yes, but it shouldn't be! We've done other projects like this before and they went fine. I just feel like everything is piling up right now. I know that you and Katharine are **pulling your weight**[2], but I feel like Caroline's given me more than I can be expected to handle.

G I think that Caroline's made the schedule too **tight**[3]. We're all **frazzled**[4], but you're **shouldering**[5] the bulk of the workload and there just might not be enough time to get it all done. **Something's got to give.**[6]

A Yes—and right now, it's my sanity! I'm going to have to talk to Caroline about my **workload**[7]. Maybe she'll assign someone to help me out—though I can't think who.

G 妳還好嗎，安？

A 老實講，我**快不行了**。

G 這專案讓妳很煩惱嗎？

A 沒錯，但不該如此！我們以前做過其他類似的案子，都很順利啊。我就是覺得事情堆積如山。我了解你跟凱薩琳都很**盡職**，但我認為卡洛琳交付給我的工作已超過我能處理的分量。

G 我想是卡洛琳把時間表排得太**緊湊**了。我們全部人都快累死了，但妳**擔下**大量工作，卻沒有足夠的時間全數完成。總要放掉一些工作吧。

A 沒錯，這正是目前我在想的！我要與卡洛琳談談我的**工作量**，或許她會派某人來幫忙我——雖然我想不到誰可以來幫我。

1 **at the end of one's rope** 達到極限（被拴在柱子上的牛羊只能吃到繩子被拉到最遠範圍內的草。用來形容窮途末路，無計可施。）

2 **pull one's weight** 盡到本分

3 **tight** [taɪt] (adj.) 緊湊的

4 **frazzled** [ˋfræzəld] (adj.) 筋疲力盡的

5 **shoulder** [ˋʃoldɚ] (v.) 承擔

6 **Something's got to give.** 必須做出取捨。

7 **workload** [ˋwɝk͵lod] (n.) 工作量

Useful Expressions

A Asking about workloads 詢問工作量 (175)

1 Haven't you got enough on your plate without taking on this presentation?
你不用負責這次的簡報，事情就夠多了吧？

2 Has the new supervisor got you **keeping your nose to the grindstone**[8]?
新上司有要你**努力幹活**嗎？

3 Is Eliza still the same old **slave driver**[9]?
伊萊莎還是那副**苛刻上司**的老樣子嗎？

B Complaining about overwork 抱怨工作量過多

4 I've been **working like a dog**[10] for months and I'm tired of it.
我**拼命工作**了數月，對此很厭倦了。

5 I just can't keep up with this **breakneck pace**[11].
我就是無法跟上那趕死人不償命的速度。

6 Jorge has us working day and night, but he's never here. There's **something fishy**[12] going on.
霍黑讓我們日以繼夜不停地工作，自己卻從未出現。事情有點**不對勁**。

7 I've been here late every night this week, and I just know I'm not going to get any **overtime**[13] out of it.
本週我每天都留到很晚，但我知道不會有**加班費**可拿。

8 I'm trying to juggle three new accounts, plus putting together the monthly sales figures, and mentoring a new employee! I'm **working my fingers to the bone**[14].
我試圖同時處理三個新客戶、統計月銷售數字，還要指導一位新員工！我**一直都在工作**。

8 **put/keep sb's nose to the grindstone** 努力工作

9 **slave driver** 苛刻的上司（奴隸的監工，比喻逼迫他人拼命工作的人）

10 **work like a dog** 拼命工作

11 **breakneck pace/speed** 極快的步調／速度

12 **something fishy / to be fishy** 不對勁；可疑的

13 **overtime** [ˋovɚ͵taɪm] (n.) 加班費

14 **work sb's fingers to the bone** （長期）不停工作

C Complaining about colleagues 抱怨同事

9 Larry has been **slacking off**[1] all month and it's affecting us all.

賴瑞整個月工作**馬虎**，連帶影響到我們全體。

10 The rest of us are busy working on the quarterly report, but Uriah's **hardly lifted a finger**[2].

我們其他人都忙於季度報告，尤來亞卻**袖手旁觀**。

11 I think we could be in good shape if Theresa and Wendy would **step it up**[3].

若泰瑞莎跟溫蒂能**加快速度**，我想我們的情況會很好。

D Complaining to your boss and asking for help 向上司抱怨並尋求協助

12 I'm afraid I don't have time to deal with both projects at once. Is there anyone who could help me?

我恐怕沒有時間同時處理兩個專案，有人可以協助我嗎？

13 It looks to me like the workload hasn't been distributed fairly, and I'm worried that's going to affect the success of the project.

我覺得工作似乎沒有公平分配，我擔心這會影響到專案的成功與否。

14 I'm **prioritizing**[4] my tasks, and I realize that some are going to have to be **postponed**[5]. Can you tell me if you agree on the ones I've set aside as the least urgent?

我把工作排了優先順序，我知道有些工作勢必會**延後**。請問你同意我將這些案子列為較不急的工作嗎？

1 **slack off** 懈怠
2 **not lift a finger** 袖手旁觀
3 **step sth. up** 加快速度
4 **prioritize** [praɪˋɔrətaɪz] (v.) 決定優先順序
5 **postpone** [postˋpon] (v.) 延遲

Review Questions

Listen to the conversations and answer the questions below.

177 1. **What is true about the man?**

(A) He is too busy.
(B) He is slacking off.
(C) He is in water.
(D) He is rolling out.

2. **What is the man working on?**

(A) A new project.
(B) A new roll.
(C) A new product.
(D) A new letter.

3. **What can the woman help him with?**

(A) She can help him to anticipate the future.
(B) She can help him to look over a letter.
(C) She can help him to roll out the product.
(D) She can help him to edit a letter.

178 4. **What did the man just finish?**

(A) A product.
(B) A presentation.
(C) A workload.
(D) A meeting.

5. **What do they want the man to do?**

(A) Present a new product.
(B) Something fishy.
(C) Go to another site.
(D) Come up with a new marketing concept.

Ans A, C, B, B, C

UNIT 36 加班 Working Overtime

 Ⓑ Barbara Ⓐ Ann

Ann is working after hours[1] to complete a report. 安為了要完成報告而加班。

Ⓑ Oh, Ann! I thought you'd left already.

Ⓐ No, I have a feeling I'm in for a long night. I don't want to leave until I've got this section of the progress report finished.

Ⓑ Be careful **burning the candle at both ends[2]**!

Ⓐ Believe me, I can't wait for this to be done! I'm not a **workaholic[3]** by nature!

Ⓑ Good! And don't forget to keep track of your overtime. You ought to get paid for all your hard work.

Ⓐ Thanks for **looking out for me[4]**. Have a good night!

Ⓑ 哇，安！我以為妳已經走了。

Ⓐ 沒有耶，我有預感我會要留到很晚。我要把進度報告的這一部分完成才要離開。

Ⓑ 要注意，不要**一根蠟燭兩頭燒**！

Ⓐ 相信我，我等不及要完成這部分了！我又不是天生的**工作狂**！

Ⓑ 很好！別忘了要記下加班的時間。妳努力工作，應該要有加班費才對。

Ⓐ 謝謝妳的**關心**。晚上愉快！

1 **after hours** 在一般上班時間之後
2 **burn the candle at both ends** 一根蠟燭兩頭燒
3 **workaholic** [ˋwɝkə͵hɔlɪk] (n.) 工作狂
4 **look out for sb.** 關心

Useful Expressions

A Talking about overtime work 談論加班 (180)

1 I think Barry's been working 60-hour weeks since January!
我想從一月開始，貝瑞每週都工作 60 小時！

2 Everyone at the office has **put in for overtime**[5].
辦公室的全體員工全都**提出加班申請**。

3 How many double **shifts**[6] has Imogen worked this month?
這個月伊茉珍輪了多少次連續值兩**班**？

4 I'**m salaried**[7], so there's no benefit for me to work extra hours.
我領**固定的薪水**，所以加班對我沒任何好處。

5 Janet's practically living at the office lately! She'll **burn out**[8] if she keeps it up.
最近珍奈特幾乎是以辦公室為家！再這樣下去她**過度勞累**。

5 **put in for overtime** 申請加班
6 **shift** [ʃɪft] (n.)（輪）班
7 **be salaried / on salary** 受薪的
8 **burn out** 耗盡心力；勞累過度

Common Occupational Ailments 常見的職業疾病

headache 頭疼

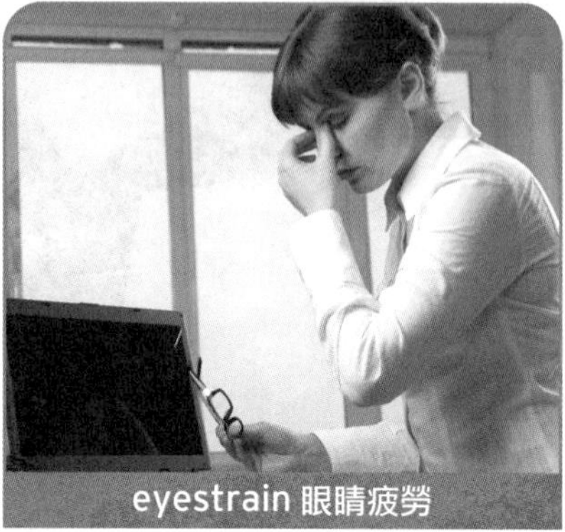
eyestrain 眼睛疲勞

obesity 肥胖

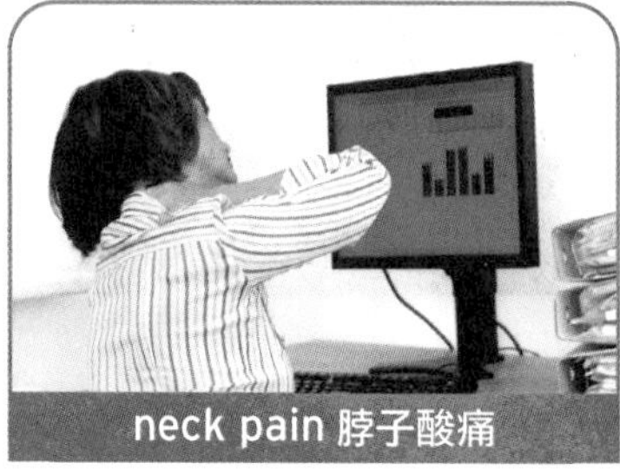
neck pain 脖子酸痛

backache 背痛

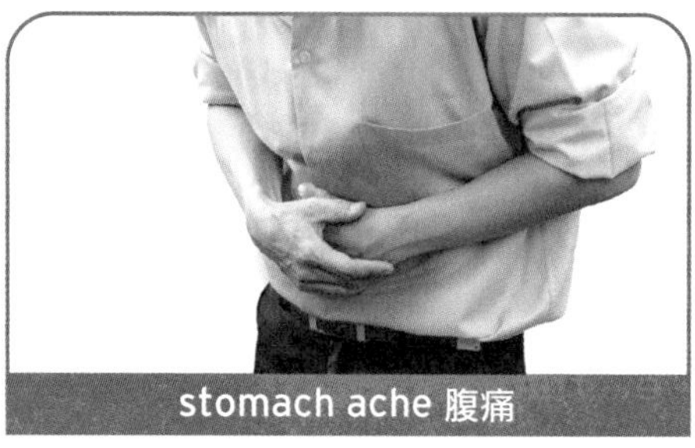
stomach ache 腹痛

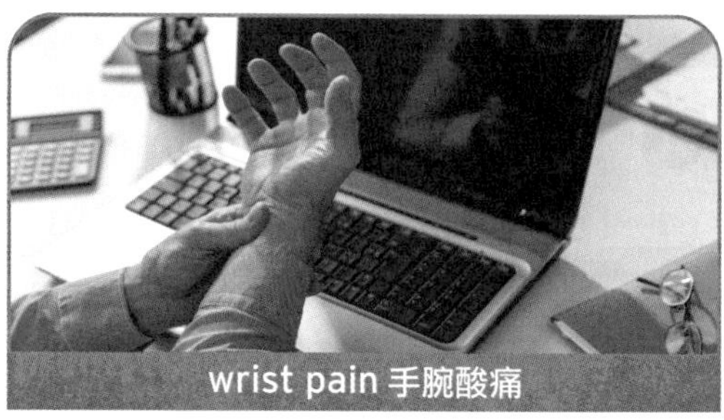
wrist pain 手腕酸痛

B Talking about overtime pay 談論加班費

6	Do you make extra for overtime?	你加班有額外收入嗎？
7	I always put in for overtime because they pay **time and a half**[1]!	由於公司付 **1.5 倍的薪水**，所以我常常申請加班！
8	My husband's company pays double for overtime.	我丈夫的公司付雙倍的加班費。
9	I'm quite happy to get the overtime pay—I'm **strapped**[2] right now.	我目前**手頭很緊**，很開心能拿到加班費。

1 **time and a half** 1.5 倍的工資

2 **strapped** [stræpt] (adj.) 缺錢的；手頭緊的

Review Questions

Listen to the conversations and answer the questions below.

181 **1. What time did the woman arrive?**

Ⓐ 6 p.m. Ⓑ 7 p.m.
Ⓒ 6 a.m. Ⓓ 7 a.m.

2. What time will the man probably leave?

Ⓐ 9 a.m. Ⓑ 9 p.m.
Ⓒ 9:30 p.m. Ⓓ 10 p.m.

182 **3. Where is Sue?**

Ⓐ In her office.
Ⓑ Out of the office.
Ⓒ It is unknown.
Ⓓ In Austin.

4. When does Sue usually leave?

Ⓐ 5 p.m.
Ⓑ 5:30 p.m.
Ⓒ 6 p.m.
Ⓓ 6:30 p.m.

5. Why is Sue behind?

Ⓐ She was away on business.
Ⓑ She was on vacation.
Ⓒ She was sick.
Ⓓ She didn't arrange her schedule wisely.

Ans C, D, A, B, A

UNIT 37 以電子郵件聯絡 Contacting by Email

Jared is sending marketing information about a new product to a potential retail partner. 傑瑞德將新產品的銷售資訊寄給一位可能合作的零售業夥伴。

MESSAGES

From:	Jared Carmody (carmodyj@abcindustries.com)
To:	Brian Swann (brianswann@swannsports.com)
Subject:	Etherkid specifications you requested
Attachment:	Etherkidoutline.doc, etherkidprojections.xls, etherkidstoresuggestions.doc

Dear Brian,

Thank you for your interest in our Etherkid line. I've attached files with the specifications you requested. Please let me know if I can give you any additional information.

As you know, we are really excited about this new line. We have thought in detail about how to market the Etherkid with the Ethersole. In the Etherkid Store Suggestions file, I outline our ideas about how to promote both shoes and how to capitalize on existing Ethersole customers.

We are really looking forward to working with our **retail**[1] partners to make the Etherkid the phenomenon we know it can be. I hope that the information attached here will convince you that the Etherkid and the Ethersole will benefit your business.

Thanks again for your interest,

Jared

Jared Carmody
ABC Industries, Inc.
carmodyj@abcindustries.com
(512) 885-6600

MESSAGES

寄件人：	Jared Carmody (carmodyj@abcindustries.com)
收件人：	Brian Swann (brianswann@swannsports.com)
主旨：	您要求的 Etherkid 詳細規格
附加檔案：	Etherkidoutline.doc, etherkidprojections.xls, etherkidstoresuggestions.doc

親愛的布萊恩：

感謝您對本公司 Etherkid 系列產品有興趣。郵件附件是您要求的詳細規格，若需任何更多資訊，麻煩請告知我。

如您所知，我們非常期待這個新系列產品。我們也縝密思考過要如何和 Ethersole 一塊來行銷 Etherkid。我在 Etherkid Store Suggestions 一檔中，概述我們的想法，該如何推廣兩種鞋款，還有如何利用 Ethersole 現有的客戶。

我們非常期待能與**零售業的**夥伴們合作，創造必定成功的 Etherkid 風潮。希望信上所附的檔案能使您相信，Etherkid 和 Ethersole 兩系列鞋款必能讓您生意蒸蒸日上。

再次感謝您對本產品的興趣。

傑瑞德

傑瑞德・卡莫迪
ABC 工業公司
carmodyj@abcindustries.com
(512) 885-6600

1 **retail** [ˋritel] (adj.) 零售的

Useful Expressions

A Contacting customers by email 以電子郵件聯絡客戶 

1 I had the pleasure of meeting you at the United Tech Trade show last week. I'd now like to follow up on our conversation and suggest a few ways our two companies could engage in some mutually beneficial strategies.

很高興能在上週的聯合科技貿易展認識您。我想就我們的談話再做進一步行動，提出幾個對我們雙方公司都能合作的互惠策略。

2 As per our discussion at the meeting on Wednesday, I'm sending along the new product line specifications.

根據我們於星期三會議上的討論，寄新系列產品的說明書給您。

3 Thank you again for the great feedback on my preliminary report. I've attached the revised report and I'd love to hear your comments on it.

再次謝謝您對我的初步報告所提供的寶貴意見。附件是我修改過的報告書，很樂意聽取您的想法。

4 I've written to all of you to outline the changes you may see in your service when we install the new system next week.

我來信是要向各位指出，下禮拜安裝新系統時，你們可能會發現服務上做出的改變。

5 Due to next week's convention, several of our office staff will be out of town. If you have any questions, please contact any of the individuals on the list below. They have all been briefed and will be able to handle any problems that come up.

我們公司的幾位職員因下週要開會而不在辦公室。若您有任何問題，請聯絡以下列表中的任何一位。他們皆收到指示，能處理任何發生的問題。

B Making and responding to appointments 訂定與回覆會面

6 I think we need to have a **review session**[1] before we start working with the new system.

在我們開始使用新系統前，我認為要先開個**檢討會議**。

7 Let's set up a meeting to explore our options. I'm **booked**[2] on Thursday, but Friday would be fine.

我們開個會來深入討論我們的選擇吧。星期四我**約**滿了，但星期五可以。

1 **review session** 檢討會議　　2 **book** [buk] (v.) 預定

8 Can we set up a time to go over the changes to the plan?

我們能安排時間來討論計畫上的變更嗎？

9 Please respond by phone, as I'll be away from my computer for the rest of the day.

我接下來的時間都不會在電腦前，所以請以電話回覆。

10 Please write back, as I won't be checking messages later.

由於我等一下不會檢查訊息，麻煩回信即可。

11 Shoot me an email to let me know what time works for you.

請寄信給我，讓我知道你什麼時間方便。

Review Questions

Listen to the conversations and answer the questions below.

185 **1. Why is the man upset?**

(A) Because he sent an email with the wrong information.

(B) Because he sent an email to the wrong person.

(C) Because he forgot to send an email.

(D) Because he forgot he sent the email already and sent it again.

2. What information was in the email?

(A) A strategy. (B) An agenda.

(C) An invitation. (D) A list of clients.

3. Who should the email not have gone to?

(A) The woman. (B) The boss. (C) The contractor. (D) The client.

186 **4. What does the woman want to set up?**

(A) A conference. (B) A date.

(C) A brunch meeting. (D) A lunch meeting.

5. When does the woman want to meet?

(A) At 2 o'clock. (B) At 12 o'clock.

(C) Any time between 12 and 2. (D) Any time between 2 and 12.

Ans B, A, D, D, C

UNIT 38 以傳真聯絡 Contacting by Fax

187 J Jared K Katharine

Jared needs to confirm changes to an order. 傑瑞德要確認訂單上的更動。

J Katharine, can you write up a fax for me?

K Sure. Who's it for?

J It's for Susan Gregory at Shoes News. She's just changed her order and I need to send her a confirmation of the changes. Then she's got to sign the confirmation sheet and fax it back to us.

K No problem. What are the changes? I should list them on the fax, right?

J Yes, here's her original order and my notes of the changes. She just wanted to add another 20 pairs of the smallest size.

K All right, I'll write it up and send it to you to review **ASAP**[1].

J Oh, I don't think I'll need to review it. Just fax it to her when you're done.

J 凱薩琳，妳能幫我寫封傳真嗎？

K 沒問題，要寫給誰的？

J 給 Shoes News 公司的蘇珊·桂格里。她剛剛改了訂單，我要傳變更確認給她。然後她要在確認單上簽名後回傳給我們。

K 沒問題。有什麼變更？我應該要在傳真上列出異動，是吧？

J 對，這是她原本的訂單，這個則是我記下的變更。她是要加訂 20 雙最小尺寸的鞋子。

K 好，我立刻寫下來，儘快寄給你檢查。

J 我不需要再看了。完成後直接傳真給她就行了。

1 **ASAP (= as soon as possible)** 儘快

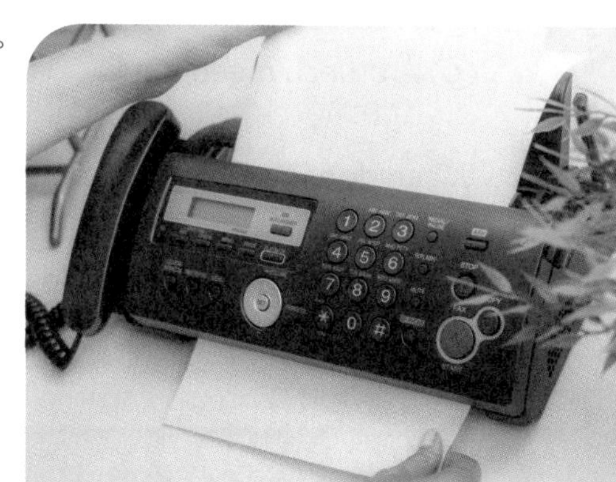

166 Elm Street; Davis, CA 95616 | Tel:530.938.9938 | Fax:530.938.8839

To: Susan Gregory	
Company: Shoes News	From: Katharine Sylvester
Fax: (907) 948-0293	Date: 10/12/2022
Subject: Changes to your order (#0908809)	Phone: (907) 948-9385
Transmitting: 2 pages	

Dear Susan,

We have changed your order (order number 0908809) to add an additional 20 pairs of the size four Etherkid shoe, according to your request. Your new total of the size four shoe is now 200 pairs. Attached is a confirmation of the changes we have made. In order to complete your order, please sign the attached confirmation sheet and fax it back to us as soon as possible. As soon as we receive your signed confirmation of the changes, we will fill your order.

As always, thank you for your business.

Katharine Sylvester

親愛的蘇珊：

我們已按照您的要求修改您的訂單（訂單編號 0908809），增加 20 雙 4 號的 Etherkid 鞋款。最新的 4 號鞋總數為 200 雙。附件為我們的確認信，請您在確認信上簽名並儘快回傳給我們以完成交易。我們一收到您簽名的確認信後，便能完成您的訂單了。

我們一如往常地感謝您的惠顧。

凱薩琳‧西爾維斯特

Useful Expressions

A Sending and receiving faxes 收發傳真 (189)

1 I don't understand the point of the fax I just got. I wonder if they didn't get our original message, or if something has **been lost in translation**[1].

我不知道剛才收到的傳真要表達什麼。我懷疑他們是否有收到我們原本的訊息，不然就是有東西被**誤譯**了。

2 I'm waiting for an important fax and I'm just going to **haunt**[2] the machine until it arrives.

我在等一份重要的傳真，便打算在傳真機附近走動，直到收到傳真為止。

3 Somehow the print on this fax got totally **garbled**[3] and now I can't read the message.

這張傳真的字不知為何整個**糊掉了**，害我現在無法辨認訊息。

4 Sophie's fax jammed, so we're all waiting for her to **put the machine to rights**[4].

蘇菲的傳真卡紙了，所以我們全部人都在等她**把傳真機修理好**。

5 I sent that fax off before I got their final message—I guess I **jumped the gun**[5].

未獲得他們的答覆前我就把傳真傳送出去了——我想我**太早行動**了。

6 I can't get this fax to **go through**[6]!

我沒辦法**傳送**這張傳真！

7 Where's the **redial button**[7]? I need to send this through again—a page dropped out the first time.

重撥鍵在哪裡？第一次傳的時候有一頁漏傳了，我要再傳真一次。

B Giving information in faxes 傳真上的資訊

8	I've attached an order sheet for you to complete.	我已附上訂購單供您填寫。
9	The changes we discussed in the meeting are marked in **script**[8] on the text.	會議上我們所討論的修改，已用**手寫字**標示在文章中。
10	Please review the attached contract and make your changes on the document.	請看過附檔的合約，並直接修改在文件中。
11	The schedule for the trade show is below.	以下是貿易展的時間表。

Review Questions

Listen to the conversations and answer the questions below.

190 **1. What event has probably just happened?**

Ⓐ A party.
Ⓑ A special sale.
Ⓒ A meeting.
Ⓓ A trade show.

2. What will the woman have to do?

Ⓐ Rewrite her notes.
Ⓑ Type out her notes.
Ⓒ Write questions in the margin.
Ⓓ Fax her notes to Wanda.

191 **3. Why does the woman need a signature?**

Ⓐ To accept changes to a contract.
Ⓑ To seal a contact.
Ⓒ To sign for a customer.
Ⓓ To make a deal with a customer.

4. When will Joan come back from headquarters?

Ⓐ Later today.
Ⓑ Tomorrow.
Ⓒ Not until Monday.
Ⓓ Before Monday.

5. What else might Joan want to do?

Ⓐ Make changes on the faxed contract.
Ⓑ Agree to the faxed contract.
Ⓒ Take the contract to headquarters.
Ⓓ Decline the terms of the contract.

Ans C, D, A, C, A

1 **be lost in translation** 失去原意
2 **haunt** [hɔnt] (v.) 經常去（某地）
3 **garbled** [ˋgɑrbl̩d] (adj.) 意思模糊不清的
4 **put sth. to rights** 使某物恢復正常
5 **jump the gun** 過早行動
6 **go through** 傳送
7 **redial button** 重撥鍵
8 **script** [skrɪpt] (n.) 筆跡；手寫字

UNIT 39 以電話與客戶預約會面 Making Appointments With Customers on the Phone

192 J Jared J Jenny

J Jenny, it's Jared. How are you doing?

J I'm great, Jared, how are you? **How's the missus?**[1]

J We're both terrific, thanks. Listen, I'm calling to see if we can make a time to talk about your orders for next quarter sometime this week. Do you have any free time?

J Honestly, this week is **a tight squeeze**[2] for me. I was hoping we could do a **conference call**[3].

J I really think it would be better to meet in person.

J We're **in luck**[4]. I had another meeting rescheduled, so I've got a few hours on Thursday afternoon.

J Terrific. Let's say 2 p.m.?

J That's fine. Listen, I'm going to **pencil you in**[5] for the moment because I've got to make sure my secretary hasn't added anything to the mix, but I'll write you to confirm later today.

J 珍妮，我是傑瑞德。妳過得怎麼樣？

J 我很好。你呢，傑瑞德？**你太太好嗎？**

J 我們都很好，謝謝。我打來是要看看這禮拜能否約個時間，談談妳下一季的訂單。有空嗎？

J 老實說，這禮拜我**抽不出空來**。我希望能開**電話會議**。

J 我真的認為當面談會比較好。

J 我們**真走運**。我有個會議改時間了，所以星期四下午有幾個小時的時間。

J 太好了，兩點可以嗎？

J 好。聽著，由於我要先與秘書確認她沒有排任何事，所以我目前先與你**暫定**這樣，不過今天晚點我會再寫電子郵件跟你確認。

1 **How's the missus/Mrs.?** 太太好嗎？
2 **a tight squeeze** 無法抽身
3 **conference call** 電話會議
4 **be in luck** 運氣不錯
5 **pencil sb./sth. in** 草擬；暫定
6 **face time** 會面時間

Personal Planning Accessories 個人計畫小幫手

yearly calendar 年曆

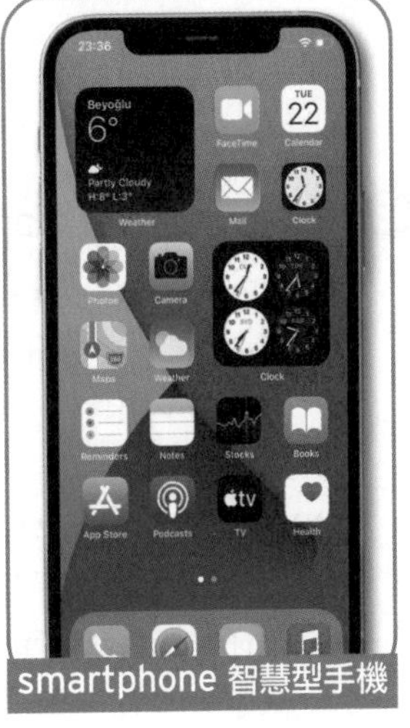
smartphone 智慧型手機

organizer 記事本

monthly calendar 月曆

Planning Applications/Websites 計畫 app／網站

Sketchboard

Evernote

Todoist

Trello

Google Calendar

Useful Expressions

A Talking about types of appointments 談論會面類型

1 Can we have a quick meeting to talk through the changes in your order?
我們可以快速地開個會，討論你訂單的變更嗎？

2 Let's schedule some **face time**[6] so I can explain the new options we are offering.
我們來安排**會面的時間**吧，這樣我才能說明我們提供的新方案。

3 I think you'll love our new line. Let's do lunch.
你一定會愛死我們的新產品。我們一起吃個午飯吧。

B Leaving messages about appointments 有關會面的留言

4 Hi, John, this is Jessica. I think we should schedule a time to go over our new account procedures, just so I'm sure you're comfortable with everything. I'm free this afternoon, but that's probably too short notice for you. I could also do Wednesday afternoon or Thursday morning. Please get back to me about what time is right for you and we'll schedule something.

約翰你好，我是潔西卡。我認為應該安排個時間仔細看看新的會計流程，只有這樣我才能確認你都放心。我今天下午有空，但這麼突然你可能沒辦法。星期三下午或者是星期四上午我也可以，請回電告訴我你何時方便，這樣就可以確定時間。

5 Lindsay, this is Allison from ABC Tech. I'm calling to see if you would be available for a breakfast meeting this week—say, Wednesday, at nine? Please give me a call as soon as you can to let me know if you can make it.

琳賽，我是 ABC 科技公司的艾莉森。我打來是要詢問您本週是否有空參加早餐會議，像是星期三的上午九點？麻煩儘快回電告訴我您是否能參加。

6 Hi, Tabitha, this is Glenda. I'm responding to your message requesting a meeting. This week is really **hectic**[1] for me, but would you be open to a dinner? I could do a dinner any night this week. Get in touch when you can and we'll make a plan.

泰碧莎妳好，我是格蘭達。我是要回覆妳有關召開會議一事。我這週真的很**忙**，但可以改吃晚餐嗎？這禮拜每天晚上我都有空。等妳方便的時候請跟我聯絡，我們來訂個時間。

7 Hi, Tim, it's Bob. I was calling to see if we could possibly **bump our appointment up**[2] from two o'clock to one o'clock tomorrow. Sorry for the change; I've just got some things that have come up here at the office. Let me know if this will work. Thanks!

你好，提姆，我是鮑伯。我打來是要詢問我們能否把明天下午兩點的會議**提早**到下午一點。公司正好有事，真不好意思跟你改時間。請告知我是否可以，謝謝！

1 **hectic** [ˋhɛktɪk] (adj.) 忙碌的
2 **bump sth. up** 提早

Review Questions

Listen to the conversations and answer the questions below.

194 1. **What day are they meeting?**
   (A) Sunday. (B) Monday. (C) Tuesday. (D) Wednesday.

2. **When was the original appointment time?**
   (A) 4:30 p.m. (B) 4 p.m. (C) 3:30 p.m. (D) 3 p.m.

3. **Who needed to reschedule?**
   (A) The man. (B) The woman.
   (C) Both of them. (D) It is unknown.

195 4. **What time, other than Tuesday morning, will the man be free?**
   (A) This Wednesday morning.
   (B) This Thursday morning.
   (C) Any morning next week.
   (D) Any afternoon next week.

5. **What are they probably going to talk about?**
   (A) The man's order.
   (B) The woman's new products.
   (C) The man's new brand.
   (D) The man's new products.

Ans B, B, A, D, B

UNIT 40 與客戶的餐會 A Lunch Meeting With Customers

(196) J Jared L Lucy

Jared is meeting with Lucy, a customer, who currently stocks[1] Etherkid shoes. 傑瑞德正在跟一位目前販賣 Etherkid 鞋子的客戶露西見面。

J I'm glad you could come—and you**'re in for a treat**[2]. This is a great place.

L Great! What do you **recommend**[3]?

J I always like to hear what the specials are first, since I find they're always delicious. Otherwise, the tenderloin is terrific, as is the rack of lamb.

L I don't eat meat. Do they offer a good **vegetarian**[4] option?

J Oh, certainly. They've got great pastas, for example.

L Terrific. Now, why did you want to meet here, Jared? I haven't made any changes to my orders. Have you **had something up your sleeve**[5]?

J Ha, no, not at all. It's just been a while since we sat down and I was hoping to get an informal account **update**[6] from you. What's new in the office?

L Oh, nothing really. It looks like Cindy might be leaving, but that's all **up in the air**[7] . . .

J 很高興妳能前來，這是一家很棒的餐廳，妳一定**會喜歡的**。

L 太棒了！你**推薦**什麼？

J 我通常會先詢問特餐是什麼，因為我發現特餐通常很美味。不然菲力牛排還是羊小排也很棒。

L 我不吃肉，餐廳有供應美味的**素食**選擇嗎？

J 當然有。像他們的義大利麵就很好吃。

L 太好了。好了，傑瑞德，說說你怎麼約在這裡吧？我又沒改訂單，你**葫蘆裡賣的是什麼藥**？

J 哈，沒有啦。只是有好一陣子沒與妳坐下來聊聊，想問問妳公司的**最新消息**。公司最近有發生什麼事嗎？

L 其實沒有什麼事。只是欣蒂好像要離職了，但**還沒確定**……

1 **stock** [stɑk] (v.) 存（貨）
2 **be in for a treat** 會喜歡的；好好享受
3 **recommend** [ˌrɛkəˋmɛnd] (v.) 推薦
4 **vegetarian** [ˌvɛdʒəˋtɛrɪən] (adj.) 素食的
5 **have/keep (something) up one's sleeve** 藏有想法或秘密
6 **update** [ˋʌpdet] (n.) 更新
7 **up in the air** 懸而未決的

Useful Expressions

A Opening lunch meetings 午餐會面的開場白 197

1 It's so nice to get out of the office once in a while, isn't it?
偶爾離開公司還不賴，你說是嗎？

2 I guess it's time to **talk shop**[8].
該是**談公事**的時候了。

B Reasons for lunch meetings with customers 與客戶午餐會面的理由

3 I suppose it's time for us to get down to business. This is the time of year when we scout for **referrals**[9], and I was wondering if you knew of anyone in your industry who isn't satisfied with their current shipping agent and might be interested in giving us a try.
我想我們該談正事了。現在是本年度尋找**介紹人**的時間，想請問您是否知道同業中是否有誰不滿意他們目前的貨運公司，可能可以給我們一個機會試看看。

4 I wanted to meet here today to ask you for a **testimonial**[10].
我今天跟您約在這裡，是要向您要**推薦信**。

8 **talk shop** 談公事
9 **referral** [rɪˋfɝəl] (n.) 推薦；介紹
10 **testimonial** [ˏtɛstəˋmonɪəl] (n.) 推薦信

❶ appetizer/starter 開胃菜
❷ salad 沙拉
❸ soup 湯品
❹ main course 主餐
❺ side dish 副餐
❻ dessert 甜點
❼ beverage 飲品

5 We really need someone to **put in a good word for**[1] us with potential clients. Would you be willing to act as a **reference**[2] for Hadley Brothers?

我們非常需要有人向潛在的客戶為我們**美言幾句**。您是否願意當 Hadley Brothers 的**推薦人**呢？

6 I wanted to **walk you through**[3] our new ordering process.

我要**為您逐步解說**公司新的訂購流程。

C Planning lunch meetings 計畫午餐會面

7 Are you up for a **working lunch**[4]?

你要開**工作午餐會**嗎？

8 Where do you think I should take the clients for lunch? I want to go someplace nice, but not overly showy.

你覺得我要帶客戶到哪裡用午餐？我想去不錯但又不會太過豪華的餐廳。

9 Who's going to **cater**[5] this meeting?

誰要**承辦**這次會議的**餐飲**？

Review Questions

Listen to the conversations and answer the questions below.

198 **1. Who is the man likely to be?**

Ⓐ A colleague. Ⓑ A client.
Ⓒ A supervisor. Ⓓ A caterer.

2. What does the woman want?

Ⓐ A promotion. Ⓑ A meeting.
Ⓒ A recommendation. Ⓓ A guarantee.

199 **3. What is ProChef, probably?**

Ⓐ A client. Ⓑ A stakeholder.
Ⓒ A reference. Ⓓ A caterer.

4. What is being created now?

Ⓐ A lunch. Ⓑ A transition team.
Ⓒ A new account. Ⓓ A meeting.

5. Who probably called this meeting?

Ⓐ The woman. Ⓑ The man.
Ⓒ ProChef. Ⓓ It is unknown.

Ans B, C, D, B, A

1 **put in a good word for sb.** 為某人說好話
2 **reference** [ˋrɛfərəns] (n.) 推薦人
3 **walk sb. through sth.** 為某人逐步解說
4 **working lunch** 工作午餐會
5 **cater** [ˋketɚ] (v.) 承辦宴席

UNIT 41 介紹與推薦公司產品 Introducing and Promoting Your Product

 Ⓢ Samuel Ⓒ Client 

Samuel is introducing his company's new power vacuum cleaner.
山繆正在介紹公司新的動力吸塵器。

Ⓢ We are convinced that our new vacuum cleaner will **blow you away**[1]. We are so excited to be bringing such a revolutionary product to the market.

Ⓒ What's new in the world of vacuum cleaners? What makes this one so special?

Ⓢ Well, have you ever wished you didn't have to move back and forth over the same patch of rug with your vacuum?

Ⓒ Sure.

Ⓢ We've just solved your problem! The unique design of our WindPro uses a ball rather than two wheels, giving our vacuum cleaner 360 degree **maneuverability**[2]. But that's only one of the many aspects of the WindPro that puts it **head and shoulders above**[3] the competition. Take a look at this video we've put together to explain the WindPro **revolution**[4].

Ⓢ 我們深信，我們的新式吸塵器絕對會**讓您大開眼界**。很高興在市面上能推出如此具革命性的產品。

Ⓒ 到底新式吸塵器是什麼？有什麼特別之處？

Ⓢ 這個嘛，您有沒有夢想過，吸地時不需要在同一塊地毯上前後走動只為了吸塵呢？

Ⓒ 當然有。

Ⓢ 我們正好解決了您的麻煩！WindPro 利用球體取代兩輪的獨特的設計，讓我們的吸塵器可 360 度操作。但這只是 WindPro **遠勝出**他家競爭者的其中一點而已。請看我們準備要用來說明 WindPro **大變革**的影片。

1 **blow sb. away** 令某人大為驚喜或高興
2 **maneuverability** [mənuvərəˋbɪlətɪ] (n.) 機動性
3 **head and shoulders above** 遠遠勝出
4 **revolution** [ˌrɛvəˋluʃən] (n.) 革命；大變革

Useful Expressions

A Promoting products to customers 向客戶推銷產品

1. You'll love what this new vacuum cleaner will do for your home.
   你將會愛上這台吸塵器為你家中所帶來的幫助。
2. You can't beat our prices for these new models.
   我們新商品的價格是無人能敵的。
3. Let's compare our product with our competitor's and see which **comes out on top**[5].
   我們來比較同業與我們的產品，看哪一個**勝出**。
4. If you're looking for processing speed and memory, this is the computer for you.
   若你要的是處理速度與記憶體，這正是你要的電腦。
5. No one has equaled our chip's processing capabilities.
   沒有任何產品比得上我們晶片的處理性能。
6. Imagine what we could do by **cross-selling**[6] this product with your tile scrubber.
   試想我們能搭配你們的地磚刷來銷售此商品。

5 **come out on top** 取得勝利
6 **cross-selling** [ˌkrɔsˋsɛlɪŋ] (n.) 交叉銷售
（指讓消費者購買商品同時一併購入其他相關產品或服務）

B Making recommendations to customers 向客戶提供建議

7 I suggest you buy the stock immediately.

我建議你馬上買下這支股票。

8 Having compared all the **pros and cons**[1], my suggestion is to recommend adopting the new system.

在比較所有的**優缺點**後，我的建議是採用新的系統。

9 You should take the price now while there is still a discount.

你應該趁現在有優惠的時候接受這個價格。

10 From my point of view, the deal seems equally **advantageous**[2] for both sides.

以我的觀點看來，這筆交易似乎對雙方都是**有利的**。

11 Why don't you take a look at the slide show to **penetrate** deeper **into**[3] our product?

您要不要觀看這份投影片，好對我們的產品有更**深入的了解**呢？

1 **pros and cons** 〔拉丁文〕正反兩面的意見；利與弊
2 **advantageous** [ˌædvənˋtedʒəs] (adj.) 有利的
3 **penetrate into** 深入了解；深入研究

Review Questions

Listen to the conversations and answer the questions below.

202

1. What is the main feature of the woman's product?

Ⓐ Packaging. Ⓑ Functions.
Ⓒ Price. Ⓓ Brand.

2. What do the users value about the woman's product?

Ⓐ Fancy appearance.
Ⓑ Consumer feedback.
Ⓒ Speed and efficiency.
Ⓓ Ease and reliability.

3. Where does this conversation probably take place?

Ⓐ At a staff outing. Ⓑ At a trade show.
Ⓒ At a meeting. Ⓓ At an interview.

4. Where does this conversation probably take place?

Ⓐ In a meeting.
Ⓑ In a trade show.
Ⓒ In a business lunch.
Ⓓ In a presentation.

5. Why is the man interested in cross-selling?

Ⓐ Because the two companies already have a working relationship.
Ⓑ Because the two companies sell products with similar qualities.
Ⓒ Because the two companies are in competition.
Ⓓ Because the two companies are going to merge.

Ans B, D, C, B, B

UNIT 42 說明與比較產品 Describing and Comparing Products

Jared is describing their new shoe line to Rose, a stakeholder, and other stakeholders. 傑瑞德正在向蘿絲等利害關係人說明新的鞋子產品線。

R So how is the Etherkid different from our other kids' shoe lines?

J First of all, unlike our other children's shoes—and other company's children's shoes—the Etherkid is designed with function as well as form in mind. That means that we've spent time and money testing how the shoe's performance on young feet would be. It's a shoe that is actually good for growing feet, not only good-looking.

R And other children's shoes aren't marketing themselves this way?

J No! Our initial market research showed that there was a huge hole in the market for this kind of product. In addition to being a performance kids' shoe, the Etherkid is also closely aligned to the adult Ethersole, so adults and children in athletic families can have associated shoes. Other lines don't have this kind of family association.

R And how does the shoe look?

J The shoes have rubber **soles**[1] and leather and **synthetic**[2] uppers. The design follows the same pattern as the adult shoe, but the Etherkid comes in brighter **hues**[3] than the adult shoe.

R So the colors and design are just like other kids' shoes?

J No, in fact, the design is totally different—our shoe design is much better for young feet than any other shoe on the market. The colors are similar to those of other kids' shoe lines, but as they are related to the colors of the adult shoes, we believe families will be more interested in buying the same brand for the entire family.

R 那麼 Etherkid 與我們其他的童鞋產品有什麼不同？

J 第一，跟我們與別家的其他童鞋不同之處為 Etherkid 兼具功能與外型。也就是說，我們投注金錢與時間在測試鞋子在兒童足部上的性能。這是一款不僅外型好看，且適合成長中的足部的鞋款。

R 那其他的童鞋沒有主打這些功能嗎？

J 沒有！我們初步的市調指出，市場很缺這類商品。除了是功能性的童鞋外，Etherkid 還與成人鞋 Ethersole 結合。如此一來，運動家庭中的大人小孩就能有同組鞋款，其他產品並沒有針對家庭做這樣相關的設計。

R 那麼鞋子的外型如何？

J **鞋底**是膠底，鞋面和鞋幫則是真皮與**合成**皮。沿續成人鞋款的設計，**色調**則是比成人款來得亮麗。

R 這麼說來，顏色與設計跟其他童鞋差不多囉？

J 不，其實設計上是截然不同的。我們的鞋款設計對兒童足部來說，要比市面上其他童鞋要來得舒適。顏色與其他童鞋產品相差不遠，不過由於顏色和成人鞋款相似，我們相信一般家庭會傾向為全家購買同個品牌。

Useful Expressions

A Describing products 說明產品

1 This soap creates a rich, creamy **lather**[4].
此肥皂能產生大量綿密的**泡沫**。

2 This is a classic woman's watch.
這是一支經典女錶。

3 Our **patented**[5] new processor makes this lightweight laptop the fastest on the market.
我們**獲得專利的**新式處理器讓此台輕量筆記型電腦成為市面上速度最快的電腦。

4 If you want affordable luxury, this is the bedroom set for you.
若您要可負擔的奢華享受，這正是您要的臥室寢具。

5 As you can see, this is the **state-of-the-art**[6] technology.
如您所見，這是**最先進的**科技。

1 **sole** [sol] (n.) 鞋底
2 **synthetic** [sɪnˋθɛtɪk] (adj.) 合成的；人造的
3 **hue** [hju] (n.) 色調；顏色
4 **lather** [ˋlæðɚ] (n.)（肥皂水等的）泡沫
5 **patented** [ˋpætn̩tɪd] (adj.) 已取得專利的
6 **state-of-the-art** [ˋstetəvðiˋɑrt] (adj.) 最先進的

6 We have designed the first self-cleaning microwave!

我們設計出首台可自行清理的微波爐！

7 Because of its soft, nontoxic material and bright colors, this toy is perfect for children under age four.

因這個玩具使用柔軟無毒的材質與明亮的顏色，正適合四歲以下的兒童。

8 We are at the head of a revolution in personal planning **applications**[1].

我們是個人規劃**應用程式**業界的先驅。

B Making comparisons 做出比較 

9 This shoe has a better fit than the other.

這款鞋比其他鞋款來得合腳。

10 I don't think these boots will **hold up**[2] as long as those.

我不認為這幾雙靴子會比那些來得**耐穿**。

11 This is definitely the most **user-friendly**[3] model I've ever tried!

這絕對是我使用過最**容易操作**的產品！

12 I've tried other shampoos, but none made my hair as shiny as this one.

我試洗過其他洗髮精，沒有一種能像這一個一樣讓我的頭髮柔柔亮亮。

13 Our machine's unique process will enable you to wrap and ship products twice as fast as your competitors.

我們機器獨特的處理方法能讓您包裝與運送產品的速度比同業還要快上一倍。

14 Let's take a look at the **trunk**[4] space in these two models. As you can see, our trunk offers space for almost twice as many suitcases, without adding length to the car! That's our **thoughtful**[5] design at work.

我們來看看此兩種車款的**後車廂**空間。如您所見，在不增加車長的情況下，我們的後車廂幾乎多了兩倍的行李空間！這是我們的**貼心**設計。

15 Our headphones give you the same sound quality as other top sellers, but with a new, more comfortable design.

我們的頭戴式耳機提供您與暢銷耳機同等的音質，並且有更為新穎、舒適的設計。

1 **application** [ˌæpləˋkeʃən] (n.)（可在智慧型手機等行動裝置上使用的）應用程式
2 **hold up** 耐穿；保持良好
3 **user-friendly** [ˋjuzəˋfrɛndlɪ] (adj.) 容易使用的
4 **trunk** [trʌŋk] (n.) 後車廂
5 **thoughtful** [ˋθɔtfəl] (adj.) 貼心的

Review Questions

Listen to the conversations and answer the questions below.

207

1. **Which machine has a lower price?**
   (A) The woman's company's machine.
   (B) The competitor's machine.
   (C) It isn't clear.

2. **Which model has been on the market longer?**
   (A) The woman's company's.
   (B) The competitor's.
   (C) It isn't clear.

3. **What is one difference between the two machines?**
   (A) The woman's company's machine has better name recognition.
   (B) The woman's company's machine was redesigned two years ago.
   (C) The woman's company's machine offers three more stitch settings.
   (D) The woman's company's machine is state-of-the-art.

208

4. **What is the man writing?**
   (A) A blurb. (B) A research.
   (C) A website. (D) A reference.

5. **What is the woman thinking of adding?**
   (A) A blurb. (B) A business model.
   (C) A technique. (D) A comparison.

Ans C, B, C, A, D

UNIT 43 與客戶議價 Price Negotiation With Customers

  Jane  Jared

Jared is trying to agree on a price with a customer, Jane.
傑瑞德正試圖與一位客戶珍取得價格的共識。

J We love the Etherkid line and we think it would do well at our urban locations. But the Etherkid is one of the most expensive kid's shoes on the market today! At the current price, we're afraid that our profits will be too low to justify keeping them in stock.

J Well, I appreciate your honesty. We're aware that the Etherkid costs more than some other shoes on the market, but the reason for that is we use quality materials and **legitimate**[1] labor. We believe that our prices are quite **competitive**[2] for the quality of the product we provide.

J I agree that the shoe is great, but we're afraid we aren't going to be able to **crack the market**[3] at these prices. Can we talk **concessions**[4]? Are you willing to **meet us halfway**[5]?

J Honestly, we have come down as far as we can on the price. However, I've been looking into other ways we could meet your needs. One possibility is to offer you a discount in exchange for your taking on the shipping costs of your orders.

J OK, that might be a possibility. I'll have to take that back to my supervisors.

J Good, I'm glad we can consider that. The other option would be to enter into a **consignment**[6] agreement at the original price. We hope this might relieve some of your anxiety about your ability to **move**[7] the Etherkid.

J That's another interesting option.

J 我們喜歡 Etherkid 的產品，並認為這在都會區會賣得不錯。不過 Etherkid 是目前市場上價格最高的其中一款童鞋！依目前的價格來說，我們擔心利潤會太低而無法持續供貨。

J 這個嘛，感謝您據實以告。我們知道 Etherkid 鞋款比市面上的其他鞋子來得貴，但這是因為我們使用高級的材質與**合法的**人力。我們相信我們的價格以我們的產品品質來說，是很**有競爭力的**。

J 我認同鞋子很不錯，但我擔心以這樣的價格是無法**打進市場**的。我們能談談折衷辦法的價格嗎？你願意**配合我們**嗎？

J 老實說，我們已經盡可能壓低價格了。我也在思考其他能符合您需求的辦法。可能可以給您打個折，但您要自行負擔運費。

J 好，這也許會是個辦法。我要回去問問我的上司。

J 很好，很高興我們能考慮看看。另一個方案就是以原價寄售的方式，希望能減輕您販售 Etherkid 的壓力。

J 這是另一個有趣的選擇。

Useful Expressions

A Talking about negotiation styles 談論議價類型 

1	She **drives a hard bargain**[8].	她**猛力殺價**。
2	I don't like dealing with Stan; he's such a **hard sell**[9].	我不喜歡跟史坦打交道，他總是**強迫推銷**。
3	I think the **soft sell**[10] approach works much better with these clients.	我認為**軟性推銷**的方法比較適合這些客戶。

1 **legitimate** [lɪˋdʒɪtəmət] (adj.) 合法的
2 **competitive** [kəmˋpɛtətɪv] (adj.) 有競爭力的
3 **crack the market** 打進市場
4 **concession** [kənˋsɛʃən] (n.) 讓步
5 **meet sb. halfway** 遷就（某人）
6 **consignment** [kənˋsaɪnmənt] (n.) 寄賣品
7 **move** [muv] (v.) 銷售
8 **drive a hard bargain** 狠狠地殺價
9 **hard sell** 強迫推銷
10 **soft sell** 軟性推銷（指以柔性說服的方式進行推銷）

B Suggesting compromises 建議折衷辦法

4 We would appreciate it if you could increase our discount, in light of our large volume of sales.

若您能看在我們龐大的銷售量的分上，而給予更多折扣的話，我們會很感謝您的。

5 Can you offer us free shipping in exchange for a certain number of orders per year?

每年的訂單到達一定數目時，您是否能以免收運費做為交換？

6 We can offer you a 4% cash discount on accounts that you pay within 30 days.

若您於 30 天之內付款，我們會提供 96 折的現金折扣優惠。

7 Do you have a lower-cost version of this product?

你有這個產品的低價版本嗎？

8 Is it possible to save money by being flexible about our delivery dates?

可以透過維持運送日期的彈性來節省費用嗎？

9 In order to agree to that, we would need you to **compromise**[1] on some of your other positions.

為了要同意這件事，我們要請您放棄一些其他的想法。

C Rejecting compromises 拒絕妥協

10 We think if you consider our position, you'll understand why we can't agree to that.

我們認為若您能考慮我們的立場，便能理解為何我們無法同意那件事。

11 I'm afraid my supervisors won't agree to that.

我的主管恐怕不會答應那件事。

12 That's a pretty **steep**[2] discount you're asking for. I don't think it's likely to be approved.

你要的折扣**幅度太大了**，我覺得不會獲准。

13 As much as I want to work with you, I know my supervisor will **reject this proposal out of hand**[3].

雖然我很想與您共事，但我知道我的上司必定會**斷然拒絕**此提案。

14 As it stands now, this contract is not something we can move forward with.

依照現況來說，我們無法繼續這份合約了。

1 **compromise** [ˋkɑmprə͵maɪz] (v.) 妥協；讓步

2 **steep** [stip] (adj.) 急降的；急升的

3 **reject sth. out of hand** 不假思索地拒絕

Review Questions

Listen to the conversations and answer the questions below.

211

1. **Where can the man find a lower price?**
   (A) In the next shop.
   (B) Across town.
   (C) Across the country.
   (D) From an online shop.

2. **Why can't the man have a discount?**
   (A) The woman doesn't have the power to change the price.
   (B) The price is already as low as it can go.
   (C) The man isn't qualified for a discount.
   (D) The woman doesn't want to give him one.

3. **What helps seal the deal?**
   (A) A 10% discount.
   (B) Free shipping.
   (C) Free delivery and installation.
   (D) The man's manner.

212

4. **What does the man want to do?**
   (A) Increase the discount.
   (B) Reach a compromise.
   (C) Be competitive.
   (D) Revise the terms of the contract.

5. **How much of a discount does the woman want?**
   (A) 15%.
   (B) 5%.
   (C) 50%.
   (D) 10%.

Ans B, A, C, B, D

Part 5 對外的聯絡 Outside Correspondences and Contacts

UNIT 44 採購產品與比價 Making Purchases and Comparing Prices

213 B Barbara J Jacob

Barbara and Jacob are talking about new laptop options for the office. 芭芭拉跟雅各在談論選擇辦公室的新筆記型電腦。

B I've made up a matrix for comparing all the brands, but it's still a tough choice.

J Nothing stands out? What's the fastest?

B Oh, they've all got the same processors, so I don't think they'll be very different. There are two that have more memory than the others, but one is the most expensive by far and might **be out of our range**[1].

J What about the other one with more memory?

B It's the second-most expensive, but it also has a small screen and doesn't get good reviews.

J Gosh, it's not going to be easy to decide, is it? What's the cheapest model like?

B It looks **serviceable**[2], though it's heavy, which people won't be happy about.

J Well, I guess we've got to decide what we value the most here and guess how much management will be willing to **fork over**[3].

B 我已經做了一個品牌比較矩陣，但還是很難選擇。

J 沒有較突出的嗎？哪一種是最快的？

B 它們的處理器都是同款的，所以我覺得不會有太大的差別。有兩款的記憶體較大，但其中一款是目前價位最高的，而且可能會**超出**預算**範圍**。

J 那另一款有較大記憶體的呢？

B 那是第二貴的，但它螢幕小，評價也不佳。

J 哎呀，要決定還真不簡單對吧？那最便宜的那台怎麼樣？

B 雖然大家都不喜歡重量重這點，但似乎還挺**耐用的**。

J 這樣的話，我們要決定最重視哪一點，還有想想高層會**願意付**多少。

1 **be out of sb's range** 超出……範圍

2 **serviceable** [ˋsɝvɪsəbḷ] (adj.) 耐用的

3 **fork over** 心不甘情不願地給

Useful Expressions

A Talking about purchases 談論採購

1 I think the Bueno laptop was the best choice.
我認為 Bueno 的筆記型電腦是最佳選擇。

2 I'm having such a hard time deciding on which scanner to buy!
決定要買哪一台掃描機讓我想破頭了！

3 Both of the design houses have great **attributes**[4], but they're like **apples and oranges**[5]. They're so different, it's hard to choose between them.
這兩家設計公司都很好，但各具**特色**。他們風格是如此地**不同**，要從中選擇真是困難。

4 It was **like pulling teeth**[6] to get management to **pony up**[7] for new office equipment, but we finally convinced them.
要高層**支付**新的辦公器材費用**非常困難**，但我們最後還是說服了他們。

5 I'm glad they finally **coughed up**[8] the money for new laptops.
我很高興他們最後還是**不得不支付**了新的筆記型電腦的費用。

B Comparing prices 比價

6 The ValuePro model is cheaper, but all the online reviews say it's unreliable. I think it might be worth it to spend more.
ValuePro 牌的產品較便宜，不過所有的網路評價都說它不可靠。我認為或許多花點錢會比較好。

7 I can't believe this company's rate is half as much as the other's!
我真不敢相信這家公司的價格比另一家的便宜一半！

8 We just found out that a new alternator is going to **cost an arm and a leg**[9].
我們剛剛才知道一台新的交流發電機**要價非常昂貴**。

4 **attribute** [ˋætrɪbjut] (n.) 特色
5 **apples and oranges** 完全不同
6 **like pulling teeth** 非常困難的
7 **pony up** 不情願地付錢
8 **cough up** 不甘心地給（錢）
9 **cost an arm and a leg** 所費不貲

9 There's no sign-up fee at this gym, but the monthly rate is higher. On the other hand, the other gym charges a sign-up fee, but has a cheaper monthly rate. It's **six of one, a half dozen of the other**[1].

雖然這家健身房不用付入會費，但月費比較高。另一方面，另一家健身房要收入會費，但月費較便宜。這根本就是**半斤八兩**。

10 I think it's worth it to spend more on the new one. It's "**pay me now or pay me later**[2]."

我認為在新設備上多花點錢是值得的，就看是要**現在花大錢還是以後花大錢**。

1 **six of one, a half dozen of the other**
半斤八兩

2 **pay me now or pay me later**
現在給或以後再支付

More Words About Computer Accessories 更多電腦相關配備

router 路由器

motherboard 主機板

modem 數據機

internal hard drive 內接硬碟

RAM (random access memory) 記憶體

CD-ROM drive 光碟機

CPU (central processing unit) 中央處理器

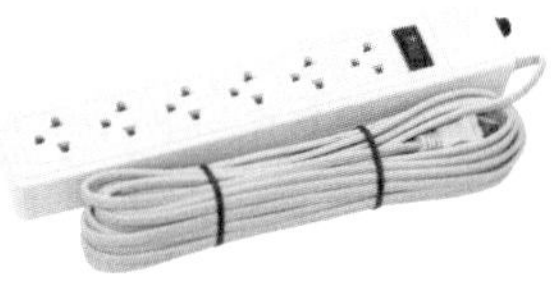

power strip 延長線

webcam 網路攝影機

HDMI cable HDMI 傳輸線

cable 網路線

Review Questions

Listen to the conversations and answer the questions below.

215 **1. What is the man thinking of doing?**

Ⓐ Getting a new phone.
Ⓑ Recommending the MyPhone.
Ⓒ Buying a MyPhone.
Ⓓ Discouraging use of the MyPhone.

2. Who will get a new phone?

Ⓐ The whole office.
Ⓑ The boss.
Ⓒ The man.
Ⓓ The woman.

3. Which is true about the MyPhone?

Ⓐ It has all the same features as the ProPhone.
Ⓑ It costs significantly less than the ProPhone.
Ⓒ It is easier to use than the ProPhone.
Ⓓ It has a better reputation than the ProPhone.

216 **4. What is the man recommending buying?**

Ⓐ A less expensive monitor.
Ⓑ A smaller yet clearer monitor.
Ⓒ A bigger and cheaper monitor.
Ⓓ A more expensive but better monitor.

5. What does the man say about the price?

Ⓐ That the Sol is just a little bit less expensive than the competitor's.
Ⓑ That the price is not important.
Ⓒ That the price matters a lot.
Ⓓ That it's worth the price to get the best quality.

Ans B, A, B, D, D

UNIT 45 接單與送貨 Accepting and Shipping Orders

217 S Susan C Customer

Susan is taking orders for shoes. 蘇珊正在接洽鞋子的訂單。

S Good afternoon, Ethershoe headquarters, may I take your order?

C Yes, I'd like to order twenty pairs of women's shoes and thirty pairs of men's shoes. I've got a question though—do your sizes **run small**[1]?

S No, the sizes are accurate. Now, what sizes do you want?

C I'd like five each of the women's six and a half, seven, eight, and nine. For the men's, let's do five each of seven through twelve.

S Great. And colors? For women, we have pink, yellow, and sage green. For men, we have yellow, blue, and sage green.

C How about a mix of all the colors?

S That's easy. Now, let me get your address.

C No problem. It's 134 Portsmouth Drive, Victoria, BC, Canada, and the ZIP code is V9C 1R9.

S OK, great. And will you be paying by credit card?

C Yes.

S And before I take your credit card information, is your **billing address**[2] the same as your **shipping address**[3]?

C Yes, it is.

S Thanks. We'll send you the **invoice**[4] with your shipment, then. Now, let me get your payment information. Can you tell me the card type and the **expiration date**[5]?

1 **run small** 版型較小
2 **billing address** 帳單地址
3 **shipping address** 收件地址
4 **invoice** [ˋɪnvɔɪs] (n.) 出貨單
5 **expiration date** 到期日

S 午安，這裡是 Ethershoe 總公司，請問您要訂購什麼嗎？

C 是，我要訂 20 雙女鞋，還有 30 雙男鞋。我有個疑問，那就是你們的鞋子**版型**有**偏小**嗎？

S 沒有，尺寸是準確的。請問您要什麼尺寸的？

C 女鞋我要六號半、七號、八號跟九號各五雙，男鞋則是從七號到十二號各五雙。

S 很好，那顏色呢？我們女鞋的顏色有粉紅、黃與灰綠色。男鞋則有黃、藍與灰綠色。

C 所有顏色都各來幾雙如何？

S 這還不簡單。請給我您的地址。

C 好。地址是加拿大卑詩省樸茨茅斯路 134 號，郵遞區號是 V9C 1R9。

S 好的。請問您是要刷卡嗎？

C 是的。

S 在我與您確認您的信用卡資料前，請問您的帳單地址跟送貨地址是同一個嗎？

C 是一樣的地址。

S 感謝您，那麼我們會將出貨單連同貨物一起寄給您。現在我要詢問您的付款資訊，可以麻煩您告訴我您的信用卡類型與到期日嗎？

Words About Payment 付款方式

credit card 信用卡

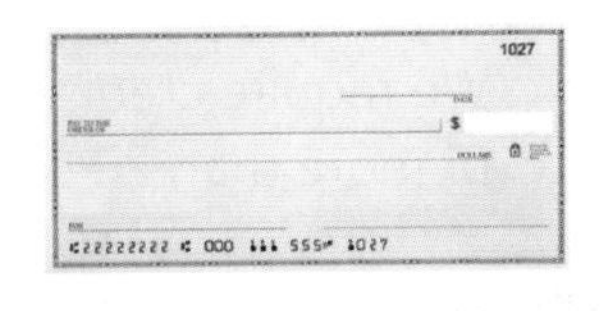
personal check 私人支票

coupon 折價券

cash (coins) 現金（硬幣）

third party online payment 第三方線上支付

gift card 禮物卡

cash (bills / notes) 現金（紙鈔）

Useful Expressions

A Taking orders 接受訂購 (218)

1	I'll be happy to take your order now.	現在很高興能為您訂購。
2	Would you like to place an order?	您要訂購商品嗎？
3	First, let me ask you a few questions. To begin with, what models are you interested in?	讓我先問您幾個問題。首先，您對哪些產品感興趣？
4	What size would you like?	您要什麼尺寸的？
5	Is this your first order with us?	這是您第一次購買我們的產品嗎？
6	I'll pass you to a manager to discuss your **bulk**[1] order.	我將替您轉接給我們經理來談您**大量**訂購。
7	For placing a bulk order, we have a slightly different process.	我們處理大量訂單的流程有些許不同。
8	We offer a discount of 5% for orders of more than US$500.	購買超過 500 美金，我們會打 95 折。
9	We require credit card payments for orders of more than 20 pairs.	我們要求超過 20 雙的訂單要以信用卡付款。

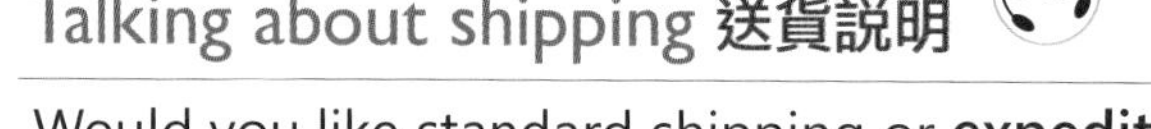

B Talking about shipping 送貨說明 (219)

10 Would you like standard shipping or **expedited shipping**[2]?
您要用標準寄送還是**快速寄送**？

11 Our express shipping options include overnight and two-day shipping.
我們的快速運送的選項有隔日到貨與兩日到貨。

12 Is your shipping address the same as your billing address?
您的收件地址跟您的帳單地址是一樣的嗎？

13 Have you checked our international shipping options online?
你在網路上看過我們國際運送的方案嗎？

14 We offer free shipping on orders of $25 and up.
訂購超過 25 美元的訂單我們會提供免運費的優惠。

1 **bulk** [bʌlk] (adj.) 大量的
2 **expedited shipping** 快速運送
3 **P.O. box (= post office box)** 郵政信箱
4 **maritime** [ˋmærə͵taɪm] (adj.) 航海的

15 I'm sorry, we can't ship to a **P.O. box**[3].
很抱歉，我們無法寄到**郵政信箱**。

16 Do you offer **maritime**[4] insurance?
你們有保**海上**保險嗎？

Review Questions

Listen to the conversations and answer the questions below.

220 **1. What is the problem with the new shipping company?**

Ⓐ It is too expensive.
Ⓑ It messed up an order.
Ⓒ It's difficult to communicate with.
Ⓓ It gets blamed for all the problems.

2. How was the order shipped?

Ⓐ Overnight. Ⓑ Two-day air. Ⓒ Day. Ⓓ Free.

3. What seems to have happened with the order?

Ⓐ It arrived late.
Ⓑ It was the wrong size.
Ⓒ It got combined with another customer's order.
Ⓓ It was overcharged.

221 **4. How will this order be paid for?**

Ⓐ By credit card. Ⓑ By check.
Ⓒ By cash on delivery. Ⓓ By PayPal.

5. Which address is a P.O. Box?

Ⓐ The shipping address. Ⓑ The billing address.
Ⓒ The supplier's address. Ⓓ The man's address.

Ans B, A, C, A, B

Part 5 對外的聯絡 Outside Correspondences and Contacts

UNIT 46 與客戶達成協議 Making a Deal With a Customer

  Jane  Jared

Jared is making a deal with Jane to sell his company's products in her shops. 傑瑞德正在與珍討論要在她的店裡販售他們公司的產品。

J I think this will work. I'm sure my bosses will be satisfied with this. I think we've got a deal.

J I'm so glad. I know this partnership is going to benefit us both.

J We're pleased as well. I'm really looking forward to having your products in our stores. I know they're going to be very popular.

J Shall we **shake on it**[1] now, and I'll have my team send you the formal offer tomorrow morning?

J Wonderful. I'll look for the offer tomorrow. A pleasure doing business with you.

J And you.

J 我認為這會成功的，我有信心我老闆會很滿意，我想就這樣說定了。

J 我很高興，我們雙方必定能從這次合作中獲益。

J 我們也感到很高興，我真的很期待能在店裡販賣你們的商品，一定會大受歡迎的。

J 我們來**為此握個手**吧，明天早上我請組員把正式的報價寄給您好嗎？

J 太好了，我明天再來看。跟你做生意很愉快。

J 我也是。

Agreement 達成協議

1. **shaking hands 握手**
2. **presenting a contract 出示合約**
3. **signing an agreement or contract 簽約**
4. **clapping/applauding 鼓掌**

1

2

3

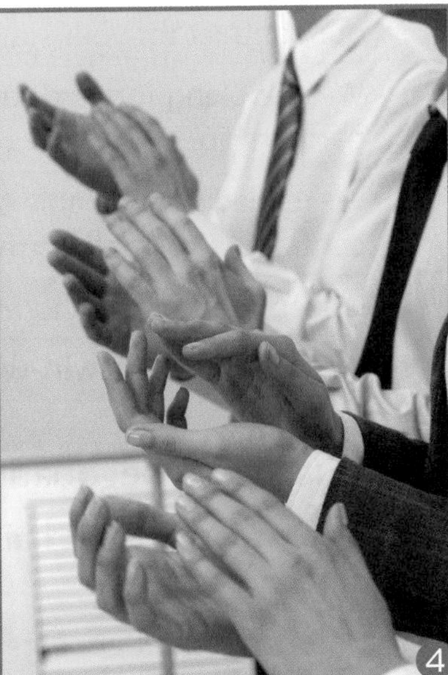

4

1 **shake on it** 握手表示完成交易

Useful Expressions

A Continuing negotiations 持續協商 

1 We've made good progress today. I think our next step should be to work on a formal contract.
我們今天的進展不少，我想接下來就是要準備簽正式的合約了。

2 I'm confident we'll be able to finalize our agreement in our next meeting.
我有信心，我們在下一次的會議便能確定協議了。

3 Let's set a date for the next stage of negotiations.
我們為下階段的協商訂下日期吧。

4 Next time, let's get everyone **around the same table**[1].
下一次，我們要請**全體都到場**。

B Reaching agreements 達成協議

5	We accept the terms stated and will forward our contract for your signature.	我們接受列出的條款，而且會將合約寄給您簽名。
6	We're looking forward to continuing our partnership.	我們期待能與您持續合作。
7	We're glad we'll be able to draw up a contract to **formalize**[2] these terms.	我們很高興能草擬合約，以確定這些條款。
8	It seems we're ready to move forward, then.	看起來我們準備好能再進一步了。
9	We've arrived at a **win-win situation**[3].	我們雙方達成了**雙贏的局面**。

C Cutting off negotiations 終止協商

10	It's a pity we couldn't **hammer out an agreement**[4] today.	很可惜今天我們無法敲定協議。
11	Unfortunately, it appears we won't be able to settle our differences.	很可惜，看來我們無法解決我們之間的分歧。
12	I think it's clear that we have **incompatible**[5] goals at the moment.	我想，我們目前雙方的目標很明顯是**相牴觸的**。
13	I'm afraid that's a **deal-breaker**[6] for us.	恐怕我們的**交易**出現了**阻礙**。
14	I'm sorry, but this is a **no-win situation**[7] for us.	我很抱歉，但這對我們來說是個**非常不利的狀況**。

Review Questions

Listen to the conversations and answer the questions below.

224 1. **How did the negotiations go?**

(A) They were successful.
(B) They are still ongoing.
(C) They were not successful.
(D) It is unknown.

2. **What had the woman hoped?**

(A) That the negotiations would be cut off.
(B) That an agreement could be reached.
(C) That a discount would be offered.
(D) That the situation could stay the same.

225 3. **What is the outcome of the negotiation?**

(A) It is a no-win situation.
(B) It is a win-win situation.
(C) It is a hard sell.
(D) It is ongoing.

4. **Why does the man think the negotiations were successful?**

(A) Because all parties participated.
(B) Because they could meet privately.
(C) Because they won.
(D) Because all paperwork has been signed.

Ans C, B, B, A

1 **around the same table** 全體到場
2 **formalize** [ˋfɔrməlaɪz] (v.) 確定；使成形
3 **win-win situation** 雙贏的局面
4 **hammer out an agreement** 敲定合約
5 **incompatible** [ˌɪnkəmˋpætəbl̩] (adj.) 不相容的
6 **deal-breaker** [ˋdilbrekɚ] (n.) 交易阻礙
7 **no-win situation** 注定失敗的局面

UNIT 47 討論合約條款 Discussing Contract Terms

Jacob and Katharine are discussing contract terms with the website designer, Aaron. 雅各跟凱薩琳正在和網站設計師亞倫討論合約條款。

J Thanks for coming in this morning. You've had a chance to look over the contract, right?

A Yes, and everything seems nearly **in order**[1], at least **on my end**[2].

J I'm glad to hear that. We tried to set up the deliverable schedule exactly according to your work specifications.

A Thank you; yes, the schedule looks great. I have one question about the conditions for **voiding**[3] the contract. The section is here, article seven.

J Oh, I see. Yes, that just means that if you knowingly put out something damaging about this company on our website, you might be **liable**[4] for our lost income.

A OK, I see. And one last thing—I'm not exactly clear on the process for extending the contract, should we want to. Would we really have to go through the whole process again?

J Oh, no. I'm sorry if that wasn't clear. We have a pretty simple process for extending existing contracts if both parties are happy with their relationship. I'll send a description of the process to you and we can add it as an **addendum**[5] to the contract, if you want.

1 **in order** 安排好的
2 **on sb's end** 就某人這邊來說
3 **void** [vɔɪd] (v.) 使無效；使作廢
4 **liable** [ˋlaɪəbḷ] (adj.) 負有（法律）責任的
5 **addendum** [əˋdɛndəm] (n.) 合約附錄，針對部分條款的必要補充

J 謝謝您今早過來。您已經看過合約了對吧?

A 看過了,看來大概都**安排**得差不多了,至少**我這邊**是如此。

J 很高興聽到您這麼說,我們試著按您的工作計畫來安排可行的時間表。

A 謝謝您,時間表安排得很不錯。我對這部分,也就是條款七合約**無效**的條件有個疑問。

J 我知道了。沒錯,這是指若您蓄意在我們網站上散布對敝公司有害的資訊,就要為我們的損失**負責**。

A 好,那我懂了。還有最後一件事,那就是若我們要續約的話,我不太清楚流程是如何。我們要整個流程再跑一遍嗎?

J 很抱歉我講得不夠清楚,不是這樣的。若雙方都對合作關係感到滿意的話,延長既有合約的流程是很簡單的。我會寄流程説明給您,您要的話,我們可以用**附錄**的方式將它補充到合約中。

Useful Expressions

A Talking about contract terms 談論合約條款 

1 What happens if we're found **in breach of**[1] contract?
如果我們**違**約會怎麼樣?

2 Will we have to pay **damages**[2] if we break our contract?
如果我們違約會需要付**賠償金**嗎?

3 Any serious problems will go to **arbitration**[3].
任何重大問題都將交付**裁決**。

4 There's no way for him to get out of it—it's an **airtight**[4] contract.
他無從脱身了——這可是份**無懈可擊的**合約。

5 The **contract period**[5] will be one year.
合約期將為一年。

B Talking about contract language 談論合約用語

6 I read the first part carefully, but I just **skimmed**[6] the **boilerplate**[7].
我詳讀了第一部分,但只**大概看過標準條款**。

7 Do I really need to understand all this legal **mumbo jumbo**[8]?
我真的需要搞懂這些**令人難以理解的**法律用語嗎?

8 Be sure to read the **fine print**[9]!
要記得看**附屬細則**!

9 Are you sure this is **legally binding**[10]?
你確定這**有法律效力**嗎?

10 They seem confident, but I don't think this contract will **hold water**[11].
他們一副有信心的樣子,但我認為這份合約根本**站**不**住腳**。

1 **in breach of** 違反
2 **damage** [ˋdæmɪdʒ] (n.) 賠償金
3 **arbitration** [ˏɑrbəˋtreʃən] (n.) 仲裁
4 **airtight** [ˋɛrˏtaɪt] (adj.) 無懈可擊的
5 **contract period** 合約期
6 **skim** [skɪm] (v.) 概略瀏覽
7 **boilerplate** [ˋbɔɪləˏplet] (n.) (合約的)標準條款;定型化條款
8 **mumbo jumbo** [ˋmʌmbo ˋjʌmbo] (n.) 難以理解的話語

Review Questions

Listen to the conversations and answer the questions below.

228 **1. What is difficult for the man?**

Ⓐ Understanding the new client.
Ⓑ Protecting themselves.
Ⓒ Holding up the new project.
Ⓓ Making a contract with the new client.

2. What won't the company lawyers agree to?

Ⓐ The new project.
Ⓑ Accepting liability.
Ⓒ Accepting benefits.
Ⓓ Accepting problems.

3. What is holding up the new project?

Ⓐ Trouble creating the contract.
Ⓑ A lawyer.
Ⓒ Trouble with new employees.
Ⓓ Trouble with the man.

229 **4. What kind of contracts are being discussed?**

Ⓐ Employee contracts.
Ⓑ Benefits contracts.
Ⓒ Management contracts.
Ⓓ Insurance contracts.

5. Who is opposed to the new contracts?

Ⓐ The man.
Ⓑ The woman.
Ⓒ The benefits administrator.
Ⓓ The new manager.

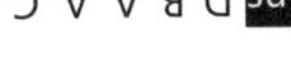

9 **fine print** 附屬細則（合約中用較小字印刷，可能不利簽約者且易被忽略）

10 **legally binding** 具法律效力的

11 **hold water** 合情合理（原意是「〔容器〕能盛得住水，滴水不漏」，引申為所提出的理論是確實的、站得住腳的）

UNIT 48 簽署正式合約 Signing an Official Contract

Jacob and Katharine are completing the contract with the website designer, Aaron. 雅各與凱薩琳正在和網站設計師亞倫一起完成合約。

J So, are all the **amendments**[1] clear? Are we ready to sign?

A Absolutely. I'm excited to get on with the project.

J So are we! Now, here are our copies and here's yours. We need three copies, for the legal section, HR, and for my files. I'm sorry to make you sign so many times.

A It's no problem. Today is the 12th, right?

J Yes. Alright, I'll sign after you . . . and here we are. All done.

A Wonderful. I can't wait to get to work on the website!

J 所有**修改**都清楚了嗎？準備好要簽約了嗎？

A 當然沒問題。我很期待要開始進行這項案子。

J 我們也是！這份是您的合約，這份是我們的。我們需要三份合約，分別要給法務部門、人資還有我這邊。不好意思要讓您簽這麼多次。

A 沒關係。今天是 12 號，對吧？

J 對。那我在您之後簽名……好了，都完成了。

A 太棒了。我等不及要開始進行網站的工作了！

1 **amendment** [əˋmɛndmənt] (n.) 修改；修正條款
2 **initial** [ɪˋnɪʃəl] (v.) 簽姓名的首字母
3 **stipulation** [ˏstɪpjəˋleʃən] (n.) 契約；規定；條文
4 **lawsuit** [ˋlɔˏsut] (n.)（尤指非刑事案件的）訴訟
5 **termination** [ˏtɝməˋneʃən] (n.) 終止
6 **penalty** [ˋpɛnl̩tɪ] (n.) 懲處

Useful Expressions

A Talking about changes to contracts 談論合約的修改 

1 I'm forwarding the contract for your review. Please **initial**[2] the changes we've agreed to.

我把合約寄出給您看了,請在我們彼此都同意的修改上**簽下姓名的第一個字母**。

2 As you can see, we've included the amendments we discussed in the last meeting. Once we've initialed the amendments, we can move on.

如您所見,我已加入我們在上一次會議所討論出的修正條款。一旦在修改上簽下姓名的首字母,我們就能繼續了。

3 I've got to ask you to include a **stipulation**[3] in this section that protects us from **lawsuits**[4].

我要請您在這部分加入能保護我們免於**訴訟**的**條文**。

4 They won't sign if we don't cut these early-**termination**[5] **penalties**[6].

我們如果不把提前**終止**合約的**罰則**刪除,他們就不簽約。

B Talking about signing contracts 談論簽約

5 Who are the **parties**[1] to this contract?

這份合約的**當事人**是誰？

6 Put your **John Hancock**[2] here.

在這裡**簽名**。

7 Let's look over everything before we put our names on the **dotted line**[3].

在**簽名處**簽名前，我們先來檢查所有東西吧。

8 I've attached two copies of the contract, one for your files and one for you to sign, date, and return.

我附上了兩份合約，一份是要供您存檔，另一份是請您簽完姓名日期之後要寄回來的。

9 Can you believe the **signing bonus**[4] they offered the new CEO?

你能相信他們給了新任執行長**簽約獎金**嗎？

1 **party** [`pɑrtɪ] (n.)（契約的）一方；當事人

2 **John Hancock** 〔俚語〕親筆簽名

3 **dotted line** （文件上指示簽名處的）虛線

4 **signing bonus** 簽約獎金

Please put your John Hancock here. = Please sign here.（請在這簽名。）

John Hancock（約翰·漢考克）是美國開國元老之一，也是第一位在《美國獨立宣言》上簽下自己名字的人，由於他將名字簽得華麗醒目，又大又花俏，自此以後，在美國「John Hancock」就成為「親筆簽名」的同義詞。

Review Questions

Listen to the conversations and answer the questions below.

232 **1. Why does the man want the contract to be signed?**

(A) Because he wants to get better benefits.
(B) Because he wants to work on the project.
(C) Because he wants to wrap up the project.
(D) Because he wants to start the project.

2. How long is the contract period?

(A) Two years.
(B) One year.
(C) Two months.
(D) One period.

233 **3. What was the man hoping?**

(A) That the amendments would be made.
(B) That the contract would be void.
(C) That the contract could be signed today.
(D) That the contract would be effective.

4. What needs to be changed in the contract?

(A) Some of the language.
(B) Some contractors.
(C) Some terms.
(D) Some amendments.

5. When will the contract be signed?

(A) Today.
(B) Thursday.
(C) Friday.
(D) Tomorrow.

Ans D, A, C, A, B

Part

5 對外的聯絡 Outside Correspondences and Contacts

UNIT 49 處理客訴 Dealing With Customer Complaints

C Client D David

A client who ordered Etherkid shoes calls the company's customer service center to complain. David, a customer service representative, answers the phone. 一名訂購 Etherkid 鞋款的客戶打到客服部客訴，客服專員大衛接到了電話。

C Hello, I need to talk to someone about a problem with my order.

D I can help you, **ma'am**[1]. What was the problem you had?

C Well, first of all, my order was late.

D I'm sorry to hear that. What product had you ordered?

C It was the Etherkid shoe. My order was two days late, but I didn't bother calling to check on it because we were so busy. But then, when it did come, the order was wrong! You'd sent me adult shoes, not the new kids shoes! And to **top things off**[2], I've had a terrible time getting through to someone to speak about this.

D Again, I'm sorry to hear that. Do you have your **order number**[3] on hand?

C Yes, I have it here. The order number is 19822.

D Alright, I'm looking up your order now. Here it is—OK, I can see that you ordered 40 pairs of the Etherkid on June 12. The order was shipped on June 14, which would have made it late, as I see it was sent with our standard shipping service. Now, according to our records, we sent you the Etherkid, but it seems that someone made a mistake in filling that order.

C So what should I do now?

D First of all, let me apologize for this difficulty. If you still want the Etherkid, I can send you a rush order today. When the delivery person arrives, he can pick up your original order for return.

C Yes, that sounds fine. Will I be **charged**[4] for the return?

D No, of course not!

C 你好，我有訂單的問題要找人談談。

D 我可以協助您，**女士**。請問有什麼問題呢？

C 這個嘛，首先，我訂的貨延誤了。

D 我很抱歉，請問您訂購了什麼商品呢？

C 是 Etherkid 鞋款。我訂的貨慢了兩天才到，不過由於我們很忙，所以沒有打電話確認。然而等貨品好不容易送達之後，居然送錯了！你們寄了成人鞋款給我，而不是新款的童鞋！**更糟的是**，要找人說明這個情況還非常的困難。

D 再次跟您說聲抱歉。請問您手邊有**訂單編號**嗎？

C 有，我這裡有。訂單編號是 19822。

D 好的，我現在正為您查詢訂單。現在出來了—您在 6 月 12 日訂購了 40 雙 Etherkid 童鞋，而商品於 6 月 14 日寄出。不過這是用標準運送服務寄送，所以會比較晚到。還有從我們的紀錄看來，我們是寄 Etherkid 童鞋給您，不過好像有人把訂單給寫錯了。

C 那我現在要怎麼辦？

D 首先，我要為給您造成的不便致歉。若您還要 Etherkid 童鞋，我今天可以寄急件給您。等送貨員到達時，他可以取回您原本的貨品。

C 這似乎是個可行的方法。退貨要跟我**收費**嗎？

D 當然不用囉！

1 **ma'am** [mæm] (n.) 女士
2 **top things off** 更糟／棒的是……
3 **order number** 訂單編號
4 **charge** [tʃɑrdʒ] (v.) 收費

Useful Expressions

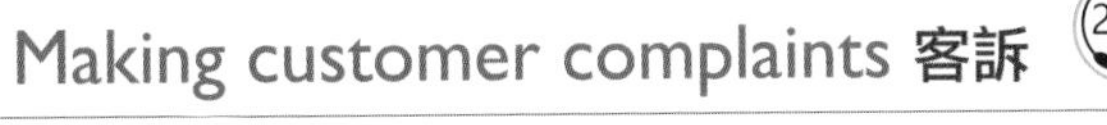

A Making customer complaints 客訴 (235)

1 The product you sent me was simply unacceptable.
你寄給我的產品完全令人無法接受。

2 I regret to inform you of the rude behavior of one of your service technicians.
很抱歉，我要告知你，你們有位技術人員行為無理。

3 It has come to my attention that the tablets you recently delivered are defective.
我收到通知說你們近期寄來的平板電腦是有問題的。

4 I am writing to express my dissatisfaction with the BlendTru blender I purchased from your company last week.
我寫信是為了表達對上星期，在貴公司購買 BlendTru 攪拌機的不滿。

B Apologizing for mistakes 為錯誤致歉

5 We are so sorry for the inconvenience caused by our mistake.
我們對因我們出錯所造成的不便感到非常抱歉。

6 Please accept our sincerest apologies for the problems with your order.
關於訂單錯誤，請接受我們最誠摯的歉意。

7 We deeply regret sending you a **faulty**[1] product.
我們對將**有瑕疵的**產品寄給您一事感到非常抱歉。

C Suggesting ways to solve a problem 建議解決問題的方法

236

8 Have you tried **troubleshooting**[2]?
你有嘗試過**疑難排解**嗎？

9 The first thing I would suggest is calling technical support.
我會先建議您打電話尋求技術支援。

10 Instead of a **refund**[3], we can offer you **store credit**[4].
我們可以提供**店內抵用金**來取代**退款**給您。

11 Before we accept the return, I have to ask you to go through the steps you took that led to the error.
接受退貨前，我必須要請您再操作一次導致錯誤的那個步驟。

12 Did you follow the instructions in the **owner's manual**[5]?
您有遵照**使用說明書**上的操作說明嗎？

13 Would you like to **exchange**[6] the product or would you like your money back?
您想要**換貨**，還是退款呢？

D Explaining actions that will be taken to solve a problem 說明解決問題所採取的行動

14 We're sending your replacement shipment right away.
我們將立即寄給您更換的貨物。

15 We will refund your credit card for the full amount.
我們會全額刷退至您的信用卡。

16 We are going to review our shipping procedures to ensure that **mix-up**[7] like this doesn't happen again.
我們將會檢討我們的運送流程，以確保類似這次的**混亂**未來不會再發生。

Review Questions

Listen to the conversations and answer the questions below.

237 1. **When did the man buy his lawn mower?**

Ⓐ Yesterday. Ⓑ Last week.

Ⓒ Today. Ⓓ The day before yesterday.

2. **What is wrong with the lawn mower?**

Ⓐ It is troubleshooting. Ⓑ It is too loud.

Ⓒ It won't start. Ⓓ The man didn't know.

3. **What does the man want?**

Ⓐ He wants to exchange the lawn mower for another one.

Ⓑ He wants to fix the lawn mower.

Ⓒ He wants the woman teach him how to fix it.

Ⓓ He wants to get a refund.

238 4. **Why does the man make this call?**

Ⓐ Because he wants to fix his order.

Ⓑ Because he wants to return a faulty product.

Ⓒ Because he wants to check his order.

Ⓓ Because he wants to make a new order.

5. **When should the man's order have been shipped?**

Ⓐ It should have been processed and shipped on the same day.

Ⓑ It should have been shipped the day after it was processed.

Ⓒ It should have been shipped using standard shipping.

Ⓓ It should have been shipped using express shipping.

Ans A, C, D, C, A

1 **faulty** [ˋfɔltɪ] (adj.) 有瑕疵的

2 **troubleshooting** [ˋtrʌbḷ,ʃutɪŋ] (n.) 疑難排解

3 **refund** [rɪˋfʌnd] (n.) 退款

4 **store credit** 儲值點數；店內抵用金

5 **owner's manual** 使用說明書

6 **exchange** [ɪksˋtʃendʒ] (v.) 更換

7 **mix-up** [ˋmɪks,ʌp] (n.) 混亂

Part 6 人事相關事宜 Personnel Matters

UNIT 50 面試應徵者 Interviewing a Job Applicant

Jacob is interviewing Thomas for a research assistant position.
雅各正在為研究助理一職面試湯瑪斯。

J Well, Thomas, your **résumé**[1] looks fine. You've clearly had some experience in the kind of work we do here, and we are definitely looking for someone with some experience.

T Yes, I've been working in **qualitative research**[2] in different **capacities**[3] for a few years now.

J Why don't you tell me a little bit about yourself? What are your career goals? Where do you see yourself in the future?

T I suppose my goals right now are to continue on this career path and take on positions of increasing responsibility. Eventually, I'd like to take on a management role, after I've had some more time to build my skills. So I guess that's where I see myself **down the road**[4]: managing and organizing projects.

J And what do you think are the most important qualities in a manager?

T That's an interesting question. I'd have to say leadership, and the ability to **motivate**[5] people and make tough choices.

J Have you ever **taken on a leadership role**[6] in a team situation? We frequently work very closely in teams here and it's important to be able to work well with others and to lead when necessary.

T Yes, there was a time, on a project I worked on last year, when I . . .

J 嗯，湯瑪斯，你的**履歷**還不錯。顯然你對我們從事的領域有些經驗，我們當然也是在找有經驗的人。

T 是的，我一直在不同的**職位**上從事**質化研究**，至今也已經好幾年了。

J 你何不向我介紹你自己？你的職涯目標是什麼？你對你個人未來的期許是什麼？

T 我想我目前的目標是繼續在這條職業道路上深造，並取得需要負擔更多責任的職位。在我有更多時間培養技能之後，希望最後能擔任管理職。這就是我對自己**未來**的期許——管理與組織專案。

J 那你認為一位經理最重要的特質是什麼？

T 這真是個有趣的問題。我必須說是領導能力，以及**激勵**人心和做出困難決定的能力。

J 你曾在團體中**擔任領導的角色**嗎？我們這裡時常要在團體中緊密合作，與團隊一起順利共事並在需要時能領導是很重要的。

T 是的，我有經驗。在去年曾經有個案子⋯⋯

1 **résumé** [ˋrɛzə͵me] (n.) 履歷表
2 **qualitative research** 質化研究
（一種非量化、非制式化的研究分析法）
3 **capacity** [kəˋpæsətɪ] (n.) 職位；工作
4 **down the road** 未來
5 **motivate** [ˋmotə͵vet] (v.) 激勵
6 **take on a leadership role**
擔任領導的角色

Useful Expressions

A Questions from job interviews 面試問題 

1	Tell me about yourself.	請介紹一下你自己。
2	Tell me about your educational background.	請介紹一下你的教育背景。
3	How has your college experience prepared you for this job?	你的大學經驗對於這份工作有何幫助？
4	What do you think you can **bring to the table**[1]?	你認為你能**帶來**什麼**貢獻**？
5	What would you say are your best and worst qualities?	你認為自己最大的優點跟缺點是什麼？
6	Are you more detail-**oriented**[2] or are you a **big-picture**[3] type?	你是更注意細節還是關注大方向的類型？
7	Where do you see yourself in five years' time?	你對於這五年的時間有什麼規劃嗎？
8	Can you tell me about a time you had to work on a team? What did you contribute and what was the result of your work?	你能告訴我你在團隊中工作的一次經驗嗎？你有什麼樣的貢獻以及成果為何？
9	What **qualifications**[4] do you have that you believe would make you successful here?	你認為自己有什麼**條件**能在這裡成功發展？
10	How do you handle stressful situations?	你如何處理壓力大的情況？
11	What questions do you have for us?	你有什麼問題想問我們嗎？

B Answering questions in job interviews 回答面試問題 

12 I focused on social media marketing during my degree. I learned how to target and engage with online communities on various social media networking sites and, in this way, spread a brand's message to new audiences.

在學期間我特別關注社群媒體行銷。我學習到如何在各種社交媒體網站中，找到目標的網路社群而加以融入，並藉由這些方法傳播品牌訊息給新的受眾。

13 Many of my courses were practice oriented and involved working with real cases, so I had had a lot of exposure to the business world during my studies. I also joined several business projects and completed a six-month long internship.

我所修習的許多課程都是以實務為導向，包含執行實際專案，因此在學期間我已有大量接觸企業界的經驗。我也參與過幾個商業專案，並且完成為期六個月的實習。

14 I believe that by joining your company I'll be able to **leverage**[5] everything that I have already learned and also gain more hands-on experience.

我相信成為貴公司的一員後，能夠**發揮**所學的一切，並且獲得更多實務經驗。

15 I joined the Georgia Institute of Technology, where students and teachers work with real companies to solve real problems. We completed several projects for local organizations, the biggest one being a fundraising campaign for a local charity.

我就讀於喬治亞理工學院。在那裡，師生與實體企業合作，一起解決實際的問題。我們為當地機構完成了許多專案，其中最大的案子是為了當地慈善機構所籌畫的募捐活動。

1 **bring (sth.) to the table** 做出貢獻
2 **-oriented** [ˋorɪɛntɪd] 以……為導向的
3 **the big-picture** 大方向
4 **qualification** [ˏkwɑləfəˋkeʃən] (n.) 能力；資歷；條件
5 **leverage** [ˋlɛvərɪdʒ] (v.) 以現有資源盡可能取得最多的利潤或好處

16 I took a course called Social Media Marketing for Community Work, which involved cooperating with a local charity. I was shocked by the poverty in many of the surrounding communities, and so I decided to take the lead in initiating a community funding drive to raise contributions. I developed a content marketing strategy with my classmates, as part of which I wrote articles for the campus paper and organized a benefit concert. Eventually, we generated over $300,000 in donations. As a result of this experience, I went on to lead other major projects as you can see from my resume.

我曾修過一門名為「社區工作的社群媒體行銷」的課程，其中包括與一間當地慈善機構合作。許多鄰近社區相當貧困，這讓我非常震驚。為了提高捐款，我於是決定帶頭舉辦社區募款活動。我和同學發展出一種內容行銷策略，其中包括為大學報撰寫報導，以及籌畫慈善演唱會。最後，我們募得超過 30 萬美元的善款。有了這次的經驗後，我持續帶領其他重要的專案，詳情可參閱我的履歷。

17 I would love to bring my innovative mindset, drive, and love for the community to the work that you have been doing for a long time.

我想帶著創新的思維、決心與對社區的熱愛，投入這份您經營已久的工作中。

18 I'm creative and analytical, and also experienced in the specific product-design **conventions**[1] of this industry. So, in this role, I'll be able to propose exciting but workable projects and ensure that the results meet customer needs.

我很有創意、善於分析，同時對這行特定產品的**傳統設計手法**有豐富的經驗。因此，在這個職位上，我能夠提出令人興奮且可行的專案計畫，而且成果能滿足消費者的需求。

19 I'm particularly skilled at writing. I've worked for CBA Magazine for six years and produced numerous **compelling**[2] articles. Readers especially appreciate my articles on travel and **cuisine**[3] around the world. I believe my skills in this area can **substantially**[4] benefit your team.

我尤其專精於寫作，曾在 CBA 雜誌社任職六年，撰寫出無數**引人入勝**的文章。讀者特別喜歡我寫的世界各地旅遊文和**美食**文。我相信，我在這方面的技能對於您的團隊助益**良多**。

20 I tend to focus too much on details and sometimes be too self-critical. However, I am aware of these habits and now **deliberately**[5] stop for a moment after I've being working for a long period of time and review my project outline. This helps me reorient myself and focus on the big picture so that I can properly manage my time and complete the project before the **deadline**[6].

我常太過於專注細節，有時對自己太吹毛求疵。不過，我知道自己有這些習慣，所以現在我在工作了很長一段時間後，會**刻意**停下來，反思一下專案計畫的要點。這有助於我重新調整自己，專注於大局，這樣我就能妥善管理自己的時間，在**期限**之前完成專案。

21 In five years' time I would like to be a successful professional in marketing and advertising. I'd like to have substantially developed my skill set—in particular my **proficiency**[7] with design software—and also have gained valuable industry experience by working with a variety of clients.

五年後，我想成為一名成功的行銷廣告方面的專業人士。我希望我的專業技能得到充分的發展，尤其是我設計軟體的**能力**，同時希望透過與各種客戶的合作，從中獲得寶貴的產業經驗。

22 In addition to creativity, I very much enjoy working with other people, which is also **vital**[8] for a **copywriter**[9]. I always get along well with my colleagues, and I love working in groups and exchanging ideas with people. I feel this keeps me and the others in my team motivated and inspired, which in turn leads to successful projects.

除了創意特質之外，我非常喜歡與人共事，這對**廣告企劃文案**來說**相當重要**。我和同事向來相處融洽，也喜歡團隊合作、與人交換想法。我認為這會讓我和同組的組員們不斷有動力和靈感，而這反過來又促成許多成功的專案計畫。

1 **convention** [kənˋvɛnʃən] (n.) 慣例
2 **compelling** [kəmˋpɛlɪŋ] (adj.) 引人入勝的；激動人心的
3 **cuisine** [kwɪˋzin] (n.) 美食
4 **substantially** [səbˋstænʃəlɪ] (adv.) （程度上）大大地
5 **deliberately** [dɪˋlɪbərətlɪ] (adv.) 故意地
6 **deadline** [ˋdɛdlaɪn] (n.) 截止期限
7 **proficiency** [prəˋfɪʃənsɪ] (n.) 精通；熟練
8 **vital** [ˋvaɪtl̩] (adj.) 極其重要的
9 **copywriter** [ˋkɑpɪraɪtɚ] (n.) 廣告企畫文案撰稿人

23 I tend to **concentrate**[1] on tasks rather than on the stress they cause. For example, I usually have two or more projects **ongoing**[2] at the same time, and to stay on top of them, I break them down into individual tasks and create a schedule for their completion. So rather than getting stressed over the enormity of **juggling**[3] several large projects, I simply stay focused on completing one task after the other. By working in this way I am able to **minimize**[4] stress and complete projects to deadline without becoming overwhelmed.

與其一直聚焦在工作帶來的壓力上，我更**專注於**工作本身。例如，我手上通常同時有兩個或更多專案在進行。為了掌控每個專案的進度，我會把它們分解成單個任務，然後製作任務的進度表。因此我只要專注於完成一個接一個的任務就好，不用因為**同時處理**許多大案子而倍感壓力。透過這種工作方法，我能夠**將**壓力**降到最低**，並且在期限內從容地完成專案。

24 I'd like to ask what you would expect me to achieve in the first two months.

我想請問，您期望我在到職後兩個月內達成哪些目標。

C Talking about aptitude[5] and chances for a job 談論才能與工作機會

25	I'm afraid you might be **overqualified**[6] for this position.	你的**資歷**就這個職位來說恐怕**過高**。
26	He's definitely a **team player**[7].	他一定是位優秀的**團隊合作者**。
27	Zach's a **shoo-in**[8] for Vice President of Operations.	札克選營運副總一定**穩贏**的。
28	Her qualifications are **impeccable**[9].	她的條件**好極了**。
29	His **CV**[10] is very impressive, but he didn't do well in the interview.	他的**履歷**非常出色，但他在面試時卻表現不佳。
30	I just don't think he can **cut it**[11] here.	我就是認為他**無法勝任**。

Review Questions

Listen to the conversations and answer the questions below.

1. **How did the man feel at his previous job?**
   - (A) He was usually relaxed.
   - (B) He was usually swamped.
   - (C) He was usually energetic.
   - (D) He was usually motivated.

2. **What has the woman probably already read?**
   - (A) The man's résumé.
   - (B) The man's resignation letter.
   - (C) The man's job description.
   - (D) The man's cover letter.

3. **What kind of characteristics does the woman probably have?**
   - (A) She is detail-oriented.
   - (B) She sees the big-picture.
   - (C) She is a team player.
   - (D) She has self-discipline.

4. **Where did the woman learn teamwork?**
   - (A) From her previous job.
   - (B) From her volunteer work.
   - (C) From her student days.
   - (D) From her neighborhood.

5. **How long has the woman been working in teams?**
   - (A) At least three years.
   - (B) Three months.
   - (C) Since her last job.
   - (D) For four years.

Ans B, A, C, B, A

1 **concentrate on** 專注於……
2 **ongoing** [ˋɑn͵goɪŋ] (adj.) 持續進行的
3 **juggle** [ˋdʒʌgl̩] (v.) 同時做兩種或以上的事情
4 **minimize** [ˋmɪnə͵maɪz] (v.) 使減到最少
5 **aptitude** [ˋæptə͵tjud] (n.) 才能；資質
6 **overqualified** [ˋovɚˋkwɑlə͵faɪd] (adj.) 資歷過高的
7 **team player** 擅於團隊合作者
8 **shoo-in** [ˋʃu͵ɪn] (n.) 必勝者
9 **impeccable** [ɪmˋpɛkəbl̩] (adj.) 無懈可擊的
10 **CV** 履歷表
11 **cut it** 勝任工作

UNIT 51 說明公司福利 Explaining the Benefits of the Company

Jacob is explaining company benefits to a prospective research assistant, Thomas. 雅各正在跟未來的研究助理湯瑪斯解釋公司福利。

J We think our benefits package is pretty competitive. We offer a **cafeteria plan**[1] of benefits, so you can choose the ones that are most important to you. All employee benefits, except for stock options and vacation time, begin immediately.

T That sounds great. What is your vacation policy?

J You are **eligible**[2] for vacation days after six months; then, you start accruing vacation days at the rate of two per month. Any days that you don't use in one year can be rolled over to the next. After two years with the company, you get three days per month. And, of course, even though you don't get vacation days during the first six months, you can take sick leave.

T Fair enough. And I remember from the manual that you have a retirement plan and an employer matching program. I'm very happy about that.

J Yes, I think it's a pretty good deal. I'm not sure what the **cap**[3] is on employer contributions, but I can look that information up for you.

T Terrific.

J In addition to that, I think we've got a very open and welcoming **corporate culture**[4]. We really do encourage **innovative**[5] thinking, and we do our best to promote people from within, so this is a good place to start out.

1 **cafeteria plan** 有彈性的福利計畫
2 **eligible** [ˋɛlədʒəbl̩] (adj.) 有資格的
3 **cap** [kæp] (n.) 最高限度
4 **corporate culture** 企業文化
5 **innovative** [ˋɪnə͵vetɪv] (adj.) 創新的

J 我認為我們提供的公司福利相當具有競爭力。我們提供**有彈性的福利計畫**，所以你可以選擇對你來說最重要的福利。除了股票選擇權跟年假之外，所有的員工福利都立即生效。

T 聽起來很不錯的樣子。那公司放假的規定呢？

J 六個月之後你便**享有**年假，並且每個月可累積兩天的假期，一年內沒放完的假期可以累積到明年。在公司做滿兩年後，一個月變成有三天假期。當然，即便你在前六個月沒有年假，你還是能請病假。

T 相當合理。我記得在手冊上有看到退休計畫與雇主提撥方案，對此我感到很滿意。

J 沒錯，我認為這非常的划算。不過我不清楚員工提撥的**上限**，我能替你查看那項資訊。

T 太好了。

J 除此之外，我們**公司的文化**非常開放而寬容。我們相當鼓勵**創新的**思考，盡其所能提拔公司內的員工，這裡是個大展身手的好地方。

Useful Expressions

A Talking about company benefits 談論公司福利 

1 We offer complete medical and dental insurance.
我們提供完整的醫療與牙醫保險。

2 We offer an **employer-matched** 401k **retirement plan**[1].
我們提供了 401k **員工退休計畫**。

3 How long will it be until I'm fully **vested**[2]?
要多久我才能全**權使用**?

4 We provide **paid leave**[3] for all **Federal holidays**[4] as well as ten days of sick leave per year.
所有**國定假日**我們都提供**有薪假**,一年也有十天的病假。

5 After six months, you are eligible for two weeks of **paid vacation**[5] per year.
你在工作六個月後,每年便享有兩個禮拜的**有薪假**。

6 You may want to take advantage of our employee **stock options**[6].
或許你會想使用我們的員工**股票選擇權**。

7 You might be interested in our **profit-sharing**[7] plan.
你可能會對我們的**分紅**計畫有興趣。

B Talking about positive aspects of a job 談論工作的優點

8 Many of our employees are eligible for **telecommuting**[8] for at least a few days a month.
我們許多的員工每個月都可在家**遠距工作**幾天。

9 They don't pay as well as some other places, but they have a great corporate culture.
他們的薪水不如其他家公司來得優渥,但他們的企業文化極佳。

10 I find the people there to be very supportive and collaborative, not **cutthroat**[9], as they can be in other companies.
我覺得那裡的人不像其他家公司的人一樣**競爭激烈**,反而是非常相互支持合作的。

1 **employer-matched retirement plan** 員工退休計畫
2 **vested** [ˋvɛstɪd] (adj.) 有權使用的
3 **paid leave** 有薪假
4 **Federal holidays** (美國的)國定假日
5 **paid vacation** 有薪假

Review Questions

Listen to the conversations and answer the questions below.

248 **1. What would the man like more of?**

Ⓐ Sick leave. Ⓑ Vacation time.
Ⓒ Dental time. Ⓓ Retirement plan.

2. What is good about the company benefits?

Ⓐ They offer paid holidays.
Ⓑ They offer medical insurance.
Ⓒ They offer brand new office supplies, including a laptop.
Ⓓ They offer profit-sharing.

249 **3. When will the man be 100% vested in the company's matching contributions?**

Ⓐ Immediately. Ⓑ After one year.
Ⓒ After three years. Ⓓ It is up to his supervisor.

4. How much will the employer match?

Ⓐ 3% per month. Ⓑ 13% per month.
Ⓒ 30% per month. Ⓓ 100% per month.

5. What is the limit the employee can contribute?

Ⓐ 3% per month. Ⓑ 30% per month.
Ⓒ The cap. Ⓓ There is no known limit.

Ans B, D, C, A, D

6 **stock options** 股票選擇權
7 **profit-sharing** [ˋprɑfɪtˌʃɛrɪŋ] (n.) 分紅
8 **telecommuting** [ˌtɛlɪkəˋmjutɪŋ] (n.) 遠距離工作
9 **cutthroat** [ˋkʌtˌθrot] (adj.) 猛烈的

UNIT 52 交涉薪資 Negotiating the Salary

 J Jacob T Thomas

J Let's talk about **compensation**[1]. What kind of salary are you hoping for?

T Well, I'd like to be earning a salary that reflects the current standard for my position.

J And that is . . . ?

T 32,000 to 39,000 US dollars per year.

J Right. That sounds like a reasonable range. Now, I see that at your current position you're making 34,000 US dollars per year. Would you consider that a reasonable salary?

T I would really be hoping for an increase, based on my previous performance and on the responsibilities in this position.

J I've got to tell you, our **base rate**[2] for this position is 33,000. I could try for more, but you've got to tell me what it will take to **bring you onboard**[3].

T I guess I've got to ask for more than 34,000. But if the salary is going to become a **sticking point**[4], maybe we can talk about adding benefits.

J 我們來談談**薪水**吧，你希望的待遇是多少？

T 我希望的薪資是能反映我目前職位的標準。

J 所以那是……？

T 一年 32,000 到 39,000 美金。

J 好，聽起來在合理範圍內。我知道你目前的工作一年是 34,000 美金，你認為這是合理薪資嗎？

T 按我之前的表現與此職位的職責看來，我真的希望可以加薪。

J 我必須跟您說，我們這個職位的**基本薪資**是 33,000 美金。我可以替您爭取加薪，不過您要先告訴我，要有什麼條件您才會**接受這個職位**。

T 我想我要有 34,000 美金以上才行，不過要是薪水成為**癥結點**，或許可以談談多一點的福利。

Useful Expressions

A Negotiating salary 交涉薪資 

1 I think you'll find that my current worth in this industry is at the higher end of this salary range.
我想您會發現以我目前在業界的價值，遠超過此薪資的範圍。

2 Let's talk about **alternative compensation**[5].
我們來談談**彈性待遇**吧。

3 Can you tell me what has been budgeted for this position?
您可以告訴我此職位有多少預算安排嗎？

4 I'm afraid that's more than we can offer for this position.
這恐怕超出我們能提供給此職位的範圍了。

5 I want to be fairly compensated for my skills and experience level.
我希望以我的技能與經歷能得到同等的報酬。

6 I think the national average for this position is higher than what you're offering.
我認為此職位在國內的平均薪資都比您的開價來得高。

7 We're prepared to offer you a signing bonus.
我們已準備好要提供簽約獎金給你了。

8 What was your **final level of compensation**[6] at your last position?
你在上一個工作中的**最高薪資**是多少？

1 **compensation** [ˌkɑmpənˋseʃən] (n.) 報酬（包含薪資、福利等）
2 **base rate** 基本薪資
3 **bring sb. onboard** 使接受職位
4 **sticking point** 癥結點
5 **alternative compensation** 彈性待遇
6 **final level of compensation** 最高的薪資

B Talking about salary negotiations 談論薪水的交涉

9 If the company is **booming**[1], I will ask for your top range.
如果公司**發展得很好**的話，我會替你爭取最高範圍的薪資。

10 The company is really **tightening its belt**[2], and it's definitely going to affect salaries.
公司正在盡量**縮減成本**，薪資勢必會因此而受到影響。

11 Don't go into your salary negotiation and wing it; be prepared!
別在交涉薪資時隨性發揮，要做好準備才行！

12 I think the salary they offered me reflects the **wage gap**[3] between men and women.
我認為他們提供給我的薪水反映出男女**薪資的差異**。

13 Make sure you get what you want! Don't **sell yourself short**[4]!
要確保自己得到想要的！可別**小看自己**了！

14 There's always some **wiggle room**[5] in these negotiations.
這幾次的談判總還有討論的**餘地**。

1 **booming** [ˋbumɪŋ] (adj.) 蓬勃發展的
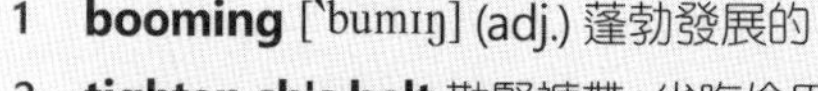
2 **tighten sb's belt** 勒緊褲帶；省吃儉用
3 **wage gap** 薪資差異
4 **sell sth./sb. short** 小看某事／某人
5 **wiggle room** 彈性空間

Review Questions

Listen to the conversations and answer the questions below.

252 **1. What is happening in the industry?**

Ⓐ It is getting smaller.
Ⓑ It is trying to reduce costs.
Ⓒ It is booming.
Ⓓ It is fragmented.

2. What does the woman ask the man?

Ⓐ What the key components of the position are.
Ⓑ What the minimum acceptable salary for the position is.
Ⓒ What the company planned to pay for the position.
Ⓓ Whether there is the possibility to have more paid leave.

253 **3. Which best describes the company's attitude to offering salary?**

Ⓐ The company was flexible about the salary range offered.
Ⓑ The company was inflexible about the salary range offered.
Ⓒ The company was unwilling to add other benefits to the salary.
Ⓓ The company offered a higher salary than the man expected.

4. What is the man thinking?

Ⓐ He is hoping for a raise later.
Ⓑ He is satisfied with the salary he accepted.
Ⓒ He is not going to take the job.
Ⓓ He is going to negotiate more later.

Ans B, C, B, A

UNIT 53 聘用新員工 Hiring a New Employee

254 J Jacob C Caroline

Jacob and Caroline are talking about looking for a new receptionist.
雅各跟卡洛琳正在談找新的接待員一事。

J I'm really busy right now, as you know, so I was hoping you could be the one to run interviews and pick the new hire.

C Certainly! Is there a job description or a **skills inventory**[1] somewhere that I could look at? Do you look for any particular qualifications that don't seem **self-evident**[2]?

J No, nothing you wouldn't think of. **Familiarity**[3] with phones is great; someone who's **punctual**[4], who's a **self-starter**[5], who's organized. To put a notice on the website, you'll have to get in touch with the **webmaster**[6] and ask him to put the job posting in the "Careers" section.

C Do you ever place **want ads**[7] in the paper or on other websites?

J We usually **garner**[8] enough interest through our own website, but you are welcome to put more ads out if you want. When you put the ad out, make sure you ask for at least one reference.

J 妳也知道我目前真的很忙，所以我希望妳能負責應徵流程，選出新員工。

C 沒問題！有職務說明或是**技能清單**能給我看看嗎？你有沒有特定的隱含條件呢？

J 沒有，全部妳都想得到。最好對電話很**熟悉**、**準時**、**自動自發**，還有做事要有條理。要在網站上刊登消息的話，妳要聯絡**網站管理員**，請他將職缺放在「工作機會」那區。

C 你有在報紙上或其他網站刊登過**徵才廣告**嗎？

J 通常透過我們的網站就能**獲得**不少的關注了。不過妳要的話，也能多刊些廣告。刊出廣告時，務必要求至少一位推薦人。

1. **skills inventory** 技能清單
2. **self-evident** [sɛlf`ɛvədənt] (adj.) 顯而易見的
3. **familiarity** [fə,mɪlɪ`ærətɪ] (n.) 熟悉
4. **punctual** [`pʌŋktʃuəl] (adj.) 守時的；準時的
5. **self-starter** [,sɛlf`startɚ] (n.) 做事主動的人
6. **webmaster** [`wɛb,mæstɚ] (n.) 網站管理員
7. **want ad** 徵才廣告
8. **garner** [`garnɚ] (v.) 獲得

Useful Expressions

A Talking about needing a new employee 談論徵才需求 (255)

1 We definitely need **another pair of hands**[9] around here.
我們這裡絕對需要**額外的援手**。

2 With Jeremy moving up, we'll need someone to **fill his shoes**[10].
傑若米升遷後，我們需要找個人**接手他的工作**。

3 They really need a new engineer—they're **swamped**[11].
他們真的需要一位新的工程師——他們**忙得不可開交**。

4 There's so much **turnover**[12] here. As soon as we hire someone new, another person leaves.
這裡的**員工流動率**很高。每當我們找到新員工，就又有人離職了。

9 **another pair of hands** 額外的援助
10 **fill sb's shoes** 接替某人的位置或工作
11 **swamped** [swampt] (adj.) 忙得不可開交的
12 **turnover** [ˋtɝnovɚ] (n.) 員工流動率

B Talking about orienting a new employee 談論新進員工訓練

5 The half-day **orientation**[1] will help you get **up to speed**[2].

為期半天的**新進員工訓練**會幫助你了解最新狀況。

6 We're going to have you **shadow**[3] Charles for a day, to get a sense of your day-to-day duties.

為了要讓你知道你的日常工作職務，今天我們要讓你**跟**在查爾斯的身邊一天。

7 Would you be willing to **buddy up**[4] with the new salesperson for a day?

你願意**陪**新來的業務人員訓練一天嗎？

C Describing jobs 說明職務

8 In this position, you will identify major gift prospects, write, edit, and analyze reports, and assist the development manager in identifying and meeting the division's ongoing needs/activities.

在這個職位上，你將確認主要的潛在捐贈者，撰寫、編輯與分析報告，以及協助研發經理找出並達成部門正在進行的需求／活動。

9 The lead systems engineer coordinates with R&D to incorporate customer requirements into system features, **delineates**[5] system specifications, and provides technical **expertise**[6] and training to business development teams.

首席系統工程師與研發人員相互協調，將客戶的要求納入系統特點中，**說明**系統規格以及提供**專業技術**與訓練給商業發展團隊。

10 Project managers must create, **execute**[7], and revise project work plans according to the changing needs of the project; they must also **allocate**[8] resources and assign responsibilities to team members, manage daily implementation of work plan, and review deliverables before presenting them to the client.

專案經理必須設計、**執行**以及依照專案的需求變化來修改專案的工作計畫；還必須**分配**資源、指派職務給團隊的隊員，管理每日執行的工作計畫，並在交給客戶之前，先檢查過待送的貨物。

1 **orientation** [ˌorɪɛnˋteʃən] (n.) 員工訓練
2 **up to speed** 了解最新情況
3 **shadow** [ˋʃædo] (v.) 跟隨
4 **buddy up** 陪同
5 **delineate** [dɪˋlɪnɪet] (v.) 描述
6 **expertise** [ˌɛkspɚˋtiz] (n.) 專門知識；專門技術
7 **execute** [ˋɛksɪˌkjut] (v.) 執行
8 **allocate** [ˋæləˌket] (v.) 分配；分派

Review Questions

Listen to the conversations and answer the questions below.

256 **1. Why does the man want to hire a new employee?**

(A) Because an old employee has left.
(B) Because the company is growing.
(C) Because he is too busy.
(D) Because he is asked to do so by his supervisor.

2. What will the woman do?

(A) Speak to acquaintances about the new opening.
(B) Advertise on a website.
(C) Apply for the new job.
(D) Recommend this position to all of her friends.

3. When would they like to start to interview?

(A) Within the week.
(B) Within the month.
(C) Within the quarter.
(D) As soon as possible.

257 **4. What does the man ask the woman to do?**

(A) Become a shadow.
(B) Produce a shadow.
(C) Be quiet.
(D) Follow Glenda's actions.

5. What won't the woman read in the handbook?

(A) Employment law.
(B) Insurance benefits.
(C) Company policies.
(D) Other employee's profile.

Ans B, A, D, D, D

UNIT 54 稅務事宜 Tax Issues

  Jacob　T Thomas

Jacob is giving Thomas his new hire tax forms to fill out.
雅各把新進員工的稅單交給湯瑪斯去填寫。

J Here you go, Thomas, I suppose you've seen these before.

T Yes, they're just the standard forms, right?

J That's it. Here's the **IRS Form W-4**[1], to set up your **income tax withholding**[2]. You don't have any **dependents**[3] yet, do you?

T No, it's just me.

J Then you won't end up with many **exemptions**[4]. I'll let you fill these out now. If you have any questions, please come and get me. Oh, and did you bring your **Social Security Card**[5] or passport? I need to copy some government identification.

T Yes, I have my passport right here.

J Thomas 這給你。我想你之前就看過這些了吧？

T 是的，這些就是標準表格對吧？

J 正是。這是要給你設定**所得稅預扣稅額**的**國稅局 W-4 稅單**。你沒有任何**受撫養人**吧？

T 沒有，只有我一人而已。

J 那你就沒有辦法**減免稅額**了。你現在就把這些填好吧，有疑問的話再來找我。對了，你有帶**社會安全卡**還是護照嗎？我要影印幾張政府的身分證明。

T 有，護照就在這裡。

1 **IRS Form W-4 (Employee's Withholding Allowance Certificate)** 美國國稅局 W-4 表格，員工預扣稅證明書
2 **income tax withholding** 所得稅扣繳稅額
3 **dependent** [dɪˋpɛndənt] (n.) 受撫養人
4 **exemption** [ɪgˋzɛmpʃən] (n.) 稅金減免
5 **Social Security Card**（美國）社會安全卡

Useful Expressions

A Talking about tax forms and procedures 談論稅務表格與流程

1 We've got to report the new hire to the state **registry**[6].
我們要將新聘職員的資料呈報到國家**登記處**。

2 Has the company sent out **W-2s**[7] yet?
公司寄**報稅單**了沒？

3 There's always so much **red tape**[8] to work through in a new position.
要開始新職務前，總是要經過一堆**繁瑣的手續**。

4 Do you think I can list my home repairs as a **tax deduction**[9]?
你認為我能將房子整修列入**減稅**項目中嗎？

6 **registry** [ˋrɛdʒɪstrɪ] (n.) 登記處
7 **IRS Form W-2 (Wage and Tax Statement)**
美國國稅局 W-2 表格，工資與稅務證明書
8 **red tape** 多餘繁瑣的政府規定或手續
9 **tax deduction** 減稅

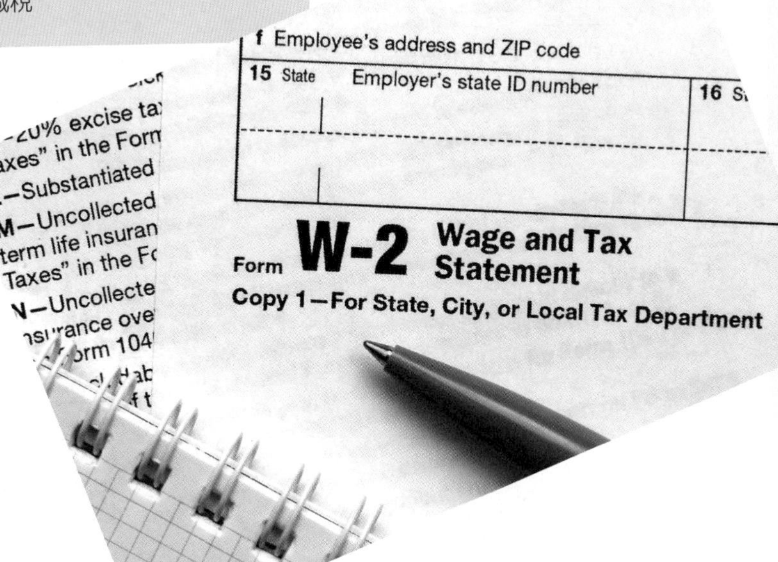

B Talking about taxation 談論稅收制度

5 I can't believe how high **payroll taxes**[1] are.

我真不敢相信**薪資稅**這麼高？

6 I just moved into a new **tax bracket**[2] and the additional amount I have to pay is unbelievable!

我剛換到另一個**稅率級距**，真無法相信要額外付這麼多的稅金！

7 I've waited until the last minute to file my **tax return**[3].

我到了最後一刻才辦理**納稅申報**。

8 We've only got three more days to file our taxes.

我們只剩三天能報稅。

1 **payroll tax** 薪資稅
2 **tax bracket** 稅率級距
3 **tax return** 納稅申報單

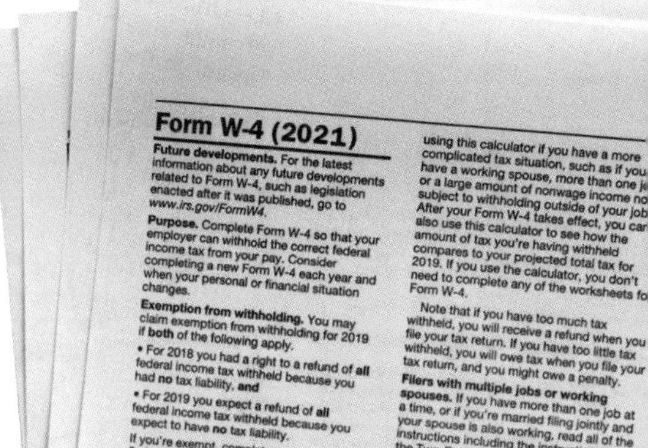

Review Questions

Listen to the conversations and answer the questions below.

1. **What has the man forgotten?**
   Ⓐ His résumé or CV.
   Ⓑ His Social Security Card or passport.
   Ⓒ His credit card or wallet.
   Ⓓ His membership card or driver's license.

2. **Where will the man pay taxes?**
   Ⓐ In the state where he lives.
   Ⓑ In the state where he works.
   Ⓒ In the state where he was born.
   Ⓓ It doesn't matter.

3. **Who deals with tax paperwork**?
   Ⓐ The woman.
   Ⓑ The man.
   Ⓒ The state.
   Ⓓ Human Resources.

261

4. **What is the woman afraid of?**
   Ⓐ That too much tax will be taken out of her paycheck.
   Ⓑ That too little tax will be taken out of her paycheck.
   Ⓒ That tax will be taken out of her paycheck.
   Ⓓ That there will be no tax taken out of her paycheck.

5. **What does the woman prefer to do?**
   Ⓐ Pay more taxes now.
   Ⓑ Pay more taxes later.
   Ⓒ Pay more exemptions.
   Ⓓ Pay less taxes forever.

Ans B, A, D, B, A

UNIT 55 保險事宜 Insurance Issues

Thomas is talking to the human resources officer, Justine, about the insurance plan at his new job.
湯瑪斯正在和人資部主管賈斯汀討論他新職務的保險方案。

J So, have you got any questions about your insurance package?

T Well, I can't see what my **premium**[1] is. Can you show me how much it will be?

J Sure, but remember, there are different premiums for different insurance packages. We pay 90% of your premium, so if you choose this package, you'll pay 100 dollars a month. If you choose the lower premium option, you'll pay 50 dollars a month.

T Oh, alright. And then what's my **deductible**[2] going to be?

J Well, that depends on the package you choose. The package with a lower premium has a higher deductible, and **vice versa**[3].

T OK, I get it. And do the plans cover the same things?

J Not exactly. The more expensive plan has more extensive **coverage**[4], including **dental**[5] care and eye exams.

T Hmm. It would be nice to have that coverage.

1 **premium** [ˋprimɪəm] (n.) 保險費用
2 **deductible** [dɪˋdʌktəbl̩] (n.)（保險）自付額
3 **vice versa** 反之亦然
4 **coverage** [ˋkʌvərɪdʒ] (n.) 涵蓋範圍
5 **dental** [ˋdɛntl̩] (adj.) 牙科的

J 你對自己的保險方案有任何疑問嗎？

T 這個嘛，我不知道**保險費**是多少耶。你可以告訴我要多少費用嗎？

J 當然沒問題，不過不同的保險方案，保險費用也會不同。90% 的保費由公司負擔，所以如果你選擇此方案，每個月便需負擔 100 美元。要是你選保費較低的方案，每個月便只需負擔 50 美元。

T 好的。那我的自付額是多少？

J 這個嘛……這要視你選的方案而定。保費較低的方案**自付額**就會比較高，**反之亦然**。

T 好，那我知道了。那這些方案都提供相同的給付項目嗎？

J 並不全然是如此。較貴方案的給付**涵蓋項目**較廣，還包含了**牙科**保健與視力檢查。

T 嗯……有這樣的給付很不錯呢。

Useful Expressions

A Talking about types of insurance 談論保險類別

1 Do I really need to get **life insurance**[1]?
我有需要保**壽險**嗎？

2 Have you got **homeowners or renters insurance**[2]?
你有保**屋主或是承租人保險**嗎？

3 The company **medical insurance**[3] doesn't cover dental procedures.
該公司的**醫療保險**無給付牙科常規的項目。

4 If Uriah gets laid off, at least he can get on **COBRA**[4].
要是尤來亞遭到裁員，至少還有**「統一綜合預算協調法案」保險方案**可使用。

B Talking about insurance coverage 談論保險給付

5 They're telling me that my **policy**[5] doesn't cover this procedure.
他們告知我的**保單**無法給付此項療程。

6 Does this policy cover **liability**[6] or only damages?
這份保單有給付**責任險**，還是只有損失費用呢？

7 Will my **spouse**[7] be covered by my policy?
我的保單能保障我的**配偶**嗎？

8 Is there a **pre-existing condition**[8] **clause**[9] in this plan?
此方案有**既有疾病條款**嗎？

1 **life insurance** 壽險
2 **homeowners/renters insurances** 屋主／承租人保險
3 **medical insurance / health insurance** 醫療險／健康保險
4 **COBRA (Consolidated Omnibus Budget Reconciliation Act)**
統一綜合預算協調法案方案（即失業健保補助）
5 **policy** [ˋpɑləsɪ] (n.) 保單
6 **liability** [ˏlaɪəˋbɪlətɪ] (n.) 責任險
7 **spouse** [spaʊz] (n.) 配偶
8 **pre-existing condition** 既有疾病
9 **clause** [klɔz] (n.)（法律文件的）條款

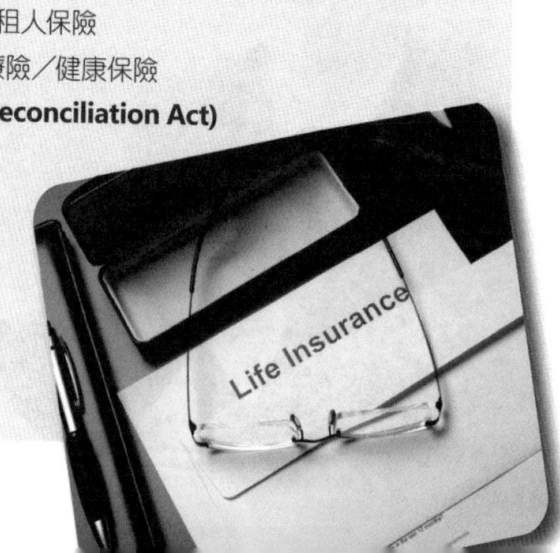

Review Questions

Listen to the conversations and answer the questions below.

264 **1. Who is the woman most likely?**

(A) A hiring manager. (B) A receptionist.
(C) A new employee. (D) An interviewee.

2. At this company, who pays for most of the monthly health insurance costs?

(A) The company.
(B) The employees.
(C) It is unknown.
(D) The company and employee share the cost equally.

3. Why is the woman unsure about working for the company?

(A) Because she would like better medical insurance.
(B) Because she would like higher premiums.
(C) Because she would like other benefits.
(D) Because she would like a higher level of compensation.

265 **4. What did the man just find out?**

(A) His health insurance is canceled.
(B) His health insurance won't pay for dentist visits.
(C) His health insurance is minimal.
(D) His health insurance costs too much.

5. Whom will the man go speak to?

(A) The woman. (B) His boss.
(C) Human resources. (D) The CEO.

Ans D, B, A, B, C

UNIT 56 升遷 A Promotion

266 J Jacob K Katharine

Jacob tells Katharine they'd like to give her more responsibility.
雅各告知凱薩琳他們要讓她負責更多職務。

J I'm sure you know that we're very pleased with the work you've done as a research assistant here. We've noticed how you take initiative and really **think outside the box**[1] in order to get things done.

K Thank you.

J Well, thank you. The point of this is that due to our recent growth and the several new projects we're working on, we need a new analyst, and we'd like you to take on this new role. It would mean more responsibility in terms of assisting project managers and learning to do more complex analyses—and, of course, it would also mean an increase in your salary. Do you think you would be interested in taking on this new role?

K Absolutely! Thank you very much.

J That's great news. I'll send you a specific job description and salary range so you can understand a little more about what your different duties would be. Can you give me your official answer by the end of the week?

K Of course. Thank you for this opportunity.

J 相信妳也清楚，我們對妳擔任研究助理任內的表現感到非常滿意。我們也注意到妳為了達成目標，採取主動積極的態度並**跳脫框架去思考**。

K 謝謝你。

J 我們才要謝謝妳。重點是由於最近的成長和我們在做的幾個新專案，我們需要一名新的分析師，希望妳能接下這個職位。這也表示會有更多的責任，包括協助專案經理、學習做更加複雜的分析，當然這也代表會幫妳加薪。妳有意要接下這個新職務嗎？

K 當然沒問題！非常謝謝你。

J 這真是個好消息。我會將具體的職務說明以及薪資範圍寄給妳，妳可以稍微了解職務的不同之處。這週結束前可以給我正式的答覆嗎？

K 沒問題。謝謝你給我這個機會。

1 **think outside the box**
跳出傳統的思維框架去思考

Useful Expressions

A Talking about increased responsibilities 討論增加的職務

1	I'm really excited to **take on**[1] more responsibilities.	我迫不及待要**接下**更多職務了。
2	She's going to have to learn to **delegate**[2] in this new role.	她在新職位要學會**分派**工作。
3	He's really **moving up the ranks**[3]!	他真的**升官**了呢!

B Talking about improved positions in the company 討論公司內部升遷

4 Kim will **be in the corner office**[4] pretty soon!

金不久後就要**升遷**了!

5 Lila's networking really paid off—she's **got the boss's ear**[5] now.

莉亞的交際總算有代價——她現在**受到老闆的重視**了。

6 I want to connect with upper management, but I'm just not good at **schmoozing**[6].

我想與高層有所交流,卻又不擅於**閒聊**。

7 Olivia **is up for**[7] **supervisor**[8], I think.

我想奧莉薇亞被**列入主管職位**的**考慮**之中。

C Talking about changed salaries 討論薪資的改變

8 I hear Jorge is going to get a huge **raise**[9] for this.

我聽說霍黑會因此而受到大幅**加薪**。

9 They say we're going to get a 4% increase **across the board**[10].

他們說我們會**全體**加薪 4%。

10 After the promotion, my whole **compensation**[11] package changed.

我的整體**薪資**在升遷後改變了。

11 Jane said there won't be a **cost of living**[12] increase this year!

珍說今年不會有**生活津貼**!

Review Questions

Listen to the conversations and answer the questions below.

268

1. Who has worked for the company longer?

Ⓐ The man. Ⓑ The woman.
Ⓒ Sam. Ⓓ Uriah.

2. What is Uriah probably not good at?

Ⓐ Delegating. Ⓑ Schmoozing.
Ⓒ Analyzing. Ⓓ Giving presentations.

3. What is one of the benefits of the promotion being discussed?

Ⓐ Travel. Ⓑ Late nights.
Ⓒ Interesting work. Ⓓ Networking.

4. What is one of the drawbacks of the new position?

Ⓐ Travel. Ⓑ A raise.
Ⓒ Different work. Ⓓ Networking.

5. Is the woman more inclined to take the job or refuse the job?

Ⓐ Take the job. Ⓑ Refuse the job.
Ⓒ It is unclear.

Ans D, B, C, A, A

1 **take on** 承擔
2 **delegate** [ˋdɛləget] (v.) 分派
3 **move up the ranks** 升遷
4 **be in the corner office** 升遷
5 **have/get sb's ear** 受到某人的重視
6 **schmooze** [ˋʃmuz] (v.) 閒聊
7 **be up for** 被列入考慮
8 **supervisor** [ˋsupɚˏvaɪzɚ] (n.) 主管
9 **raise** [rez] (n.) 加薪
10 **across the board** 全面性的
11 **compensation** [ˏkɑmpənˋseʃən] (n.) 薪水
12 **cost of living** 生活津貼

Part 6 人事相關事宜 Personnel Matters

UNIT 57 人事異動 A Change in Personnel

  Jacob　Ⓐ Ann　Ⓚ Katharine　Ⓒ Caroline

Jacob tells his team that he'll be moving to another branch.
雅各告訴所有團隊成員他要調任到別家分公司。

Ⓙ Thanks for coming, everybody. I wanted to make sure that you all heard this from me: I'm going to be **transferring**[1] to the Austin branch next month. I'm sad to be leaving all of you, but I'm very excited about the opportunities I'm going to have in Austin, so this is both good and bad news.

Ⓐ Oh no! I'm happy for you, Jacob, but we're going to miss you.

Ⓙ And I'll miss this team!

Ⓚ You're leaving next month?

Ⓙ Yes, my last day here will be the fifth. They aren't sure who is going to step into my position yet, but I'll let you know as soon as I do. I do know that they are probably going to bring in an **outsider**[2], so there will be some new faces around here. That's always a positive thing, I think. A little **fresh blood**[3] **rejuvenates**[4] everyone!

Ⓒ So, is this going to affect any of our current projects?

Ⓙ No, it shouldn't. By next month, we'll be in the **home stretch**[5] of all our current projects. It may mean that we don't start anything new until my replacement is here, so he or she won't have to **play catch-up**[6].

J 感謝各位前來，我想確認各位是從我口中得知此事，那就是——下個月我就要**調**到奧斯汀的分公司了。我很捨不得離開各位，卻又對即將能在奧斯汀大展身手的機會感到期待，所以這是個好壞參半的消息。

A 噢不！雅各，我真替你感到開心。我們會想念你的。

J 我也會想念大家的！

K 你下個月就要離開了嗎？

J 沒錯，我在公司的最後一天是五號。他們尚未確定誰來接我的職務，但等我一知道就會立刻告訴大家。我是知道他們可能會請**外面的人**，所以會有幾位新成員加入。我想這是件好事，**新成員**的加入可以**使**大家**精神為之一振**！

C 那這樣會影響到我們目前手上的案子嗎？

J 不，應該不會。我們目前所有的案子到下個月就進入**最後階段**了，也就是說在替補我的人到職前，我們都還不用著手新計畫，所以新人也用不著**趕進度**。

1 **transfer** [træns`fɚ] (v.) 調任
2 **outsider** [ˌaʊt`saɪdɚ] (n.) 外人
3 **fresh blood** 新人；新血
4 **rejuvenate** [rɪ`dʒuvənet] (v.) 使恢復活力
5 **home stretch** 最後階段
6 **play catch-up** 趕進度

Useful Expressions

A Talking about movement within a company 談論公司內部異動 

1 Is this going to be a promotion or a **horizontal move**[1]?
這會是升遷還是**同層調動**?

2 I'm really hoping to be transferred soon.
我非常希望很快就能調職。

3 She just feels ready to **part ways**[2] with ABC, Inc., and we wish her the best.
她覺得是**離開** ABC 公司的時候了,我們祝她一切順利。

4 I'm glad it's only a **transfer**[3] and I'm not being let go. This isn't really a place with great **job security**.[4]
我很高興只是**調職**,而不是被裁員。在這裡工作還真沒保障。

5 It's a **double-edged sword**[5]: on the one hand, I'm really glad to have been promoted. On the other, I'm so sad about leaving all of you!
這**有好有壞**:我一方面很開心能得到升遷,一方面又捨不得離開大家!

B Talking about company changes that affect personnel 談論影響公司人事的異動

6 All this **downsizing**[6] is causing big changes around headquarters.
所有的**裁員**都造成總公司的重大異動。

7 A lot of people are going to be **laid off**[7] or moved due to the **restructuring**[8].
許多人因為公司重整而即將被**解僱**或是**調動**。

8 I don't know what's going to happen to Alan and Marcia when they **eliminate**[9] their department.
不知道高層將艾倫與瑪希亞的部門**裁撤掉**後,接下來他們會怎麼樣。

1 **horizontal move** 同層調動
2 **part ways** 分離
3 **transfer** [ˋtræns͵fɚ] (n.) 調職
4 **job security** 工作的穩定性
5 **double-edged sword** 人、事、物的正反兩面
6 **downsizing** [ˋdaʊn͵saɪzɪŋ] (n.) 裁員
7 **lay off** 解僱
8 **restructuring** [riˋstrʌktʃɚɪŋ] (n.) 重整;改組
9 **eliminate** [ɪˋlɪmə͵net] (v.) 去除

Review Questions

Listen to the conversations and answer the questions below.

1. **What will happen to the assistant managers who are not let go?**
   - (A) They will continue with their current jobs.
   - (B) They will assume new positions with less pay.
   - (C) They will continue managing with less pay.
   - (D) They will stay on the same team.

2. **Why are the assistant managers leaving?**
   - (A) Because the company no longer wants assistant managers.
   - (B) Because they are being fired for poor performance.
   - (C) Because they are asking for too much money.
   - (D) Because there will be new hiring in the near future.

3. **What is the man worried about?**
   - (A) Restructuring.
   - (B) Fresh blood.
   - (C) Being asked to take a pay cut.
   - (D) Losing his job.

4. **What is Abdul's position?**
   - (A) A team member.
   - (B) A computer engineer.
   - (C) A manager.
   - (D) A temp.

5. **What is going to happen to the two departments?**
   - (A) They are going to be eliminated.
   - (B) They are going to be merged.
   - (C) They are going to be downsized.
   - (D) They are going to be extended.

Ans B, A, D, C, B

UNIT 58 辭職 Resignation

J Jacob　A Ann

J Hi, Ann. What did you want to see me about?

A Well, there's no easy way to say this: I'm **giving my notice**[1]. I've been offered a management position at a company in New York. I've always wanted to work there, and I feel I've got to take this opportunity.

J Wow! Well, that's a **bombshell**[2]. I'm happy for you, of course. When do you plan to leave?

A Oh, I can stay through the end of the month. I just got the offer, but I wanted to give you as much advance notice as possible.

J I appreciate that. Oh dear, we'll be sorry to see you go. Are you sure there's nothing we can do to keep you here?

A Thanks, but I don't think so. I am very sad to leave, but I think it's the right time.

J 嗨，安。妳找我有什麼事？

A 嗯，很難啟齒……我是要**遞辭呈**。我獲得紐約一家公司所提供的管理職位，我一直想要到那裡工作，所以覺得要把握這個機會。

J 哇！這可真是個**震撼彈**。我當然替妳高興囉，那妳何時要離職？

A 我可以待到月底。我才剛得到這個工作機會，不過想儘早通知你。

J 謝謝妳這麼做。哎呀，我們很捨不得妳離開，妳確定沒有任何辦法可以挽留妳嗎？

A 謝啦，不過不用了。我很難過要離開這裡，但我想也是時候了。

1 **give (one's) notice**
遞交辭呈；（事先）提出離職通知

2 **bombshell** [ˋbɑm͵ʃɛl] (n.) 震撼彈

Useful Expressions

A Telling your boss you are resigning 告知老闆你要離職

1 It is difficult for me to tell you this, but I've decided to leave the company.
我很難向你開口說這件事，但我已決定要離開公司了。

2 I think it's time for me to go in a different direction.
我想是時候要邁向另一個領域了。

3 I'm sorry to say I've got to give notice.
我很抱歉要提出離職通知。

4 I wanted to let you know that I'm **resigning**[3].
我想跟你說，我要**離職**了。

B Announcing your resignation in a letter 以信件告知辭職消息

5 It is with sadness that I am **submitting**[4] my written notice of **resignation**[5] from TechPro, **effective**[6] two weeks from today.
我很難過要**遞交**從科技專業公司離職的書面通知，從今天起兩個星期後**生效**。

6 I **hereby**[7] announce my resignation as Sales Director of Home Pro.
我**特此**宣布辭去家庭專門公司業務主管一職。

7 I am writing to officially **tender**[8] my resignation from AtoZ Industries.
我來函**正式提出** AtoZ 企業的離職聲明。

8 Please accept this letter as formal notification of my resignation, effective immediately.
請接受此封信為我的正式離職通知信，並立即生效。

9 This letter is to inform you that my last day will be Friday, June 24, two weeks from today.
此信是要通知您，從今天算起兩個星期後，6 月 24 日的星期五將會是我最後的工作日。

10 This letter confirms my resignation as Office Manager.
此信批准我辭去公司經理一職。

3 **resign** [rɪˋzaɪn] (v.) 辭職
4 **submit** [səbˋmɪt] (v.) 提交
5 **resignation** [͵rɛzɪgˋneʃən] (n.) 辭呈
6 **effective** [ɪˋfɛktɪv] (adj.) 生效的
7 **hereby** [͵hɪrˋbaɪ] (adv.) 特此（用於公文）
8 **tender** [ˋtɛndɚ] (v.) 正式提出

C Talking about time with a company 談論在公司的時光 (276)

11 I will always appreciate the opportunities I was given at Next, Inc.
我會永遠感謝奈克斯特公司曾給過我的機會。

12 My years at Western, Inc. have been a time of great personal and professional growth.
在我任職於威斯頓公司多年的時間，是一段個人與專業上獲益良多的時光。

13 Working at Innovation, Inc. has been a wonderful experience and one I will always **hold dear**[1].
任職於創新公司是一個很棒的經驗，我會永遠**好好珍惜**。

D Explaining reasons for resigning 說明離職原因

14 I will be accepting a position at Berkely Brothers, Inc.
我會接受柏克利兄弟公司提供的職務。

15 I have accepted the position of Marketing Manager at Yosemite Clothing.
我已答應了優仙美蒂服飾的行銷經理一職。

16 I realize that I need to spend more time with my family.
我發現我要多花一點時間與家人相處。

17 In the end, I realized I had to **quit**[2] in order to **pursue**[3] my art full-time.
我最終還是覺得要**辭去**工作，全力發展我的藝術專長。

1 **hold dear** 珍惜；重視
2 **quit** [kwɪt] (v.) 辭職
3 **pursue** [pɚˋsu] (v.) 追求

Review Questions

Listen to the conversations and answer the questions below.

1. **What is Sara planning to do?**
   - (A) She is going to resign.
   - (B) She is going to go home.
   - (C) She is going to finish a project.
   - (D) She is going to take a long break.

2. **Why is Sara quitting?**
   - (A) Because she is getting a promotion.
   - (B) Because she's found a job with a higher salary.
   - (C) Because she's happy here.
   - (D) Because she's not happy here.

3. **Why is the woman quitting?**
   - (A) Because she wants to spend more time at home.
   - (B) Because she thinks it is the time to visit a school.
   - (C) Because she was offered another position.
   - (D) Because she wants to go back to school.

4. **When will the woman's last day be?**
   - (A) This Friday.
   - (B) Next Friday.
   - (C) This Monday.
   - (D) Next Monday.

5. **Why is the man in a difficult position?**
   - (A) Because the woman's position is difficult to fill.
   - (B) Because the woman hasn't given him much notice.
   - (C) Because the woman has classes to take.
   - (D) Because he and the woman are very close friends.

Ans A, B, D, A, B

UNIT 59 同事間的聚餐 A Lunch Gathering Between Colleagues

 W Waiter K Katharine A Ann C Caroline

Katharine, Ann, and Caroline are having lunch at a restaurant.
凱薩琳、安和卡洛琳正在一家餐廳享用午餐。

W The soup **du jour**[1] is gazpacho.

K I'll have that. Does anyone else want an **appetizer**[2]?

A I would. I'd like the pear salad. Can I make a **substitution**[3], though? Could I please have it with walnuts instead of almonds?

W That should be no problem.

C And we'll all **split**[4] the fried calamari.

W I'll be back in a moment with your drinks.

A OK . . . I feel bad saying this, but have you noticed what Carla's been wearing lately?

C Oh, my goodness, I'm so glad you brought it up! I can't believe she's going to sales meetings like that! She looks so sloppy!

A I know! I wonder if Jonas even notices. If she keeps it up, someone might have to talk to her about it.

K I don't think Jonas is paying attention to much these days. He always seems to be **flustered**[5]. I think he's finding he **bit off more than he could chew**[6] in his new role.

A I've been getting that feeling also. I hope he **gets it together**[7]. I really like working with him.

W **今日**湯品是西班牙番茄冷湯。

K 我要點那個。還有人要點**開胃菜**嗎?

A 我要梨子沙拉。可是我可以**換**東西嗎?我能把沙拉的杏仁改成胡桃嗎?

W 應該沒問題。

C 我們一起**共享**炸花枝圈。

W 我即刻回來送上您們的飲料。

A 好了……說到這就覺得不太好意思,不過你們有沒有注意到卡拉最近的穿著?

C 我的天啊,很高興妳提到這個!我不敢相信她穿成那樣出席業務會議,看起來有夠邋遢的!

A 沒錯!不知道喬納斯有沒有注意到,如果她繼續這樣,可能會有人找她談談這件事。

K 我不認為喬納斯最近有在管事,他老是一副慌慌張張的樣子。我認為他可能在新職位上發現自己接下過多工作而無法處理。

A 我也是這麼覺得。希望他能早日上手,我很喜歡與他共事。

1 **du jour** [du`ʒur] (adj.) (法語)當日的
2 **appetizer** [`æpə͵taɪzɚ] (n.) 開胃菜
3 **substitution** [͵sʌbstə`tjuʃən] (n.) 更換;代替
4 **split** [splɪt] (v.) 分享
5 **flustered** [`flʌstɚd] (adj.) 慌張的
6 **bite off more than one can chew** 自不量力;貪多嚼不爛
7 **get it together** 將事情處理妥當

Useful Expressions

A Restaurant etiquette 餐廳禮儀 

1	I think we need a few more minutes before we order.	我們還需要幾分鐘才能點餐。
2	Can we get another menu, please?	可以再給我們一份菜單嗎?
3	Could we move to a quieter table, please?	請問能換到安靜一點的座位嗎?
4	I'm sorry, I'm afraid I didn't order this.	不好意思,我沒有點這個。

B Ordering food 點餐

5	I'll take the corn chowder, please.	麻煩你，我要點玉米巧達濃湯。
6	Could I please get an order of onion rings?	能麻煩給我一份洋蔥圈嗎？
7	We're going to share a large pizza, so could we have an extra plate?	我們要共享一份大披薩，所以能多給我們一個盤子嗎？
8	Please put my **dressing**[1] **on the side**[2].	請把我的**沙拉醬另外放**。
9	Is it possible to get the pasta special without ham?	義大利麵特餐可以不要加火腿嗎？

C Discussing the bill 討論帳單 

10	OK, **what's the damage**?[3]	好，**總共多少錢？**
11	I've got this one.	這次我來付。
12	Let me **cover you**[4] this time—you paid last week!	上禮拜是你請的，這次讓我**請你**！
13	This is **my treat**[5].	這次**我請客**。
14	This one**'s on Sally**[6]—she just got a big raise!	這攤**算莎莉的**——她才剛被大大加薪呢！

D Office gossip 辦公室八卦

15	Have you heard what they're saying about Jordan?	你有聽說他們說了喬丹什麼嗎？
16	You've got to keep this very **hush-hush**[7].	你一定要保守這個秘密。
17	I'll tell you when they're going to announce the results, but you've got to **keep it under your hat**[8].	等他們要宣布結果時我再告訴你，但你一定要**保守秘密**。
18	What do you think I should tell Uma when I hand in my resignation?	你覺得當我交出辭職信時，要跟烏瑪說什麼？
19	I can't believe Tom **spilled the beans**[9] about Jim being **canned**[10].	我真不敢相信湯姆把吉姆被炒的事說出來了。

Review Questions

Listen to the conversations and answer the questions below.

282 1. **What does the man mean by "what's the damage"?**

Ⓐ How much is the bill? Ⓑ What was damaged?

Ⓒ How much did the woman pay? Ⓓ How bad is the situation?

2. **What will the woman do?**

Ⓐ She will split the bill. Ⓑ She will pay the entire bill.

Ⓒ She doesn't want the bill. Ⓓ She will pay next time.

3. **What does the woman expect her new position to be?**

Ⓐ Lucrative. Ⓑ Busy. Ⓒ Exciting. Ⓓ Boring.

283 4. **What does the woman want for her meal?**

Ⓐ Some Ketchup. Ⓑ Minestrone soup.

Ⓒ Handmade fish. Ⓓ Rockfish.

5. **What does the woman want the man to do?**

Ⓐ Keep a secret. Ⓑ Tell her a secret.

Ⓒ Give her the news. Ⓓ Gossip with her.

Ans A, B, B, B, A

1 **dressing** [ˋdrɛsɪŋ] (n.) 沙拉醬
2 **on the side** 裝在另一個盤子裡
3 **What's the damage?** 多少錢？
4 **cover sb.** 替某人付費
5 **my treat** 我請客
6 **be on sb.** 由（某人）請客
7 **hush-hush** [ˋhʌʃ,hʌʃ] (adj.) 秘密的
8 **keep sth. under one's hat** 保守秘密
9 **spill the beans** 洩密
10 **can** [ˋkæn] (v.)〔美國口語〕解僱

UNIT 60 年終獎金 Year-end Bonuses

 K Katharine T Thomas

K I'm glad they're giving bonuses this year. That'll really help me with my Christmas shopping.

T Yeah, you're not the only one.

K Apparently, they couldn't give them last year, though they still had the big holiday party. I'd rather have a bonus than a party, to be frank.

T Me, too. Do you know what they base the bonuses on? Is it **seniority**[1], performance, or something else?

K I'm really not sure. I think the amounts are based on some mathematical **equation**[2] that has to do with salaries and time with the company, but performance might have something to do with it as well. After all, the bonuses come right after our year-end **performance reviews**[3].

T Yes, I'd think they'd have something to do with performance. How are the performance reviews? Painful?

K No, they're really not bad. If you're not doing well, someone will let you know long before your review time. There aren't any surprises.

1 **seniority** [sinˋjɔrətɪ] (n.) 年資
2 **equation** [ɪˋkweʒən] (n.) 方程式
3 **performance review** 績效考核

K 今年有發獎金我真是太高興了。這對我的耶誕採購幫助不少。

T 對啊，妳不是唯一的一位。

K 雖然去年有盛大的假期派對，但他們明顯發不出年終獎金。老實說，我寧願要獎金而不要派對。

T 我也是。妳知不知道獎金是以何作基準？是**年資**、績效，還是其他的呢？

K 我真的不確定。我想獎金金額是依據某些數學**公式**，跟在公司的薪資與年資有關吧。不過績效應該也有影響，畢竟是在年終**績效考核**後才發獎金的。

T 沒錯，我覺得獎金一定跟績效有關。績效考核進行得如何，很慘嗎？

K 不，還不差。如果你做不好，會有人在考核之前告訴你，不會有出乎意料的事。

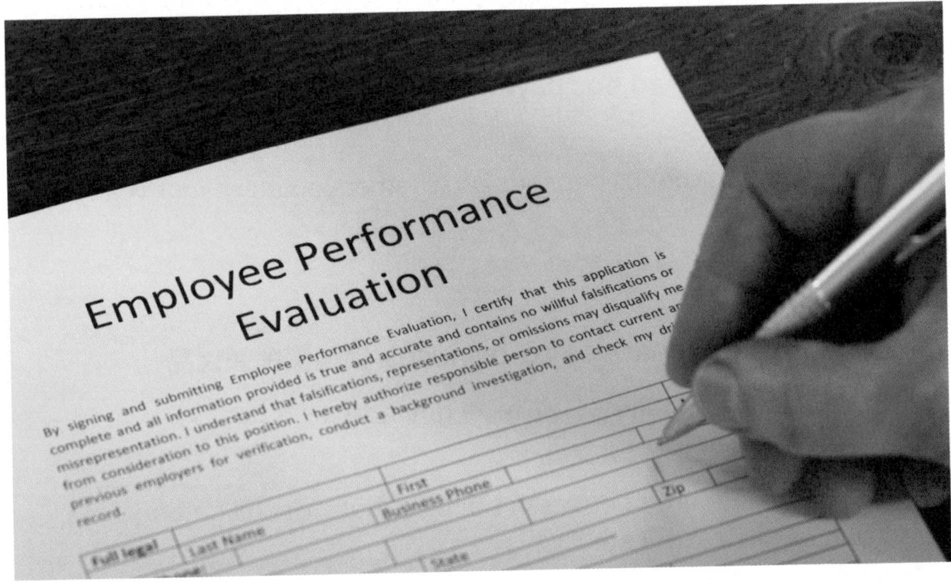

▲ performance review 績效考核

▼ year-end party/banquet 尾牙

Useful Expressions

A Talking about bonuses 談論獎金

1 It's important for us to give some kind of bonus, just to keep **morale**[1] up.

為了要提振**士氣**，給予一些獎金對我們來說是很重要的。

2 I'm not sure how we're going to **divvy up**[2] the year-end **bonus pool**[3].

我不確定我們要如何**分配**年終**獎金**。

3 Our bonuses count as **ad hoc payments**[4].

我們的獎金被當做**特別款**。

4 The amount of your bonus depends on whether you meet your yearly sales goals.

你的獎金金額取決於你是否有達到年度的業績目標。

B Talking about alternatives to bonuses 談論獎金替代品

5 Jenny says instead of bonuses, we're all going to get a ham.

珍妮表示我們會拿到火腿，而不是獎金。

6 They've cut the amount of our cash bonuses, but we're all getting some kind of **gift certificate**[5].

他們刪除了我們的現金紅利，但我們有拿到幾種**禮券**。

7 The profits this year weren't enough to cover employee bonuses.

今年的獲利不足以支付員工的獎金。

1 **morale** [mə`ræl] (n.) 士氣
2 **divvy up** 分配
3 **bonus pool** 獎金總額
4 **ad hoc payment** 特別款（專門為了某種目的、個案或場合而特別提撥的款項，不算在正式薪水中）
5 **gift certificate** 禮券

Review Questions

Listen to the conversations and answer the questions below.

1. What does the woman want to know?

(A) She wants to know how much her bonus will be.
(B) She wants to know when bonuses will be given.
(C) She wants to know what bonus amounts are based on.
(D) She wants to know whether they will have the bonus.

2. How does the company give out bonuses?

(A) Equally across the board.
(B) Based on yearly performance.
(C) Based on employee salaries.
(D) Based on customer feedback.

3. Why does the woman feel disappointed?

(A) Because she thinks equal bonuses are the worst.
(B) Because she thinks performance-based bonuses make people work harder.
(C) Because she thinks the bonus pool is too small.
(D) Because she thinks she deserves more bonus.

287

4. What is true about the man?

(A) He is angry about the bonus situation.
(B) He is going to complain to his supervisor.
(C) He was expecting a big bonus.
(D) He just learned about the bonus situation.

5. Why is the woman so angry?

(A) Because she has hated the bonus situation since she got in.
(B) Because she doesn't like gift certificates.
(C) Because her contract was violated.
(D) Because she feels she is being cheated.

Ans C, A, B, D, D

UNIT 61 員工旅遊 Staff Outings

(288) K Katharine A Ann

Katherine and Ann are at an annual staff outing.
凱薩琳和安正在參加一年一度的員工旅遊。

K It's funny, I'm never excited about these corporate **outings**[1], but I always have fun when I get here.

A Ha, I feel the same way. I think it's because management gets so enthusiastic about it. It's hard not to **get swept up**[2] in their excitement.

K Absolutely. Now, are the afternoon **team-building exercises**[3] **mandatory**[4]?

A I think so, but you can choose which ones you want to participate in.

K That's good. And then the CEO will give us his annual **pep talk**[5] before dinner?

A Yes. I'm interested in how he's going to **spin**[6] the recent **layoffs**[7] into something to be cheerful about!

K 說來有趣，我從未期待過公司**旅遊**，但每次參加又會玩得很開心。

A 哈，我也這麼覺得。我想這是因為高層對這非常熱衷，很難不**被**他們的興奮之情所**影響**。

K 正是。下午的**團隊建立活動**是**強制**參加嗎？

A 我想是的。不過妳可以選擇自己想參加的。

K 太好了。然後執行長會在晚餐前向大家發表年度**激勵演說**嗎？

A 是的。我很好奇他要如何將最近的**裁員**風波說得令人開心。

1 **outing** [ˋaʊtɪŋ] (n.) 郊遊；短途旅遊
2 **get swept up (in sth.)** 受到（某事的）影響
3 **team-building exercise** 團隊建立活動（用來提升工作成員之間的信任和溝通的一種活動）
4 **mandatory** [ˋmændə͵torɪ] (adj.) 強制性的
5 **pep talk** 鼓勵性演說
6 **spin** [spɪn] (v.) 編造
7 **layoff** [ˋleɔf] (n.) 解僱

Useful Expressions

A Types of staff outings 員工旅遊類型

1	Are we going to have another **retreat**[8] this year?	我們今年又有**旅遊**了嗎？
2	Is it time for the company picnic already?	是時候舉辦公司野餐會了嗎？
3	The staff trip to Arizona is next month.	要去亞利桑那州的員工旅遊就在下個月。
4	Everyone loves the yearly golf outing.	大家都非常喜歡一年一度的高爾夫球之旅。

B Planning staff outings 策劃員工旅遊

5	Next year I'm going to join the **events committee**[9] to see if I can plan a retreat that will actually be fun.	明年我將要加入**活動事務委員會**，看是否能策劃一次真正好玩的旅遊。
6	What kind of **facility**[10] will we need for the activities?	這些活動要辦在哪種**場地**才好？
7	We need to set up the **duty roster**[11] as soon as possible.	我們要儘快訂出**輪值表**。
8	Let's ask if they have a **party suite**[12].	我們來詢問他們是否有**團體房**。
9	Should we ask people who plan to attend to register for seats?	我們應該讓想參加的人去登記座位嗎？
10	I think we should suggest that staff members arrange **carpools**[13].	我想我們要建議員工們安排**共乘**。

8 **retreat** [rɪˋtrit] (n.) 旅遊（一般指到度假勝地，一邊進行團隊訓練、一邊度假之活動）
9 **events committee** 活動事務委員會
10 **facility** [fəˋsɪlətɪ] (n.) 場所
11 **duty roster** 輪值表
12 **party suite** 團體房
13 **carpool** [ˋkɑr͵pul] (n.) 共乘

Types of Staff Outings 員工旅遊的形式

hiking 健行

bicycle riding 騎自行車

golf 高爾夫球

paintball 漆彈

barbecue 烤肉

water activities 水上活動

dinner party 聚餐

karaoke 卡拉 OK

board game 桌遊

picnic 野餐

kart racing 卡丁車競賽

movie night 電影之夜

C Staff outing activities 員工旅遊活動

11	It's time for the speeches to start, I think.	我想是時候開始演講了。
12	There's going to be a volleyball **tournament**[1] between all the **remote offices**[2]!	所有的**分公司**將有一場排球**錦標賽**!
13	We can have hayrides and treasure hunts for the kids.	我們可以替小孩辦農車搭乘活動跟尋寶遊戲。
14	I'm hungry. Where's the **buffet**[3]?	我肚子好餓，**自助餐區**在哪裡?

1 **tournament** [ˋtɝnəmənt] (n.) 錦標賽
2 **remote office = branch office** 分公司
3 **buffet** [bəˋfe] (n.) 自助式吃到飽餐廳

Review Questions

Listen to the conversations and answer the questions below.

290 1. **What event is the company going to arrange?**

Ⓐ A baseball tournament against a business competitor.

Ⓑ A free live television baseball game-watching in the meeting room.

Ⓒ A meetup for baseball fan.

Ⓓ A baseball outing.

2. **What is the company going to charge for?**

Ⓐ Tickets. Ⓑ Refreshments.

Ⓒ Transportation. Ⓓ Registration.

291 3. **How often the retreat is probably held?**

Ⓐ Annually. Ⓑ Monthly.

Ⓒ Weekly. Ⓓ Irregularly.

4. **Why does the company want to host a retreat according to the woman?**

Ⓐ Boost profitability. Ⓑ Increase team spirit.

Ⓒ Promote team sales. Ⓓ Seek honor.

5. **When will the retreat be this year?**

Ⓐ In October.

Ⓑ In December.

Ⓒ Sometime in September. The exact dates will be voted.

Ⓓ Sometime in September. The exact dates will be decided by the board.

Ans D, C, A, B, C

UNIT 62 安排出差
Arranging a Business Trip

 292  Jared  Caroline

Jared and Caroline are discussing a business trip to another state.
傑瑞德和卡洛琳正在討論到別州出差一事。

J The first meeting's been scheduled for 9 a.m. on Thursday, which means we should probably get to town on Wednesday night. That means taking a Wednesday morning flight, I suppose, to **be on the safe side**[1].

C Agreed. We've **accumulated**[2] a lot of **miles**[3] with Jetways Airlines; I suggest we get a ticket from them.

J Good idea. I'll tell Katharine to take care of that. So, we'll need a hotel Wednesday night and Thursday.

C And don't forget that we have dinner plans with our other clients on Thursday night. I think it would be better to come back on Friday morning than to rush through dinner in order to make a late Thursday night flight.

J You're right. So sometime today we should give Katharine our hotel preferences. I'd prefer to stay near the airport, if it's all the same to you.

C Sure. We'll need a car, too, won't we? There's no public transportation from the airport there, is there?

J I don't think so. The other big issue is our presentation materials. I don't really want to carry them through the airport. It's best to **travel light**[4].

C But I don't know if I want to trust them to a shipping company!

- Ⓙ 第一場會議的時間訂在星期四早上九點，也就是說我們應該星期三晚上就要到城裡了。我想，**保險起見**，我們要搭乘星期三早上的班機。
- Ⓒ 我同意，我們**累積**了許多傑特威航空的**里程數**，不如就向他們購票吧。
- Ⓙ 好主意，我會請凱薩琳去安排。那麼，星期三晚上跟星期四我們都需要住旅館。
- Ⓒ 別忘了我們星期四晚上還要跟其他客戶用晚餐。我想比起為趕搭星期四的深夜班機而匆忙結束晚餐，還是星期五早上回來比較好。
- Ⓙ 妳說的對，那看今天哪時候再告訴凱薩琳我們偏好的旅館。如果這對妳來說沒差的話，那我較偏好機場附近的旅館。
- Ⓒ 沒問題。那我們還需要一輛車是吧？從機場到那裡沒有大眾運輸工具可搭，對嗎？
- Ⓙ 我想沒有。另一個大問題就是簡報的器材了。我不想帶著大包小包進出機場，最好是**輕便地旅行**。
- Ⓒ 不過我不知道把那些器材交付給運輸公司可不可靠。

1. **be on the safe side** 謹慎起見
2. **accumulate** [əˋkjumjə͵let] (v.) 累積
3. **miles / frequent flyer miles** 里程數
4. **travel light** 輕便旅行

Words About Traveling 有關旅遊的物品

passport 護照

boarding pass 登機證

visa 簽證

carry-on baggage 隨身行李

airport trolley 機場推車

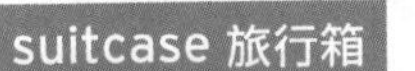
suitcase 旅行箱

briefcase 公事包

baggage tag 行李吊牌

Part 7 社交與旅遊
62 安排出差 Arranging a Business Trip

Useful Expressions

A Talking about making travel arrangements 談論旅遊的安排

1 I'm going to **be away on business**[1] for the next three days. Please tell customers they can reach me on my cell phone.
接下來三天我要**出差**，客戶找我的話，請他們打我的手機。

2 We'll have to ask Jim to reserve another room for our party.
我們要請吉姆替我們一行人再訂一間房。

3 I know it's the cheapest, but I really don't want to take a **red-eye**[2]. I'd rather be fresh for our presentation.
我知道它是最便宜的，但我真的不想搭**紅眼航班**。我希望能神清氣爽地做簡報。

4 I don't want to **check**[3] any bags. I'll fit everything into a **carry-on**[4].
我不想要**託運**任何行李，我會把所有東西都塞到**隨身行李**中。

5 We can ask at the gate if they'll **upgrade**[5] us.
我們可以在登機門那邊問問他們能不能幫我們**升等**。

B Talking about business trip activities 談論出差活動

6 I really hope we have time for a little **sightseeing**[6] while we're here.
我真的很希望我們在這裡能稍微留個時間**觀光**一下。

7 Do you think our lunch meeting will be in the hotel restaurant, or will they take us out somewhere?
你認為午餐會議會辦在飯店的餐廳，還是他們會帶我們去別的地方呢？

8 Do we have to **tip**[7] here? I don't want to make a mistake and look foolish in front of the client.
這裡要**給小費**嗎？我可不想在客戶面前犯錯出糗。

9 Have you gotten any feedback on your presentation yet?
你有獲得任何對你簡報的意見嗎？

1 **be away on business** 出差中
2 **red-eye** [ˋrɛd,aɪ] (n.) 紅眼航班
3 **check (a bag)** 託運（行李）
4 **carry-on** [ˋkæri,ɑn] (n.) 隨身行李
5 **upgrade** [ˋʌp,gred] (v.) 升等
6 **sightseeing** [ˋsaɪt,siɪŋ] (n.) 觀光
7 **tip** [tɪp] (v.) 給小費

Review Questions

Listen to the conversations and answer the questions below.

294

1. **When will the man be away on business?**
   - (A) Next week.
   - (B) Next month.
   - (C) The next day.
   - (D) Next Monday.

2. **What did the man react after he was informed about the business trip?**
   - (A) He felt a great responsibility.
   - (B) He looked forward to it.
   - (C) He was anxious about it.
   - (D) He was reluctant to go.

3. **How will the man probably spend his free time?**
   - (A) Participate in meetings.
   - (B) Go sightseeing.
   - (C) Work in his hotel room.
   - (D) Go shopping.

4. **What does the woman tell the man to do?**
   - (A) To upgrade the airline tickets.
   - (B) To sign for the materials.
   - (C) To book another night at the hotel.
   - (D) To change the flight from Friday morning to Saturday night.

5. **How will headquarters receive the meeting materials?**
   - (A) The meeting materials will be brought by the man and the woman.
   - (B) The meeting materials will be shipped by the man and the woman.
   - (C) The meeting materials will be emailed by the man and the woman.
   - (D) The meeting materials will be shared on cloud storage by the man and the woman.

Ans A, D, C, C, B

UNIT 63 訂房 Booking a Hotel Room

 Ⓗ Hotel receptionist Ⓐ Amanda

Amanda is booking a hotel room for her boss.
亞曼妲正在為上司訂旅館房間。

Ⓗ Good afternoon, Pine Top Hotel, how may I help you?

Ⓐ Hello, I'd like to reserve a **single room**[1] from September 11 to the 13. Can you tell me your rates, please?

Ⓗ A standard single room during those dates will be US$89 per night.

Ⓐ That's fine.

Ⓗ Wonderful. Do you have a floor preference? Would you like smoking or non-smoking?

Ⓐ No floor preference, and non-smoking, please.

Ⓗ And what is the name of the guest?

Ⓐ John Wallace.

Ⓗ And I'll need a credit card number to hold the room.

Ⓐ I've got that right here. Are you ready?

Ⓗ Go ahead.

Ⓐ OK, it's a Visa. The name is . . .

1 **single room** 單人房

Room Types 房間類型

ingle room 單人房

twin room 雙人房(兩小床)

double room 雙人房（一大床）

:riple room 三人房

suite 套房

quadruple room 四人房

Ⓗ 午安，這裡是松頂飯店。請問需要什麼服務嗎？

Ⓐ 妳好，我想要訂一間**單人房**，日期從 9 月 11 日到 13 日。能請妳說明房價嗎？

Ⓗ 該期間內的標準單人房每晚為 89 美元。

Ⓐ 那可以。

Ⓗ 太好了。請問您有偏好住哪一層樓嗎？吸菸房或非吸菸房呢？

Ⓐ 哪一樓都可以，麻煩要非吸菸房。

Ⓗ 請問客人貴姓大名呢？

Ⓐ 約翰·沃斯勒。

Ⓗ 我還需要信用卡號來保留房間。

Ⓐ 卡在這裡了，妳準備好要記了嗎？

Ⓗ 請說。

Ⓐ 好，是 Visa 卡，持卡人姓名是⋯⋯

Useful Expressions

A Talking about accommodations 談論住宿 297

1	Do you have smoking rooms available?	你們有空的吸菸房嗎？
2	I don't have a reservation. Do you have any vacancies tonight?	我沒有預約訂房。請問今晚還有空房嗎？
3	Can I request a room on **the ground floor**[1]?	麻煩能給我一間**一樓**的房間嗎？
4	I'd like a king-size bed, please.	我要特大尺寸的床，麻煩你。
5	I'm calling to **book**[2] a **double room**[3].	我打來是想要**訂**一間**雙人房**。
6	How much is it per night?	住一晚多少錢？
7	Does it include tax and service charge?	這個價格有含稅和服務費嗎？
8	Could you give me a discount if I stay for three nights?	住三晚的話有沒有折扣？
9	Is breakfast included?	有附早餐嗎？

B Asking about hotel features 詢問旅館設施

10	Is there a swimming pool?	那邊有游泳池嗎？
11	Do you offer **room service**[4]?	你們有提供**客房服務**嗎？
12	Do you have a gym or fitness room?	你們有體育館或是健身房嗎？
13	Do you have a business center?	你們有商務中心嗎？
14	Is wireless Internet available in the rooms or in the lobby?	房間或大廳內有無線網路可以使用嗎？

C Talking about checking in and out and payment 談論入住、退房與付款

15 What time is **check in**[5]?
入住時間是何時?

16 I know **check out**[6] is at noon, but my flight isn't until three. Can I please leave my luggage behind the desk until my taxi arrives?
我知道**退房**時間是中午 12 點,但我的班機是下午 3 點的。請問我可以將行李暫放在櫃台,等我的計程車抵達再拿走嗎?

17 I want to pay with a **corporate credit card**[7], but can I make the reservation now with a different card? I don't have the corporate card **on hand**[8].
我想以**公司的信用卡**來付款,但公司的卡目前不**在手邊**,是否能先以別種信用卡訂房呢?

18 Can I pay for my reservation in cash when I arrive?
能等我抵達時再用現金支付訂金嗎?

19 Do you accept **traveler's checks**[9]?
你們收**旅行支票**嗎?

20 I made the reservation online through a hotel-booking confirmation.
我是在一個訂房網站上預訂的。

21 Can I check in? My name is David Ridgeway, and I made a reservation through an online travel agency.
我可以辦理入住嗎?我是大衛·瑞奇衛,我是透過線上旅行社訂房的。

1 **the ground floor (= the first floor)** 〔英〕一樓
2 **book** [buk] (v.) 預定
3 **double room** 雙人房
4 **room service** 客房服務
5 **check in** 入住
6 **check out** 退房
7 **corporate (credit) card / company (credit) card** 公司信用卡
8 **on hand** 在手邊
9 **traveler's check** 旅行支票(現已少用)

Booking a Hotel Room Online 線上預訂飯店房間

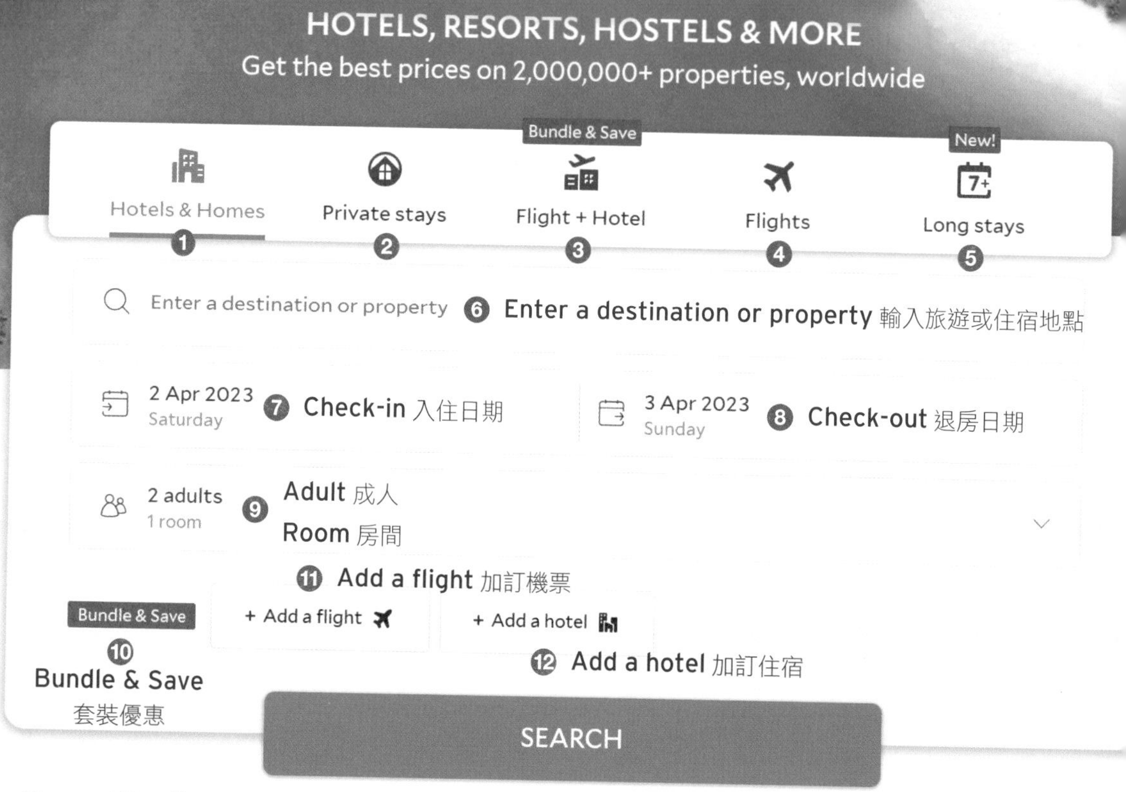

HOTELS, RESORTS, HOSTELS & MORE

Get the best prices on 2,000,000+ properties, worldwide

Bundle & Save

New!

Hotels & Homes ❶ Private stays ❷ Flight + Hotel ❸ Flights ❹ Long stays ❺

Enter a destination or property ❻ **Enter a destination or property** 輸入旅遊或住宿地點

2 Apr 2023 Saturday ❼ **Check-in** 入住日期

3 Apr 2023 Sunday ❽ **Check-out** 退房日期

2 adults 1 room ❾ **Adult** 成人 **Room** 房間

⓫ **Add a flight** 加訂機票

Bundle & Save + Add a flight + Add a hotel

⓬ **Add a hotel** 加訂住宿

⓾ **Bundle & Save** 套裝優惠

SEARCH

(Source: https://www.agoda.com)

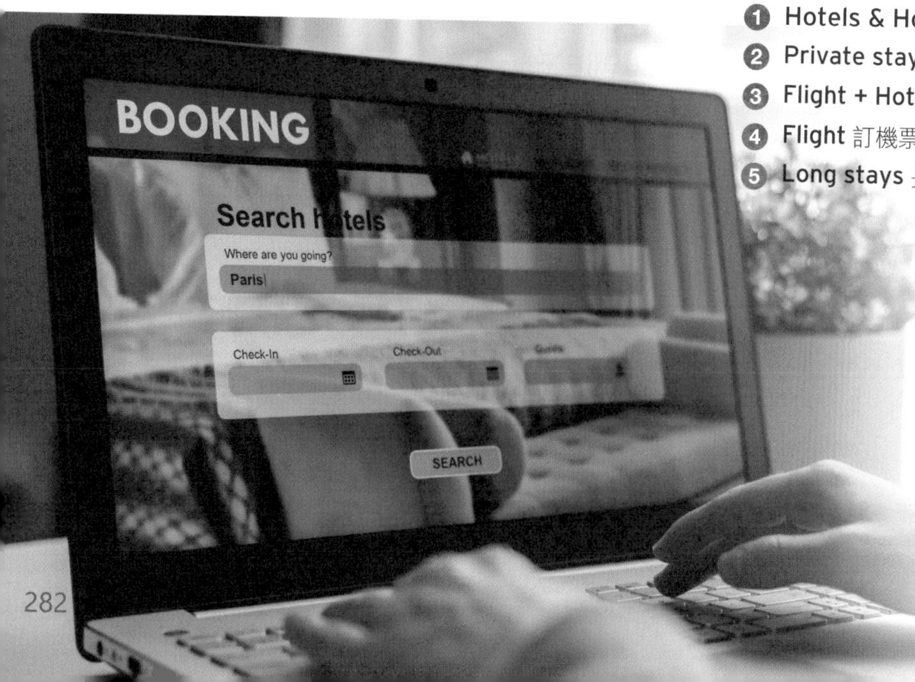

BOOKING

Search Hotels

Where are you going?

Paris

Check-In Check-Out

SEARCH

❶ **Hotels & Homes** 找住宿

❷ **Private stays** 民宿

❸ **Flight + Hotel** 機票＋住宿

❹ **Flight** 訂機票

❺ **Long stays** 長住方案

Review Questions

Listen to the conversations and answer the questions below.

300 **1. When will the man go on his trip?**

Ⓐ April 1st to 7th. Ⓑ April 2nd to 7th.
Ⓒ April 2nd to 9th. Ⓓ April 2nd to 10th.

2. Does the man smoke?

Ⓐ Yes, he smokes.
Ⓑ No, he doesn't smoke.
Ⓒ It isn't clear.

301 **3. What hotel does the woman want to stay in?**

Ⓐ The Marriot. Ⓑ A hotel with a pool.
Ⓒ The Hilton. Ⓓ A hotel with high floors.

4. What is the woman's preference?

Ⓐ She prefers an upper floor.
Ⓑ She prefers a non-smoking floor.
Ⓒ She prefers a lower floor.
Ⓓ She prefers a smoking floor.

5. How will the woman reserve the room?

Ⓐ With a personal credit card. Ⓑ With wire transfer.
Ⓒ With a company card. Ⓓ With cash.

Ans C, B, B, C, A

Part 7 社交與旅遊 Socializing and Travel

UNIT 64 確認班機與訂機票 Confirming Flights and Booking Air Tickets

 Ⓚ Katharine Ⓐ Airline representative

Katharine is confirming her boss's flight. 凱薩琳正在替她的上司確認班機。

Ⓚ Hi. I'm calling to confirm a flight this afternoon from Washington, D.C., to Seoul.

Ⓐ Certainly. What was the flight number?

Ⓚ It's 19a.

Ⓐ And do you have your reservation number?

Ⓚ I don't, but the passenger's name is John Clarkson.

Ⓐ One moment, please. Yes, you are booked for flight 19a departing from Washington Dulles Airport at 1:45 p.m., and arriving in Seoul the next day at 4:15 p.m. This is not a **direct flight**[1]. There will be a **transfer**[2] at Chicago O'Hare.

Ⓚ Right. And how long is the transfer time? I don't want to cut things too close.

Ⓐ Your flight is scheduled to land at 3:15 and the flight to Seoul leaves at 5:10. That should be plenty of time.

Ⓚ Thanks very much. Oh, and one more thing—I'd like to double check that the passenger will have window seats on all flights.

Ⓐ I'll check that now.

1 **direct flight** 直飛班機
2 **transfer** [ˋtrænsˌfɚ] (n.) 轉乘（如轉機、轉車）

Ⓚ 你好，我打來確認今天下午從華盛頓特區飛往首爾的班機。

Ⓐ 好的。請問航班編號是？

Ⓚ 19a。

Ⓐ 請問您有訂位編號嗎？

Ⓚ 沒有，但乘客姓名是約翰·克拉克森。

Ⓐ 請稍候。是的，您訂的為航班 19a 班機，下午 1:45 從華盛頓杜勒斯機場出發，於隔日下午 4:15 抵達首爾。這不是**直飛班機**，需要在芝加哥歐海爾機場轉機。

Ⓚ 好，那轉機時間是多久？我不希望時間太趕。

Ⓐ 您的飛機預計在 3:15 降落，前往首爾的班機是 5:10 起飛，時間應該相當充裕。

Ⓚ 非常謝謝。噢，還有一件事，我想確認這位乘客在所有航班中的座位都是靠窗座位。

Ⓐ 我立即為您查詢。

1. **Leaving From** 出發地
2. **Going To** 目的地
3. **Departure Date** 出發日期
4. **Return Date** 回程日期
5. **Passenger Details** 旅客資料
6. **Class** 艙等
7. **One Way** 單程行程
8. **Round Trip** 來回行程
9. **Multi-City** 多航點行程

Airport 機場

check-in counter 航空公司櫃檯

immigration 入境海關

duty free shop 免稅商店

currency exchange 貨幣兌換處

boarding gate 登機門

baggage claim 行李領取處

Travel Class 飛機艙等

first class 頭等艙

business class 商務艙

economy class 經濟艙

Useful Expressions

A Booking and confirming flights 預訂與確認航班

1	I'm looking for **round-trip**[1] flights from **TPE**[2] to **LAX**[3].	我要查詢從**桃園國際機場**飛往**洛杉磯國際機場**的**來回**航班。
2	Could I book the 10 a.m. **departure**[4] from Heathrow?	可以預訂早上十點從希斯洛機場**出發的航班**嗎？
3	I'd like to confirm my seat on flight 298 to Kyoto.	我要確認我前往京都的 298 號班機的座位。
4	I need a **one-way**[5] flight from Tokyo to New York leaving as soon as possible.	我需要一張從東京飛往紐約的**單程**機票，越快越好。
5	I'll send you your **itinerary**[6] right away.	我會立刻把**行程表**寄給您。

B Talking about airline seating 談論機上座位

6	Is it possible to get an **aisle seat**[7]?	可以安排**靠走道的座位**嗎？
7	Can I request a seat in the emergency exit row?	我能要求在緊急出口這一排的座位嗎？
8	I always try to sit behind the **bulkhead**[8].	我每次都想坐在**座艙隔板**後的位子。
9	I always fly **business class**[9]—it's so much more comfortable.	我向來搭乘**商務艙**，這要舒適得多了。
10	The service in first class is beyond belief!	頭等艙的服務好得超乎想像！
11	I've never flown anything but **coach**[10]. The other seats are just too expensive.	我只搭乘過**經濟艙**，其他種的座位太貴了。
12	They say it's best to travel later in the week, as earlier flights are often fully booked.	由於稍早的班機通常全被訂滿了，他們說最好搭乘這週後面幾天的班機。

1 **round-trip** [ˋraund,trɪp] (adj.) 來回的
2 **TPE** 桃園國際機場（國際航空運輸協會機場代碼）
3 **LAX** 洛杉磯國際機場
4 **departure** [dɪˋpɑrtʃɚ] (n.)（交通工具）出發
5 **one-way** [ˋwʌn,we] (adj.) 單程的
6 **itinerary** [aɪˋtɪnə,rɛrɪ] (n.) 行程表
7 **aisle seat** 靠走道座位
8 **bulkhead** [ˋbʌlk,hɛd] (n.) 隔板
9 **business class** 商務艙
10 **coach (=coach class)** [kotʃ] (n.) 經濟艙

C Talking about flight events 談論機上事件

13	How many meals are we going to get on this flight?	這趟航程中機上會提供我們幾餐？
14	That last patch of **turbulence**[1] was frightening.	最後一波的**亂流**真是嚇死人了。
15	We've got a seven-hour **layover**[2] in Sydney. I think we should go out and see some of the city!	我們會在雪梨**停留**七小時，我想我們應該出去參觀一下這座城市！

1 **turbulence** [ˋtɝbjələns] (n.) 亂流
2 **layover** [ˋleˏovɚ] (n.) 中途短暫停留

On the Plane 機上設施

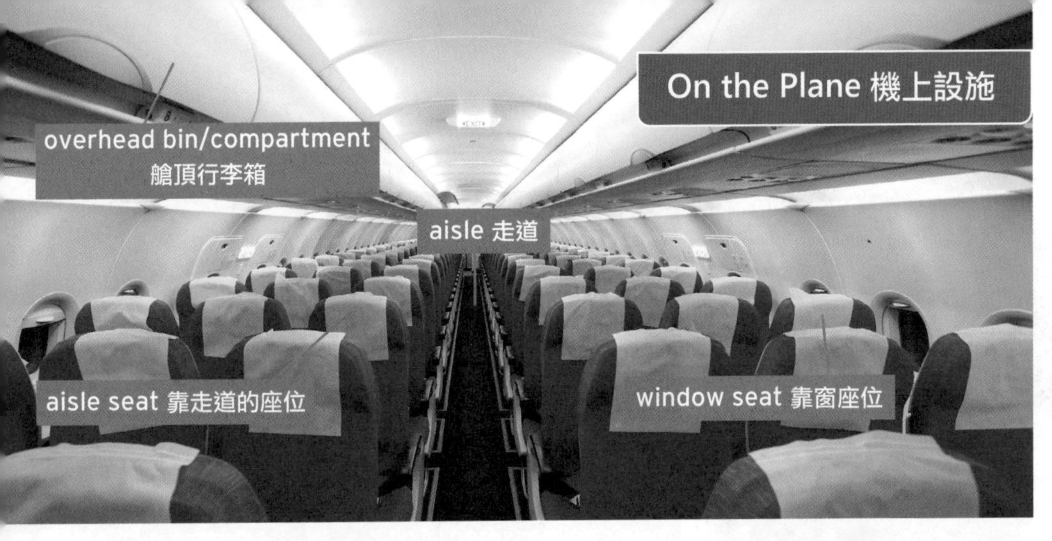

airsickness bag 嘔吐袋

emergency exit 逃生

oxygen mask 氧氣罩

vacant 廁所無人使用

headphones 耳機

seat belt 安全帶

occupied 廁所使用中

Special Meal 特殊餐點

- vegetarian oriental meal (VOML) 中式素餐
- vegetarian lacto ovo meal (VLML) 蛋奶素餐
- raw vegetarian meal (RVML) 生鮮素餐
- vegan/vegetarian meal (VGML) 嚴格素餐
- baby meal 嬰兒餐
- child meal 兒童餐
- diabetic meal (DBML) 糖尿病餐
- gluten free meal (GFML) 麩質不耐症餐
- low fat meal (LFML) 低脂肪餐／低膽固醇餐

Review Questions

Listen to the conversations and answer the questions below.

304 1. **How many days will the woman's trip last?**

Ⓐ About 7 days. Ⓑ About 10 days.
Ⓒ About 30 days. Ⓓ From the 10th to the 12th.

2. **What does the woman mean when she said "I don't mind transfers"?**

Ⓐ She prefers to stay on one flight the whole time.
Ⓑ Changing planes doesn't bother.
Ⓒ She dislikes flying directly.
Ⓓ She is willing to fly luxuriously.

3. **What is the woman's priority in booking a flight?**

Ⓐ Travel time. Ⓑ Airline company.
Ⓒ The cost. Ⓓ Transfer time.

4. **What does the man need to do?**

Ⓐ He needs to cancel a flight.
Ⓑ He needs to change his itinerary.
Ⓒ He needs to book a flight.
Ⓓ He needs to book a flight for another person.

5. **What is true about the man's trip?**

Ⓐ It will be cancelled. Ⓑ It will be the same.
Ⓒ It will be shorter. Ⓓ It will be longer.

6. **What is the man's destination?**

Ⓐ Boston. Ⓑ Penang.
Ⓒ Randal. Ⓓ It hasn't been decided.

Ans A, B, C, B, D, A

UNIT 65 租車或搭乘大眾運輸工具 Renting a Car or Taking Public Transportation

306 J Jared C Car rental representative

Jared is renting a car for a business trip.
傑瑞德正為了出差而租車。

J Hi, I'd like to rent a car from Tuesday, June 1 to Friday, June 4.

C Great. What class of car would you like? We offer **economy, compact, standard, premium, and luxury vehicles**[1], as well as trucks . . .

J An economy car, please. And is it possible to pick the car up from one office and drop it off at another? We're flying in to one airport and out of another.

C That will be fine—you'll just have to tell me the codes for the two airports after I enter your information. Now, to make your reservation, I'll need your **driver's license number**[2].

J Let me find that . . .

J 你好，我想租車，時間是從 6 月 1 日星期二到 6 月 4 日星期五。

C 好的，請問您想租哪一種車型呢？我們有**經濟型、小型、標準型、高級型，還有豪華型**的，也有貨車……

J 麻煩訂經濟型的。還有，可不可以在一地取車，然後在異地還車？我們打算從某個機場出發，然後由另一個機場返回。

C 這沒有問題——您只需在我輸入您的資料後，告知這兩處機場的代碼即可。現在我需要您的**駕照號碼**以完成訂車手續。

J 我找一下……

1 **economy, compact, standard, premium, and luxury vehicles** 經濟型／小型／標準／高級／豪華車型

2 **driver's license number** 駕照號碼

Useful Expressions

A Discussing car rental 討論租車 (307)

1	I'd like to rent a luxury car for the week of March 15.	我想預訂豪華車型，日期是 3 月 15 日那個禮拜。
2	We have an economy vehicle reserved for you, but for 5 dollars more a day you can upgrade to a mid-sized one.	我們已為您預訂經濟車型，但只要一天加 5 美元即可升級至中型車。
3	Would you like to purchase optional insurance coverage?	您要購買附加車險嗎？
4	Do you have **stick-shift**[3] cars available?	你們有**手排**車嗎？
5	Should we keep the **rental agreement**[4] in the car?	我們需要將**租賃合約**留在車上嗎？
6	What is the rate for the car per day?	租金一天多少？
7	Do I have to fill up when I check in?	我還車的時候需要把油加滿嗎？

B Using buses, trains, and subways 使用公車、火車還有地鐵 (308)

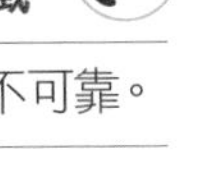

8	I don't know how reliable the bus system is.	我不知道公車系統可不可靠。
9	Is there a **bus stop**[5] nearby?	附近有公車站嗎？
10	Can I have a bus **transfer**[6], please?	麻煩可以請給我一張公車轉乘券嗎？

3 **stick-shift** [ˋstɪkˏʃɪft] (adj.) 手排的
4 **rental agreement** 租賃合約
5 **bus stop** 公車站
6 **transfer** [ˋtrænsfɝ] (n.) 轉乘票

Classification of Cars 車種

compact 小型汽車

sedan 轎車

SUV (sport utility vehicle) 休旅車

convertible 敞篷車

sports car 跑車

limousine 大型豪華轎車

11	Which **platform**[1] is for northern-**bound**[2] trains?	哪一個是北上的**月臺**?
12	Should we take a **local train**[3] or is there an **express**[4]?	我們應該搭乘**區間車**,還是有**特快車**可搭?
13	Excuse me, where is the nearest subway station?	請問最近的地鐵車站在哪?

C Using taxis 使用計程車

14	I'd like to go to 14th and P Streets, please.	我要到 14 街和 P 街的交叉口,麻煩你。
15	Would you turn on your **meter**[5]?	能請你將**計費錶**打開嗎?
16	Right here is fine, thanks. What's the **fare**[6]?	這邊停就可以了,謝謝。**車資**是多少?

1 **platform** [ˋplæt,fɔrm] (n.) 月台
2 **bound** [baʊnd] (adj.) 前往(某地)的
3 **local train** 區間車
4 **express** [ɪkˋsprɛs] (n.) 特快車
5 **meter** [ˋmitɚ] (n.)(計程車的)計費錶
6 **fare** [fɛr] (n.) 車資

Booking a Car Rental Online 線上預訂租車

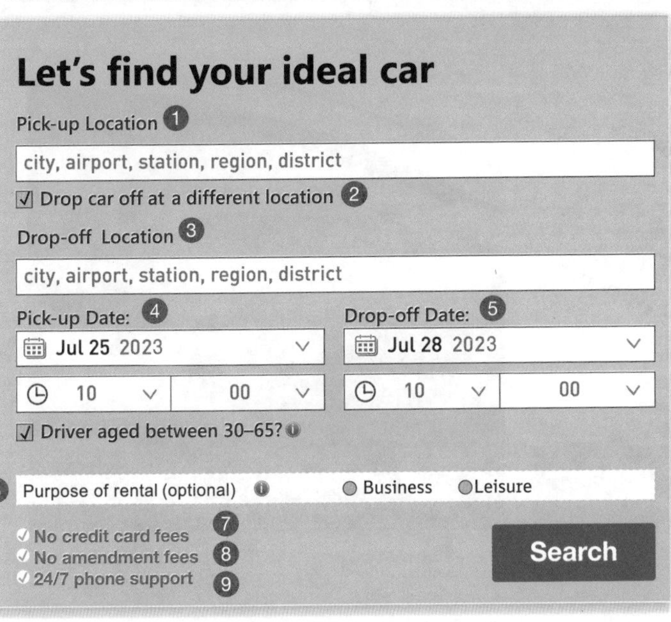

1. Pick-up location 取車地點
2. Drop car off at a different location 甲地租乙地還
3. Drop-off location 還車地點
4. Pick-up date 取車日期
5. Drop-off date 還車日期
6. Purpose of rental (optional) Business / Leisure 租車用途（選填）出差／出遊
7. No credit card fees 無信用卡衍生費用
8. No amendment fees 無改單費用
9. 24/7 phone support 24 小時電話支援

Using an App to Get a Ride 使用應用程式叫車

❶ **Enter the destination and set your pickup time.** 輸入目的地，設定乘車時間。

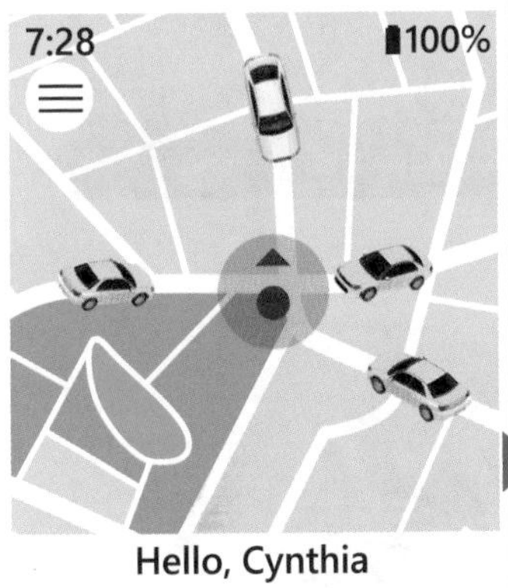

❷ **Select your preferred vehicle type and see price estimates.** 挑選喜好車型，了解預估價格。

Choose a ride

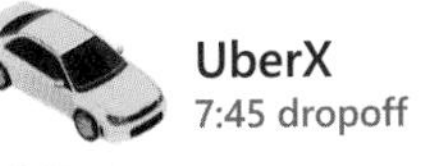

UberX $12.10
7:45 dropoff

Black $35.15
7:47

UberXL $19.90
7:50

❸ **Meet the driver and check the ride.** 與司機會合並確認搭乘正確的車輛。

Car Rental 租車

international driver's license / international driving permit 國際駕照

check in / return 歸還車子
check out 租走車子

rent 費用

road map 地圖

van 廂型車

under construction 道路施工

parking space 停車位

parking lot 停車場

parking meter 停車計費表

one-way 單行道的；單向的

No U-turn 禁止迴轉

speed limit 速限

mileage 哩程數

automatic car 自排車

manual car 手排車

be broken down 拋錨／
walk-through 檢視車子是否有毀損

flat tire 爆胎

dead end 此路不通

Review Questions

Listen to the conversations and answer the questions below.

309 1. **Which costs less, the bus or the train?**

Ⓐ The bus. Ⓑ The train.

2. **Why do the man and the woman choose the option they did?**

Ⓐ Because it is closest to their hotel.

Ⓑ Because it is less expensive.

Ⓒ Because it is closer to where they are now.

Ⓓ Because they don't want to pay for a taxi.

310 3. **Whom is the woman talking to?**

Ⓐ A taxi driver. Ⓑ A train conductor.

Ⓒ A police officer. Ⓓ A pedestrian.

4. **What are the woman's travel options?**

Ⓐ Bus or subway. Ⓑ Taxi or subway.

Ⓒ Taxi or bus. Ⓓ Taxi or car renting.

5. **Why doesn't the woman know the fare?**

Ⓐ Because it isn't known until the end of the journey.

Ⓑ Because the man doesn't know how much her ticket will cost.

Ⓒ Because the woman isn't clear about where she is going.

Ⓓ Because the man doesn't want to let her know.

Ans A, C, A, B, A

聽力內容＋中譯

Unit 1 P. 9 04

M: I'm Jordan Shih; I'm starting in the tech department today.

W: Lovely to meet you, Jordan. I'll call the IT manager to have her show you around. Please take a seat for a moment.

M: Thank you.

男：我是喬丹．石，今天開始到技術部門上班。

女：很高興認識你，喬丹。我會打電話聯絡資訊科技部的經理，請她帶你到處逛逛。請坐一下。

男：謝謝妳。

05

W: Good morning, Matthew. It's nice to meet you.

M: Pleased to meet you as well.

W: It's such a nice sunny day outside—it seems like a pity we have to spend it indoors!

M: I completely agree!

女：早安，馬修。很高興認識你。

男：我也很高興認識妳。

女：外面天氣好晴朗——有點可惜我們得待在室內！

男：我完全同意妳的看法！

Unit 2 P. 15 10

This is Robert, who manages financial projects, and that's John, our new research assistant.

這位是羅伯特，他是我們的財務專案經理；那位是約翰，我們新到任的研究助理。

11

W1: I'd like you to meet Leslie, Bill, and June. Leslie and June are accounts administrators, and Bill works in sales.

M1, W2, W3: Hello.

M2: It's nice to meet all of you. Will we all be working on the same floor?

M1: I work quite closely with Leslie and June, but the sales offices are actually one story up, on the 3rd floor.

W2: You'd never know it from Bill, though.

女1：我想讓你認識一下萊斯莉、比爾和瓊恩。萊斯莉和瓊恩是會計行政人員，比爾是業務。

男1、女2、女3：你好。

男2：很高興認識大家。我們都會在同一層樓上班嗎？

男1：我工作的位置和萊斯莉與瓊恩很近，但業務部辦公室其實是在往上一層樓，也就是在三樓。

女2：不過比爾人在哪就很難說了。

12

M1: These are the other call center trainees that you'll be training with today. Why don't you all introduce yourselves?

W1: I'm Karen.

W2: Hi, I'm Stephanie.

M2: George, nice to meet you.

W3: And I'm Christine.

M1: And this is your trainer, Gloria. I'll let her take over from here.

W4: Thanks, John. OK, why don't you sit down and look over your orientation packets.

男1：他們是妳今天要訓練的另一批客服中心受訓人員。大家何不自我介紹一下呢？

女1：我是凱倫。

女2：嗨，我是史蒂芬妮。

男2：喬治，很高興認識妳。

女3：還有我是克莉絲汀。

男1：這位是你們的訓練講師葛洛莉亞。我讓她從這裡開始接手。

女4：謝謝你，約翰。好，大家何不坐下，看一下新進人員的說明資料。

Unit 3 P. 19 15

M: I have a lot on my plate most of the time, so I don't get as much time to talk to employees as I'd like to. That's why I like to take a minute to chat with all new employees when they start. Of course, my door is always open to employees with questions.

W: Well, that's reassuring.

M: Oh, we don't want people to feel they have to wing it for their first few weeks. If you're unsure of anything, there is always someone who'll be happy to help you get the hang of things.

男：我多數時候都忙得不可開交，所以雖然我很想多跟員工聊聊，卻沒有太多時間。這就是為什麼我喜歡在新員工入職的時候，花點時間跟他們聊一下。當然，員工有任何問題，我辦公室的們永遠為他們敞開。

女：唔，這樣很令人安心。

男：噢，我們也不希望讓大家以為，剛開始上班的頭幾週都要靠自己發揮臨場反應。如果大家對任何事感到不太確定，一定會有人很樂於協助你們掌握工作的竅門。

Unit 4 P. 23 19

M: Excuse me. Could you tell me where the restrooms are?

W: Of course. There aren't any on this floor. Walk down this hallway and take the stairs on the left. Go down to the second floor. The bathrooms are just to the right as you walk out of the stairway.

男：不好意思，可以請妳告訴我廁所在哪裡嗎？

女：當然可以。這層樓沒有廁所。沿著走廊走到底，然後從左邊的樓梯走下去到二樓。廁所就在你走出樓梯間的右邊。

20

W: May I help you?

M: I'm sorry, I'm a little lost. I'm looking for Cutting Edge Design.

W: They're upstairs. Take the elevator. It's just down the hall.

女：我可以幫你什麼忙嗎？

男：不好意思，我有點迷路。我在找「前衛設計公司」。

女：這家公司在樓上。請搭電梯，電梯就在走廊的盡頭。

21

W: Are there any vending machines in this building?

M: Yes, there are several on the first floor.

女：這棟大樓裡有自動販賣機嗎？

男：有的，一樓有好幾台喔。

Unit 5 P. 27 25

M: Excuse me, do you know how far we are from the Turner Building?

W: You're just a few blocks away. Go up to the next traffic light and turn right. It's down that street—I'm not sure how far, but it's not too bad a walk.

M: Thanks a lot.

男： 不好意思，請問妳知道我們離透納大樓有多遠嗎？

女： 只有幾個街區的距離。先往前走到下一個紅綠燈，再右轉。大樓就在街的那一頭，我不太確定有多遠，但走過去的時間還好。

男： 多謝妳。

26

W: Can you remind me where the post office is?

M: Sure. Go left out of the building and walk to the next light, at Rosebud Street. Turn right and the post office will be on your right, halfway down the street.

女： 你可以提醒我一下郵局在哪裡嗎？

男： 當然可以。從大樓出去後往左，走到下一個紅綠燈，在羅斯布德街。右轉，那條街走到一半距離左右，就會看到郵局在妳的右手邊。

Unit 6 P. 33

30

M: So Anne and Bob both work for Joseph?

W: Yes, and Joseph answers to the VP, Aaron Kline.

M: VP of what?

W: Marketing.

男： 所以安和鮑伯都是約瑟夫的下屬？

女： 是的，而約瑟夫的直屬上司是亞倫・柯林恩副總。

男： 什麼部門的副總？

女： 行銷部門。

31

W: Who do you have to speak to to get the project approved?

M: Well, everything has to go through Ron, but the finance director has the final word.

W: What's her name again?

M: Gloria Shue.

女： 專案要得到批准的話，該找誰呢？

男： 是這樣的，所有事情都得經過朗恩那邊，但是財務總監有最後的決定權。

女： 你剛說她叫什麼名字？

男： 葛洛莉亞・舒。

Unit 7 P. 37

35

W: Joe, I've been waiting to find out what I should do with the new market research data. Can you tell me what my next step should be?

M: Haven't you sent it up to the manager's office for review?

W: No! Was I supposed to do that?

M: Yes—in the report instructions, it says to send all drafts to the manager's office immediately! How long have you been waiting?

W: Oh . . . not long. I'll send it there now.

女： 喬，我一直在等人來跟我說要怎麼處理新市場的研究資料。你可以告訴我，我下一步該怎麼做嗎？

男： 妳還沒送去經理辦公室審核？

女： 沒有啊！我應該這麼做嗎？

男： 是啊——報告說明裡有說，所有的草擬資料都得立刻送交經理辦公室！妳已經等多久了？

女： 喔……沒有很久。我現在就送過去。

36

M: Oh no, Chloe is out sick today and she doesn't know when she'll be back in.

W: I guess we're going to need to call a temp to handle the phones until she's back.

M: Yes—the only problem is that only Chloe knows the number to the temp agency!

男： 喔不，克蘿伊今天請病假，她不曉得什麼時候能回來上班。

女： 我想在她回來上班前，我們得找短期派遣人員來處理接電話這個部分。

男： 好——但唯一的問題是，只有克蘿伊知道短期派遣公司的電話號碼！

Unit 8 P. 43 41

M: How was your weekend, Christy?

W: Absolutely wasted. I spent the weekend in bed with a fever.

M: Oh no! I'm sorry to hear that.

男： 克莉絲緹，週末過得怎麼樣啊？

女： 整個泡湯。週末我因為發燒，都待在床上。

男： 喔不！我替妳感到難過。

42

W1: I love your shoes. Are they new?

W2: Oh, I've had these forever. I don't get to wear them often, though.

W1: They're beautiful. Where did you get them?

女1： 我很喜歡妳的鞋子，是新買的嗎？

女2： 喔，我已經買很久了，只是不常穿。

女1： 很好看耶，妳在哪裡買的？

Unit 9 P. 49 50

M: Good morning, Phoenix Pharmaceuticals. How may I direct your call?

W: Jonathan Busey, please.

M: And who may I say is calling?

W: This is Leah Hammer.

男： 早安，這裡是菲尼克斯製藥公司。請問需要我把您的電話轉接給誰？

女： 請幫我轉接給強納森．布塞。

男： 請問您是哪位？

女： 我是莉亞．漢默。

51

M: Hi, may I speak to Glenn Dover, please?

W: I'm sorry. Mr. Dover is away from his desk at the moment. Would you like his voice mail?

M: No, thanks. I'll call back later.

男： 嗨，能請葛連恩．多佛接一下電話嗎？

女： 不好意思，多佛先生目前不在位子上。您要不要在他的語音信箱留言？

男： 不用了，謝謝。我待會兒回撥。

52

M: Would you put me through to Rachel Ravin, please?

W1: Certainly. One moment. Ms. Ravin, you have a call.

W2: Can you take a message for me, Karen? I'm very busy right now.

W1: I'm sorry, Ms. Ravin isn't available right now. May I take a message?

男： 可以請妳幫我轉接給瑞秋．瑞文嗎？

女1： 當然可以。請等一下。瑞文小姐，有妳的電話。

女2： 凱倫，可以請妳幫我請對方留言嗎？我現在很忙。

女1： 不好意思，瑞文小姐現在無法接聽電話。我可以幫您留言嗎？

Unit 10 P. 54 56

W1: Good morning, ABC Industries. This is Shannon speaking; how may I help you?

W2: Good morning! I'd like to speak to the person who handles your long distance phone service.

W1: That would be our office manager, but I'm afraid she's not available at the moment.

W2: Well, if you tell me her name, I can call her back at a more convenient time.

W1: We don't usually accept solicitations over the phone. Would you like to leave a message that I can pass along to her? Then she can get back to you if she's interested.

W2: Sure. This is Gloria with Strong Telecom. We are offering a fantastic VoIP package for new customers. It can save you up to half of your current monthly phone bill and almost eliminate your long distance bills.

W1: Come again? What kind of package?

W2: V o I P. It stands for "voice over Internet protocol."

W1: Thank you. And you are Gloria with Strong Telecom. Now, what's your phone number?

W2: (07) 285-3394 and I'm extension 19.

W1: Thank you. OK, (07) 285-3394, extension 19. I'll pass the message along to our office manager.

女1：早安，這裡是ABC工業公司，我是雪儂。我可以幫您什麼忙？

女2：早安！我想找負責處理長途電話服務的人。

女1：那應該是辦公室主任，但她恐怕目前無法接聽您的電話。

女2：呃，如果您跟我說她的名字，我可以等比較方便的時候再回撥電話給她。

女1：本公司通常不接受電話推銷。您要不要留言，我再轉達給她？如果她有意了解的話，她會再和您聯絡。

女2：沒問題。我是史特隆電信公司的葛洛莉亞。我們目前為新客戶提供了很棒的VoIP配套服務，每月可以為貴公司省下最多一半的電話費，而且幾乎去掉了長途電話費。

女1：再說一遍，是什麼樣的配套服務？

女2：VoIP，是「IP網路語音傳輸服務」的縮寫。

女1：謝謝您。您是史特隆電信公司的葛洛莉亞。那您的電話號碼是幾號？

女2：(07) 285-3394，我的分機是19。

女1：謝謝您。好的，(07) 285-3394，分機19。我會將此留言轉達給辦公室主任。

57

W1: Good morning, ABC Industries. This is Shannon speaking; how may I help you?

W2: Hi . . . actually, I was calling for Barbara, the receptionist.

W1: I'm sorry. Barbara is working on another project for the next few days. May I take a message?

W2: Yes, would you please tell her that the catering for next week's senior management meeting is all set?

W1: Sure. Can I get your name, please?

W2: Of course, I'm Sue Granger of Your Way Caterers.

W1: And does Barbara have your number?

W2: She does, and there's no need for her to contact me unless she needs to change her order. We'll be there next Thursday at 10:45 a.m. to set up.

W1: I'll give her the message. Thank you.

女1：早安，這裡是ABC工業公司，我是雪儂。我可以幫您什麼忙？

女2：妳好⋯⋯其實我想找接待員芭芭拉。

女1：不好意思，芭芭拉接下來幾天都會處理另一項專案。我可以幫您留言嗎？

女2： 好的，麻煩妳告訴她，下週高階主管會議的外燴服務都安排好了。

女1： 好的，可以請問您貴姓大名嗎？

女2： 當然可以，我是「客製外燴公司」的蘇·葛倫格。

女1： 那芭芭拉有您的電話號碼嗎？

女2： 她有。除非她要改餐點內容，否則不用打給我唷。我們下週四早上10:45會到場開始準備。

女1： 我會轉告她，謝謝您。

Unit 11 P. 59 61

W: Hi, John. I wanted to talk to you about possibly taking a day off next week; say, on Thursday. What do you think?

M: To be honest, we're really busy right now. If you have to, I understand. But if you could possibly postpone your personal day, I'd appreciate it.

女： 嗨，約翰，我想和你談一下，我下週是不是可以請一天假。比如說，下週四，你覺得怎麼樣？

男： 老實說，我們現在真的很忙。如果妳非得請假不可，我可以理解。但如果妳可以儘量延後時間請事假，我會很感激。

62

W: Good morning, Gilbert Communications, Sara speaking.

M: Hi, Sara, it's Joe. Listen, I'm really sick this morning and I don't think I'm going to be able to come in.

W: Oh no! I'm sorry you're not feeling well. You should probably tell Alex— do you want me to put you through to his office?

M: Yes, please.

女： 早安，這裡是吉伯特通訊公司，我是莎拉。

男： 嗨，莎拉，我是喬。我跟妳說，我今天早上真的很不舒服，我想我沒辦法去上班了。

女： 哦，不！聽到你生病了，我也覺得難過。你可能要跟艾力克斯說一聲，你要我幫你轉接到他的辦公室嗎？

男： 好，麻煩妳了。

Unit 12 P. 63 66

W1: Good morning, Aster Institutes for Science.

W2: Hi, Carla, it's Leslie. Listen, there's been some kind of accident on the highway and all the lanes are shut down. Traffic is backed up for miles. I have no idea when things will be moving again, but I'll get to the office as soon as I can.

女1： 早安，這裡是艾斯特科學機構。

女2： 嗨，卡拉，我是萊斯莉。我跟妳說，高速公路好像發生車禍，所有的車道都封閉了。車輛回堵了好幾英里。我不知道什麼時候才動得了，但我會儘快趕到公司。

67

W1: Good afternoon, Sally's Graphic Design.

W2: Gail, hi, it's Margaret. I can't believe it—I went to pick up a salad for lunch and while I was in the shop, my car got towed! This is so annoying. I've got to go down to the impound lot and pick it up.

W1: Oh no!

W2: The worst part is, I have a client coming in at 1:15 and there's no way I'll make it before then. Can you please call her and reschedule our appointment? Her number's in the book.

女1：午安，這裡是莎莉繪圖設計公司。

女2：蓋兒，嗨，我是瑪格莉特。我真不敢相信，我只是去買個生菜沙拉當午餐，我人還在店裡，車子就被拖吊了！好煩啊。我得去拖吊保管場把車領回來。

女1：哦，不會吧！

女2：最慘的是，我有個客戶1:15會到公司，但我不可能在那之前趕回來。可以請妳打電話給她，另外安排我們開會的時間嗎？她的電話號碼在通訊錄裡。

Unit 13 P. 69 72

M: Did you get the email I sent about the design changes?

W: Yes. Didn't you get my response?

M: No. That's strange; I've been at my computer all day.

男：妳有收到我寄的那封跟設計更動有關的電子郵件嗎？

女：有，你沒收到我的回信嗎？

男：沒收到。好奇怪，我今天一整天都在用電腦。

73

W: Would you send around a message to the whole office to let them know the carpet cleaners will be here tomorrow?

M: Sure. Is there anything they need to know?

W: Just that it'll be loud in here for a little while.

M: I'll send it now.

W: Thanks. And cc me on it, please.

女：可以請你傳個訊息給辦公室的全體同仁，讓大家知道地毯清潔人員明天會過來嗎？

男：好啊。他們還需要知道什麼資訊嗎？

女：就是這裡有一小段時間會很吵。

男：我現在就傳送。

女：謝謝，也請傳副本給我。

74

M: Did you see the email Frida sent this morning?

W: No. What did she say?

M: I'll forward it to you. You should read it.

男：妳有看到佛莉妲今天早上傳的電子郵件嗎？

女：沒有，她說了什麼？

男：我再轉寄給妳，妳應該看一下。

Unit 14 P. 73 77

W: I agree. Does Friday afternoon work for everyone?

M: Sorry, Friday's out for me. Can we make it Thursday morning?

W: That's fine for me.

女：我同意。大家週五下午都能參加嗎？

男：抱歉，我週五沒辦法參加。我們可以安排在週四早上嗎？

女：我可以喔。

78

M: I think we need to arrange a meeting between the project managers and the contractors.

W: Alright. I'm not really in contact with the project managers. Can you talk to them?

M: Sure. If you can get the contractors to come in next Tuesday, I'll make sure the project managers are here.

W: I'll get right on it.

男：我覺得我們需要安排一場會議，讓專案經理和承包商一起開個會。

女：好喔。我沒有真正跟專案經理接觸過，你可以和他們談一下嗎？

男：好啊，如果妳可以讓承包商下週二進公司，我會確保專案經理都到場。

女：我馬上去辦。

79

M: I don't understand all these delays on the project. Can you get the team together for a meeting?

W: I'll try, but it's going to be hard. We're all so busy right now.

男：案子一再耽擱，我不懂這是怎麼回事。妳可以把小組召集起來一起開個會嗎？

女：我試試，但是會很難，因為大家現在都忙得不得了。

Unit 15 P. 77 82

M: I'm out of window envelopes. Do you have any? I need two.

W: Sure . . . here you go.

M: Thanks a lot.

男：我的橫式開窗信封都用完了，妳那邊還有嗎？我需要兩個。

女：有啊……給你。

男：多謝啦。

83

M: Are we supposed to print business letters on letterhead?

W: Yes, always.

M: Do you know where I can get some?

W: You're supposed to apply for it through the mail room. I've got some if you only need a few sheets, though.

M: Great, thanks.

男：我們應該用有信頭的信紙來印商務信函嗎？

女：對的，每次都要喔。

男：妳知道哪裡可以拿到印有信頭的信紙嗎？

女：你應該透過收發室申請。但如果你只需要幾張，我這裡有。

男：太好了，感謝。

84

W: I'm out of staples. Do you know where they're kept?

M: That kind of stuff is usually in the cabinet in the corner. If you don't see them there, you'll have to ask Sally.

女：我沒有釘書針了。你知道釘書針放在哪裡嗎？

男：這類東西通常是放在角落的櫃子裡。如果那裡還找不到，就要去問莎莉。

Unit 16 P. 83 87

M: I've run into a problem on the report and I think I'm going to need a little more time. Can I give it to you at close of business, rather than 2:30?

W: That should be fine. Thanks for letting me know!

M: OK, I'll get back to it now.

男：我的報告遇到了一個難題，我想我需要多一點的時間來處理。我能不能改成下班的時候交給妳，而不是兩點半交？

女：應該沒關係。謝謝你跟我說！

男：好，那我現在繼續處理。

88

M: I'm afraid my chair is giving me back pain. Would it be possible to get a new one?

W: I think we've already made our furniture order, but check with Sam. Maybe it hasn't gone through yet. If it has, you can always fill out a special request form. It just might take a while.

M: Well, do you think I could pick one up myself and get reimbursed?

W: It doesn't really work that way around here.

男：我覺得我坐的椅子讓我的背很痛。有沒有可能買張新椅子？

女：我想我們已經下單買辦公家具了，但你可以去跟山姆確定一下。也許訂單還沒送出。如果已經送出，你隨時都可以填寫特殊需求表，只是可能要等一陣子。

男：那妳覺得我可以自己去買，然後跟公司報帳嗎？

女：那種方式在公司這裡是行不通的。

Unit 17 P. 87 91

M: Do you know how to work the new fax? I can't get my document to feed.

W: Let me try. Oh, I see the problem. There was another fax in it still trying to send.

M: Thanks a lot.

男：妳知道怎麼使用新的傳真機嗎？我的文件沒辦法進紙。

女：我試試看。喔，我知道問題出在哪。有另一份檔案還在試著傳真出去。

男：多謝啦。

92

W: Hi, Joe, I've got a fax for you. It came through while I was sending one.

M: Thanks! Ah yes, I've been waiting for this.

W: You're welcome.

女：嗨，喬，我這裡有你的傳真。我今天在傳真的時候收到的。

男：謝謝妳！啊，對了，我一直在等這份傳真。

女：不客氣。

93

W: I'm going to load some scrap paper in the fax—do you know if I should put it face up or face down?

M: I'm pretty sure you want to load it print-side down, but you should check with Sally.

女：我要把一些廢紙放進傳真機的紙匣裡——你知道我應該要把空白面朝上或朝下嗎？

男：我滿確定要印出傳真內容的那面要朝下，但妳還是跟莎莉確認一下吧。

Unit 18 P. 91 96

M: Can you please make 10 copies of the meeting agenda? You can use recycled paper if there is any.

W: Sure. When do you need them?

M: Any time before the meeting at 2:30 p.m.

男：妳可以印10份會議的議程表嗎？如果有回收紙可用，就用喔。

女：好啊。你什麼時候要用到？

男：下午兩點半開會前拿到就可以了。

97

W: I keep printing this the wrong way and wasting letterhead!

M: Try using tray two; it's easier. Just load the letterhead in face down.

W: OK, thank you!

女：我一直印錯，浪費了信頭紙啊！

男：試試看第二個紙匣，會比較容易。只是要把信頭的那面朝下放進紙匣裡。

女：好的，謝謝你！

Unit 19 P. 95

101

M: Do you know how to use cut and paste shortcuts?

W: Yes. In this program, alt-c cuts and alt-p pastes.

M: Thanks! That will make things go much faster for me.

男：妳知道剪下和貼上的快速鍵要怎麼用嗎？

女：知道。在這個程式裡，按alt-c鍵是剪下，按alt-p鍵是貼上。

男：謝謝！這樣我處理事情就會快很多。

102

W: Hi, John. I just wanted to let you know that I've made up a new expense report sheet that I think is much easier to use.

M: Really? That's great! The old one was such a pain, I ended up doing all the calculations by hand anyway.

W: Wow! No, this one should be no trouble. The functions are all embedded in the columns this time. All you have to do is enter in the figures. I'm going to send it around to everyone later today.

M: Terrific! Now, if I could only keep track of my receipts . . .

女：嗨，約翰，我只是想跟你說，我新編了一張費用報告表，我覺得會比較容易使用。

男：真的嗎？太好了！舊版的太麻煩了，到最後全部都是我自己手動計算。

女：哇！這個新版的應該不會那麼麻煩。這次所有的函數都嵌入欄位裡了，你只要輸入數字就好。我今天晚一點會傳給每個人。

男：太棒了！如果我能只記錄收據⋯⋯

Unit 20 P. 99

106

M: I don't think I can email a file this large to everyone.

W: Don't email it! FTP it.

M: I'm never sure how to do that. Can you show me?

W: Sure. It's simple—all you have to do is log in, open a session, and then follow the prompts.

M: I'm lost already. I don't know if I have a username or password. Can I watch while you help me?

男：我覺得我沒辦法把這麼大的檔案用電子郵件傳給每個人。

女：別用電子郵件信箱！用FTP傳。

男：我一直不會用FTP，妳可以教我嗎？

女：好啊。很簡單，你只要登入、打開一個上傳程序，然後按照指示操作就行了。

男：我已經昏頭了。我不知道我有沒有使用者名稱和密碼。我可以在旁邊看妳幫我操作嗎？

107

W: Hey, would you save that database to the server so the whole network can access it?

M: Sure. Where should I save it? I haven't set up my own folder yet.

W: Oh, we don't use our own folders there. Files are organized by project, so just look for the name of the project you're working on.

女：嘿，你可以把那個資料庫儲存到伺服器，讓整個網絡都可以存取它嗎？

男：好啊，我該存在哪裡？我還沒設定我自己的資料夾。

女：喔，我們不在那邊使用自己的資料夾。我們以專案的名稱來分類檔案，所以只要找到你在處理的專案名稱就好。

Unit 21 P. 103 110

M: I didn't bookmark the site I was using and now I can't find it for the life of me.

W: Have you looked in your search history?

M: No. I'm not sure I'd recognize the URL, but it's worth a shot. Thanks.

男：我之前沒有把我在用的網站加入書籤，現在我怎麼找也找不到那個網站。

女：你有去看看瀏覽紀錄嗎？

男：沒有。我不太確定我是不是能認出那個網址，但還是值得一試。謝謝妳。

111

W: Do you know anything about repairing books?

M: No, but I bet you can find something online.

W: Really?

M: Yes, try searching "book," "repair," "service" or something.

女：你懂修復書籍的任何資訊嗎？

男：不懂，但我想妳可以上網找到相關資訊。

女：真的嗎？

男：是啊，試著搜尋「書籍」、「修復」、「服務」之類的關鍵字。

Unit 22 P. 107 115

M: You should really use instant messaging. Everyone else in the office is using it.

W: Really? I just assumed it would be blocked.

M: No, we use it all the time. I'm sure the program is on your computer already.

男：妳真的該用即時通訊軟體，辦公室裡的每個人都在用。

女：真的嗎？我只是以為會被公司封鎖。

男：沒有，我們一天到晚都在用。我敢肯定地說，即時通訊軟體已經在妳的電腦上了。

116

W: I'm running out the door—can you IM Sylvia and tell her I'm leaving?

M: Sure, but her status is "idle." She might not get the message.

W: Oh well. Send it anyway and she'll see it when she comes back.

女：我要出門了——你可以用即時通訊軟體發訊息給席薇亞，跟她說我要走了嗎？

男：好啊，但她的狀態是「閒置中」，她可能不會收到訊息喔。

女：喔，這樣嗎，還是傳吧，她回來的時候就會看到了。

Unit 23 P. 111 120

M: Hey, I'm just about to do a really long print job. You don't have anything you need to send now, do you?

W: Nothing that can't wait.

M: Good. I'll let you know when mine is done.

男：嘿，我要開始列印東西，會花很久的時間。妳沒有什麼是需要現在傳送的，對吧？

女：沒關係，我這邊都可以等。

男：好喔，那我印完後跟妳說。

121

W: I didn't preview this document and I didn't realize the page breaks had gotten all messed up.

M: Oh, what a waste!

W: I know. Do you need any recycle paper?

女：我列印之前沒有先預覽一下文件，沒發現到分頁符號全部都亂掉了。

男：喔，好浪費哦！

女：我知道。你需不需要回收紙？

Unit 24 P. 115 125

M: Can you take a look at my computer? For some reason, I can't get into my email.
W: Hmm . . . have you changed your password?
M: No. Everything was fine yesterday. I just don't get it.
W: You should probably call tech support.

男：妳可以看一下我的電腦嗎？不知怎麼一回事，我進不去我的電子郵件信箱。

女：嗯……你有改密碼嗎？

男：沒有，昨天都還好好的。我真的不懂。

女：你可能要聯絡技術支援部門。

126

W: Do you know Glenda Harris's email address?
M: I've got it here somewhere. Let me pull it up. Ah, here it is: gl underscore harris at global ship dot net.
W: Is "gl harris" all one word?
M: No, it's gl_harris.
W: Of course, silly me. Thanks!

女：你知道葛蘭達・哈里斯的電子郵件信箱地址嗎？

男：我有記在某處。我找一下。啊，在這裡：gl 底線 harris 小老鼠 global ship 點 net。

女：「gl harris」是同一個字嗎？

男：不是，是gl_harris。

女：喔，對耶，我真傻。謝謝啦！

Unit 25 P. 119 129

M: There's something wrong with my computer. When I looked online for a solution, it said I should do a system restore. But I don't know what that is.
W: Oh, I can help you with that. Some of this stuff is much easier than it seems.
M: Thank you.

男：我的電腦有問題。我上網找解決辦法的時候，網路上說我應該要進行系統還原。但我不知道那是什麼。

女：喔，我可以幫你處理。有些東西比想像中的要容易得多。

男：謝謝妳。

130

W: I'm really not confident about the company's antivirus software. I have a feeling it's not the best.
M: They say it protects against all known viruses and worms.
W: Yes, but I don't think it updates often enough—and the whole network is vulnerable if one of us gets hit.
M: Why don't you find another one that's better, then?

女：我對這家公司的防毒軟體實在沒什麼信心，我覺得這不是最好用的。

男：他們說可以阻擋所有已知的病毒和蠕蟲程式。

女：對，但我覺得它更新得不夠頻繁——如果我們有一個人中標，整個網絡都岌岌可危。

男：那妳何不另外找一個更好用的呢？

Unit 26 P. 123 135

W: So, who's going to handle travel arrangements this time?

M: I'd like to suggest that we use a travel agent.

W: But I thought we'd agreed that travel agents were too expensive.

M: Yes, but I think we all underestimate the amount of time we spend making these arrangements. I think if we break down the amount of time one of us spends doing all the travel arrangements, and consider the lost work time on the project, we'll find we're actually losing.

女：那麼，這次由誰負責安排旅遊的事呢？

男：我想建議我們找一家旅行社來辦。

女：但我以為大家都贊同旅行社太貴了。

男：沒錯，但我覺得我們都低估了自己安排行程所需要花的時間。我想如果我們把我們當中某個人花在旅遊安排上的時間細分一下，同時考量一下少了多少處理專案的時間，就會發現我們其實是在損耗時間。

136

M: I like Bob's suggestion, but if we really want to start generating word of mouth, I think we need to hold an open house.

W: How do you mean?

M: We should set up our own miniconference and invite our current clients and others we're interested in. We could even invite some of our contractors to set up booths. You know, get out information about what we do and who we already work for.

W: Interesting. I've never thought of something like this before. What do you all think? How could we make it work?

男：我喜歡鮑伯的建議，但如果我們真的想要開始創造口碑，我想我們必須舉辦開放參觀的活動。

女：你指的是什麼？

男：我們應該舉辦一場小型會議，邀請現有的客戶還有我們有意接洽的其他客戶來參加。我們甚至可以邀請部分的承包商來設置活動攤位。就是把我們的專業和服務對象等資訊傳達出去。

女：有意思。我以前從沒想過這樣的方式。大家覺得怎麼樣？我們要怎麼順利進行這件事？

Unit 27 P. 129 140

M: It's nice to see all of you. Thanks for being here. There are copies of the agenda right here for everyone who doesn't have one.

W: Would you pass me one of those, please?

M: Sure. Now, let's go over some of these points before we get into anything else . . .

男：很高興見到大家，謝謝大家到場。這裡有會議的議程表，沒拿到的人過來這邊拿。

女：可以請你幫我傳一份過來嗎？

男：沒問題。現在，在我們討論其他問題之前，先來看一下這些重點……

141

W: Before we begin, I'd like to make a few suggestions. The first is that we talk about item 5 on the agenda first, because Jason will have to leave early and I don't want him to miss that discussion. Is that OK with everyone?

女：在我們開始之前，我想提出一些建議。首先，我想我們先討論議程上的第5點，因為傑森要早點走，我希望他不會錯過這項討論。大家都可以接受嗎？

Unit 28 P. 137 145

W: I guess I'm back to cold calling. Ugh.

M: Did you finish your last project?

W: Yes, and now all they've got for me to do is get back on the phones. I really don't see how these calls are effective.
M: Maybe while you're waiting on the line, you can come up with some new marketing ideas!

女：我想我又要回去做聯絡潛在客戶的事了，呃。

男：妳結束上一份專案了嗎？

女：結束了，現在他們要我做的就是再回到打電話找潛在客戶的做法。我真的看不出來，這種聯絡方式會有什麼效果。

男：也許妳在等對方接聽的時候，會想到一些新的行銷點子！

146

W: Our target market for the new game is tech-savvy adult men. We aren't going to try to dumb-down our commercials to attract people who don't understand the technology.
M: I still find it surprising that we can't attract women to these games in higher numbers.
W: We've tried, but they're a really hard market to crack. They just don't seem to be interested in our kinds of products.
M: Maybe we should rethink our marketing plan.

女：我們新電玩的目標市場針對的是精通科技的成年男性。我們不打算讓廣告內容通俗化來吸引不了解這項科技的人。

男：我覺得奇怪的是，我們無法吸引更多的女性來玩這類電玩。

女：我們曾試過，但是女性市場真的很難打入。她們就是對我們這類產品不太感興趣。

男：也許我們應該重新思考行銷計畫。

Unit 29 P. 141 150

M: I'd like to present my proposal for getting back the teen market. You all have a copy of the proposal to look over in-depth later, but for now let's talk about the main points.
W: First of all, how do you plan to staff this?
M: Well, the main burden would be on my team of five. We would outsource the print and layout to a contract we've been happy with in the past.
W: And you could do it all with your team of five? In this time frame?
M: Yes, I think three months will be enough.

男：我想簡報奪回青少年市場的提案。大家手上都有一份提案副本，稍後可以深入了解一下。但是現在我們先來談談重點。

女：首先，你要怎麼規劃人員分配的部分？

男：是這樣的，大部分的事情由我的五人小組承擔，我們會將印刷和排版的工作外包給過去合作愉快的約聘人員。

女：你靠你的五人小組就能搞得定這一切？在這樣的時間範圍內？

男：能，我覺得三個月就夠了。

151

W: My proposal aims to reduce our overhead costs by relocating warehouses and selling advertising space on those and other buildings.
M: Are you speaking regionally or does your proposal cover our international branches as well?
W: For now, the scope is limited to this region.
M: I think this is a sound idea. Can you tell me more about the advertisers you've contacted?

女：我的提案主要是希望藉由遷移倉庫、出售倉庫還有其他大樓上的廣告空間等方式，降低我們的間接成本。

男：妳指的是地區性的做法，還是國際分公司也包括在內？

女：現階段的提案範圍先侷限在本地區。

男：我認為這個點子滿合理的。妳可以多說一下，妳已經聯絡哪些廣告公司了嗎？

Unit 30 P. 145 154

W: And here it is, the newest, slimmest cell phone on the market, the Skinny Phone!

M: In terms of capabilities, what's different about this phone compared to the last one?

W: The Skinny Phone has all the same functions as our previous model, but in a smaller package!

M: But does it have any new functions?

女：就是這個，目前市面上最新、最輕薄的手機——「纖薄手機」！

男：以性能來說，這款手機與上一款相比，有什麼不同呢？

女：纖薄手機的功能和上一款手機的功能都一樣，只是尺寸比較小！

男：但這款有什麼新功能嗎？

155

M: So how is this model going to extend our brand?

W: Well, with the lower price, we believe we can reach buyers who were interested, but who just couldn't afford the bigger, more expensive model.

M: Are you sure there's an untapped market for this product? Won't they have bought cheaper models from our competitors?

W: I think our brand has a desirable reputation, so even consumers who have bought competing products will come back to us if they can afford it.

男：那麼，這個型號會如何拓展我們的品牌？

女：是這樣的，在價格較低的情況下，我們相信可以吸引到有意購買卻又買不起那款較大、較貴的買家。

男：妳確定這種產品還有未開發的市場嗎？難道消費者不會從競爭品牌那裡買更便宜的型號嗎？

女：我認為我們的品牌聲譽良好，所以即使是已經購買競爭品牌產品的消費者，在可以負擔的情況下，還是會回籠購買我們的產品。

Unit 31 P. 149 159

W: I've got to do something about my computer.

M: What's the matter with it?

W: It's just too old! It crashes all the time and it runs really slowly, so all my work takes twice as long.

M: Have you talked to Thomas about it?

W: Yes, and he's blown me off twice. This time, though, I'm going to demand a new one.

女：我要幫我的電腦想想辦法。

男：妳的電腦怎麼了？

女：真的太老舊了！老是當機，而且跑得很慢，我所有的工作都要花兩倍時間才能做完。

男：妳跟湯瑪斯談過這情況了嗎？

女：談過了，他已經拒絕我兩次了。但我這次一定要要求一台新電腦。

160

M: Sophia just realized she put the wrong date on the board meeting invitation letters she sent last week.

W: Oh dear! What are you going to do about it?
M: Well, we can't change the date, so we'll have to send a correction letter. It's embarrassing.

男： 蘇菲亞剛剛才發現，她上週寄出的董事會會議邀請函上的日期寫錯了。

女： 喔，天啊！你要怎麼處理？

男： 這個嘛，我們無法更改開會的日期，所以只好寄出更正日期的通知函。真的好糗。

Unit 32 P. 153 163

W: I think I see where our calculations went off.
M: Where?
W: Someone entered the March numbers in for April as well. After that, all our numbers and projections went wrong, and the whole quarterly budget ended up short.

女： 我想我知道我們的計算結果哪裡出錯了。

男： 哪裡？

女： 有人把三月分的數字也輸入到了四月分裡。此後，我們所有的數字和預測數字都出錯，導致整個季度的預算出現短缺。

164

M: I can't believe the trouble we're having with this conference!
W: Why, what's going on?
M: First, Joan booked the convention center for the wrong dates! Then Keith sent out invitation letters that hadn't been spell checked and had a few typos. And now it looks like our keynote speaker is going to cancel!
W: What a mess!

男： 我真不敢相信這場會議居然惹出了這麼大的麻煩！

女： 怎麼了，發生了什麼事？

男： 首先，喬安把會議中心的日期訂錯了！然後奇斯寄出的邀請函沒有檢查過拼字，上面有幾個錯別字。現在看來，我們的主講人要取消行程，不來了！

女： 真是一團亂啊！

Unit 33 P. 157 168

W: I called you in here to talk about the state of the report.
M: OK. First of all, I'd like to say that I take full responsibility for the schedule problems. I haven't been able to work as fast as I'd thought.
W: Do you know why that is? Because you've been able to finish other projects on time.

女： 我找你過來是想談一下報告的狀態。

男： 好的。首先，我想說的是，我要對日程安排的問題負起全部的責任。我的動作沒有我想的那麼快。

女： 你知道為什麼嗎？因為你都能夠準時完成其他的專案。

169

M: Can somebody tell me who gave a quotation to Mr. Ryan?
W: I did.
M: The quote you gave him was seriously short! Now he's refusing to pay the full price.
W: Oh no! Let me look through my files and see what happened. I'm so sorry. I can't believe I did that.
M: I'd like you to speak to him, please.
W: Of course. I'll handle this as best I can.

男：有人可以跟我說一下，是誰報價給萊恩先生的嗎？

女：是我。

男：妳給他的報價過低了！現在他拒絕支付全額費用。

女：喔，天啊！我看一下我的檔案，看看是發生了什麼事。我很抱歉，我真不敢相信我報錯價了。

男：我想請妳和他談談。

女：沒問題，我會盡力處理這件事。

Unit 34 P. 161 172

W: Who is the head honcho in Sales?

M: Gosh, I really don't know.

W: How is it that nobody here knows his own department?

M: I only started yesterday!

女：誰是業務部的主管？

男：天啊，我真的不知道。

女：怎麼會有人不清楚自己的部門？

男：我昨天才剛開始上班！

173

M: I've created a system to keep this project running. Joel, you will be responsible for all correspondence with the client. Tim, you answer to Joel and help him with drafting and research.

W: And the rest of us?

M: I'm getting there. Linda, you'll be our representative onsite, since you like to travel. You report to Jade, who will be working with me on the final program.

男：我已經設計了可以讓此專案持續運行的系統制度。喬伊爾，你負責客戶方面的所有聯絡事宜。提姆，喬伊爾是你的直屬上司，請協助他草擬文件與研究的部分。

女：那我們其他人呢？

男：我正要說。琳達，因為妳喜歡四處趴趴走，那就由妳來擔任駐場代表。妳的上司是傑德，他會和我一起處理最後的階段 。

Unit 35 P. 165 177

W: How are you holding up?

M: I'm drowning here, to be honest. The new product roll out has been a lot harder than I anticipated.

W: Is there anything I can do to help?

M: Actually, yes. Bill wanted me to look over this letter of his, but I just don't have time. Could you do it?

女：你還好嗎？

男：老實說，我快累死了。新產品的上市籌備比我預想的還要難許多。

女：有什麼我可以幫忙做的嗎？

男：其實有喔。比爾要我幫他看一下他寫的這封信，但我就是沒時間。妳可以看看嗎？

178

M: Just when I thought I could take a breather, they toss another project at me!

W: What do you mean?

M: I just got finished presenting the new marketing concept, and now they want me to go help another site with their product trials! I really don't think it's fair.

W: Yeah. Did you know they've never asked Harriet to visit a site?

M: There's something fishy here.

男：正當我以為可以喘口氣的時候，他們又丟了另一個專案給我！

女：什麼意思？

男：我才剛簡報完新的行銷概念，現在他們要我去另一個據點協助他們進行產品測試！我真的覺得很不公平。

女：對啊。你知道嗎？他們從來沒有叫過哈瑞特去據點。

男：事情有點不太對勁喔。

Unit 36 P. 169 181

M: Boy, I'll be happy when we get these annual reports done.

W: You're telling me! I've been here since 6 a.m., and what time is it now?

M: Almost 9 p.m. And I'll be slaving away for another hour for sure.

男：天啊，等我們把這些年度報告做完，我就開心了。

女：可不是嘛！我早上六點就來了，現在都幾點了？

男：快晚上九點。我肯定還要再辛苦一個小時。

182

W: Oh no, have I missed Sue?

M: No, she's still in her office.

W: I can't believe she's here so late! She usually leaves at 5:30.

M: She's been working a lot of overtime this week.

W: She must be catching up on things she missed when she was sent to that conference in Austin.

女：喔，不會吧，我錯過蘇了嗎？

男：沒有，她還在她的辦公室裡。

女：我真不敢相信，這麼晚了她還在！她通常五點半就離開了。

男：她這禮拜一直在大量加班。

女：她一定是在趕工，把她被派去奧斯丁開會期間錯過的工作補上。

Unit 37 P. 173 185

M: Oh no, I think I'm going to be in trouble.

W: What happened?

M: I sent an email to everybody outlining our strategy for Thursday's meeting—but I accidentally sent it to the client as well! I'm so embarrassed.

W: Oh no, you couldn't recall it?

M: No, by the time I realized what I had done it was too late.

男：喔，慘了，我想我有麻煩了。

女：發生了什麼事？

男：我傳了一封電子郵件給大家，裡面概述了週四會議討論出的策略，但我不小心也傳給客戶了！太丟臉了。

女：喔，不會吧，你沒辦法回收信件嗎？

男：沒辦法，我發現我誤傳的時候，已經來不及了。

186

W: Bob, I need to set up a lunch with George at HomePro. Can you email him for me?

M: Sure. When do you want to meet, and where?

W: Ask him if he's free between 12 and 2 tomorrow or Wednesday. And I suggest going to The Palm or Ray's Steakhouse.

M: Alright. And do you want me to mention what you'd like to discuss?

W: No, that's alright; he'll know.

女：鮑伯，我必須跟「生活專家公司」的喬治吃午餐。你可以幫我寄電子郵件給他嗎？

男：好啊。你們要幾點見面，地點在哪裡？

女：問他明天或週三的12點到2點之間有沒有空。我建議去「棕櫚樹」或「雷斯牛排館」。

男：好喔。妳要我提到你們要討論的事項嗎？

女：不用，這樣就可以了，他會知道的。

Unit 38 P. 177 190

M: Can you fax the meeting notes to Wanda? I'm sure she'll want to see them.

W: Sure. Do I need to type them up, though? I was just going to work with my handwritten notes.

M: No, as long as they're neat, that's fine. Wanda might write questions in the margins, though.

男：你可以把會議紀錄傳真給汪達嗎？我確定她會很想看這些內容。

女：好啊。我需要把會議內容打出來嗎？我原本打算傳手寫的紀錄。

男：不用打字喔，只要字跡工整就可以。不過汪達可能會在旁邊空白處寫下問題。

191

W: I need to get Joan's signature on the contract changes before we can move on, but she's going to be at headquarters until Monday.

M: Just fax it to her. I'm pretty sure a fax signature is acceptable in this case?

W: Really? That's great. I can also let her mark up the contract directly in case she wants to make any last minute additions.

女：在我們繼續之前，我要先請喬安在合約異動處簽名，但是她要在總部待到禮拜一。

男：傳真給她就好了。我很確定在這樣的情況下，傳真簽名也是可以接受的吧？

女：真的嗎？太好了。萬一她最後想新增什麼內容，我也可以請她直接在合約上標示出來。

Unit 39 P. 181 194

M: Hi, Karen. I'm calling about our appointment on Monday—I'm afraid I need to reschedule.

W: OK. Do you know which day you'll be able to meet?

M: Actually, Monday is still fine. I just need to bump things up from four to three. Will that still work for you?

W: That's fine. See you at three, then.

男：嗨，凱倫。我打電話來討論我們下週一開會的事，我恐怕要改時間。

女：好的，你知道你哪一天可以開會嗎？

男：其實週一還是可以的，只是我需要把事情從四點提早到三點進行。妳這個時間也可以嗎？

女：可以喔。那到時候三點見。

195

W: So, when can I tell you about this new line in person?

M: Let me see . . . it looks like I can do this Tuesday morning, or any afternoon next week.

W: Hmm . . . I have a breakfast meeting at 8:30 on Tuesday, but I'll be done before 10:30. Is eleven too late for you?

M: Eleven will work—but if we run too long, you'll have to buy me lunch!

女：那麼，我什麼時候可以當面向您說明這個新系列產品？

男：我看一下……看來這個星期二早上我可以，或下週任何一天的下午也可以。

女：嗯……我週二八點半有早餐會議，但十點半前會結束。十一點對你來說會太晚嗎？

男：十一點可以，但如果我們開會開太久，妳就要請我吃午餐喔！

Unit 40 P. 185 198

M: Everything looks great. I can't decide what to order.
W: I recommend getting whatever the day's special is—they're always good. And speaking of recommendations . . .
M: Ah ha, straight to work, I see.
W: Well, we really are hoping that TrueStat can put in a good word for us with AccuQuote, as the competition for that account is really stiff.

男：每樣餐點看起來都很棒，我沒辦法決定要點哪一道。

女：我推薦點當日特餐，這類餐點一向都很讚。那說到推薦的事……

男：啊哈，開門見山談工作，我懂了。

女：是這樣的，我們真的希望「真數據」公司能幫我們跟「艾可引言」公司美言幾句，因為要爭取到這個客戶的競爭真的很激烈。

199

W: I'm really glad you could join us. We're just waiting for ProChef to finish setting up and then we'll be able to get started.
M: What are your objectives for this meeting, June? You didn't give us anything to think about in advance.
W: Oh, I only want to update you on some changes that have been happening here. You may have heard that Karen is leaving, and Arthur has decided to go, too. We are in the process of creating a transition team to handle their accounts, and we wanted to assure you that nothing will change in terms of the way your accounts are handled.

女：我真的很高興大家可以來開會。我們只是在等「專業廚師」公司把會場布置好，然後我們就可以開始了。

男：瓊恩，公司召開這次會議的目的是什麼？妳事先沒有給我們任何思考的機會。

女：喔，我只是想跟大家更新一下公司最近發生的一些變動。你們可能有聽說凱倫要離職了，亞瑟也決定要離開。我們正在成立一個過度小組來處理他們手上的客戶，我們向大家保證，你們各自應對客戶的方式不會有任何改變。

Unit 41 P. 189 202

W: Good morning! Thanks so much for taking the time to meet with me today. I'm sure you'll consider it time well spent after we show you what our new model can do for your office.
M: We hope so as well.
W: This product is about speed, efficiency, and reliability. After working with consumer feedback from using other products, we realized that our users valued ease and reliability, not fancy packaging or extraneous features that detract from the model's most important functions. So we've built this product with you in mind all the way, and in every detail.
M: I'd love to have an opportunity to play with it, if it's as good as it sounds.

女：早安！承蒙您今天在百忙之中撥空與我見面，非常感謝。我相信待會您看過敝公司的新產品對貴公司辦公室將會有何助益後，您就會認為花這個時間很值得。

男：我們也希望如此。

女：本產品集速度、效率、可靠性於一身。在了解消費者使用其他產品的意見回饋後，我們發現本公司產品的使用者看重的是產品是否容易上手以及可靠性，而非精美的包裝或無關緊要的功能，那些都會影響到產品最重要的作用。因此，我們在打造此產品的過程中，一直有考慮到使用者的需求，每一個細節皆是如此。

男：如果這個產品真有聽起來這麼好的話，我很樂意有機會試一試。

203

M: Hi, there. Great booth. I'm with GreenPro, on the second floor.

W: Thanks very much. GreenPro? What do you guys do?

M: We manufacture environmentally friendly detergents and housecleaning products. I was looking at your water-saving and low-electricity line and I think we might have a great chance for cross promotion with our two lines.

W: I think you might be right. Why don't you leave me your card and I'll see if we can set up a time to meet and talk about this before the event is over?

男：嗨，妳好。你們的展位很棒啊。我是綠專公司的人，展位在二樓。

女：謝謝誇獎。綠專？你們公司是做什麼？

男：我們公司生產環保清潔劑跟家用清潔產品。我剛在看你們的省水節能產品，我覺得我們可能有很大的機會可以交叉宣傳彼此的產品。

女：我想你可能說得對。你何不留一張名片給我？我看看能不能在活動結束前雙方安排個時間見面談談這件事。

Unit 42 P. 193

207

W: Our competitor has better name recognition than we do, but I think if you'll look at the facts about our two products, you'll change your mind. Their model has been on the market in the same form for the past two years; ours has been redesigned recently to incorporate up-to-the-moment advances in technology.

M: Well, your prices are going to be almost the same. What difference will your redesign make for me?

W: We offer three more stitch settings than they do. We also have a new, more durable spool system that lasts longer and makes for quicker and easier threading.

女：競爭對手的知名度比我們高，但我認為如果您看了我們這兩款產品的實際情況，您或許會改變想法。在這兩年來，他們上市產品的款式一直沒有推陳出新；我們的產品最近才重新設計過，納入了最新的先進技術。

男：嗯，你們的價格都快要一樣了。你們重新設計的產品對我來說又有何不同？

女：我們內建的針法比他們的多了三種，而且我們的捲軸系統既新穎又更耐用，使用時間更長，穿針引線也更快速、更方便。

208

M: Want to help me come up with a better blurb for the section on "our work" for the website?

W: Sure. What have you got so far?

M: We use research-based methods to track how your audiences respond and react. Our expertise can help your company communicate more effectively and efficiently with the people you need to reach.

W: That sounds fine! But do you think you can add something that compares us with other companies? Like "clients prefer our science-based approach to other, old-fashioned techniques?"

男：要不要幫我們的官網「實例分享」部分想個更棒的推薦廣告？

女：沒問題。你目前想到了哪些？

男：本公司採用以研究為基礎的方法來追蹤貴公司客戶端有何回應以及如何應對。我們的專業知識有助於貴公司與欲接觸的客戶進行更有效、更高效的溝通。

女：聽起來很好啊！不過，你有沒有想過可以把我們與別家公司進行比較的內容加進去？像是「與其他老掉牙的技術相比，客戶更喜歡本公司以科學為主的方法」之類的？

Unit 43 P. 197 🎧211

M: I've looked around, and I know I can get this TV at a lower price across town.

W: I'm surprised to hear that. We think our prices are competitive for this area. I'm not authorized to provide you a discount, but I can offer you free delivery and installation.

M: If you throw that in, I think we have a deal.

男：我已經貨比三家了，我知道我能以更低的價格在本鎮的另一頭買到這款電視。

女：聽到這個消息，我很驚訝。我們認為本店的價格在這一帶很有競爭力。我沒有權力給您折扣，但是我可以為您提供免費送貨到府與安裝服務。

男：如果妳加上這兩點，那我想我們成交了。

🎧212

W: We were hoping for more favorable terms than your first offer.

M: Well, we do think our prices are very competitive for this market. However, we are eager to reach a compromise that will benefit both of us.

W: Since we are willing to order in bulk, and since we believe that we will be able to sell a great deal of your monitors, we hope you can reduce your price by another 10%.

M: We are willing to bring the offer down by 5%, but we can't go lower than that.

女：我們原本希望你們這次的條件會比第一次報價的時候更優。

男：呃，我們確實認為我們開出的價格在這個市場上很有競爭力。不過，我們希望能達成妥協，讓雙方都能受益。

女：由於我們願意大批訂貨，也因為我們相信我們能大量賣出貴公司的螢幕，所以我希望你們的價格可以再降10%。

男：我們願意將報價調低5%，不能比這更低了。

Unit 44 P. 201 🎧215

W: Have you heard that they're going to ask us all to get ProPhones for office work? I hear they're terrific.

M: But, wow, they're really expensive. Are we supposed to buy them ourselves?

W: I don't know that yet.

M: I've been using the MyPhone I just got—it's not nearly as costly, but it has almost all the same features and works great. I wonder if I can recommend that we all use this one instead.

女：你們聽說了嗎？公司打算讓我們每個人都買ProPhones來處理公事。我聽說這款手機很棒耶！

男：哇，可是很貴耶。我們得自己掏錢買嗎？

女：我還不知道這一點。

男：我最近都在用剛買的MyPhone手機，這款手機沒那麼貴，可是所有的功能幾乎一模一樣，而且超好用的。不知道我能不能跟公司建議，大家都改用這款手機好了。

216

M: I think we should go with the Sol monitor.

W: Instead of the Luna? Why?

M: Well, we spend so much time looking at our screens that I think we need the biggest and clearest on the market. The Sol is supposed to be the best. And since it costs only a little bit more than its nearest competitor, I think we should take this as an example of "getting what we pay for" and pay a little bit more for the best.

男：我認為我們應該選「明光牌」的螢幕。

女：不用「夜光牌」的？為什麼？

男：嗯，因為我們盯著螢幕的時間實在太長了，所以我想我們需要市面上最大、最清晰的螢幕。「明光牌」應該就是最好的了。而且這個品牌的價格只比它的最大競爭對手高一點點，我認為我們應該秉持著「一分錢，一分貨」的原則，多付點錢買最好的。

Unit 45 P. 205 220

W: I think we made a mistake when using this new shipping company.

M: Oh no, what happened?

W: Well, we sent our first bulk order to a new customer and they made a big mess of it. They shipped everything to the customer overnight and charged us a fortune, though we'd told them expediting the order wasn't necessary. Then we got a call from the customer about missing several boxes—it seems like they mixed up boxes from different orders, so each customer only ended up with about half of what they actually ordered.

M: Oops. I guess we will get blamed for the problems in the end.

W: Of course. It is definitely the last time we use them.

女：我想我們錯了，我們就不該用這家新的貨運公司。

男：噢，不會吧，發生了什麼事？

女：唉，有個新客戶下了一大筆訂單，我們出了第一批貨，然後貨運公司把事情搞得一團糟。他們連夜把所有的貨都一股腦地送到客戶那裡，然後跟我們收了一大筆錢，儘管我們已經跟他們說過這批貨不必加急處理。之後客戶打電話過來說，有好幾箱沒收到，看樣子是貨運公司把不同張訂單的箱子混淆了，結果每個客戶都只有收到實際訂購的一半的貨。

男：這下慘了，到頭來是我們要為這個差錯背黑鍋。

女：當然。這絕對是我們最後一次叫這家貨運公司。

221

M: OK, let me ask you a few questions in order to enter your order into our system. What is your address?

W: 321 Richmond Court, Bridgewater, New Jersey, 08807.

M: And you're paying for this order with a corporate credit card, correct?

W: That's right.
M: Is the billing address the same as the shipping address?
W: No, the billing address is P.O. Box 118, but also in Bridgewater.

男：好，現在我要把您的訂單輸入系統，所以得請教您幾個問題。請問您的地址是什麼？

女：08807 紐澤西州橋水市里奇蒙路 321 號。

男：您要用公司的信用卡來支付這筆訂單，對嗎？

女：沒錯。

男：請問帳單寄送地址跟收件地址一樣嗎？

女：不一樣，帳單地址是郵政第118號信箱，不過也是在橋水市。

Unit 46 P. 209 224

W: Well, I really regret that we weren't able to move forward today as I'd hoped.
M: As do I. At least we can be confident that you understand our position, and if the situation changes, maybe there will be a chance to reopen negotiations in the future.
W: Of course. And if you rethink your price point in the future, please inform us.

女：唔，我真的覺得很遺憾，今天沒能如我所願的那樣取得進展。

男：我也是。至少我們確信您理解我們的立場，如果情況有變，也許將來會有機會重新談判。

女：當然。假如您以後要重新考慮價格點，請通知我們。

225

M: I'm so glad we could all come to the negotiating table today. I don't think we could have worked things out otherwise.
W: Likewise. I'm very pleased with this agreement.
M: Our next step will be to sign all the necessary paperwork—shall we get started on that right now?

男：我很高興今天大家都能上談判桌。不然的話，我還真不認為我們還有其他達成共識的方法。

女：君子所見略同。我對這個合約很滿意。

男：我們下一個步驟就是在所有必要的文件資料上簽名。我們現在可以開始了嗎？

Unit 47 P. 213 228

M: We're having a really hard time hammering out a contract with the new client.
W: Why is that?
M: Oh, they aren't leaving us room to protect ourselves! They want us to be liable for absolutely any problems that occur, which our lawyers of course won't agree to.
W: I hope they can work things out soon. They're really holding up the project.

男：我們跟新客戶在敲定合約一事上遇到了很大的難題。

女：為什麼會這樣？

男：哦，對方不留給我們保護自己的空間。他們要我們為發生的任何問題負完全的責任。我們的律師當然不會同意這樣做。

女：希望他們很快就能把事情解決。他們真的耽擱了案子的發展。

229

W: What's going on in there?
M: Oh, they're arguing about the new employee contracts.
W: What's the problem?

M: Well, we've never had them, but the new manager wants everyone to be issued one now. There's also going to be a non-compete agreement. The employee benefits administrator doesn't want her to do it because it'll be so much work.

W: And because some of us are careful about what we sign!

女：裡面發生了什麼事？

男：哦，他們正在為新的勞動契約吵個不停。

女：有什麼問題嗎？

男：嗯，我們從來沒簽過勞動契約，可是新來的經理希望現在每個人都要簽。還有一份競業禁止合約。員工福利的行政人員並不希望經理進行這件事，因為工作量太大了。

女：也因為有些員工對於要簽名的文書很謹慎！

Unit 48 P. 217 232

W: Are they really going to sign the contract today?

M: I hope so. They've been working on it for ages and we're really being held up.

W: I want to get to work, too, but I don't want us to be stuck in an unfair working situation for the next two years!

女：他們今天真的要簽約了嗎？

男：希望如此。他們已經為此努力了很久，連我們也給耽誤了。

女：我也想回去上班，但是我不想在未來兩年被不當的工作條件綁手綁腳！

233

M: I was hoping we could sign today, but there were a few amendments to make.

W: Really? Anything important?

M: Not really. We just wanted to change some of the language to prevent us from being unduly penalized over potential problems with outside contractors.

W: Right. So when are you meeting again?

M: On Thursday. Everything should be ironed out by then.

男：我原本希望我們今天就能簽約，但是有幾條條款有待修正。

女：真的嗎？是什麼重要的條款嗎？

男：算不上。我們只是想變更幾個用語，避免我們因跟外部承包商發生什麼潛在問題，而遭受到不應有的懲罰。

女：了解。那麼你們打算什麼時候再簽約？

男：這個星期四。到那時，一切都應該被擺平了。

Unit 49 P. 221 237

W: May I help you?

M: Yes, I bought this lawn mower yesterday and it won't start.

W: I'm sorry to hear that. Have you tried troubleshooting with the owner's manual?

M: Yes, of course. It just doesn't work and I'd like my money back.

W: Would you like to exchange it for a different mower of the same model?

M: No, I'd like to take my money and go to another shop.

女：請問您需要幫忙嗎？

男：要，我昨天買了這台割草機，可是它都發動不了。

女：聽到這個消息我很抱歉。請問您有沒有試著按照使用說明書寫的來排除故障問題？

男：當然有。它就是發不動，我要退款。

女：您要不要換一台型號相同的割草機？

男：不要，我想要把錢拿回來，然後去別家店買。

238

M: I'd like to speak with someone about a missing order.

W: I can help you. What's the problem with your order?

M: Well, it's not here. I ordered it to be overnighted, and it's been two days.

W: Please tell me your order number.

M: It's 203948. And my name's William Bell.

W: OK, I see your order here. Unfortunately, it wasn't shipped on the same day as it was processed, so it won't arrive until tomorrow.

M: Well, you can cancel it then. I needed the goods today.

男：我訂的貨不見了，我想找負責此事的人。

女：我可以協助您。請問您訂的貨怎麼了嗎？

男：好吧，訂的貨都沒送來。我訂的是隔日配，可是已經兩天了。

女：請告訴我您的訂單號碼。

男：號碼是203948。我叫做威廉・貝爾。

女：好的，我這裡看到了您的訂單。不幸的是，它沒有在您訂購的當天寄出，所以要到明天才會到貨。

男：這樣啊，那妳可以取消訂單了。我今天就需要這批貨。

Unit 50 P. 229 244

W: So tell me something about you that I can't learn from your résumé.

M: Gladly. Well, I love to fish. I spend most of my weekends fishing—that is, the weekends I wasn't working.

W: Did you work a lot on weekends?

M: Oh, yes. At my previous job we were chronically understaffed, so all of us had to work a lot of weekends. I loved the work, but I didn't like the pace.

W: I guess fishing provided a very different experience.

M: Absolutely.

女：那麼，跟我說說你自己吧，說一些我沒辦法從你的履歷上得知的事。

男：樂意之至。嗯，我喜歡釣魚，我週末大部分的時間都在釣魚，也就是不需要工作的週末。

女：你週末要做很多事嗎？

男：哦，是的。我上一份工作的公司就是長期人手不足，所以我們所有人在許多個週末就不得不工作。我很喜歡那份工作，但是我不喜歡這樣的節奏。

女：我想，釣魚是一個非常不同的體驗。

男：絕對是。

245

M: In your previous position, you mostly worked alone, didn't you? Can you tell me in what way you've developed as a good team member?

W: Well, it's true that I often worked alone before, which certainly required a great deal of self-motivation and discipline. But outside of work, I'm a member of a volunteer committee that organizes opportunities for underprivileged women.

M: Really? How long have you been doing that?

W: For three years now. And my volunteer work was all done in teams.

男：妳之前的工作基本上都是一個人單打獨鬥，對吧？那妳能告訴我，妳如何能夠勝任團隊工作？

女：唔，我以前的確經常獨立作業，這當然需要大量的自我激勵與自律。但在工作之餘，我也在為弱勢婦女提供機會的志工委員會當志工。

男：真的嗎？妳在那邊當志工多久了？

女：到現在已經三年了。而且我的志工工作全都是以團隊的方式進行的。

Unit 51 P. 233 248

W: So, how was your job interview?

M: Oh, it went well. I liked the interviewer, but I'm not really thrilled about the company's benefits package.

W: What's the matter with it?

M: They don't offer much vacation time and they don't provide dental coverage. They do offer a pretty good profit-sharing plan, though.

女：那麼，你工作面試得怎麼樣？

男：喔，很順利啊。我喜歡面試官，但是那家公司的福利並沒有讓我很興奮。

女：有什麼問題嗎？

男：他們給員工的假不多，而且也不提供牙醫保險。不過，他們的員工分紅制度倒是相當優渥。

249

M: How long does the vesting process take?

W: Well, you are 100% vested in all your contributions at all times. As for our matching contributions, you become 100% vested after three years of employment. That's the standard for our industry.

M: Wonderful. And can you tell me the cap for employer matching?

W: We match up to 3% of your monthly salary.

M: But I can contribute more than that amount, right?

W: Of course.

男：請問工作多久的時間才能拿到全部的退休金？

女：嗯，所有你自行提撥的部分，任何時候都100%歸屬於你所有。至於公司為你提撥的配額，在你為公司服務滿三年後就100%歸屬於你所有。這是我們這行的標準做法。

男：太好了。您能告訴我公司提撥配額的上限是多少嗎？

女：我們最多提撥你月薪的百分之三到你的退休帳戶。

男：但是我可以自行提撥更高的金額，對嗎？

女：當然。

Unit 52 P. 237 252

W: I must say, I think that the salary for someone of my experience and background should be in the upper part of this range.

M: But you must be aware that with all the belt-tightening in the industry, salaries are bound to fall.

W: I understand the need to be frugal, but I don't think it should come at the expense of fair compensation packages. Maybe if you tell me what you have set aside from this position, we can work something out.

女：我得說，我認為以我這種學經歷背景的人來說，薪資應該落在這個範圍的前半部分。

男：可是妳一定也有注意到，我們這個行業大家都在縮減成本，薪資勢必會因而下降。

女：我能理解節儉的必要性，但是我不認為這應該以犧牲公平的薪資待遇為代價。也許你可以告訴我你們打算給這個職位的薪資是多少，我們可以商量一下。

253

W: How did the interview go?

M: Oh, it was great—until they asked me about the salary I wanted.

W: What went wrong?

M: Nothing went really wrong, I was just surprised at what they'd budgeted for the position. It was a lot less than I expected.

W: Did you negotiate?

M: Yes, but they really didn't have a lot of wiggle room. I did my best. Eventually, I got some other benefits out of it, but the salary only went up a jot.

W: Too bad. Well, next time around.

M: Oh, no, I took the job. I really like the company, and I figure, maybe I can get more out of them after I've proven myself.

女： 面試進行得怎麼樣？

男： 哦，在他們問我預期的薪資之前都很順利。

女： 什麼地方出錯了？

男： 沒有真的出錯，我只是對他們為這個職位所編列的預算感到很驚訝。比我預期的要少很多。

女： 你有跟他們交涉薪資嗎？

男： 有，但是確實沒有什麼討價還價的餘地。我已經盡力了。最後，我跟他們要到了一些其他的福利，但是薪資只增加了一點點。

女： 太可惜了。好吧，下次再來。

男： 哦，不用了，我接受了這份工作了。我真的很喜歡這家公司，而且我想等我證明了自己的能力後，我也許可以跟公司要求更多。

Unit 53 P. 241

256

M: I think we need to hire a new project manager. We've got so much new business coming in.

W: It's great that we're growing so much. How are you going to look for project managers? Are you going to use an employment website?

M: I guess so. I was also hoping to use a little word of mouth. Do you know anyone you could recommend?

W: I can certainly think about it and ask around. When are you hoping to interview?

M: As soon as possible, I guess. The new project kick-off is going to be within the month!

男： 我想我們需要聘請一位新的專案經理。我們最近有很多新業務進來。

女： 公司生意做得越來越大，真是太好了。你想要怎麼應徵新的專案經理？你打算用徵才網站嗎？

男： 大概吧。我原來也希望靠別人介紹一些人來。妳知道有什麼人可以推薦的嗎？

女： 我當然可以想一想，再去四處問問。你想要什麼時候面試？

男： 我想，越快越好。新專案在這個月內就會啟動了！

257

M: We're going to have you shadow Glenda for the day, to get the hang of things.

W: Terrific.

M: Unfortunately, Glenda's running a little late. She'll be here within half an hour, so why don't you sit down and look over the employee handbook until she gets here?

男： 我們打算讓妳跟在格蘭達的身邊一天，學學怎麼處理事情。

女： 好極了。

男： 不巧的是，格蘭達今天有點遲到。她會在半小時內到這裡，所以妳要不要坐下來，在她來之前先把員工手冊看一遍呢？

Unit 54 P. 245 260

M: I'm sorry. I seem to have forgotten my ID.

W: That's alright. You can still fill out these tax forms now. I'll just copy your identification when you bring it tomorrow.

M: Great. Sorry about that. Now, I live in another state. Am I going to pay taxes here or in the state where I live?

W: I'm glad you mentioned that. You'll pay taxes in the state where you live, so I'll have to call HR and make sure they handle your paperwork with that in mind.

男： 對不起，我好像忘了帶身分證。

女： 沒關係。你現在還是可以把這些稅務表格填好。等你明天把身分證帶過來，我再影印就行了。

男： 太好了，真不好意思。嗯，我住在別的州。所以，我的稅是要在這一州繳，還是在我居住的那一州？

女： 我很高興你提到了這件事。你要在居住的那一州繳稅，所以我得打電話給人資部，確定他們在處理你的資料時有考慮到這一點。

261

W: Excuse me, I think I made a mistake on my tax forms. Is it possible to redo them?

M: Sure. What do you think happened?

W: I'm pretty sure I accidentally claimed too many exemptions. I really want to double check, because I'd rather be owed money at tax time than have to pay.

M: Wouldn't we all? OK, I'll see if I can find your forms. I don't think we've filed them yet, so it should be easy to make changes.

女： 不好意思，我想我的稅單上面弄錯了。有可能重寫嗎？

男： 當然可以。妳覺得是哪裡弄錯了？

女： 我很肯定我不小心申報了太多的免稅額。我真的很想仔細檢查一遍，因為我寧願在繳稅時先溢繳，也不願到時要補繳。

男： 我們不都是這麼想的嗎？好吧，我看看找不找得到妳的稅單。我想我們還沒有去申報，所以要改應該很容易。

Unit 55 P. 249 264

W: I'm interested in the position I just interviewed for, but the company's benefits really aren't great.

M: What's wrong—or what's missing?

W: Their health insurance is pretty minimal, and on top of it, they make employees pay for most of the premiums!

M: Yes, that doesn't sound great. Are the other benefits alright?

W: They're fine, I suppose. But health insurance is important to me.

女： 我對剛剛面試的那個職位很感興趣，但是那家公司的福利真的不太好。

男： 有什麼問題嗎，或者應該問，少了什麼？

女： 他們的健康保險只保最基本的，除此之外，他們居然讓員工自行負擔大部分的保費！

男： 對，聽起來不是很好。其他的福利還可接受嗎？

女： 我想，還可以吧。可是健康保險對我來說很重要。

🎧265

M: I just found out that our medical insurance doesn't cover dental work.

W: You didn't know that?

M: I guess I just assumed it was covered. I'm annoyed because I have to have a bunch of dental work done and it's going to cost a fortune.

W: That's too bad. If you have time, you could buy extra dental coverage. Do you think that would be worth it?

M: I don't know. I'll have to look into it. Do you think I can speak to HR about it?

W: Why not?

男： 我剛剛發現，我們的醫療保險居然不支付牙科的醫療費。

女： 你以前不知道嗎？

男： 我想我當時以為有保到這項。我很火大，因為我的牙齒得做一大堆的治療，這要花很一大筆錢。

女： 真糟糕。如果你有時間的話，你可以加買牙科保險。你覺得這樣做划得來嗎？

男： 我不知道。我必須研究一下。妳覺得我可以跟人資部談談這個問題嗎？

女： 有何不可？

Unit 56 P. 253 🎧268

M: I hear that Sam is up for regional director.

W: Wow! But he hasn't been here nearly as long as Uriah.

M: I know. I guess they like his work, though. And Uriah's never been good at networking. I think that's hurting his chances.

W: I wonder if Uriah knows.

男： 我聽說山姆被列入地區總監一職的名單裡。

女： 哇！可是他進公司的時間還沒有尤來亞來得久耶。

男： 我知道啊。不過我猜是因為他們喜歡他的工作成果。而尤來亞從來就不擅長交際。我認為這影響到了他的升遷機會。

女： 不知道尤來亞曉不曉得這件事。

🎧269

W: Corin just offered me the lab director position!

M: Wow, congratulations! Are you going to take it?

W: I'm thinking about it. I could use the raise, and the work seems interesting. On the other hand, there'll be a lot of travel.

M: And a lot of work—the other lab directors are always staying late.

W: Right. There's a lot to think about. But I'm leaning toward taking it.

女： 科林剛剛給了我實驗室主任的職位！

男： 哇，恭喜！妳會接受嗎？

女： 我還在考慮。我很想要加薪，而且這份工作似乎也滿有意思的。另一方面，這個工作要常常出差。

男： 而且工作一大堆——其他的實驗室主任總是待到很晚。

女： 沒錯。有很多事情需要考慮，但是我個人傾向於接下這個工作。

Unit 57 P. 257 🎧272

W: Did you hear they're eliminating several assistant management positions?

M: No—wow, that's not good news. What does that mean for the current assistant managers?

W: Well, they're going to try to find places for some of them on different teams, but they're going to have to take pay cuts. And some of them will have to be let go.

M: That's rough. I really hope the market recovers soon. I'm starting to get worried about layoffs myself!

女：你聽說了嗎？公司打算裁掉幾個副理職位。

男：不會吧——那可不是什麼好消息。這對那些現任的副理來說，結果會怎麼樣？

女：嗯，公司會想辦法把其中幾位安插在別的團隊裡，但是前提是他們必須要接受減薪的條件。剩下的人就得面臨被解僱的局面了。

男：好慘啊。真希望市場很快就能復甦。我也開始擔心自己被裁員的問題了！

🎧 273

M: What's going to happen when they combine the two departments?

W: I'm still not sure. They've said they're going to retain most of both departments. I think we'll all be working under one manager, though, and I'm pretty sure that'll be Abdul.

M: So where will Wendy go?

W: I don't know. She might be transferred.

男：公司把兩個部門合併之後會發生什麼事？

女：我也不是很清楚。公司說兩個部門的員工大多都會留任。不過，我覺得我們都會在某個經理的手下工作。我很肯定那個人就是阿布度。

男：那麼溫蒂將何去何從？

女：我不知道。她可能會被調職吧。

Unit 58 P. 261 🎧 277

M: I hear Sara's quitting.

W: Really? Wow. She seemed so happy here.

M: Yes, but I guess she's been looking for other jobs on the side and she's found one that'll pay way more than this.

W: Gosh . . . maybe I should ask her about it!

男：我聽說莎拉要辭職了。

女：真的嗎？哇。她在這裡似乎還滿快樂的。

男：是啊，不過我猜她私下一直有在找別的工作，而她找到了一份薪水比這高得多的工作。

女：天啊……或許我該去問問她是怎麼找到的！

🎧 278

W: I'm really sorry to tell you this, Frank, but I'm leaving.

M: You mean you're resigning?

W: Yes. I have to.

M: Well, this is sudden. Why are you leaving?

W: I've always wanted to go back to school and I think now is the time.

M: OK, well, I wish you luck, of course. So, when will your last day be?

W: That's bad news also—classes start on Monday, so my last day has to be Friday.

M: Oh dear. That puts us in a very difficult position.

女：法蘭克，我真的很抱歉要跟你說這件事，我要離開了。

男：妳的意思是你要辭職了？

女：對，我不得不走。

男：嗯，這太突然了。妳為什麼要辭職？

女：我一直想再回學校讀書，我認為現在就是時候了。

男：好吧，那當然要祝妳一切順利。那麼，妳最後一天上班是在哪一天？

女：那也是個壞消息——下星期一就要開始上課了，所以我的最後一個工作日是這星期五。

男：噢，天啊。這就讓我們很為難了。

Unit 59 P. 265 282

M: That was a great lunch. Now, what's the damage?
W: Oh, this is on me. I didn't get to tell you all the big news yet!
M: What's the news?
W: I'm being promoted! So this lunch is my treat—since I probably won't have much time for these long lunches in the future!

男：這頓午餐很好吃。好吧，總共多少錢？

女：哦，這頓飯算我的。我還沒來得及跟你們大家說一個大消息！

男：什麼樣的消息？

女：我要升官了！所以這頓午餐我請客，因為我以後大概不會有太多時間吃這麼久的午餐了！

283

W: Are there any specials today?
M1: Well, our soup du jour is homemade minestrone, and our catch of the day is rockfish.
W: The minestrone sounds great. I'll have that and the pasta.
M1: I'll be right back.
W: Listen, Greg, I've got great news—but you've got to keep it under your hat for now.
M2: My lips are sealed! Tell me!

女：今天有什麼特餐嗎？

男1：哦，我們今天供應的例湯是自家做的義大利蔬菜濃湯，還有今天的漁獲是石狗公。

女：義大利蔬菜濃湯聽起來不錯。我要點這個湯跟義大利麵。

男1：請稍等一下，我馬上回來。

女：聽我說，格雷格，我有個好消息——不過你暫時得保密。

男2：我會守口如瓶！說吧！

Unit 60 P. 269 286

W: Do you mind if I ask you a question about our bonuses?
M: Sure, what is it?
W: I'm curious about how they're calculated. Are they a percentage of our salaries? Does everyone get the same amount? Do they reflect our performance?
M: As far as I know, everyone gets the same amount.
W: Really? That's disappointing.
M: Why?
W: Well, that doesn't give us a lot of incentive to perform well, does it? I mean, money motivates!

女：你介意我問你一個跟獎金有關的問題嗎？

男：當然不介意，是什麼問題？

女：我很好奇獎金是怎麼算出來的。是薪水的一部分嗎？每個人拿到的獎金都一樣多嗎？獎金是不是反映出我們的績效？

男：據我所知，每個人的金額都一樣。

女：真的嗎？真令人失望啊。

男：為什麼？

女：唔，這樣我們不會有太大的動力想要好好表現，不是嗎？我的意思是說，錢就是動力！

🎧 287

W: I'm so angry about the bonus situation this year.

M: Why, what's wrong?

W: Haven't you heard? We aren't getting bonuses this year, just gift certificates to the mall.

M: Wow, that's disappointing.

W: It is—and I feel really misled. When I took this job, they were pretty clear that good work would result in big bonuses. I guess I should have gotten their promises in writing.

女：我對今年發的獎金很生氣。

男：為什麼，怎麼了？

女：你還沒聽人家說嗎？我們今年不發獎金，只有購物中心的禮券。

男：哇，這也太令人失望了吧。

女：是啊——而且我覺得我真的被坑了。當初我接受這份工作的時候，他們說得很清楚，工作表現出色就會有豐厚的獎金。我想我那時就該讓他們將承諾用白紙黑字寫下來。

Unit 61 P. 273 🎧 290

M: I just heard that they're going to charge for the baseball outing this year.

W: Really? I love that trip. How much are they charging?

M: Oh, I think it's not very much. They're doing it because they're providing a bus rather than asking staff to carpool. I think the bus fee is about five dollars.

W: Oh, that's no big deal! I thought they were going to make us pay for our own food and drink.

男：我剛聽說今年的棒球之旅公司要收費。

女：真的嗎？我很喜歡這個行程。公司要收多少錢？

男：哦，我想不會很多。公司會這麼做是因為公司今年會提供一輛巴士，而不是要求員工共乘便車前往。我想巴士費大概是五美元吧。

女：哦，這沒什麼大不了的！我還以為公司要我們自行負擔吃喝的費用呢。

🎧 291

W: When is the retreat this year?

M: Sometime in September, but I'm not sure of the exact dates. I think they're going to put it to a vote.

W: That's great. I'm really looking forward to this year's event. I think we could all use a little morale boost.

M: I agree. I feel like communication is always so much better after these retreats.

女：今年的員工旅遊是在什麼時候？

男：九月的某個時候吧，不過我不確定是哪一天。我想他們會讓大家投票表決。

女：那太好了。我真的很期待今年的旅遊活動。我覺得我們大家都需要點鼓舞士氣的活動。

男：我同意。我覺得每次旅遊完回來，溝通都會變得非常順暢。

Unit 62 P. 277 🎧 294

M: I'm really not happy about being away on business next week. It's going to disrupt everything I had scheduled.

W: Are you sure you absolutely have to go?

M: Oh, yes, they made it clear that they expect me to be there. I just wish I'd gotten more notice about it.

W: Oh well. At least you can do some sightseeing, or try some interesting food.

M: Oh, no. The head office is in a really boring town. I'll probably just spend my nights in my hotel room, working.

男：我真的很不高興下個星期要出差的事。這會打亂我安排好的每件事情。

女：你確定你一定要出差嗎？

男：哦，確定。他們說得很清楚，他們希望我到場。我只是希望我能早一點收到通知。

女：哦，好吧。至少你可以去那邊觀光或是吃點什麼有趣的食物。

男：哦，不會吧。總部是在一個很乏味無趣的小鎮。晚上我大概會待在飯店房間裡工作吧。

295

W: I need to make a few changes to the plans for our trip on Tuesday. First of all, we're going to need the hotel rooms for four nights instead of three.

M: OK. Anything else?

W: Yes, we're going to need all our flights changed from Friday night to Saturday morning. I hope we can still do that. And we need to call headquarters and tell them we'll be shipping our meeting materials and they'll need to sign for them when they arrive on Tuesday morning.

M: Alright. I'd better get started!

女：星期二的出差行程我有些地方要修改。首先，我們的飯店房間要訂四個晚上，而不是三個晚上。

男：好的，還有嗎？

女：有，我們必須把所有的航班從星期五晚上改到星期六早上。希望我們還能更改航班。然後我們要打電話給總部，跟他們說我們會把會議資料寄過去，他們需要在星期二早上資料送達時簽收。

男：沒問題。我最好現在就開始工作了！

Unit 63 P. 283 300

M: Sarah, can you handle the hotel bookings for this trip?

W: Sure. What are the dates again?

M: Let's see . . . we'll arrive on April 2 and we'll leave a week later. There will be four of us, so we'll need four rooms.

W: OK. Non-smoking for all of them?

M: Definitely for me, but you might want to ask the others.

男：莎拉，妳可以處理這次出差的訂房事宜嗎？

女：當然可以。日期是什麼時候來著？

男：我看看……我們會在4月2日抵達，一個星期後離開。這次有四個人出差，所以會需要四間房間。

女：好。四人全部都訂禁菸房嗎？

男：我肯定要訂的，但是妳可能要問問其他人。

301

W: Please check if they have a pool—if they don't, I don't want to stay there. You can try the Marriot instead.

M: OK. Is there anything else I should know?

W: Yes. I want to stay on the first or second floor, but no higher. And you can make the reservation with my personal card, but I'm going to pay for it when I get there with the corporate card.

M: Alright. And if for some reason I can't do that?

W: Then don't make the booking and we'll just wait until I can find the card.

女：請確認一下飯店有沒有游泳池——如果沒有，我不想住那裡。你可以問萬豪飯店看看。

男：好的。還有什麼是我需要知道的嗎？

女：有。我想住在一樓或是二樓，但是不要比這更高的樓層。還有你可以先用我個人的信用卡訂房，等我到飯店後再用公司商務卡付房費。

男：沒問題。要是有什麼原因我沒辦法這樣做呢？

女：那麼就不要訂房，等我找到卡以後再說。

Unit 64 P. 291 🎧304

W: Hi there. I need to book a flight from Beijing to Toronto, please.

M: Alright. What dates would you like to travel?

W: Well, my dates are flexible. I can leave anytime between the 10th and the 12th of March, and I'd like to return a week later. Can you search for the cheapest fares within those dates?

M: Of course. And would you like a direct flight?

W: No, I don't mind transfers, and I know direct flights are usually more expensive.

女：你好，我要訂一張從北京到多倫多的機票，謝謝。

男：沒問題。請問您要訂哪一天的班機？

女：嗯，我的時間很彈性。3月10日到12日之間的航班我都可以，還有我想一個星期後回來。你可以幫我找找這段期間內有沒有最便宜的機票？

男：當然可以。您想要直飛的班機嗎？

女：不用，我不介意轉機，我知道直飛的班機通常會比較貴。

🎧305

M: I need to change a flight reservation I'd made.

W: OK. Can you please tell me your reservation number?

M: Sure. It's 6BX3RT.

W: Thank you. Are you Mr. John Randal, and is your flight from Boston to Penang?

M: That's right. I was supposed to leave Penang and return to Boston on April 15, but I'm going to have to extend my trip by another five days.

W: So instead of leaving on the 15th you would like to leave on the 20th?

M: That's right.

男：我想要更改之前預定的班機行程。

女：好的。可以請您告訴我您的訂位編號嗎？

男：當然好。編號是6BX3RT。

女：謝謝您。請問是約翰·藍道先生嗎？您是搭從波士頓飛往檳城的班機？

男：沒錯。我本來應該要在4月15日當天離開檳城返回波士頓，但是我現在必須將行程再延長五天的時間。

女：所以您是想要在20日這天出發，而不是15日囉？

男：沒錯。

Unit 65 P. 299 🎧309

M: What makes more sense, train or bus?

W: The train is closer. It'll be more expensive, but it means less walking with our bags.

M: That's true. But does it stop near our hotel?

W: Hmm . . . it looks like it stops about a kilometer away. We could take a taxi from there.

M: Sure, that's fine. Let's just get going.

男：哪一種比較合理，火車還是公車？

女：火車站比較近。雖然車資會比較貴，但是這表示我們背著行李可以少走一點路。

男：這倒是真的。可是我們住的飯店附近有火車停靠嗎？

女：嗯……看起來距離飯店一公里遠的地方有火車停靠。我們可以從那裡搭計程車過去。

男：好，那也行。我們出發吧。

310

W: Excuse me, can you tell me how much it will cost to go from here to the corner of 2nd and Main Streets?

M: I'm sorry ma'am, we use the meter here. I can guess, but I can't tell you for sure.

W: Well, what's your guess?

M: About ten dollars. Maybe up to 13.

W: And is there a bus that goes there?

M: No, not that far. You could try the subway, but it's very crowded at this hour.

W: Oh no, I guess I'll just go with you.

女：你好，你能告訴我從這裡到第二大街與緬因街的路口需要多少錢嗎？

男：女士，很抱歉，我們這裡採跳表計費。我可以估計一下，但是我沒辦法肯定地跟您説多少錢。

女：呃，你估計要多少錢？

男：十美元左右吧。可能會到13美元。

女：有公車到那裡嗎？

男：沒有，沒開到那麼遠。您可以試試搭地鐵，但是這個時候地鐵非常擁擠。

女：哦，不會吧，我想我還是搭你的車好了。

辦公室英語會話必勝課
職場溝通即戰力

作　　者　Michelle Witte
協同作者　王于瑞（Part 6: Unit 50 Useful Expressions）
譯　　者　謝雅婷／劉嘉珮／黃詩韻
審　　訂　Helen Yeh
編　　輯　陳彥臻／王婷葦
校　　對　黃詩韻／陳慧莉
主　　編　丁宥暄
內文排版　蔡怡柔
封面設計　林書玉
製程管理　洪巧玲
出 版 者　寂天文化事業股份有限公司
發 行 人　黃朝萍
電　　話　+886-(0)2-2365-9739
傳　　真　+886-(0)2-2365-9835
網　　址　www.icosmos.com.tw
讀者服務　onlineservice@icosmos.com.tw
出版日期　2022 年 4 月 初版一刷
（寂天雲隨身聽 APP 版）

國家圖書館出版品預行編目 (CIP) 資料

辦公室英語會話必勝課：職場溝通即戰力
(寂天雲隨身聽 APP 版)/Michelle Witte 著：
謝雅婷，劉嘉珮，黃詩韻譯 . -- 初版 . -- 臺北
市：寂天文化事業股份有限公司，2022.04
　面；　公分
ISBN 978-626-300-115-2(平裝)

1.CST: 商業英文 2.CST: 會話

805.188　　111003426

郵撥帳號 1998-6200 寂天文化事業股份有限公司
・ 劃撥金額 600 元（含）以上者，郵資免費。
・ 訂購金額 600 元以下者，請外加郵資 65 元。
〔若有破損，請寄回更換，謝謝。〕